A CHANGED MAN

A CHANGED MAN

a novel

F r a n c i n e   P r o s e

HarperCollins*Publishers*

HarperCollins books may be purchased for educational, business, or sales promotional use. For information, please write: Special Markets Department, HarperCollins Publishers Inc., 10 East 53rd Street, New York, NY 10022.

FIRST EDITION

Designed by Jaime Putorti

Printed on acid-free paper

Library of Congress Cataloging-in-Publication Data

Prose, Francine
  A changed man : a novel / Francine Prose.—1st ed.
    p.   cm.
  ISBN 0-06-019674-2
  1. White supremacy movements—Fiction. 2. Human rights workers—Fiction.
  3. Holocaust survivors—Fiction. 4. Change (Psychology)—Fiction. 5. Divorced
  mothers—Fiction. 6. New York (N.Y.)—Fiction. 7. Suburban life—Fiction.
  8. Teenage boys—Fiction. 9. Neo-Nazis—Fiction. I. Title.

PS3566.R68C48 2005
813'.54—dc22   2004047448

05 06 07 08 09   ❖/RRD   10 9 8 7 6 5 4 3 2 1

IN MEMORY OF SPALDING GRAY

I used to call you Chop Chop. My sweet Chop Chop.
I don't go to those places no more.
I've given up my bad habits.
I've seen the light.
I'm a changed man.

—"A Changed Man"
The Fatback Band

I have a belief on my own, and it comforts me. . . .
That by desiring what is perfectly good, even when
we don't quite know what it is and cannot do what we
would, we are part of the divine power against evil—
widening the skirts of light and making the struggle
with darkness narrower.

—George Eliot, *Middlemarch*

PART ONE

N OLAN PULLS INTO THE PARKING GARAGE, braced for the Rican attendant with the *cojones* big enough to make a point of wondering what this rusted hunk of Chevy pickup junk is doing in Jag-u-ar City. But the ticket-spitting machine doesn't much care what Nolan's driving. It lifts its arm, like a benediction, like the hand of God dividing the Red Sea. Nolan passes a dozen empty spots and drives up to the top level, where he turns in beside a dusty van that hasn't been anywhere lately. He grabs his duffel bag, jumps out, inhales, filling his lungs with damp cement-y air. So far, so good, he likes the garage. He wishes he could stay here. He finds the stairwell where *he* would hide were he planning a mugging, corkscrews down five flights of stairs, and plunges into the honking inferno of midafternoon Times Square.

He's never seen it this bad. A giant mosh pit with cars. Just walking demands concentration, like driving in heavy traffic. He remembers the old Times Square on those righteous long-ago weekends when he and his high school friends took the bus into the city to get hammered and eyeball the hookers. He's read about the new Disneyfied theme park Times Squareland, but that's way more complicated than what he needs to deal with right now, which is navigating without plowing into some little old lady. A fuzzball of pure pressure expands inside his chest, stoked by patches of soggy shirt, clinging to his rib cage.

It's eighty, maybe eighty-five, and he's the only guy in New York wearing a long-sleeved jersey. All the white men seem to be running personal air conditioners inside their fancy Italian suits, unlike the blacks and Latinos, who have already soaked through their T-shirts. What does that make Nolan? The only white guy sweating. The only human of any kind gagging from exhaust fumes. While Nolan's been off in the boondocks with his friends and their Aryan Homeland wet dream, an alien life-form has evolved in the nation's cities, a hybrid species bred to survive on dog piss and carbon monoxide. Nolan needs to stop thinking that way. Attitude is crucial.

Last night, at his cousin Raymond's, he'd watched the TV weather-chipmunk chirping about the heat wave, so *unseasonable* for April, reassuring local viewers with his records and statistics lest anyone think: Look out, global warming, the world is ending *right now*. Why is everyone so surprised that the planet's cutting them loose? Ecological Armageddon was just what the doctor ordered to take Nolan's mind off his own problems as he'd faced the dark hours ahead until it was time to get up and borrow Cousin Raymond's truck, his money and pills, and vanish into the ozone. Nolan's hardly slept for two weeks, ever since he decided to turn. Two Xanax did nothing to stop his lab-rat brain from racing from one micro-detail to another.

Like, for example, sleeve length. Should he hide the tattoos? Or just wear a T-shirt and let *them* do the talking? If one picture's worth a thousand words, that's the first two thousand right there, two thousand minus the hi howareya nicetameetcha. Which was one reason to get the tats: cut through a load of hot air. On the other hand, strolling into the office of World Brotherhood Watch with Waffen-SS bolts on one bicep and a death's-head on the other might make it harder for Nolan to get his point across—let's say, if the people he's talking to are hiding under their desks. Nolan wouldn't blame them. It hasn't been all that long since that lone-wolf lunatic in L.A. shot up the Jewish temple preschool.

In any case, it's going to be tough, explaining what he's doing at Brotherhood Watch, especially since Nolan himself isn't exactly sure. There are some . . . practical issues involved with stealing Raymond's truck plus the fifteen hundred bucks that, if you want to be literal, belongs to the Aryan Resistance Movement. But there's more to it than that. If it were just a question of disappearing and starting over, Nolan could have some fun. Sell SUVs in Palm Springs, deal blackjack in Las Vegas. Go to Disney World, put on a Goofy suit, let toddlers fuck with his head.

What he'd really like to do is give every man, woman, and child in the world the exact same hit of Ecstasy, the same tiny candy, pink as a kitten's tongue, that managed to turn his head around, or more precisely, to give his head a little—well, a fairly big—push in the direction it was already headed. But that's not going to happen, free Ex for the human race, so maybe the next best thing is to help other people find a more gradual route to the place where the Ex took Nolan.

Meanwhile, he knows that thinking like this will only get in his way. He'll stay cooler if he convinces himself that he's just interviewing for a job.

Has it only been two weeks since Nolan finally made up his mind? A *long* two weeks of trying to figure it out, even—especially—after he knew how he was going to do it.

No one promised it would be easy. But Nolan has prepared. He's read up, starting with two books by Meyer Maslow, the founder and current head of the World Brotherhood Watch Foundation. He actually went out and ordered them through the bookstore in the mall. The first book, *The Kindness of Strangers*—Maslow's tribute to the people who saved his life when he was on the run from the Nazis—was what made Nolan begin to think that maybe his plan could work.

For balance, Nolan has also been reading *The Way of the Warrior*, a paperback he took from the tire shop, borrowed from the backseat of a Ford Expedition some yuppie brought in for the Firestone recall. Nolan knows the book's a fortune cookie for bond traders with samurai delusions, but still, it's filled with ancient principles of diplomacy and war that help Nolan untangle the knots into which his thoughts can get snarled. For example, *The Way of the Warrior* says: Planning is key. Planning and total freedom to change the Warrior's plan. The book suggested that Nolan wait till afternoon. The Warrior knows that the enemy is best approached after lunch. So Nolan has spent hours cruising the suburbs, killing time.

Driving into the city, Nolan went over the plan. Park truck. Find Fifty-first Street. Find building. Enter lobby. Locate elevator. Push button. Board elevator. Hold breath. Assume that every passenger carries a different contagious disease.

The plan is working better than planned. The elevator is empty. He finds 19, pushes the button, leans against the wall. Just before the doors close, a dwarf hops into the car. Young, tan, streaky surfer hair, oddly handsome for a guy with a mashed-in pumpkin head. A blindingly bright white T-shirt shows off his gym-buffed chest. Great, thinks Nolan. My luck. Our man is being tested. The old Nolan would have been pissed, forced to ride up nineteen floors with a mutant. The newly reconstructed Nolan wills himself to imagine what the short dude went through on his first day of kindergarten. Or asking a girl to the prom. Nolan had a hard enough time, and he's on the tall side.

The trouble with changing your attitude is that the old one doesn't disappear. It hides in the creases of your brain, sending out faint signals. He can hear what Raymond would have said about the elevator dwarf. The hungriest chromosome is the broken one. The weak and the damaged will multiply and conquer the earth like a virus. Nolan remembers one of those boozy, late-night "discussions" with Raymond and his friends. One guy said that people used to think dwarfs had magical powers, which, they all agreed, just went to show how stupid people are. Nolan never bought it. He never believed that freaks were having lots of sex and millions of freaky children.

The elevator seems to have stopped. Is this Nolan's floor?

"Nineteen," says the mind-reading dwarf. He got on after Nolan. He couldn't have seen him hit the button. What if Work-Out Dwarf *is* a magical being? And what's with the knowing smile? Maybe he works in the building and sees a thousand guys like Nolan, every week some Nazi punk turns and heads for Brotherhood Watch. That worm-colored geek with the shiny head? Send the guy up to nineteen. Nolan has to remind himself that he's dressed in such a way that there's nothing to distinguish him from your normal, fashionably bald dude in jeans and a long-sleeved shirt.

The elevator releases Nolan into a carpeted hall paneled in gleaming wood. Behind the reception desk sits a beautiful Asian chick in stylish black ninja pajamas. How classy, how predictable for a famous human rights outfit to hire PC Dragon Lady to guard the front door. Nolan recalls a Hong Kong film where the secretary rockets up from her desk and does triple flips, slinging nunchaks around the office. He wishes he'd brought six other guys. He wishes his tattoos showed.

In the end, what he *can't* hide is enough to give Suzie Wong the willies. The duffel bag is a problem, as he knew it would be. Of course, it would have been smoother if he could have left it somewhere. As Nunchak Girl eyes the bag, Nolan watches a little fight-or-flight thing take place in her face, until her receptionist training wins out over her basic human instinct not to be anywhere *near* him. Nolan has the feeling she's got one finger on the panic button. Just in case.

"May I help you?"

"I'd like to see Mr. Maslow. Uh, Dr. Maslow. Whatever."

"Do you have an appointment?"

He doesn't know what the gentleman's called. Does it *sound* like he has an appointment?

"No," says Nolan. "I need to talk to him." So do millionaires. Politicians. Nolan can expect about five more seconds of Miss Yin Yang's attention. He says, "I've got some information I think he might want to have. I guess you know what ARM is, right? The American Rights Movement?"

A definite yes from Ice Princess. Now she's *really* eyeing the duffel bag, obviously wondering if this is her time, if her bullet-riddled body will be all over tomorrow's front page. And is that a tiny *twitch* pulling her hand beneath the desk? Call security! Red alert! Hitler's in the building looking for Meyer Maslow! Nolan can't decide if he wants to pop her in the nose or fall on his knees and promise he won't hurt her. He follows her glance toward the duffel bag.

"I'm in a kind of . . . transitional state," he says. "And if you're thinking what I think you're thinking . . ." He turns his palms outward and tries to smile. "I'm harmless. I promise. Unarmed. There's nothing in the bag but some books and clothes and dirty laundry."

The receptionist's lip curls. She doesn't want to think about Nolan's dirty laundry.

"I was in ARM for five years." Lie number one, and Nolan's only been here two minutes. So what. It's a detail. They can hash out the fine points later.

"Congratulations." She gives him the freeze-out look she learned in Bitch Receptionist 101. She hesitates, thinks, thinks some more. Then she picks up the phone and keeps pushing the same button. Security isn't answering. So she's pretty much on her own. Is that fear on her face? Just a trace, and it's gone, either because she's a *professional*, a professional receptionist, or because she doesn't want to give Nolan the satisfaction. Or because he's charmed her. That's always a possibility. She listens, pushes another button, listens, then another. So the person about to deal with the fact of Nolan's existence is several rungs down the food chain here at World Brotherhood Watch.

"Bonnie?" she says. "There's someone here you might want to talk to." *Bonnie?* Maslow's secretary, probably. Did Nolan think Madame Butterfly was going to ring the boss's direct line? She looks at Nolan. "Ms. Kalen will be out shortly."

Nolan strolls across the foyer and checks out the art on the wall, a mammoth canvas gunked with gobs of that shit-brown color kids mix up just to piss off the art teacher. A finger painting of train tracks. Some genius got a fortune.

"Excuse me?"

Nolan wheels around to find himself standing way too close to what's got to be Bonnie. Putty-colored business suit, thin blondish hair tied back into the same limp pigtail she probably wore in college, fortyish, a couple of kids, bossy psychiatrist husband. Nolan worked for a hundred women like her, that summer he spent around Woodstock humping chlorine and skimming bugs for Skip's Pool and Spa.

Bonnie's eyes, two magnified blue jellyfish swimming toward him from behind her glasses, look slightly psycho. Another female nutcase. One of those women, like his mom, always trying to be a good person. Except that they're clueless as to what *good* is, so they're always checking in with a dozen inner opinions on what they should do and say. If only chicks like Bonnie and his mom would stop trying so hard to be good, the world might be a better place. Certainly their world would be. With Mom, it was a problem. But this Bonnie's functioning up to speed—and beyond. She's working overtime, just standing still, revving her engine. She's an orgasm waiting to happen. Or a nervous breakdown. Whichever gets there first. Nolan doesn't want to be around to see which way it goes down.

She says, "I'm Bonnie Kalen? From the development department?"

Develop my ass, thinks Nolan. But what's his problem, exactly? She's really *trying*, smiling for so long it must hurt. She's a little slower than her receptionist friend at IDing Nolan. Which is fine. Back to Plan A. Hide the tattoos and get his good intentions across before she figures out who he is. But what will the tattoos tell her about who Nolan is, and what he's been through? Except for the fact that one drunken, stoned night at the Homeland Encampment, it felt great to be so out of it that the tattoo needle felt good. He could talk himself blue in the face and never make her understand the sweetness of feeling that the buzzing and pain was happening in a parallel universe, happening to some other guy, some fool who bought the entire Aryan Homeland program. Maybe he thought that getting the tats was a way of thanking Raymond for his hospitality. More likely, Nolan was letting the codeine and beer think for him. And now he's thanked Raymond, all right, by stealing all his stuff.

"Nice to meet you. I'm Vincent Nolan. What do you develop?"

Loser. Nolan knows what she means. He got thrown off by the silence.

Bonnie's trapped in another smile. "Actually, we do fund-raising."

How brilliant. Psychic blackmail. Rich people writing out checks to keep this Bonnie from exploding like those blobs of hot dough Nolan had to scrape off the walls when he worked in the doughnut shop.

No need to feel sorry for Bonnie. She's got a fat scene going. She—or someone—must be a whiz. Somebody's bankrolled the woodwork, the painting, the carpets. The gold letters above the receptionist desk: WORLD BROTHERHOOD WATCH. PEACE THROUGH CHANGE. Somebody paid the bills for that. And it's not like they're selling a product.

"Well, great. Whatever," says Nolan. "I want to work with you guys."

Bonnie eyes the Asian receptionist. What is Ninja Girl supposed to say? She's hanging Bonnie out to dry. Or maybe she's just bewitched by the spell of this magical situation. An incoming call blinks on and off, but no one moves. Is Bonnie from outer space? Nolan should just push up his sleeves, flash his tattoos, and cut to the chase.

"That's wonderful," Bonnie rattles on. "Actually, we do have a volunteer auxiliary which has been *very* helpful with mailings and phone calls and stuff. Mostly it's older women, but we also attract some really cool energetic kids."

Older women? Really cool energetic kids? "Wait a second," says Nolan. "Do you know who I *am?*"

Good question. Bonnie takes a step back. God only knows what she's seeing.

"Listen," says Nolan. "I'm not pretending I understand anything about you or your organization, but I'll bet most of the people you deal with are pretty much like yourself." Jesus, don't let her think he means Jews.

"We reach out to all kinds of people. I'm sorry, Mr. Nolan. There's something I'm not—"

"*Reach out? All* kinds? Can I ask how many white supremacists you guys have reached out to?" He runs one hand over his bald head. Does he have to draw her a map? He'd rehearsed saying "white suprema-cist."

"Not. So. Far," says Bonnie. "I see." And she does. So this is where they would have started if he'd showed his tattoos up front. It's just that they have gotten there by a smoother road. Even so, Nolan can watch revulsion and fear warring with something she believes, or wants to believe: the filthiest skinhead slimeball is some mother's son.

Only now does she notice the duffel bag. She's not the world's most observant person. Maybe it's the glasses. But once she sees it, she can't stop staring. Or looking paler and more afraid. Nolan draws the line at going through the books-and-dirty-laundry rou-tine again.

"World Brotherhood Watch. May I help you?" The sound of the other shoe dropping has roused the receptionist from her trance. "To whom may I direct your call?"

Bonnie's face takes on the strangest look, as if she's trying to place Nolan, almost as if she thinks she might have met him before. As if she *knows* him from somewhere. She does a guppy thing with her mouth several times before she says, "Why don't we go to my office? Would you like to leave your bag at the desk?"

"No, thanks, it's light." Obvious lie number two. But there's no way he's going to leave it and let Kung Fu Girl help herself to his drugs and ARM's fifteen hundred bucks.

"Actually," says Bonnie, "it would be a good idea if you left it out here."

The chick can get tough if she needs to! Nolan's not going to fight her on this. Anyhow, it's an ultimatum: Lose the duffel or forget the invite back to the inner sanctum. It's a test Nolan has to pass, a test of faith. If he's going to put his life in these people's hands, he might as well trust them not to root around in his stash. Nolan walks around behind the desk and shoves the bag in an empty corner.

"Guard it with your life," he says, grinning into the steely center of the receptionist's glare.

Bonnie punches a code into the wall, and Nolan follows her

through a door, past cubicles and offices full of busy worker bees. Nolan glances at Bonnie's ass, mostly because it's there, modestly announcing itself under her unsexy business skirt. Something about it breaks his heart. She's got a nice ass, and she doesn't know it, and now it's almost too late. The ass has got another couple years. The husband's already stopped caring. It's funny, how a woman always knows when you're looking. Even Bonnie stops and turns.

"Listen, I have a better idea. Let's take you to meet Dr. Maslow."

Nolan hopes this change of plans doesn't mean she knows he was checking her out, and now she's scared to be alone with the punk storm-trooper rapist. Or maybe Bonnie finally gets what Nolan can do for Brotherhood Watch. The alien's made itself understood. Take me to your leader.

Bonnie knocks on a half-open door.

"Come in!" cries a voice. You'd think that, with his history, Maslow would ask who's knocking. Nolan watches Bonnie's posture change as she pushes open the door. Hesitant, girlish, slightly stooped—she's shrinking in front of his eyes. Is it terror? Awe? Respect? Sex? You've got to consider sex first.

Outside the windows, the silvery jaws of the city yawn and snap shut, gobbling Nolan and spitting him out, spiraling toward the horizon. The view leaves him slightly motion-sick, and the inrush of sunlight starts him sweating again, though the air conditioner is set to maintain the climate control of heaven.

Maslow's on the phone, one elbow on the desk, cradling his head in his hand as he uses their entrance to end his conversation. "Come in! Excuse me, yes, of course, I'll try to get there, Mount Sinai. Give my love to Minna, all right, see you later. Good-bye."

Bonnie's jumping out of her skin. "Is something wrong? Is someone sick?"

"Nothing serious." Maslow's lying. "An old friend's wife needs a cheer-up visit." Nolan imagines patients in ICUs all over the town, waiting for Maslow to arrive so they can yank out their tubes and die happy. But he can see why Maslow might have that effect. His presence is working on Bonnie like a Valium IV drip.

"Meyer Maslow," says Bonnie. "I'd like you to meet Vincent Nolan."

Maslow stands and extends his hand, not quite far enough, so that reaching for it throws Nolan slightly off balance. Nolan recognizes Maslow from the photos on his books. The same crisp features, untouched by the putty that old age likes to stick onto old guys' faces. Maslow's movements have a catlike grace. Useful, Nolan thinks. For all those times he had to get small and slip through the cracks and vanish.

Maslow's book-jacket gaze meets Nolan's straight on. Does he look that way at everybody? Bonnie doesn't bring *everybody* back into his office. Maslow gives Bonnie a funny look. An I-told-you-so look. As if Maslow had been . . . expecting him. A shiver runs down Nolan's spine.

The Warrior faces and analyzes the forces he has to deal with. And what is Nolan facing? It depends on which Nolan you ask. The old Nolan sees a fat-cat Jew with a million-dollar corner office. The new Nolan sees a hero who survived Hitler to fight for justice and tolerance, to write books and start this foundation. According to their Web site, Brotherhood Watch has saved thousands of lives worldwide. Nolan can only hope that Maslow will step up to the plate and save his.

Maslow's hand is dry and powdery, and like the rest of him, perfect. Every white hair clipped to perfection, like the mane of a show dog, and his eyes are the eyes of the Lassie or Rin Tin Tin you tell all your little-boy secrets. That face will wait forever for Nolan to explain why he's come. If Nolan had a dog like that as a kid, he wouldn't be here now.

"Thanks for taking time," says Nolan. "I read about you guys on the Web. And in the newspapers. I read all your books. I especially liked *The Kindness of Strangers*. And *Forgive, Not Forget*. And the new one, *One Heart at a Time*."

Maslow wasn't expecting that. Score ten points for Nolan.

"You read the new one?"

"I read them all," Nolan lies. "And reading them really changed

me. They made me think that I should come in here and . . . offer
my services. See if you guys wanted to, like, debrief me. There's a
couple of things I could tell you from the years I spent in ARM.
The American Rights Movement?"

"Yes. We know what ARM is. And we know its other name: the
Aryan Resistance Movement." Maslow's eyelids flutter shut. He can
hardly stand the thought. Nolan doesn't blame him. Considering what
he survived—escaping the Nazis, in hiding for years, half a dozen
close calls and near-death experiences, and after all that they caught
him and sent him to the camps—how's the guy supposed to feel about
a bunch of white punks stomping around and giving each other the
Hitler salute? Nolan wouldn't blame Maslow for hating guys like him.
Once again he hears Raymond's voice: To the Jew, we're all the same.

The hate stuff was never what Nolan liked about ARM. Of
course, he agreed that the big bucks weren't going to honest working men like himself, but he was never fully convinced that his tax
dollars were being raked in by the eight Jewish bankers who secretly own the Federal Reserve. Anyway, the ARM guys got
steamed if they so much as heard the word *hate*. They claimed they
didn't hate anyone. It was just that they *loved* the white race. Which
was also a problem for Nolan. Loving a race is a lot to ask. It's hard
enough loving a person. He'd thought he'd loved Margaret, right
up until and including the morning when she'd patiently waited till
he'd finished moving out of their place, loading the last of his stuff
into his truck, and then she got in her UPS van and drove off, smiling and waving.

Mostly, Vincent got into ARM because its take on the government
was so dead-on. ARM said things that no one else had the brains or
the balls to say about those greedy slobs in Washington, figuring out
how to turn a dime by taking away Nolan's freedoms. Clinton, Bush, it
was all the same shit. What sensible person would give a rat's ass who
was in the White House? Those twenty-one babies in Waco weren't
old enough to vote. That stuff was pretty persuasive, Waco and Ruby
Ridge, the shock of finding out that the government you paid taxes
and pledged allegiance to could massacre women and children just for

trying to live the way the Constitution guaranteed. Also, being in ARM had a certain . . . entertainment value. Sometimes the ARM guys could be funny, especially when they got loaded.

Raymond would never have been so hospitable if Nolan hadn't pretended to go along with the entire ARM program, and probably Nolan would never have joined ARM if not for Raymond's hospitality. Not that Nolan would ever admit that. Becoming a white supremacist for the free lunch seems even sleazier than joining because you believe that the white race is an endangered species, or because you like wearing the camouflage gear and the boots.

Nolan *wasn't* a racist, in the sense that he didn't believe in hating people unless you knew them personally. But look, it wasn't lost on him that the Jewish swimming pool owners who contracted with Skip thought nothing of calling Vincent at dawn, ordering him to hustle over to Woodstock just because they'd found a mouse floating at the deep end. Let the Jew get a net and drag the mouse out himself. Or better yet, let the Jew share his wealth and give poor bastards like Nolan a shot at the weekend house and the pool.

The absolute low point was the incident with Mrs. Regina Browner, a Jewish woman, as it happened, an *old* Jewish woman, as it happened, but with plenty of energy left for being a pain in the ass. She kept insisting that frog died in her pool because Nolan had overdosed it with chemicals, when obviously the frog had drowned without any chemical help. She said frogs didn't drown. What did she want Nolan to do? Autopsy the slimy fucker?

She'd been *at* him, bitching and carrying on. When she threatened to complain to Skip, Nolan lifted all starved-down, nipped and tucked ninety pounds of her in his arms. He'd never done anything like that. He felt awful the minute he picked her up and saw how light she was, like those balsa-wood model planes he used to make as a kid. But by then he'd set something in motion and couldn't put her down until he'd gently deposited her in the shallow end of the pool.

Of course he'd jumped in and fished her out, apologizing the whole time, because he was sorry and also because he knew that, if she pressed charges, she could do some damage. He was glad she didn't drown. That's what he said in the letter he wrote her that night. He wrote that he'd meant her no harm. He'd been having a miserable summer. He said his doctor thought he might have an allergy to algaecides, which made him act weird around pools. That was the only lie he told. It was true that he was sorry. If only she had stopped yelling at him five minutes sooner. He couldn't believe he'd become a guy who could drop old ladies in pools. He was glad—he deserved it—when Skip let him go.

After a hairy couple of weeks, Mrs. Browner agreed not to press charges if Nolan took twenty hours of anger management class.

Bonnie and Maslow are staring at him.

Nolan smiles. Okay. It's the moment.

"And I want to help you guys," he says. "I was thinking . . ." Deep breath. Count to ten. "I want to help you guys save guys like me from becoming guys like me."

Nolan can't help grinning. He got that sucker right! The line he'd practiced, chanting it in his head to put himself to sleep during some very rough nights. I want to help you guys save guys like me from becoming guys like me. Tough, tongue-twisting sonofabitch. But he did it. He meant it. *Means* it.

But *what* does he mean, precisely? I want to help you save guys who happen not to have a place to crash from becoming the kind of guys who could keep quiet and go along with Raymond's bonehead ideas in return for a chance to camp out on his lumpy living room couch? And sure, you *would* want to save guys from becoming a guy like that.

The atmosphere stutters, like a thermostat clicking on. Maslow and Bonnie swap long looks. Whatever *that* exchange was about, score ten more for Nolan. Maslow taps his fingertips together, a gesture that reminds Nolan of a Catholic priest.

"I know how those guys think," Nolan says. "I know how they wound up where they wound up. And I know how to turn them around."

Maslow says, "Vincent. If I may call you that. . . . Help us understand. You've spent two years in one of the country's most vicious hate groups. And now you want to come and work with World Brotherhood Watch?"

"In a nutshell," Nolan says.

"I see," says Maslow. "And in that nutshell, I assume, is a major change of heart?"

Change of heart. That works for Nolan. That's exactly what it was. A heart transplant, a new pig's heart for your damaged old one, one of those total blood exchanges you get in Transylvania. Maslow's native land.

"*Major* change," Nolan says. "Correct."

"A conversion experience," Maslow says.

"Exactly."

"And how did you get to us?"

"Your Web site," Nolan says. "Like I said . . ."

Maslow eyeballs Bonnie a memo: See what the World Wide Web can do! Let's look into this further. "But something else must have happened—"

"That's right. Something did, sir." Nolan's never called anyone *sir* in his life. Like some lowlife cornball Elvis.

Maslow says, "Vincent, Bonnie, please. Sit down."

Bonnie sinks into the nearest chair. Nolan takes the other chair, and bingo, he's back in the principal's office on one of the many occasions when he and his mom were summoned in for a chat. Nolan's mom always took his side, patiently explaining why her son might be bored, ignoring the sparks of hatred shooting out of the principal's eyes. He's also thinking of the time when he and Celia Mignano got busted for having sex in the art room. Both memories give him a pleasant buzz, like a swarm of mellow bees humming between him and Bonnie.

Maslow says, "Would you mind telling us how this change of heart came about?"

How did they get so far so fast? Nolan isn't ready. He'd pictured a conversation. This is an audition. Only now he sees it's useless. He could sit here and blab all day and never explain. Still, it's not as if he didn't know that sooner or later they would ask. That's why

Nolan prepared, mentally rehearsed his account of what pushed him over the edge.

"The thing is . . . I was at this rave. . . . Two weeks ago, maybe three. That last freak hot spell before this one . . ."

"Rave?" Five seconds into the story, and Maslow's left in the dust. He smiles and hands this one off to Bonnie, their resident youth-culture expert. "Mrs. Kalen has two teenagers."

"Girls or boys?" As if Nolan cares.

"Sons. Max and Danny." Bonnie likes just mentioning them. Something loosens in her face. "Twelve and sixteen."

"You must have had them when you were a child," Nolan says.

"Right," says Bonnie. "A baby."

Maslow's fingers drum on the desk. What *is* it with Maslow and Bonnie? If only it were as simple as sex. It's some neurotic head trip. Bonnie worships the guy. And he digs it.

"A rave?" asks Maslow. "Enlighten me."

"It's like a huge party," says Nolan.

"Well," says Bonnie. "A little more than that. It's a whole . . . underground subculture. Kids get the word out, and thousands of them take over an old warehouse with giant sound systems and paint their faces and dance and—"

"Lovely," says Maslow. "Do your sons attend these events?"

"Not so far." Bonnie knocks on Maslow's desk. The woman is superstitious.

Nolan says, "This one was outdoors. In a field. The dead middle of nowhere. In March. How smart was that? They'd dragged out these gigantic generators and the screens for the lights and . . . Did I say my cousin Raymond took me?" Nolan wishes he hadn't mentioned Raymond. The urge to look over his shoulder must be visible on his face.

"Vincent," says Maslow. "May I interrupt? When you're as old as I am, everyone under forty looks the same age. But excuse me, I'm wondering . . ."

"I'm thirty-two," says Nolan. He knows where Maslow's going with this. Nolan's near the top of the age curve for rave and rock-concert attendance. "That's why I thought it would depress me, hanging out with a bunch of teens jumping around and waving glow sticks and puking. And frankly . . . I couldn't see what it would *do* for me to exchange a big group hug with the rainbow coalition."

Bonnie laughs—a good sign. Maslow doesn't—a bad one.

"Thirty miles from the rave, the sky clouded over. I started hearing thunder. I figured we were looking at some Woodstock Nation mud fest. I remember telling Raymond how embarrassing it would be to spend years preparing to die with the ARM liberation forces and then get fried by lightning with a crowd of dirt children in a meadow."

"Did you and your friends in ARM often go to these . . . raves?" What's it to Maslow? What ARM members do on their down time is none of his business.

"Never," says Nolan. "Not usually." This story has two levels. One is the truth, which makes it easy to tell. The second level is not a lie so much as a highlight, drag, and delete. You don't have to tell everyone everything. It's a lesson that comes with age. By now Nolan has learned a few things, and also anger management gave him some useful tips to remember: No need to always have the last word, to unload the last shot in the chamber. No reason to report that Raymond made fun of him for suggesting they bail because of the weather. Was chickenshit Nolan scared of getting *rained on?* What was Raymond supposed to do with those seventy hits of Ex? Shove them up his ass?

"By the time we arrived, a million kids were squirming around under these drive-in movie screens, boom boom, pulsing colored lights. Like some worm-farm lava-lamp cult. They had this huge scaffolding with disc jockeys sitting up top and techno music pounding—"

Maslow says, "It sounds like hell."

Again the sound of Raymond's voice thrums in Nolan's ears. The Jew does not believe in heaven or hell. That's why he can steal from his neighbors, provided he repents on that one day a year that the Jew sets aside to atone.

"So what happened then?" Hold on. Is Maslow *hurrying* him? Nolan will take as long as he needs to.

"Raymond splits. Disappears. And I'm thinking . . . Okay, wait. Let's back up a minute. You've got to understand. I was a different person then. I thought stuff I would never think now." Is that true? Sure it is. Maybe Nolan picked and chose from the crap he was hearing, but he definitely chose *some* of it. The part he agreed with already.

"We *do* understand," says Bonnie. "You're telling us how you *changed*."

Is that what Nolan's telling them? Peace through change. Where did he just see that? Right. The sign in the lobby. So that's what they're selling. Beautiful. Nolan can do peace through change.

"So I'm thinking it's just like Raymond to leave me alone in this mob of human hairballs. And then this girl starts dancing with me. And she hands me two light sticks."

Time for another drag and delete. The girl was young and pretty. Nolan would have stuck the light sticks in his eyes if he'd thought it would get him laid. "So okay, I wave them around. The girl's smiling, everything's cool, a second later she's gone. And I'm left with these lights. I'm trying to get to the edge of the crowd, but the mob keeps pushing me back. And it's confusing, because I'd been hanging out with guys who thought it was your patriotic duty to stomp people like that. Not that the guys I knew in ARM got into those situations much. We always kept it together."

"Meaning what?" says Maslow.

"We tried to stay in control," says Nolan. "Our particular unit was not into random violence." Enough. If they want the details, he can fill them in later. Though maybe what they want to know *most* is how many asses he kicked. Well, the truth is, not any. Which isn't to say that the guys from ARM weren't often right on the edge of wasting the next Paki convenience-store clerk who gave them attitude. Problem was, on the nights they were feeling that way, the clerk on duty was always some poor pimply white chick. Maslow and Bonnie don't have to know that yet. For now, let them dream what they want. Let them think Nolan and his pals kicked a minimum one ass per day.

"So I stopped moving and let my hands drop, and the light sticks are now, like, you know, around, like, my crotch area, and I'm looking down at them, and suddenly I get this feeling like I'm seeing my spirit or soul or something, burning inside me, shining . . ."

By now Maslow's got to be wondering what drugs Nolan was taking, and Bonnie, with her two teenage sons, thinks she *knows* what drug he was on. Which in fact he *was* on, but that's not why it happened. He'd taken Ex before. He did a hit the night he got the tattoos. So what does that tell you? He's taken so many drugs by this point, his brain's a wedge of Swiss cheese. But he'd never felt that way before. This was new. Deeper. Higher.

"I heard this roaring in my head. This pounding and thrumming. Like wings. Like that blood pressure thing in your ears, you know? You get it, and then it goes. I thought it might be some buzz in the amps. And then I looked up at the scaffolding, and there was this funny . . . halo spinning around the disc jockeys. It reminded me of this Christmas card my mom used to have, a painting of the Holy Spirit dove hovering in this circle of pale gold light. And then . . . this is the hardest part to explain, but I got this feeling of *love* for everyone around me. Everyone. Black and white, Jewish, Christian, Communist, freaks, retarded, mutant, whatever."

Is this working? Let's ratchet things up a notch. "It was like I got hit by lightning. I felt like Saint Paul getting knocked off his donkey on the road to Damascus."

"Horse," says Maslow. "Saul of Tarsus got thrown off his *horse* on the way to Damascus."

The Jew thinks he knows more than you do. That's what Raymond would say. But Nolan is the one thinking it now. It's time to let go of all that if he wants this plan to succeed. Let go of the long-nosed Jew and the Negro with the big dick. Bye-bye defending the endangered white race, hello peace through change.

Maslow says, "May I ask you something? Did you attend church as a child?"

"Irish Catholic." It's mostly true. Nolan's grandparents were Catholic. This is not the time to explain that after his dad died,

Mom dragged him around from one hippie religious clambake to another. She's been a chanting Buddhist ever since she saw Tina Turner on *Living Legends*. "One of my aunts was a Baptist who used to take me to revivals. I liked the hymns. There was this one hymn, 'Blessed Assurance.' And those two words, *blessed assurance*, kept running through my mind while I was having that . . . experience at the rave."

The part about the hymn is pure rich smoke Nolan's blowing up their asses. But sure enough, he can feel Bonnie's eyes on him. It's been Nolan's experience that women love imagining you as a kid with your hair slicked back, all sweaty and hot in your scratchy church suit. They want to go to bed with that kid. That's how weird women are.

The first time Nolan met Margaret, in a bar in Hudson, a gospel tune came on the jukebox. Nolan knew the words, he sang along. *Trials, troubles, and tribulations* . . . Nothing corny, like singing in Margaret's ear, but softly, to himself, like a man remembering something sweet from childhood. The song ended. He'd looked at Margaret, and he knew it had worked. Our man was *in*.

Maslow asks, "And did you still feel that way the next morning?"

"What way?" says Nolan. "Excuse me, I . . ."

"Loving the world," says Maslow.

Does the old guy believe him at all? It's impossible to tell.

"Even more," Nolan says. "I woke up under a tree. Somehow Raymond found me. He drove me home to his place. When I got there, I was still flashing on hate, how I used to hate everything, how hate poisoned the world, how every bad thing that's happened could be traced directly to hate."

Most of that came from Maslow's book. But the basic idea is true: Nolan couldn't stand one more minute of ARM, or Raymond and his friends. Just turning in to Raymond's driveway nearly made him puke. Maybe it was the lawn gnomes in Raymond's yard, or maybe the fact that they looked so much like Raymond and Lucy and their kids. In the end, it was a pit-of-the-stomach thing. An allergy to the guys in ARM, to the sound of their voices. None of them gave a shit about the planet. They made fun of save-the-whales types. You'd think the Ex-high residue would have left Nolan loving Raymond and his friends along with every other human creature. Loving the white race. But somehow it didn't work that way. It was time to get out of Dodge.

"So what did you do then?" Bonnie says.

"One morning, I woke up before everyone else, and I went to Raymond's desk. I went online. I typed in 'Neo-Nazi.' And then 'Help.'"

"Is that how you got to us?" says Bonnie.

"No," Nolan says. "First I got some newspaper site, with this article: 'Neo-Nazi Helps Foundation.' About this white separatist brother who saw the light and reformed—" Does *this* qualify as a lie? It's too small to matter. Nolan *did* look up the story on the Internet, but by then he'd already seen a program about it on *The Chandler Show*.

On TV, the former skinhead got the total fashion makeover. He was all duded up in a fancy suit, and they'd waited till his hair grew back enough to look like some hip, faggy buzz cut.

Harrison Chandler was nearly sobbing when the guy explained how he'd turned from the dark toward the light, from the path of hate to the path of love. Nolan would rather not think about that. Because then he'll have to think about how much Raymond and his buddies liked to watch *Chandler* and yell at the TV, because Chandler is an extremely visible overpaid Negro employed by the Jewish media. That episode really ticked them off. They were throwing beer cans at the set until Lucy shut the party down.

Maslow wants to know what they did in ARM? They watched TV and yelled.

"Oh, that guy who went to work for the Wiesenthal Foundation," says Bonnie. "Remember, Meyer?"

The old man doesn't want to remember. There's something about this he doesn't like. Better wrap up this part and move on.

"Anyway," says Nolan, "I read about this skin who had a huge . . . change of heart because he heard his four-year-old daughter calling someone a nigger." Bonnie and Meyer flinch. "Excuse me. Which, frankly, would *not* have been enough to make me turn—but then, I don't have kids." He smiles at Bonnie. *She* has kids. "The guy signed on to help with this tolerance group in L.A. And I thought if I could find a place like that, I could do something similar."

Bonnie says, "Meyer, I don't *believe* this. You were just saying before—"

Maslow gives her a look. He means her to shut up.

"So you know who we are? From the Internet."

Didn't Nolan just say that? "I read your books," he repeats. "*The Kindness of Strangers*. And the new one. *One Heart at a Time*."

"That's still in hardback," says Maslow.

"I ordered it from Amazon." Nolan intends to, when he finds a way. That is, as soon as he figures out how to get his own credit card and an account.

"We no longer patronize Amazon," says Maslow. "Not until they agree to stop carrying *The Turner Diaries*."

Normally, Nolan's proud of how much he reads, but for once he suppresses the desire to say, "I read that!" Of course he read *The Turner Diaries*. It was the only book, besides the Bible, that Raymond had in the house, which made sense, since Pierce's novel is practically like the Bible to the ARM guys, who can quote it, chapter and verse. Despite all the violence and the stuff about the major race war finally breaking out and the black people—or was it the white collaborators or race-mixers?—strung from lampposts, Nolan thought it was boring. Will it earn him points to say that? Not likely. He thinks not.

"Anyhow," says Nolan, "that's how I wound up here. I thought I could help out. I know how ARM functions, and what those guys want, why the whole Aryan thing works for them. I was *one* of those guys, so I know what makes them so vulnerable, so open to having their heads turned around."

Maslow says, "This is very interesting. Why don't you phone us in a few days? Mrs. Kalen and I and our staff will try to figure out how we can use your experience—"

Is that what they tell the ladies who volunteer to lick envelopes and make calls for the charity drive? All this hard work, and Nolan has failed to get his point across.

"I don't know how to say this, but I can't go back. Leaving ARM is not like quitting the Boy Scouts. I can't wait for you to call and have some guy at the tire place where I work, where a bunch of ARM guys work, say, Hey, Nolan, phone call. For you. World Brotherhood Watch. Those guys don't just let you go. They're not real fond of . . . defectors. This one guy who left Wyoming ARM. They found out where he was and put him in the hot seat and cut off three of his toes. They would track me down, is what I'm saying. As it is, I'm risking my life. If they knew I was here . . ."

Only when Nolan hears himself say this does he realize that it's true. If Raymond ever found out where he was, Nolan would be dead meat. Will Raymond bother to hunt him down? Probably. Sooner or later. The shiver Nolan feels makes him want to pass the fear along to someone else.

"I mean, like I said, the guys I knew in ARM, they weren't really all that violent. But they were always one step away from seriously breaking heads. The slightest insult, one word of back talk from someone of another religion or race, would have been all they needed to get things rolling. They were always jealous when they heard about guys who actually torched a synagogue or something. Or encouraged some lone wolf who went on a shooting spree."

Torched a synagogue. Shooting spree. Nolan's taking a risk here. On the one hand, he doesn't want to make them think that taking him on will be more dangerous than it's worth. On the other hand, he's hoping that the element of threat will make them want to prove how gutsy they are, and rise to the scary challenge. He looks at Bonnie and Maslow. Bonnie's gone white. The old man's harder to read.

Maslow says, "We'd be discreet. We wouldn't try to reach you at your workplace."

"We can call you at home," says Bonnie.

How could she still not get it?

"I've been staying on my cousin's living room couch," says

Nolan. "I *have* no home. I'm homeless." He hears his voice rise. "Which could get inconvenient. Listen, I was even worried the guys in ARM would find out I'd checked out your Web site on Raymond's computer."

"Maybe they'd think you were learning about your enemies," says Maslow.

"That's not how their minds work." What's making this trickier are the details that might have supplied the filler to plug up the holes in his story. The fifteen hundred dollars, the truck. The contents of Raymond's medicine chest.

"What I need is something like the Federal Witness Protection Program. Only . . . not so extreme. *The Kindness of Strangers* was what gave me the idea." In fact, Maslow's books *were* what convinced Nolan that he might be able to do this. Starting with the first line: "This is a book about being taken in and saved by ordinary people of courage and conscience." In the second book there's a conversation between Maslow and some Japanese Zen master in which they agree that history is the stick God uses to whomp you on the head. Then there's the new book—which Nolan hasn't actually read, except for the summary on Amazon—about changing one person, one heart, at a time. What he read was enough for him to understand that Maslow is working toward sainthood. So let's see how saintly you are, pal. Save me, like those strangers saved you.

"I read how you survived the war because people—even people who didn't like Jews—had consciences and hearts and souls and pitied you and took you in. And I figured you would remember. I mean, I know you must hate neo-Nazis even more than the—"

Oops. Nolan stops in mid-sentence. He can practically watch the steam pour out of Maslow's ears.

"We don't hate anyone," Maslow says. "Hate is not what we do. And young man, let me tell you that if you think protecting you from your hooligan hate-monger friends is *anything* like being saved from the Nazis—"

Bonnie startles, visibly.

I've blown it, Nolan thinks.

"I didn't mean *that*. I'm sorry if that's how it sounded. But I thought that since it . . . since something like that happened . . . I mean, I know that what's happening to me is nothing like—"

Maslow's eyelids droop. He nods wearily. Let it go.

"I thought you would understand and find some way to help me lay low till the dust settles. Plus . . . don't you think the newspapers will love it? 'Nazi Turns for Brotherhood Watch.' There were always reporters and freelance writers swarming all over the Homeland Encampment, wanting to take us out for beers and listen to our life stories. Every creep was writing a book about the white-power movement. After that skin in L.A. turned himself in to the Wiesenthal Foundation, he was on all the talk shows for a while, it was a big deal. Not that this would just be about the media. It would be about changing one heart at a time. Like you say in your book."

Nolan's had to spell it out for them. And he's had to bank on the fact that Maslow and Bonnie are no different from anyone else.

"Forgive me." The old man looks tired. Has Nolan blown it again? "It's late in the day. Somehow it's taken me all this time to understand what you're offering—and what you're asking. Which is quite a lot."

Nolan shrugs. "Offering mainly."

"And asking. Quite a lot," repeats Maslow. "You're asking us to shelter you. To give you a new life. And if we had any brains at all, or if our brains were as big as our hearts, we'd refuse. Anyone would understand. No one would know we'd turned you down. But maybe you know that Sufi story about the man who steals a chicken and goes out to the woods to kill it where no one will see, except that he knows God sees—and so he can't kill the chicken."

Nolan takes a little break during the chicken story. It's the same spiritual jive he used to hear from his mom and her friends.

"Well," explains Maslow, "God sees into this room today, and I would have to answer to Him if I turned away a young man in need, perhaps in danger, a young man determined to change—and help us. Which reminds me. One thing we ask. And that is the truth. No reconciliation, no progress, can happen without it. This is something I learned from Nelson Mandela, from the Truth and Reconciliation Program. Bonnie, do we have that film on tape? I think our friend should see it. It's very moving, what they've done in South Africa. They believe that healing cannot happen without total honesty and full disclosure. As do we. Which is why we're asking you to be completely forthcoming. We'll need to know who you are, and what you've done, and what you believe."

Nolan nods his wild approval. How cool is *that*—dropping Nelson Mandela's name? "Sure, the whole truth and nothing but the truth. My life is an open book."

"Think of that as our contract," Maslow says.

"Agreed," Nolan says. "Sir." And now Maslow smiles.

"Let's find you an empty office, and you can relax until we figure out the next step. Would that be all right?"

"That would be fine." Standing, Nolan starts sweating again, so the hand he gives Maslow to shake is a slippery mess. Maslow doesn't seem to mind.

"So if we are to be colleagues," he says, "do you think that I could make a slightly . . . unusual request?"

What does he mean by *unusual?* Nolan's staying in to find out.

"Be my guest," says Nolan.

"Would you mind pushing up your sleeves?"

"Sure." Nolan pushes his sleeves to the elbow, high enough for Maslow and Bonnie to get a good look at the Waffen-SS bolts and the death's-head. Neither shows the slightest emotion. They could be doctors trained to examine disgusting eruptions.

"Thank you, Vincent," says Maslow.

And then Maslow rolls up *his* sleeve, unbuttoning a pearly button and neatly turning his elegant cuff. And there on Maslow's spindly arm is the row of blue numbers. Nolan should have predicted this, but he's shocked, nonetheless. He's never seen anything like it. He always knew Raymond was wrong about the Jews tattooing themselves. The Holo-hoax, Raymond calls it. Maslow's quite a guy. You've got to give him credit for having the balls to go mano a mano in this weird game of dueling tattoos. Damn, Nolan's *glad* he got the tats. They're getting him into the action. At the same time he's glad he never went for that Holo-hoax crap. If he had, the old man's tattoos would be making him feel bad about himself instead of about his fellow humans.

Maslow says, "Did you know that you can tell from the number when one arrived at Auschwitz?"

When *one* arrived at Auschwitz? One *what?* Shame washes over Nolan, an oily wave of self-loathing. The guy survived the death camps, and Nolan's annoyed by how he talks? English isn't his language. He hardly has an accent. How would Nolan stack up if they were doing this in Hungarian?

Nolan says, "I didn't know that."

"And you could tell where someone came from. The Italians had the lowest numbers. Read Primo Levi. I can't remember my phone number, but I remember the one on my arm."

Nolan can't remember the last time he had his own phone number. But no matter what's happened to Nolan, Auschwitz beats it cold. So far. Unless Raymond and his buddies hunt him down and kill him. Not that they'd *mean* to kill him. They'd just try to scare him. Things get out of hand. Even then his death would be only one death, compared to millions of deaths. But the bottom line would be that Nolan would be dead, and Maslow would be alive. So *then* who would have it worse?

"A living dog is better than a dead lion," Nolan says.

"Ecclesiastes," says Meyer.

"My favorite quote from the Bible," says Nolan. "Anyway that's what tattoos do. I mean, they mark time. I remember when I got these, I—"

Maslow's face hardens from best-friend puppy to attack dog. "My tattoos and yours are *not* the same!"

"I know that," Nolan says.

"You don't. You don't know!" Maslow says.

"I'm learning," says Nolan. "Believe me."

A FTER BONNIE AND VINCENT have pretty much covered the riveting subjects of the weather (hot for April!) and the traffic (hardly moving!), there's nothing to do but sit in the van, foreheads popping beads of sweat into the hideous silence. Bonnie's fighting the impulse to fling open the door and run screaming down the highway, which would make perfect sense since it's obvious she's already lost her mind.

But why should it seem crazy, or even odd, to be taking a skinhead stranger home to spend the night alone with you and your children? Why? Because it's outrageous. Totally suicidal. How could Bonnie—a grown woman, a mother, the person more or less single-handedly responsible for raising the annual budget of a great human rights organization—have let Meyer talk her into this? Why? Because she believes that Brotherhood Watch *is* a great organization. Everything follows from that. It makes everything into a test. Is she great enough to work there? Bonnie loves the foundation, she loves her job, and above all she loves the feeling that she is doing something worthwhile with her life, something more important than what she did at her previous job, which was shaking down her suburban neighbors so that the Clairmont Museum could buy another antique print of a riverboat steaming up the Hudson.

"Tappan Zee traffic," says Bonnie, the Martian's tour guide to Earth.

"I figured." Vincent's staring straight ahead and sitting up so rigidly he could be one of those mannequins solo drivers buy so they can ride the commuter lanes. Is it nervousness? Some paramilitary thing? Or was he taught as a child to take up the minimum possible space? How sad that a child should be taught to get small. But that's what Meyer had to learn. That's how Meyer survived.

How different from her own kids—squirming, sprawling, occupying every inch of the world that exists for them to fill with their glorious bodies. Bonnie has to admit that even with their broken home, their self-involved dad, and the soulless home-wrecker he currently lives with, Danny and Max are lucky. She knocks on the little square of wood she carries on the dashboard for that purpose.

"Superstitious?" Vincent asks.

"Extremely," Bonnie replies.

It doesn't take a genius to figure out that knocking on wood means you're superstitious. Still, Vincent's getting it right might seem like an encouraging sign—he's paying attention, taking things in, he *is* from Planet Earth—except that he hasn't turned to face her or so much as twitched during their brief conversation. If that isn't creepy, what is? Perhaps he's just being polite, trying to inflate a bubble of privacy around himself in this awkward situation. It would be worse if he were, say, staring at her knee as she swivels between the gas and the brake, revealing stretches of thigh. Her skirt seems six inches shorter than it did this morning. Most men couldn't sit still, couldn't suppress their body-language critique of Bonnie's driving. Joel rarely let Bonnie drive, except sometimes after a party; then he'd slide all the way down in the seat and cover his face with his hands. The worst part was that Bonnie *laughed* at this cute married joke.

No, the most humiliating part was how Bonnie trained herself to respond to Joel's every gesture: that almost imperceptible lip-curl that meant the steak was a shade too rare. She should have made him burn it himself. Maybe they'd still be together. Not that Bonnie wants that. Since the divorce, she's begun to see many aspects of Joel that she'd chosen to overlook. But monitoring his tiny tics has turned out to be excellent training, useful now in her work as she watches a donor's face for the perfect moment to raise the subject of giving.

"Might as well relax," she tells Vincent. "Go with the flow." She's said plenty of stupid things, but not, as it happens, *that*. Vincent looks frightened to death. What's *he* got to be scared of? Plenty, Bonnie thinks.

Leaving the office, they'd had to discuss how to get to Bonnie's house. It was like a blind date from hell, matchmade by Meyer Maslow. Vincent asked where Clairmont was, as if it made a difference. He said his truck was broken. He'd taken the bus into the city. Which means that Bonnie gets to drive him home, and back and forth to work every day now that Meyer has decided to give Vincent a desk and pay him a minimal salary to do . . . what? They'll figure that out later. At least he won't be parking a pickup truck plastered with racist bumper stickers in her driveway overnight. Clairmont's a small town. People talk. Her kids go to public school.

Meyer told her to think of Vincent as a person newly escaped from a cult. These first few days would be critical. He could take off at any minute. Did Meyer miss the part where Vincent said he *couldn't* go back? It comforts Bonnie that Meyer said, "these first few days." After that they can help Vincent find his own place. What could be simpler than renting a Manhattan apartment for a homeless, tattooed neo-Nazi with nothing to his name but a duffel bag? And probably a storage unit by the side of the road crammed with explosives and canned baked beans, his emergency survival cache for the coming race war.

To break the silence, she says, "It's getting worse every day. The traffic, the pollution—"

"That's a statistical fact," Vincent says. "I read where some scientists said we've only got enough oxygen left in the atmosphere to last us thirty more years."

Where did he read *that?* The *National Enquirer?* Don't be a snob, Bonnie thinks. Working with Meyer has made her acutely aware of her middle-class prejudices. Could it be true about the oxygen supply? Bonnie doesn't care. It's the longest sentence Vincent has spoken since they got in the van, back in Midtown.

"That's what you get for chopping down the rain forest." This seems safe enough, unless it inspires a rant about the Indians bringing it on themselves, burning their habitat for firewood, or some other such proven fact.

"For Big Mac containers," says Vincent. So Bonnie and her Nazi pal share similar views on the environment.

Earlier that afternoon, while Vincent waited in Meyer's secretary's office, Meyer sat on the edge of his desk and ticked off the essential questions on his elegant fingers: What is their obligation to someone who needs their help? Why would a guy like Vincent decide to become a skinhead? Why would he change? And can some magic formula be extracted from his reversal, some miracle vaccine with which to inoculate thousands like him? Meyer went on to talk about how the species was being programmed—by overpopulation, crowding, the media, big business—to suppress its instinctive impulse to shelter the homeless, and to take in the stray.

"Who's got the room?" said Bonnie, lamely.

"Everyone," Meyer said.

That's why Bonnie admires Meyer. And it's also why Danny calls him Meyer Manson. *So, Mom, what did Charlie—I mean Meyer—say today?* Don't call him that, says Bonnie, even though she's weirdly pleased that her son knows who Charlie Manson is. By now that counts as history. Plus, she understands what he means. When Meyer gets his big ideas, his visionary plans, other people—mainly Bonnie—wind up handling the details.

Work with anyone long enough, you learn that the person is human. Bonnie has seen the great man's whole day ruined by a gravy spot on his tie. But he's a true believer, and what he believes in—saving lives, getting people out of prison and fed and taken care of, education, health care, basic human rights—is pretty high on the scale of things, no matter how you're counting. So what if Meyer might, in his secret heart, *like* to be a cult leader? He's not programming Bonnie to stab Hollywood starlets or to be raptured up into outer space.

Still, Bonnie can't help wishing that she wasn't always the one who gets to deal with the trivia that makes Meyer's dreams come true. During last summer's Pride and Prejudice ("Keep our pride! Lose our prejudice! Celebrate diversity!") camp in Maine, it was Bonnie who called the lawyer when the kids got busted for smoking pot. It was Bonnie who tracked down the surgeon when the Bosnian peace activist's appendix ruptured on Thanksgiving morning. Bonnie who found the backup caterers for the Copenhagen Conference after that BSE scare, the pharmaceutical company wanting to brighten its tarnished image by shipping penicillin to aid workers in Somalia. Why is Bonnie the chosen one? Obviously. She's female. But that can't be the whole reason. Other women in the office aren't singled out. Is it that Bonnie can't say no? She'd rather think that Meyer sees her as someone from whom heroic things can be asked.

How rare it is to have a boss who's a better person than you are. Bonnie's become a more savvy and trusting human being just from being around him. She's learned a lot by watching him take one look at someone and figure out who that person is. He's said it's a skill he had to learn fast, on the run from the Germans. He didn't have the luxury of misreading people's intentions. So if Meyer says that Vincent is a person who wants to change and not a serial rapist, Bonnie is willing to believe that Vincent is a person who wants to change and not a serial rapist. It means being braver than she really is. But that's a good thing, too.

Anyway, Vincent doesn't seem like a serial rapist. In fact, if he weren't a neo-Nazi, okay, a *former* neo-Nazi, and if Bonnie weren't your basic single-mother-of-two foundation fund-raiser nun, she might almost think that Vincent was . . . sort of attractive. A little on the rough-trade side, but some women like that. Or she might think that if the divorce hadn't left her convinced that you were better off not noticing if a man was attractive or not.

After Meyer had talked her into taking in Vincent as a houseguest, the first thing that crossed Bonnie's mind was that Vincent had made it clear: his life might be in danger. How interesting that her first response wasn't fear of Vincent but fear of Vincent's friends, the ones who'd tracked that poor guy down—that defector in Wyoming. They'd put him in the . . . *hot seat.* Cut off three of his toes. Maybe Bonnie has instincts, too. That would be reassuring. Reassuring about what? About his buddies not hunting him down and spraying the house with bullets? A stab of grief warns her away from imagining her sons asleep in their beds when the white-power drive-by erupts. How could Bonnie do this to them? For *Meyer?* It's not about Meyer. It's about saving and changing a life.

The boys are probably home by now. Bonnie would give anything to be there with them, kicking off her shoes, putting on her sweatshirt and jeans, and fooling around in the kitchen, instead of here in gridlock hell in a freak spring heat wave, stalled in traffic that hasn't moved in fifteen, twenty minutes, and just for added interest, a human time bomb in the passenger seat and, wait a minute, what's *this?* A blinking light on her dashboard.

The blinking light says, "Maintenance required." When did *that* come on? And does it mean required right now? Or required when you get to it?

Either the steering wheel's vibrating strangely, or Bonnie has some . . . neurological tremor that also wasn't there this morning. Calm down. She knows what Meyer would say: *Look for the hidden blessing.* Meyer's books are filled with stories in which he asked what God wanted, and the answer helped him escape one mortal danger after another. Let Meyer find the blessing in this five-year-old van, the heat, the traffic. Meyer *walks* home from work.

Well, one blessing of being stuck on the road is that it's delaying the moment when Bonnie has to introduce her kids to their new roommate. Another is that Vincent's presence forces Bonnie to maintain some dignity instead of pounding the steering wheel and moaning, as she might if she were alone. Vincent might know what to do if the blinking dashboard light turns out to be serious. He's a guy. He works in a tire shop.

Which would mean that her life was some cornball O. Henry short story scripted by Meyer. Our heroine does the right thing, her car breaks down, and—surprise!—the homeless skinhead is on board to help.

Vincent says, "I really appreciate your giving me a place to crash—"

"You should thank Meyer," says Bonnie. "Not me." That's not what she meant to say. *This wasn't my idea. The boss made me do it.* But isn't that partly true? She'd begged Meyer to let her call a hotel and book Vincent a room. Meyer was sure that Vincent would be gone before morning. Bonnie reminded Meyer: She's divorced. She lives in the suburbs with two teenage sons. Did he think a Nazi houseguest was really a good idea?

Meyer said, "What do I know? I'm just someone whose life was saved by men and women who acted without asking themselves if it was a good idea."

"It's not the same," Bonnie pointed out. "Hiding you was the opposite of hiding a neo-Nazi." It had only been a few minutes since Meyer said that to Vincent.

"A former Nazi." Meyer waved his hand. "A human being asking for help." Once more Meyer had made Bonnie see that she was being narrow and small-minded, caring only for her soft bed, her house, her kids, her privacy, when, if Meyer's instinct about Vincent turned out to be true, the good he could do might outweigh all that put together. Here was a person who could talk to—who could *reach*—the kind of bigots that the Anti-Defamation League and the Southern Poverty Law Center can only monitor from afar. And what if Vincent doesn't pan out? He doesn't have to make *converts*. All he has to do is scare one middle-school kid out of turning into him.

"He's quite a guy," says Vincent. "That thing he did with the tattoos blew me away."

"Me, too," says Bonnie. "Wasn't that incredible?" So it's not just their concern for the rain forest that she and her new friend have in common. They shared an *experience* back in the office.

Bonnie had been deeply moved. Meyer's thin arm, Vincent's muscular one, the difference in their ages, their colors. Every human body born into this world as a blank slate on which a life will be inscribed. Another vision she would never have had if not for Meyer Maslow.

But the really incredible part, the part that gives her the chills, started an hour or so before Meyer and Vincent got around to comparing tattoos.

Bonnie's day had begun with a string of disturbing phone calls; first the PR firm, then the events planner, then the accountant, all wanting to discuss the disappointing ticket sales for the Brotherhood Watch Annual Gala Benefit Dinner coming up in June. Nobody knew what the problem was. The economy? Everyone holding tight to see what happens with the estate tax? Their inability, so far, to find a big-draw celebrity speaker? The Middle East? That disastrous interview in which Meyer told the *Times* reporter that the Palestinians and the Israelis could *both* do more toward practicing forgiveness without forgetting? She'd thought enough time had lapsed since the article ran, but maybe she'd been wrong.

Everyone wanted Bonnie to know what she already knew: they're looking at the Temple of Dendur, the most popular party venue at the Metropolitan Museum of Art, rented for the evening with half the tables unsold, which will translate not only into a major morale problem but a black hole in the annual budget. She'd waited to tell Meyer until after lunch, when he was often sleepy and consequently more mellow.

When Bonnie mentioned the calls, Meyer seemed annoyed, then saddened. She hoped he wasn't connecting this to the modest sales of his new book, *One Heart at a Time.* Though he never mentioned it, she knew that it upset him. But finally Meyer shrugged, his personal shorthand for: It is all in God's hands. Compared to what he'd lived through, what were book sales, what was a budget, what were tickets to a dinner?

"Anyway," Meyer told Bonnie, "I have a . . . funny feeling. The faintest blip on my radar. Someone is coming. Something's going to happen. How many times have I told you, no problem is too large or small for God to fix. The important thing is to stay open to the miracle when it occurs."

It's not Bonnie's favorite side of Meyer, the part that can make him sound like some cheeseball New Age guru. Meyer insists on having it all at once: history, God, and expensive clothes. He demands his right to wear Armani while using a mystical tale from Rabbi Nachman to make a point about former Soviet bloc politics or hunger in Rwanda. Bonnie knows the contradictions make some people uneasy. But Bonnie respects him for that. Meyer's a complex person, and after all this time, there's still something mysterious and unpredictable about him that keeps her slightly off balance, guessing, impressed.

What's bothering her is the growing suspicion that he might be slipping. Not losing it so much as phoning it in, going on automatic: the Meyer Maslow Show. She's concerned about his fondness for repeating his trademark phrases: Forgive, not forget. One heart at a time. Lately, he's got a new one: the moral bungee jump. Bonnie suspects he's trying it out for his speech at the gala.

But whenever Bonnie has doubts, something amazing happens. Meyer not only talks about miracles, he actually seems to create them, or at least to be around when miracles occur. Foreign dissidents get sprung from jail, whole populations are allowed to emigrate to freedom. Meyer is, after all, a man plucked five times from the clutches of death. What was he supposed to do? Outgrow it after the war? Just today, for example, he'd begun to tell her one of those stories about the poor couple who welcome the beggar who knocks on the door and who turns out to be God's messenger and—

Meyer got a phone call and left the story unfinished. And before he was off the phone, the beggar messenger arrived, disguised as Vincent Nolan.

Ask for something, God sends it. A typical day with Meyer. Was it chance or God's will that the receptionist, Anita Shu, couldn't reach building security? How lucky it was that Anita didn't call Roberta Dwyer, their chief publicist. Had Roberta seen Meyer do that thing with the tattoos, she would have tried to commodify it and turn it into a photo op they could repeat on demand for the press. Bonnie wants attention for Brotherhood Watch. But she'd rather avoid the tabloid centerfold of the two men's arms. Not that Meyer would have allowed it.

Thank God it was Bonnie who answered, Bonnie and Meyer who recognized that Vincent could pump new energy into the foundation. When Vincent referred to how much the media might go for the story of his leaving the white power movement and coming to work for Brotherhood Watch, something clicked for Bonnie. She'd turned to Meyer and seen that, as always, he was light-years ahead.

So once more Bonnie finds herself responsible for the small stuff. So what if Meyer isn't offering Vincent *his* apartment? *Everyone has room.* Meyer has more room, plus a whole domestic staff and a powerhouse wife, Irene, who could handle all this with one hand tied behind her back, a thousand times better than Bonnie, who has a tiny guest room crammed with junk. Just enough space for Vincent and a duffel bag stuffed with guns and ammo.

The traffic starts, then stops again. "Jesus Christ," Bonnie mutters.

"How long have you worked for the guy?" Vincent asks.

"With Meyer? Three years. Almost four." It seems like another lifetime, that first day she met Meyer. She'd been a wreck, a ghost of a woman whose husband of thirteen years, the father of her children, had just left her for a gold-digging slut named Lorraine.

At that time, Bonnie had been working in development at the Clairmont Museum. A few weeks after Joel left, an old friend from college e-mailed her about a job opening at Brotherhood Watch. That e-mail from the long-lost friend was the first of Meyer's miracles—that is, the first one Bonnie experienced. Of course she had known who Meyer Maslow was. In her opinion, the greatest Holocaust witness. The saintliest and most selfless.

Bonnie had read Meyer's first book and had been moved almost as powerfully as she had when she'd read Anne Frank's diary, back when she was Anne Frank's age. She remembers herself, as a girl, feeling almost regretful that these tragic historic events hadn't so much as brushed against her life. Her family came to America half a century before the war. To Bonnie's father, an atheist, a lawyer, a man with only a sentimental and culinary attachment to Judaism, the Holocaust had seemed like a warning, evidence that, for Jews, just crossing the street was more dangerous than it was for other people. Look both ways. Never let down your guard. Take nothing for granted.

What would her parents have said if they had lived to see her bring home a neo-Nazi? Her mother would have worried. But perhaps her father would have seen Vincent—that is, Bonnie's freedom to take Vincent home if she wanted, even if it *was* Meyer's idea—as a prison break from the jail of her life with Joel, whom he never liked. How naive Bonnie was, that her father's opposition should have made her love Joel more.

Bonnie's parents had raised her to think there was nothing she couldn't do. Her mother read aloud to her, nineteenth-century classics she was too young to understand; her father drove her from White Plains into the city to visit museums, where he showed a preference for paintings with some legal connection—the murder of Holofernes, the judgment of Solomon. Bonnie always thought that those Sundays had something to do with the reason she majored in art history at Cornell. After college, she got a few museum intern jobs, then a couple of small jobs: assistant assistant curator.

And then that part of her life stopped, and she changed, with shocking ease, into Joel's idea of what a successful cardiologist's wife should be. Now, half the time, Bonnie can't understand how she became that unrecognizable person, and half the time, she thinks it could happen to anyone. Anyone female.

She quit working when the kids were born. After they started school, she took an entry-level position at the local museum, where she was rapidly transferred from curating into development, because there was nothing to curate, and because no one else wanted the job of raising money for more etchings of the Old Clairmont Ferry Landing. Meanwhile, on the home front, every meal had to be perfect, or Joel would *disapprove*. Where was the real Bonnie hiding? The Stockholm syndrome took over. Bonnie could have been Patty Hearst, falling in love with her captors. That is, if it *was* love. Or captivity, for that matter. Joel's departure saved her life. She should send Lorraine flowers.

That first day she came to apply for the job, Meyer never inquired about Bonnie's qualifications. He'd asked: Do you want to change your life? She'd wanted a life to change.

"And you?" Bonnie asks Vincent.

"And me what?" Vincent says.

"How long have you worked at the tire place?"

"The same. Three years. Little longer." Bonnie has no clue how to read this guy. What is he after? Did he think that she and Meyer were too stupid to figure out that he must have been on drugs for his big conversion? Does he imagine that Meyer fell into his arms because Vincent read his books? Or that every punk with a duffel bag who wanders into Brotherhood Watch gets whisked straight to Meyer Maslow's office? Bonnie almost wishes there were some way to tell him about her conversation with Meyer before he arrived. Meyer's story about the beggar messenger sent by God. Does Vincent think he's scamming them? Who's scamming whom, exactly?

"Amazing," Bonnie says to herself.

"What is?" Vincent asks.

"Nothing," Bonnie says, just as Vincent reflexively lifts his chin to indicate that a patch of road has opened up. Male passenger body language. Ultimately, he can't help it. Not much of a patch, as it turns out. Bonnie pulls up, then stops. "And before that?"

"Before what?"

"Before the job you have now. Had now. Had." Bonnie spends her days chatting up the city's richest, most hard-nosed donors, powerful men and women who are very good at—who secretly *like*—turning down shuffling, hat-in-hand donation requests. But somehow Bonnie talks the talk. She gets them to give money. And now she's tongue-tied, almost unable to speak to a recovering skinhead. "Before you worked at the tire shop."

"Swimming pool maintenance. Did that for a while. Worked in a doughnut shop. For a while. Nothing worth talking about."

Nothing worth talking about. Conversational homicide. Euthanasia, more like it. How could Bonnie be taking this on? She's got enough trouble with her kids. Danny watches hours of TV and chats with his friends online and does no homework, as far as she can tell. When she presses him for simple information, he rolls his eyes and leaves the room, tricks he learned from his father. Bonnie has smelled pot on Danny's hair when he's come home from a party. She knows about zero tolerance, but it would just push him further away if she made a fuss about a sixteen-year-old smoking on the occasional Saturday night. Probably she should tell Joel, but unlikely as it seems, she's always afraid he might ask for custody, even though he originally gave it up without a fight. He and Lorraine rarely take the boys, even for the alternate weekends and holidays he got in the settlement. It upsets Lorraine to be reminded that Joel had another life, one not orchestrated by her.

Traffic starts moving and keeps up for long enough to persuade Bonnie that the problem (accident? construction?) has been solved, long enough so that her blood pressure spikes when everything stops again. Bonnie should ask what that dashboard light means. But she's not going to play the helpless female asking the alpha male for car-repair advice. If Vincent thought the car was in trouble, he would say so. Maybe.

As usual, Bonnie's stuck in the slowest lane. She used to hate it when Joel whined and raged as if the sluggish lane he'd picked were a personal judgment against him. The line beside them stops, and they're practically rubbing mirrors with a car full of Hispanic kids.

Bonnie likes the salsa bass pumping through the open windows. Or she would if she were alone. Being with a white supremacist makes it way too freighted.

"Ricky Martin," Vincent says. "Is that guy supposed to be straight?"

"Compared to Marc Anthony, I guess." Great, so Bonnie and the Nazi agree, all Latin singers are gay. Not all. Not Tito Puente.

"The weird thing is, it takes balls for a Latin dude. I read where when Rican parents think a kid is going to turn queer, they lock him in his room until he swears to go straight."

Where did Vincent read *that?* Does this mean that every five minutes she's going to have to decide if something's worth arguing about, and whether or not to mention that you shouldn't say *Rican?*

"I don't think that's necessarily true," she says.

"Look, their culture isn't exactly breaking out the champagne and tequila when the *muchacho* turns *maricon*, right?"

"I guess not," Bonnie says.

"Well, then," says Vincent.

"But there are lots of gay Latin men."

"More and more," says Vincent. "It's scary."

After a silence, Bonnie says, "Can I ask you something?"

"Sure," he says. "No problaymo."

"How come you joined ARM?" Bonnie knows she's being nosy. They've practically just met. But she also knows, from experience with her kids, that sometimes being in the car, looking at the road, not having to make eye contact, is the ideal opportunity for heavy conversation. And she'd better be nosy. She needs to find out what she's dealing with. Not that she expects him to tell the truth—if he even knows what it is.

Vincent rolls up his window to shut out the salsa beat. The temperature in the car spikes. He rolls it down again.

"Sorry about the air conditioner," Bonnie says. "I meant to have it fixed. But who would have thought I'd need it yet. It's only April—"

"Global warming," says Vincent. "Anyhow, I hate air-conditioning. I read where those coolant systems are like petri dishes for respiratory viruses."

"So you were saying, why you joined ARM?" Bonnie's not letting it go.

Staring out the windshield, Vincent says, "I was having a hard time."

A hard time. Next, he'll be telling her how he suffered from low self-esteem and was abused as a child.

"Lots of people have hard times. And they don't—"

"A Book-of-Job hard time," Vincent says. "I lost my job, my girlfriend left. I had a . . . problem at work that almost turned into a court thing but luckily got settled."

What problem? What court thing? Bonnie reminds herself to ask later.

"So you joined a hate group?"

"Right. I mean, look . . . have you ever been having a really tough time, and someone told you something that made everything fall into place and make sense?"

Obviously, Bonnie has. She came to work for Meyer. But it's not like joining ARM.

A sense of belonging, an explanation for how the world works—sure, it's what everyone wants. When Bonnie tries to understand how someone could become a Nazi, that's the only explanation she can come up with. But every conversion isn't the same. What matters is what you turn into, what you do, what you believe. And what did Vincent Nolan believe? How did it help him to think that Jews should be killed and African-Americans shipped back to Africa? If he thought that. Thinks that. Is there a polite way to ask?

"Anyhow, it wasn't the hate stuff. Like I said before, it was about the government. My family had some problems with the IRS."

"So what happened? You got audited? That's why you joined ARM?" Bonnie hears the edge in her voice and instantly regrets it.

Vincent turns to face her, and now it's lucky the traffic has stopped, because Bonnie feels helpless to look away; her gaze is locked on his. It's as if they've known each other so long that she can stare at him without blinking. Though his face is chapped and abraded by years of anger, disappointment, alcohol, and boredom, he looks like a kid. Is it because he's good-looking that Bonnie was never really scared, not even in the office when she finally figured out who he was?

He says, "It might be better if you didn't talk about stuff you don't know about."

Is he warning her? Or giving advice? Or giving warning advice? She wishes Meyer were here to tell her what he means.

"Sorry," is all she can say. It's the second time she's apologized: a bad precedent for the future.

"No, I'm sorry," Vincent says. Another silence falls. And now—so there *is* a merciful God—the traffic picks up again. Bonnie's so glad to be moving, she nearly plows into the back of the car ahead of them and has to slam on the brakes.

Vincent says, "Ever notice how men and women have different driving styles?"

"Right," says Bonnie. "So they say. Men won't ask directions."

"How's that?" Vincent asks.

Is this guy Rip Van Winkle? Where's he been for the last twenty years? But it makes sense. *Men Are from Mars, Women Are from Venus* would hardly have topped the Aryan Nation best-seller list. Probably this is the lead-in to the critique of her driving skills that he finally can't help giving.

"Women protect what they have," he says. "And guys always want what *you* have. It's territorial instinct. It's why women don't start wars."

What about Indira Gandhi? Margaret Thatcher? Bonnie feels defensive. This is one discussion she doesn't want to be having with this guy. Or with anyone. She always hates it when men say anything about *women*. It feels like flirtation and criticism rolled into one neat little package.

"Human instinct," says Vincent. "Simple as that. You can't get rid of it." He flashes Bonnie a grin. Probably he's relieved that they've stopped talking about his career in ARM.

"You're saying it's hardwired?" Bonnie says.

"I hate that expression," says Vincent. "Hardwired."

"Actually, so do I. Come to think of it." Bonnie points to the dashboard. "Speaking of wires, what's that?"

"Maintenance required? Nothing. Get a tune-up sometime in the next thousand miles."

The next thousand miles? Bonnie's thrilled. She can deal with the traffic jam as long as she doesn't have to deal with a traffic jam *and* a breakdown. And now . . . look at that! The toll booth's in sight. She edges into the E-ZPass lane.

"E-ZPass is some scary shit," says Vincent. "They can track your every move."

"Let them track me," Bonnie says. "I'm going home to my kids."

It's as if saying it makes it true. The bridge opens up before them. Even after years of living in Clairmont, Bonnie still loves driving the Tappan Zee. Traveling over the causeway makes her feel like a water bird, skimming the surface before takeoff.

"These bridges?" Vincent shouts above the warm wind rushing into the car. "They have a guy stationed at the on-ramps round the clock. His whole job is to take over the wheel for drivers who panic and have to be driven across."

"Really?" Bonnie shouts back.

"I used to get that. I had it for years. Then it went away."

Terrific. A phobic neo-Nazi. And a neurotic single mother of two. Bonnie and Vincent were made for each other.

As they turn onto 9W, Vincent's sitting forward, charged with gopherlike alertness now that there's something to see, signposts to his future. It's touching how he's practically sniffing at everything they pass: the gas station, the supermarket, the garden center.

"Clairmont," Vincent says.

"Ever been here?" says Bonnie.

"Once, I think. Some . . . firemen's carnival. Years ago. Before—"

"Every July." It gives Bonnie the creeps to think of Vincent and his white supremacist pals hanging out in her town on beer night.

They pass the candle store, the antiques shops, the organic health food café, all of it seeming more precious and middle class and privileged by the minute. An African-American couple cross the street, pushing a high-tech baby stroller. Nothing like a skinhead riding shotgun to make you see your town clearly. Well, sorree! Bonnie likes what she sees, the diversity, the small businesses trying to survive, the pretty houses, the families who want the best for their kids and don't feel compelled to burn a cross on the lawn of anyone who's different.

They stop at the traffic light in front of the Methodist church, where for a couple of weeks now the billboard has read, THE TOMB IS EMPTY.

Vincent says, "Tomb. Empty. Those are two words that shouldn't exist in the same sentence. Is that some Easter thing?"

"I live on the next block," says Bonnie. "The not-so-great house on the great block." Meaning: Don't get excited or worried when we pass the huge stately Victorians. Don't judge until we pull into the driveway of the nondescript two-story frame house that seems to have been transported from another, shabbier town.

When she and Joel first moved here, they liked saying that they lived in the not-so-great house on the great block. But eventually it got old. She's gotten so used to apologizing for the house she's still apologizing, just in case her guest room happens to be a step down from the Nazi cousin's living room couch.

Bonnie should have known that Joel was planning to leave when he had the house repainted. She has to give him credit for not sticking her with that. But why he didn't do it earlier, when domestic neglect was one of many topics of low-level squabbling masking the real problem, which was Lorraine? Lorraine is the widow of Joel's former partner Jeffrey, who died suddenly of a coronary, and before that the widow of one of Jeffrey's cardiac patients. Lorraine has written a book about it, a successful memoir called *Heartbreak*, an account of how it feels to lose two husbands in a short time, both to coronary occlusion.

Maybe Joel wanted the painters around to minimize the hysterical fits he assumed Bonnie would throw when she learned he was leaving. When in fact she was admirably calm, if you don't count a few shaming episodes of weeping and begging and promising to change. Until the house is painted again, which will probably be never, she'll always be able to measure the time since he left. A marker, as Meyer and Vincent said about their tattoos.

Bonnie pulls into the driveway.

"Nice crib," says Vincent. "Good *living*."

"Thank you," Bonnie says.

"What does your husband do?"

"Ex-husband," Bonnie says. "Cardiologist."

"Got it," Vincent says.

"What's so funny?" Bonnie says.

"I don't know," says Vincent. "I figured a shrink."

"He *needed* a shrink." Why did Bonnie say *that?*

"Well, obviously," says Vincent. "The guy blew a good thing."

Should Bonnie say thank you again? She busies herself with leaving the van. Vincent waits till she's gathered her purse, keys, and briefcase, and disentangled from the seat belt. Then he goes around to the back and wrestles out his duffel bag. It's heavy. The poor guy's exhausted. He's had a tough day. He catches Bonnie watching.

"Books," he explains.

Right. *The Protocols of the Elders of Zion, Mein Kampf, The Turner Diaries.* Having Vincent along makes her so self-conscious that she enters her own house as if someone else lives there.

"Hello-o? Max? Danny? Kids?" Meanwhile she's rehearsing. Boys, this is Vincent Nolan. He's come to work with the foundation. He'll be staying with us for a few days until he gets his own place. Very up, very straightforward. Very don't-ask-me-now.

But there's no one to try it out on. She calls their names. Neither boy seems to be here. So what? Max is twelve, Danny's sixteen. There are a million places where they could be on this lovely, unseasonably warm evening. Playing basketball. Strolling up Main Street for a predinner Big Mac. Bonnie knocks on the wooden banister. The most unlikely possibility is that something bad has happened, but that's what Bonnie imagines first. At least she can suffer in private. Joel always found her maternal terrors so pitiful and annoying.

She returns to the kitchen to find Vincent still standing near the door.

"Oh, gosh, I'm sorry," Bonnie says. "Let me show you where you'll be staying."

"Are you okay?" says Vincent.

Bonnie says, "Why wouldn't I be? I'm fine. I was just wondering where my kids are."

"Out having fun?" Vincent suggests.

"Probably," admits Bonnie. "Are you hungry? Thirsty?"

"Maybe later." Vincent hasn't put down his duffel bag.

"Come on," says Bonnie. "It's this way."

Vincent waits a beat after Bonnie starts up the stairs, perhaps so his face won't be directly in Bonnie's ass. His face. Bonnie's ass. *Those* are four words that shouldn't exist in the same sentence.

If only Meyer could have trusted the guy to stay in a hotel for one night and given her time to clear out the guest room, to deal with the striated layers of family junk dumped in a space intended for a life that never happened. What guests did she and Joel imagine spending the night? Visiting friends from the city? Those friendships dropped off soon after they moved here. Even Joel's parents, in from La Jolla, stayed in Manhattan and drove up for the day.

She and Vincent linger in the doorway, contemplating the piles of boxes, old clothes, papers, outgrown toys stuffed in lumpy plastic bags. Bonnie should have predicted the hard knot of anxiety that would swell in her chest at the prospect of this stranger sleeping in a room with her kids' outgrown stuff. Their baby pictures. Does she think Vincent will hurt them? That's what Meyer would ask. Somewhere, he'd say, there's a mother with baby pictures of Vincent.

"Sorry about the mess," says Bonnie.

"Please," says Vincent. "You should see the rathole I've been staying in. Not that it was *my* mess. I'm basically a neat person—"

"Glad to hear it," says Bonnie. "I'll get you some clean sheets. And if you need to rearrange some stuff . . ."

"I'll be careful," Vincent says.

"The bathroom is at the end of the hall. You'll be sharing with the boys." Bonnie can hardly say it, the thought fills her with such revulsion. "I'll leave the dark blue towel for you. It's the only one like it, so you won't confuse it—"

"I won't," promises Vincent. "That'd be great. Man, I could use a shower."

And Bonnie? She could use getting through the lifetime from now until the boys show up. Once they're home she can relax and get on with her evening. Read, watch TV. Danny will go to his room. Sometimes Max still consents to cuddle on the couch.

Bonnie should have given Vincent the house and taken the kids to a motel. Maybe she could get comfortable there. She certainly can't, not here. At least her bedroom is on the other side of the house. At least she has her own bathroom. Everything could always be worse. She can stand it for one night.

She goes to her room and lies down without taking off her shoes. The unmade bed increases her sense of languor and self-pity. She closes her eyes and tries to calm herself by making plans for tomorrow. She and Meyer are having a staff meeting to discuss how they can use Vincent to generate some buzz. And help him in the process.

Suddenly, Bonnie jumps up. Has she fallen asleep? Are the kids home? She'd just as soon Vincent not meet the boys while she's napping upstairs.

The first disappointment is that the kids aren't home. The second is that Vincent is back in the kitchen, looking fresh and scrubbed. The duffel bag must contain some clothes. He's changed into a short-sleeved black T-shirt. Bonnie tries not to stare at his tattoos. Do Max and Danny need to see that right away? They'll see it sooner or later.

On the table before him are two books.

"What are you reading?" she says.

He says, "I like to read two books at once. "This one's *The Way of the Warrior.* That's *The Complete Pogo.*"

"Pogo?" says Bonnie. "The comic? Why?"

"I like how those swamp creatures sound like guys I know."

"*Pogo?*" repeats Bonnie. "They don't sound like anyone *anyone* knows."

Vincent shrugs. "I'm also reading *Crime and Punishment.*"

"You're reading Dostoyevsky? I haven't read that since college." What has Meyer sent her? A neo-Nazi intellectual?

"My mom was a reader," Vincent explains. "I guess I got it from her. The funny thing was, I didn't start until I was, like, twenty-five—"

"I'm always so relieved to hear that. Neither of my kids read. They'd watch TV nonstop if I let them—" What kind of mother is Bonnie? Complaining about her children for some Nazi's entertainment? If something happens to Danny and Max, Bonnie will have deserved it.

Vincent says, "Are those them? Your kids?"

Bonnie spins toward the window. The boys are walking up the back steps. Her relief is so euphoric it works like a stiff drink, persuading her that she can get through anything. Max and Danny are safe. In the face of that blessing, who could worry about something so minor as introducing her kids to a guy who's changing his life by coming to work with Brotherhood Watch?

WHAT'S STRANGE IS THAT DANNY isn't more surprised to come home and find some geek leaning his nasty tattooed arms all over the kitchen table. It's as if he's been expecting it. In fact it hasn't been that long since he and Max saw that *Chandler* show about the former skinhead working with the famous Nazi hunter in California. Danny remembers telling Max: Trust me, it won't be long until Mom and Meyer get a Nazi of their own.

Now Danny gives his brother a look: *Did I call this, or what?* But Max has already left his body, vacated, as he tends to do in tricky family situations.

"Boys, this is Vincent Nolan. He's come to work with Brotherhood Watch. He'll be staying with us for a few days until he gets his own place."

Danny says, "Mom, can I talk to you?" Six words practically guaranteed to make her start hyperventilating.

"In a minute, honey. Vincent, this is Max, that's Danny. Danny, Vincent, Max, Vincent—" Mom comes up for air.

Max rolls his eyes at Danny. Does Max know what those tattoos mean? Danny's often shocked by the gaps in his brother's basic knowledge.

"Mom," says Max. "Take a deep breath. Chill. Say it again." It's one of those annoying things Max says to Mom when she's wound tight and ready to snap. And Mom *listens*, she obeys, she gets all girly and smiles, and repeats herself more slowly. Normally, Danny resents the inside jokes Max shares with their mother. What makes it even more annoying tonight is that Max is too young to know to skip the chintzy family humor in front of the guy with the death's-head and the Waffen-SS bolts on his arms.

Obediently, Mom pauses, exhales. "Boys, Vincent Nolan, he's come to work—"

"Hi," says Danny, cutting it short.

"This is Danny," says Mom. "Did I say that?"

Vincent Nolan acknowledges him with a nod that's more like a spasm. Has Mom not noticed that her new friend is Timothy McVeigh's clone? What the hell is Mom thinking? Inviting some demented tweaker to stay here until one night, high on crystal meth, he figures out that they're Satanists and that God needs him to hack them up and stash them in the freezer. How ridiculous that Mom's not concerned about bringing this maniac home when she worries about every little thing. Danny fears that obsessive worry is an inherited trait.

Danny and Max keep sneaking glances at the tattoos, until Mom catches them looking. "You guys should have been there. The most amazing thing happened. Meyer rolled up his sleeves and put his tattoo, you know, the numbers from the concentration camp, near Vincent's, and it was so moving, seeing them like that together."

"It was something," the skinhead agrees.

The thought makes Danny want to puke. Meyer and Vincent's tattoos. Tattoos in general gross him out, though his friend Chloe has an eyeball on her shoulder blade that winks when she twitches her back. Just this morning, in homeroom, Danny longed to reach out and touch it.

Danny doesn't like Meyer. He's one of those guys who don't

have kids and think that kids are a waste of time. He can never re-member which one is Danny and which one is Max, but he fakes it as long as their mom is around. What grade are you in? How do you like school? Mainly, Danny doesn't like how Mom does what-ever Meyer tells her, how she's always quoting the guy. Meyer says this, Meyer says that. Meyer could be David Koresh. The Jewish Charlie Manson. Danny blames it on the divorce. Mom needs to be deprogrammed.

Naturally, some part of him admires what Meyer does. Even Danny has to admit that Meyer is trying to do good in the world and make a positive difference. But whenever Danny tries to tell his friends what the foundation's about—sending aid to global trouble spots, keeping tabs on hate groups at home, getting guys sprung from jail—it sounds like such a downer, he's sorry he brought it up.

Mom says what Danny knew she'd say. "Where were you guys just now?"

"Does it matter?" asks Danny.

"Danny, sweetheart, I've told you. Don't answer a question with a question."

"All right. We were out." Danny *wants* to answer, to make this easy on her. But it's as if he's possessed by a demon insisting that his independence and self-respect depend on giving her maximum atti-tude and minimum information.

"Out where?" Mom's determined to drag out the Big Interroga-tion.

"Mom, we were playing basketball in the grade-school yard."

"Thank you, Max," says Mom. "Was that so hard?"

"Whatever," Danny says.

"Anybody hungry?" says Mom.

"Starved," Max says.

"I could eat," says the Nazi.

"Sure. I guess," Danny says. "No Chinese."

"I was thinking Chinese," Mom says.

"We had it last night," Danny points out. The most irritating thing is that she's so nervous she forgot. You'd think the guy was a visiting rock star. It's how she acts around Meyer. Even though his mom and dad fought a lot before the divorce, at least they were comfortable with each other. Like normal screwed-up grown-ups.

"Then maybe we should go out . . ." Mom's voice has that wispy tremble it gets when she can't cope and makes Danny and Max decide.

They're certainly not going out. Danny would rather starve to death than run into someone he knows. By second period tomorrow it will be all over school that Danny was having dinner with a skinhead. By lunch they'll be saying the guy is Danny's mom's new boyfriend.

"Pizza," says Max. "Call."

"Sure," says Danny. "Why not?"

"Will pizza be enough?"

"Fine with me," the Nazi says.

"Simple!" Mom picks up the phone. "What about toppings? Anything you don't eat?"

"Nuts," says Vincent. "Any kind of nuts. I'm fatally allergic. I wind up in the hospital. I nearly died several times."

"God," says Mom. "How scary."

Danny says, "I guess that kind of rules out the peanut-butter pizza."

Suddenly, everyone's staring at him. He should probably smile at Mom to show that he wasn't making fun of the guest. But on the way to Mom's face he gets sidelined by the hairy eyeball he's getting from the Nazi, checking to see if he *is* making fun, because if he is, Vincent's going to kick his ass. Is Mom picking up on this?

Obviously Danny is goofing on the guy. What did the moron *think* they would order? Macadamia pizza? And why do they need to know about his loser allergy problems? Vincent narrows his eyes. Whatever passes between him and Danny is silent, scary, and over in a second, at the end of which Vincent chooses to believe that Danny *is* making a joke, but not a joke about *him*, and he laughs, a jagged dog-bark that makes Max flinch.

Danny says, "Pepperoni," his brother's favorite. He hates pepperoni. So there's usually a fight.

"Danny!" says Mom. "How generous of you! Danny hates pepperoni." As if the guy needs to know. She orders two large pies, one with pepperoni, one with mushrooms and green pepper. "Fifteen, twenty minutes," she says, first triumphant, then defeated as she wonders: What will they do until the pizza arrives?

Max saves the day. "Hey, Danny, want to watch TV?"

"Okay," says Mom. "But come upstairs the minute I call. Don't let the pizza get cold." Usually, she goes insane when he and Max get home and head straight for the TV. Danny grabs Max and fake-shoves him down the stairs to Dad's room.

They still call it Dad's room even though it's been years since Dad cleared out everything but the thirty-six-inch TV and a couple of beat-up couches. He couldn't have found a better way to yank Mom's chain. She despises the humongous TV. She never comes down to Dad's room. But then, she never did. At the time, it had seemed normal. But later Danny wondered: Wouldn't you think something was wrong if your husband came home from the office and spent every minute downstairs couch-potatoed in front of the tube? Once again, his mom worries about everything except the things she should worry about. Which is what Dad said once about Danny. So it gets confusing.

Everyone fights with their parents about how long they're allowed to watch TV. But only Danny and Max get to fight about watching it in their dad's old room, on a television so expensive that Mom can't make herself throw it out.

Brain-dead Max imagines he's getting the remote. "What's on *Chandler*?" he says.

Danny grabs the changer. "The usual bogus shit."

"Let's just see," pleads Max.

"Forget it, creep," says Danny.

It's strange how everyone watches *Chandler*. It's really just a talk show, and Chandler is an annoying rich black dude who quit a million-dollar corporate law job to get real, get down with the street. Last year the network picked up his contract for *fifty* million dollars. So Chandler came out okay. His show is such a big hit that it runs during the dinner hour to compete with the news. They advertise it that way: The *good* news is on *Chandler*. It's what all the mothers—except Danny's—watch on those miniature TVs they set up in the kitchen for when they're cooking. What's doubly strange is how the kids in school talk about what they saw on *Chandler*. And it's not just the teachers bringing it up. Maybe it's because Chandler has shows that are actually interesting, especially if you happen to be so stoned that his guests seem smart.

Every so often, Chandler gets it right, like that program with the high-school kids talking about global warming. Not the usual geeks you see on those shows. All the girls were hot *and* intelligent. The guys were guys you'd be friends with. But Danny's not in the mood for *Chandler* right now. It's creepy that when the skinhead was on *Chandler*, Danny predicted that Meyer and Mom would get a Nazi of their own.

Danny changes from the Cartoon Channel to MTV. Then he hits the mute button.

"Listen" he says. "Do you know who that guy upstairs *is?*"

"Duh," Max says. "You and I watched that *Chandler* together."

"Max, man, this is not some talk-show guest. Did you see the guy's arm?"

"I'm not stupid," Max says. "We read *Night* last semester, ass-hole. I hated it, remember. I had to write that cut-and-paste poem with phrases from the book."

"I still can't believe they made you read that. They should have made you do Anne Frank."

Max says, "Plus, do you think I'm so retarded I don't know where Mom works?"

"Sorry," says Danny. "I'm not saying you're retarded. It's just weird, is all."

"It *is* weird. Mom's out of her fucking mind."

"Language!" Danny imitates Mom.

As he turns toward the big screen, Max idly gives Danny the finger. The two boys fall silent, attempting to lip-read what the moderately hot Asian girl is saying through her tears.

"Put the sound on," Max says.

"Bite me," Danny replies.

The camera pulls back to show the Asian girl sitting by a pool, at night. It's Key West. Danny's seen this one before. Subhita has a drinking problem and has been arguing with the other girls in the house.

Max says, "Do you think we should call Dad? Should we tell him about this guy?"

This is what Danny means about the gaps in his brother's information—for example, about who Dad is. Their father's a jerk who went to live in Manhattan in a boring high-rise apartment with Lorraine, the widow of his dead partner, Jeffrey. Before she hooked up with Jeffrey, Lorraine was the wife of Jeffrey's patient, who died of a heart attack, at fifty. Then Jeffrey died of a heart attack, at forty-nine. Once Danny overheard Mom calling Lorraine the Black Widow. Danny knew she was joking, but for a while he was scared. Dad is forty-eight. Dad is not a responsible grown-up you can ask for advice and help. Dragging Dad into this will only make everything worse.

Danny says, "How can Mom *do* this? Can you explain that one thing?"

Two girls' faces fill the screen. Danny raises the sound. Amanda and Kirsten are agreeing that Subhita should put herself back in rehab.

"The guy's got no place to stay," Max says. "Otherwise he wouldn't be here. Mom's not going to leave him on the street. That's not who Mom *is*."

Trust genius Max to cut to the chase, though Danny can't recall Mom saying, in so many words, that the guy was homeless. But that's got to be the story. So it's worse than Danny thought. He could be here for months.

"Mom's just trying to be a good person," says Max, the middle-school Dalai Lama. No wonder their mother loves Max more. Max is a better person than Danny. And so grown-up for his age.

"Brilliant," says Danny. "That's the most obvious thing about Mom. Now tell me something I don't know."

"Pizza's here!" yells Mom.

Max runs upstairs. Let the others go first. Danny flips through the channels and stops, frozen by the freaked-out piglet face of Timothy McVeigh. What a coincidence. The guy's separated-at-birth twin is upstairs scarfing down pizza.

Danny trudges up to the kitchen. Surprise! They've started without him.

"Danny," says Mom. "Get a chair."

Danny gets a chair from the living room and pulls up next to Max. Everyone's eating off real plates. There are glasses, a carton of orange juice. Mom has made a salad.

"La-di-dah," Danny says to the salad.

"Excuse me?" says Mom. "What was that?"

"Nothing," Danny says. "Talking to myself."

His slice of pizza buckles, dumping the cheese in a greasy plop at the bottom of the box. He tears off a mouthful of soggy crust, chokes it down, then, just to see what will happen, says, "They're delaying the McVeigh execution. They found three thousand pages of evidence the FBI forgot to turn over."

"FBI slimeballs," says Vincent. Danny can't tell if Vincent knows that McVeigh looks just like him.

"I think it's disgusting," Mom says. "All that media frenzy, everyone so bloodthirsty, wanting to watch a human being die. It's like the Roman Colosseum. They should sell beer and popcorn and kill the guy in Yankee Stadium. I'd feel better about that than having to hear all this stuff about 'closure.' At least it would be honest. I know he's a murderer. I don't approve of what he did, but still—"

Danny guesses he agrees. But it's always so embarrassing when his mom gets fired up.

"Definitely," Vincent says. "The government loves killing. What about those women and babies they gassed and burned at Waco? What about them sending in their crack SWAT team to murder Randy Weaver's wife?"

"Yes, well . . . I don't know . . ." Mom's voice trails off. "Of course, I don't believe in the death penalty to start with."

Neither does Danny, exactly. But hasn't Mom ever seen the clips of those bloody babies outside the Murragh Building? Sometimes Danny worries about terrorists blowing up the Tappan Zee Bridge when he and Mom and Max are crossing. He wishes he never thought like that. Other kids don't seem to. And he wishes he didn't suspect that he has these fears because he's like Mom.

"Were you watching the news?" Mom says. "At least it's the news. I hate the boys watching TV."

"I try to stay away from TV," says Vincent. "Toxic parasite mind rot."

For all Danny knows, Vincent's one of those guys who think that the government is beaming mind-control rays out of the TV screen. The last thing Danny needs around here is someone who, for whatever reason, is on his mother's side about television.

"Actually, guys," says Mom, "Vincent's a reader." Meaning *unlike you two*. "And guess what? He didn't start really reading till he was twenty-five."

Danny and Max will never forgive her for comparing them negatively to a Nazi. Though it's possible that she's just trying to reassure them that, underneath the lightning bolts, the guy is a harmless book nerd.

"He's reading Dostoyevsky."

Danny says, "Who the fuck is Dostoyevsky?" Even though he knows.

"Danny!" his mom says. "Language!"

Max says, "So what do you guys do? Like, beat up black people and Jews?"

Jesus, Danny loves Max sometimes. Right now he's the perfect age. Still trading on his little-kid right to ask inappropriate questions, but grown up enough to know what the right questions are. When Dad and Mom announced they were splitting up, Max asked if they still loved each other. They both answered at the same moment. Mom said of course, Dad said not exactly, and then Dad said, I mean of course.

"*I* never did," says Vincent. "But I knew guys who did."

"You don't know them now?" Max says.

"I don't know them, and they don't know me," Vincent says.

"Good for you!" says Mom. "Boys, you can't imagine the risk Vincent is taking. He says there are guys, his former friends, who won't *like* his quitting—"

A familiar look comes over Mom's face. She wishes she hadn't said that, wishes she hadn't given in to the impulse to share her fears with them. Danny wishes she hadn't. Now he's got one more thing to worry about.

They finish their pizza in silence. Danny and Max clear the table, which they wouldn't usually do, but they can't let Mom do it, not in front of a stranger. So maybe it's good that she's brought him home. It feels like those first weeks after Dad left, when everyone was practically tiptoeing around the house. Normal rules suspended. Like having a substitute teacher, except you act better instead of worse.

After dinner Danny and Max watch more TV. Homework isn't mentioned. Danny surfs the channels. He keeps wondering what's happening upstairs. The pressure is exhausting. Danny drifts off several times before he wakes up and finds Max asleep in front of boring Ted Koppel. Propping his little brother up, he half steers, half pushes him to his room, and dumps him on his bed.

In his own room, Danny lies awake, trying to ignore the noises that always start at night when the world stops pretending to be its harmless daytime self. As a kid, he'd been scared of the dark. Way past the age when he would admit it, he used to make Mom come to his room and stay with him till he fell asleep. He'd pretended that he'd just wanted to talk. Once he overheard Dad tell Mom that kids weren't smart enough to know what to be scared of. The proof, he said, was that children were scared of the dark and not of death and airplanes. Now Danny's old enough to be scared of all that and more.

How humiliating to be sixteen and still afraid of the dark. Maybe he should phone one of his friends, or go online and see if anyone's awake. He'd like to talk to Chloe. She always makes him feel better. But what would he say? He can't tell Chloe how nervous he is. So there's nothing to do but lie here and listen to the noises that spooked him as a kid. Relax. It's only the footsteps of the Nazi moving in.

MEYER AND HIS FRIEND SOL STAND OVER Sol's wife, Minna, watching her chest rise and fall. You'd think it was fascinating. And in a way, it is. The distance Minna has traveled in a couple of days! Her face has that chalky pallor hospital patients get, camouflaged to match the walls, their doctors' coats, the skim milk on their trays, as if they're trying to disappear, fade into the woodwork so Death can't find them. But Minna isn't dying. The operation went well. She may look embalmed, but according to Sol, she'll be back on her feet in no time, hosting her famous Sunday brunches.

Those oily bounties of cheese and smoked fish will never seem the same now that Meyer has watched Minna snore in her puckered flowery pajamas. Their mutual embarrassment will be the geriatric version of how Meyer used to feel when he ran into girls he'd slept with when he first came to this country. Those sweet, warm-hearted American girls, so eager to help him *forget. Mercy fuck* was the first American slang phrase Meyer learned. But that awkwardness was about sex, and this is about death, about watching himself and his friends race each other to the grave, a race no one wants to win.

Meyer's got no cause for complaint. At seventy-one, he's in excellent health. Seventy-one? That's reason enough for self-pity. Often Meyer finds himself staring at men his age, wondering how they get through the day without lashing out in a jealous rage at everyone younger than they are. Meanwhile he's ashamed of himself for questioning the will of God, for worrying about how much time he has left when he knows he's supposed to be thinking of higher things: his work, his foundation.

Sol's describing Minna's symptoms. The pesky cough. The X ray on which they accidentally picked up the aneurysm that would have blown her artery wide apart if they hadn't caught it in time.

"How lucky was *that?*" asks Sol.

"A miracle. Miracles happen." Dear God, don't let Sol remember that's the title of the second section of Meyer's new book. But would he think it was less sincere? No, he'd think Meyer *meant* it. He'd put it in a book.

Meyer does mean it. What else but miracles can explain what happens in one lifetime? Consider the arc that took him from the hayloft in Hungary to here. He doesn't like to think about it, not so much because the memory is still painful, which it is, but because he is conscious of using it, or of using his distance *from* it, to make himself feel better about why he was spared and what he has done with his life. How shameless to use the Holocaust as an analgesic. But even that is better than using it as your trump card, to win every argument, to establish your credentials in the field of suffering. But the truth is, it *is* a trump card. And soon there will be no one left alive with the indisputable right to play it.

"Meyer," Sol's saying. "Are you all right?"

"I'm fine. You were telling me about Minna."

"I made her go to the hospital," said Sol.

"Lucky thing she has you," Meyer says. Sol's a good husband, one of the fortunate few who's satisfied with what he's got. He wants nothing more than his Minna, his library, his tenured job teaching comparative literature at Queens College. Unlike Meyer, Sol has lots of male friends: confident, athletic, expensively maintained professionals who clump together, telling jokes at Minna's brunches. Meyer has known Sol since Meyer first came to this country and supported himself by giving language lessons. Meyer tutored Sol's students. Meyer slept with them. Sol didn't.

Minna's stomach gurgles. "She looks terrific," Meyer says.

"Your nose just grew," says Sol.

"She'll be fine." Meyer turns his palm outward, a stop sign for doubts.

"So they tell me," says Sol.

Minna's pink pajamas make her sudden spasm seem like the ropy stretching of a sleeping child. She pushes the blanket down, revealing a gap between her shirt buttons. Meyer glimpses a curve of breast before he turns away.

"Sit down," says Sol. Meyer sinks into a chair, a motion Sol mirrors on the opposite side of the bed. Peering down from the TV, Tom Brokaw chants above footage of Tim McVeigh being led out in leg irons, squinting into the flashbulbs. Meyer sighs. If only Vincent Nolan looked a little less like McVeigh.

Sol says, "Imagine, the guy calling those babies *collateral damage!* That's what I can't get past. Half the time I think, Go ahead and fry the sick bastard. But then again—"

"I've got a better plan," Meyer says. "Make McVeigh *think* he's going to be killed. Then save him at the last minute. Like Dostoyevsky."

"Like you," says Sol.

"Like me," Meyer concedes. "And let me tell you, it changes you. Televise his life after that. It's the reality TV that we all want to watch."

"That's brilliant," says Sol. "Have you written about that? Maybe for the op-ed page." An almost lustful enthusiasm glimmers in Sol's eyes as he flings his idea, without envy, at the shrine of Meyer's importance. Sol wishes he could write anything for the op-ed page.

"I don't know," says Meyer. It might not be helpful, at this point, for Brotherhood Watch to support the country's most hated homegrown terrorist. A piece like that would hardly sell more benefit tickets. As if the *New York Times* would print such garbage in the first place. But shouldn't Meyer do something? Isn't McVeigh's life worth saving?

Meyer says, "Ever seen anyone hung?"

"No," says Sol. "Thank God."

"I have," says Meyer.

"I know." Of course Sol knows. Meyer described it in both of his first two books. For a guy whose mission—whose raison d'être—is remembrance, Meyer is getting forgetful. Sometimes, when someone asks a question about his war experience, he has to look it up in his memoirs. If he had to get through the war now, he probably wouldn't survive. He hates the idea that everything depended on his having been young. He wants to believe he's the same person. The same soul in a different body.

Meyer and Sol watch two men in dark suits, huddled and scowling. *McVeigh's lawyers say their client is reviewing his options.*

"What options?" says Sol. "To die or to die."

"Same options everyone gets," Meyer says.

"Thanks, I needed that," says Sol. "Okay. Listen. What did the blind man say the first time he touched a matzoh?"

Meyer shrugs. He's waiting.

"Who wrote this shit?" Sol says.

Meyer laughs out loud, then says, "I never get to laugh like that at my job."

"Poor you," says Sol. "All you have to do is keep a straight face and you get to fly the Concorde. Hey, what did I say wrong? Your face got the strangest look—"

A loud gurgle from Minna's intestines reclaims their attention.

"Great of you to come," Sol says. "Considering all you've got on your plate."

"I said I would come. I couldn't *not* come." It's not only that Meyer has known Sol and Minna for so long, that he cares about them, that it means something to them that he's here. Whether he likes it or not, and despite how lonely it makes him feel, Meyer Maslow showing up means a little something extra.

Beyond that, there's a raft of reasons he's not about to discuss with Sol, reasons why he had to come, some of which have to do with a letter Meyer received this morning.

A hate letter, as it happens.

Meyer gets plenty of hate mail. Thank God, he rarely sees it. His staff makes the first cut and passes the rest of his correspondence along to Roberta or Bonnie. But like the secretaries, Roberta had thought it was *nice* that someone had sent him, anonymously, a chapter from Charles Dickens.

It was a section from *Bleak House*, which Meyer has never read. And he might not have taken the time today, except that the minute he saw the chapter heading, his heart sank and kept sinking until he'd read to the end.

The chapter, "Telescopic Philanthropy," recounts a visit to the messy home of a certain Mrs. Jellyby, who can't be bothered cleaning house or looking after her filthy, miserable, neglected children, who are constantly falling downstairs and getting their heads stuck in railings. And why? Because Mrs. Jellyby is busy with her "African project," establishing coffee plantations and teaching the natives of Borrioboola-Gha.

Meyer knows it wasn't meant well. Someone is suggesting that he is a Mrs. Jellyby, practicing telescopic philanthropy, mistreating those closest to him in his efforts to save people on the other side of the planet. It's unfair and untrue. Meyer is kind to his staff, to Irene. Maybe someone thought it was funny and assumed that Meyer would, too. But why the anonymity? Someone was being hostile. The gesture was so overcomplicated, when one word would have done. One word like *fraud* spelled out in letters scissored from the newspaper.

Why does Meyer think it's someone who knows him well enough to know that the horror of being a telescopic philanthropist is among his worst fears? In fact, those worries have been multiplying, or maybe it's just that Meyer more often thinks of those aspects of his character that make him feel small and depress him. His vanity and his ego. How can he be shallow enough to get his feelings hurt when Bonnie tells him that tickets to the dinner haven't been selling? And neither has his new book. . . .

It reminds him of how he felt, a few months ago, when he and Elie Wiesel attended a conference in Rennes, and the French paparazzi greeted Wiesel with a hail of flashbulbs that stopped when Meyer walked in behind him. Apparently it doesn't bother them that Wiesel seems to believe that genocide is only genocide when it happens to Jews—and maybe Bosnians. But surely not gypsies or Africans. Their deaths are, at best, mass murder. All right, so Meyer's not well known in France. That was never the point. The point is his *minding* that Wiesel gets all the flashes. But is that such a sin? Dictators torture children and never lose a minute of sleep while Meyer stays up nights in terror of being a tiny bit vain?

Today, just before lunch, he'd gotten a fax saying that an Iranian cartoonist had been jailed and was at risk of being tortured. The guy has a wife and kids. Meyer met him last fall when he'd come over to the United States with a delegation of Iranian writers and artists, apparatchik stooges the government sent as propaganda. A friend in the State Department talked Meyer into showing them around New York. Meyer owed his friend a favor, so he took the Iranians to a few parties and panels where they yakked about how free they were. They'd all read Salman Rushdie. Their wives all chose to go veiled. Only one guy, the cartoonist, never said a word. And now he's the one in prison.

Meyer started making calls. Telescopic philanthropy. After that came the dreary talk with Bonnie about the ticket sales, and then Vincent Nolan walked in. Right away, Meyer saw, in Vincent, proof that he hadn't lost it, that he still had the power to make miracles happen. And to see who people *were*—in Vincent's case, a lost soul who could never have believed all the things he must have claimed to believe to belong to that hate group. He saw a nice-looking young man who truly wanted to change his life, to work for toler-ance and justice. It wasn't until Vincent and Bonnie left that Meyer remembered the Dickens chapter. At which point he *had* to go see Minna. Anything to prove that he wasn't a Mrs. Jellyby.

"What's new at the foundation?" asks Sol.

"Every day something," says Meyer. "This morning I got a fax about an Iranian artist I know who just got locked up in jail. Iran is tough, but it's worth a try. Maybe we can do something."

"That's marvelous!" says Sol. "The things you accomplish!"

Meyer nods, accepting the tribute. "The foundation does them," he says. "And then this afternoon, back on the home front, Bonnie Kalen, our development director—"

"I know Bonnie," says Sol.

"—walks into my office with this . . . skinhead. This former skinhead. Some upstate Hitler Jugend."

"You let him in?" demands Sol. "Are we forgetting the sick bastard who shot up that preschool in California?"

"We welcomed him, actually. He'd had some sort of mystical vision at a rock concert. He told us he wanted to work with us."

"Obviously, some cuckoo." That's Sol's diagnosis. But what does Sol know? He's a literature professor, not a psychiatric clinician. "I'd cut him loose in a minute. I mean, you've got to wonder what makes them racists in the first place." How much does Meyer know about this guy after half an hour in his office? Maybe he should have figured out some alternative to sending him home with Bonnie.

"I do wonder," Meyer says. "Why would a guy who's not stupid let himself get sucked into that? I'm sure there's plenty he isn't admitting. But I think he's mostly telling the truth. He's my scientific experiment. My golem. What can we extract from him to vaccinate the world with?"

"Today the foundation, tomorrow the world," says Sol. "Be careful, is all I'm suggesting." In the silence that falls between them, their focus drifts from an SUV commercial to the digital read-out of Minna's heartbeat.

Finally Sol says, "So God tells Adam: I'm going to make you a wife, a helpmate, the most beautiful woman who ever lived, fabulous in bed, uncomplaining, ready to carry out your every wish and desire. But it'll cost you.'

"'How much?' says Adam.

"'An eye, an elbow, a collarbone, and your left ball.'

"Adam thinks for a minute, then says, 'What can I get for a rib?'"

Meyer laughs, then thinks, How can a guy tell a joke like that over his wife's sickbed? Isn't Sol superstitious at all? Meyer tries to think of another joke, quick, something to counter that one. But what he thinks is: I need to call Irene. She has no idea he'll be late. He hates to worry her.

Meyer says, "Two old guys in Miami. One says, 'I forget everything lately. I go to the mall and forget how I got there.' The other one says, 'Not me. I never forget a thing.'"

Meyer stops. The punch line is, the guy knocks on wood for luck, and then forgets and says, "Come in!" But there's no wood in Minna's hospital room. Sol's looking at Meyer, wondering if he's forgotten the punch line of a joke about forgetting. Meyer knocks on Minna's nightstand. "Come in," he says, too late.

Sol doesn't get it. The joke is ruined, and worse yet, the knock has woken Minna. Traces of the recognizable Minna animate the waxy mannequin of the old woman in bed.

"Sol," she says, delightedly. "Meyer. How lovely to see you."

Meyer raises her papery hand to his lips, inhaling its faint scent of disinfectant. Soon he'll be out of here, heading back to his apartment. He'll go home, pour himself a stiff Scotch, and Irene—or Babu, their cook—will bring him a delicious dinner, which he'll enjoy as he tries not to think of Minna peeling the plastic wrap off her hospital tray.

Sol and Minna's faces swim up through Meyer's reverie. What are they waiting for?

Meyer says, "Sorry. Where were we? Minna, you're looking splendid."

Babu opens the door. How happy Meyer is to be home! Meyer shakes Babu's hand as he does every night, until Babu removes his limp palm and clasps both hands and bows. Babu is an Untouchable activist who was getting death threats in Hyderabad and needed a place to lay low until the crisis blew over. He liked it at Meyer's and stayed. Isn't that more or less what happened today with Vincent Nolan? Except that Meyer doubts that Vincent can cook, which means that Meyer got a better deal than Bonnie.

"Mrs. Maslow is starting dinner," says Babu.

It's not what Meyer imagined—first the leisurely drink in his study, then the meal. But he's a big boy. He can adjust. Irene puts up with a lot.

The candles are lit. The table is set for two. Irene's back is toward the door, and she doesn't turn, not even when Meyer kisses the top of her head.

"Sorry I'm late," says Meyer. "Minna's in the hospital. I stopped by on my way home."

Irene clutches Meyer's forearm. "What is it? What's wrong? Why didn't someone call me?" In the early days of their marriage, when it turned out that Meyer wasn't yet ready to give up the freedom he'd won at such cost, Irene used to confide her sorrows and jealousies in Minna. Everyone, including Meyer himself, had thought he would never get married. That was twenty years ago. Irene was almost forty, married to a multimillionaire businessman. She'd left Vienna just before Hitler, a different Europe from Meyer's.

"An aneurysm," says Meyer. "They fixed it. She'll be good as new. I meant to call you. I—"

"Thank God." Irene pauses, then looks down at her plate. "Thai soup with lemon grass. I wish you'd called. I would have waited five minutes."

There's no reproach in Irene's voice. She means what she says. She would have waited five minutes. With another woman, the ease with which she's segued from Minna's illness to the subject of dinner might indicate a shallow character. But that's not true of Irene, who cares deeply about Minna and whose insistence on a good meal in the face of—as a charm against—illness and pain is part of the reason Meyer married her, and why they have stayed together. Meyer takes his seat at the far end of the table and looks across at Irene. He still thinks she's beautiful, even if she doesn't. If there's one thing he would change about her, it would be her inability to accept her aging, the way Meyer tries to accept his. He knows it's easier for men. Or so Irene tells him.

Babu appears with another bowl of soup. Meyer thanks him, and Irene says, "Babu, you're a genius."

Babu bows. "It is my duty." For all Babu's formal subservience, his role in the household is more powerful than he lets on. He's Irene's second in command. Together, they keep the complicated domestic machinery oiled and running. Meyer sometimes feels like the indulged child of two loving but distant parents.

The soup is a tangle of cellophane noodles with basil and coconut milk. Irene knows that coconut's bad for Meyer's cholesterol. And she's told Babu. Meyer realizes that Irene and the cook aren't conspiring to kill him, but rather to give him pleasure. Meyer is glad that Irene isn't one of those women who make you constantly aware of your diet, your health, your mortality. She's careful, but she takes breaks in which they are free to enjoy themselves—and live.

Not until Babu clears the plates does Irene ask about Meyer's day. A weaker man might tell his wife about the Dickens letter and the unsold benefit tickets, wanting reassurance, needing her to say: You're not a telescopic philanthropist, dear! And the tickets will sell. But Meyer keeps it to himself, taking satisfaction in the fact that, after all these years, he and Irene still make an effort to preserve their own, and each other's, dignity. Perhaps it's because they're European. They haven't bought into a culture in which it's considered normal to confess your secrets on a TV talk show.

Meyer says, "Irene, do you remember when those Iranians came for dinner?"

"Of course." The sit-down dinner for twelve she arranged. She probably still knows the menu.

"Do you remember this one quiet guy, he didn't say a word, a short guy with thick black glasses?"

Irene won't remember. Because now Meyer recalls that she spent the dinner chatting with the most handsome Iranian, the leader of the group and, as far as Meyer could tell, the biggest stooge and spy. Why should Irene care what he did in his own country? He made her feel young. Should Meyer have been jealous? They give each other latitude. Which also seems European.

"What about him?" Irene says.

"He's in jail," says Meyer. "In Tehran."

"That's terrible," says Irene. "Is there anything you can do?"

Something's slightly off. Perhaps on the way to the disturbing thought of the jailed Iranian, Irene's been sidetracked by the more pleasant thought of his handsome friend, so that her sympathy feels like an afterthought. Irene believes in the foundation's work, but Meyer knows that the people they've helped blend in her mind into one battered prisoner crouched on a cold cement floor.

"Something else," Meyer says. "Today, at the foundation. A neo-Nazi came into the office."

"Oh my God," says Irene. "Is everyone all right?"

"Nothing happened, darling. Relax. He wants to work with us. He claims to have had some kind of vision. So he's come to Brotherhood Watch to—"

"Oh," says Irene. "You mean like that skinhead in California? I saw him on that *Chandler* show. Now he's become a big shot with the Wiesenthal Foundation."

Meyer remembers Vincent saying something about a TV show. Meyer chose to ignore it. Again he feels vaguely like he felt when the flashbulbs popped for Wiesel. That something like this has happened before diminishes his own satisfaction, his sense of being special. Good God, how small is *that?* The ideal would be for *every* skinhead to work for tolerance and brotherhood. To convert the entire white supremacist world.

"Who knows what the truth is? Or if the guy knows his own mind. He wants us to believe that he's already changed. That all of that is behind him. But I think he's on the edge. He could go either way. That's what interests me. So I thought we'd sign him on as . . . something like an intern. Bonnie Kalen offered to let him stay at her house—"

"Meyer," says Irene. "Excuse me. I must have heard you wrong. You let poor Bonnie Kalen, who's hanging on by her fingernails, if she *has* any fingernails she hasn't bitten, you let that poor woman take in some . . . thug."

"I didn't *make* Bonnie do it. Bonnie volunteered." *Is* he taking advantage of Bonnie? More telescopic philanthropy. He'll call Bonnie later and see if everything is all right.

"How could you even let him into your office?"

"That's what Sol asked," says Meyer.

"Someone should have searched the guy. He could have had a gun! You need to hire a bodyguard, Meyer. I've been telling you that for years. But what good would a bodyguard do if you invite these criminals—"

"*Bonnie* invited him," Meyer says.

"Oh, that poor woman," says Irene. "How do you know the guy isn't dangerous? He might be a serial killer, he—"

"Because I'm *sure*, is why." Everyone knows that Meyer is a genius at judging character. So why doesn't Irene believe that? No man is a hero to his valet. And now that there are no more valets, it's become a code word for wife.

Only a woman would think first about what this means for Bonnie. It's one of the reasons Meyer needs Irene, to keep his compassion sharp, to keep him focused on the Jellyby children as well as the African babies. But women also need men to tell them which men are dangerous, to reassure them that a guy like Vincent Nolan is harmless. How *does* Meyer know? He knows. Irene couldn't do what he did today. Nor would Irene, for all her intuition, know that Bonnie wanted to be asked to take Vincent in.

ONLY NOW THAT HE'S LIFTING THE JUNK off the bed where Bonnie said he could sleep can Nolan afford to ask himself: How messed up has he been? Now that the previous stage in his life is over, or practically over, or temporarily— and *temporarily* is the operative word—over, only now can he face the fact that he's been basically homeless. Sleeping on Raymond's living room couch is not what you'd call a life. Nolan could never decide for himself when to hit the sack. Nights, while Raymond and his friends watched TV, Nolan had to wait until some show that *wasn't* about Nazis came on the all-Hitler Channel, or until Raymond got bored or too drunk and called it a night, or until Lucy stomped in.

He'd never said it was a life. The word he'd thought then was *transition*. He'd had a life. A job, a girlfriend, a home. And the next day, he didn't. Flip-flip, like a domino chain. One thing falls, then another. First he got fired. Which turned out to be a disaster, but he doesn't blame Skip. Friendship aside, you can't afford to have your employees dumping old ladies in pools.

Margaret carried on as if he'd been screwing up ever since they met and the incident with Regina Browner was the last straw. But he hadn't been screwing up. He'd come straight home every evening and had mostly cut down drinking. Dunking Mrs. Browner was his first step off the straight and narrow.

That was Margaret's big break. Her ticket out of his life. And Margaret jumped right on it. She told him their relationship wasn't going anywhere. Relationship. Their *relationship*. She'd never used that word before. He wouldn't have been with a woman who talked that talk-show trash. Maybe that's what hurt most: that he'd spent two years with a woman who could break his heart because *their relationship wasn't going anywhere*. And Margaret *is* going somewhere. By the time she's forty, she'll be running UPS instead of just driving one of their trucks. Nolan used to think it was sexy, the brown uniform, the clipboard, the friendly little wave Margaret always gave him, pulling away in her truck. Only a fool would be turned on by how happy a woman looked to be rolling out of the driveway.

It was Margaret's apartment in Saugerties, so the breakup took care of the home part. Then it turned out that Vincent had less money saved up than he'd thought. He had some unemployment coming, so he stayed around Kingston. He found a weekly rental at the Streamside Motel. No one could blame him for heading straight to the beer and TV and pills. Right around the corner from the motel was one of those Doc-in-the-Boxes, walk-in medical clinics where the personnel were remarkably understanding about his work-related, intractable back pain.

Eventually, he stopped paying the motel owner, Mr. Derjani. The guy never fixed the hot water heater. In Nolan's mind they were even. But the word on Nolan must have gone out over the Paki-landlord grapevine. Every time Nolan walked through a door, the No Vacancy light flickered on.

Finally, he'd gone to his mom's, as if he'd forgotten that his mom was now—had been, for a decade or so—married to Warren the Warthog. As if it had slipped his mind that Warren was newly retired from the electric-fan factory and had too much time on his hands. The happy couple live in a trailer near Beacon, which Warren had gotten years ago in his divorce settlement. Warren made

Nolan feel at home by asking him several times daily how long he planned on staying.

After Warren passed out snoring, Nolan's mom droned her Buddhist chant. She asked him to chant with her. There was so much he could chant for. True love. A real vocation. Finding his path, at last. He was sorry, but he couldn't. It kills him that his mom has spent so long looking for things—a decent man, a home of her own. Peace. Love. God. Whatever. He doesn't hold it against her. He hopes she finds it before she dies.

Nolan split after two days. He hasn't been back since. He'd known better than to show up there with his shaved head and tattoos. His mom would think it was her fault for moving around so much when he was a kid. The other potential problem is that since the last time he saw his mother, Nolan has found out certain things about his father— about his father's death—that she never told him. He guesses he would probably have to bring that up, sooner or later.

After he left his mother's, he got hired for the night shift at the doughnut shop, and then after he was fired from that, at the Quik-Mart on Broadway in Middletown. The manager told him about a room he could sleep in at an old folks' home if he slipped the janitor a ten.

That's what Nolan had sunk to: working nights at a convenience store and sleeping during the day at a cockroach-infested Mafia-scam nursing home. You heard about losers falling through the cracks, through the safety net.

He fell.

Running into Raymond was his lucky break. After his little layover at the Quik-Mart and Lilyvale Manor, the chance to stay on Raymond's couch and work at the tire shop seemed like an invitation from Saint Peter to pitch his tent in heaven. At first, Nolan hardly minded being woken every morning by the whine of the blender as Lucy made those nasty health shakes for the kids. He understood that the blender was Lucy's way of sending him a big good-morning fuck-you.

Compared to that, Bonnie's storage room—sorry, *guest* room—

makes Nolan feel like Mick Jagger sipping tropical rum drinks in his Caribbean hacienda. How sad that what he likes best about his room at Bonnie's is that the door shuts. That's something you might not appreciate unless you'd had to stay up listening to Raymond and Ted Donnell and Frankie Most and Tommy Lehman have their beery conversations about how the white man is getting shafted. Nolan didn't have to say much. They assumed he was one of them. And in some ways, he guesses, he was. He shaved his head and got the tattoos. He went to the Homeland Encampment and listened to the German marching songs and the speeches about how the Jewish sons of Satan were out to destroy the white race.

He can't deny that it felt good to stop having to hide how angry he was, which was something he'd been taught to do ever since he could remember. That was what he learned about himself in anger management class. The best thing about ARM was that it gave you a place for the anger to go. Like a lightning rod, an electrical ground. You touched it, the tension discharged. Once he could have gotten a buzz off the fact that, all the time Nolan was homeless, Bonnie and her kids had a whole room they didn't even use. *Look who's maintaining the swimming pools, and look who is swimming in them.* But what good would those thoughts do him now?

Nolan shoves some boxes aside and lies on the bed and opens *Crime and Punishment.* Like the samurai book, like most of the books he's read in the last few years, it came from a vehicle someone brought into the tire shop. Vincent started to see the place as his private lending library. No one ever missed the books, no one ever came back to find them, though they'd be calling every five minutes if some kid lost his mitten.

At Raymond's he had no place to read, which was more annoying than Bonnie being shocked that he *could* read. It served her right that her kids got pissed at her for mentioning Nolan's reading. Holding him up as some kind of adult role model must mean she wants them to hate his guts before they even get to know him.

Near the end of his stay at Raymond's, Nolan spent lunch hours driving to an empty lot and sitting in the truck and reading. That

was where he read Maslow's books. And that was where his truck
died. He couldn't get it started. He'd had to call Raymond, and
when Raymond asked what he was doing parked in an empty lot,
Nolan said: Taking a piss.

Best not to think about that now. What better reason to lose
himself in a book and forget all his troubles? He pages through
Crime and Punishment, looking for his place. Past the murder, which
was great, and up to the part where the guy thinks everyone's talking about him. Someone else's persecution complex is the last thing
Nolan needs. He tries Pogo, but can't focus, then opens *The Way of
the Warrior.*

The Warrior keeps occupied to build a fortress against enemy
thoughts. But what could "occupied" possibly mean in his present
situation, holed up in a spare room crammed with family garbage?
Well, if he's going to stay here, he needs to get his living quarters
squared away.

Nolan grabs a pile of clothes, jams it into the closet, and slams
the door on the surprisingly feisty heaps of old coats. Bonnie's kids
are a little like Raymond's. It must be a generational thing. None of
them see the payoff in even pretending to be polite. Nolan doesn't
blame Bonnie's sons, coming home to find their new roommate at
the kitchen table. Together, she and the kids are like some ultra-sick
sitcom. The younger one's got some twisted love affair happening
with the mom. The older one's scared of his shadow. Nolan could
blow them both away just by looking at them funny. Maybe they
were cooler before their father bailed.

Nolan was three when his father split. He doesn't remember
much. Apparently, the guy worked twenty-four hours a day and had
money problems anyway. Nolan thinks he recalls the time when his
father began having tax troubles, but the only image he can summon up is a light shining over a kitchen table. Bonnie's kids are
spoiled rotten. They don't know how good they have it.

Nolan only left Raymond's this morning. And look what he's accomplished! A brand-new life, for starters. No wonder he's tired.
He's earned the right to kick back. Just shove some more stuff aside

and take a Vicodin and push the reset button when he wakes up tomorrow morning. Thinking of his drug stash makes him want to make sure it's still there. And he'll take just one little pill for the teensiest bumperino.

Nolan thinks, as he often does, that the medical and legal establishments have it all wrong about why a person might take drugs. They assume you want to get to that place where you're falling off your chair with your eyes rolled back in your head. When really what Nolan wants is a reason to stay *on* the chair, that mini-shift of focus that makes everything seem more fun, smoother, less boring, and minus the jittery backbeat of impatience and paranoia.

Nolan reaches into his duffel bag, past the T-shirts and underwear. He slides out a couple of books and the latest issue of *Soldier of Fortune* that, on an impulse—even though it's hardly his favorite magazine, and even though he knew that stealing it would enrage Raymond almost more than anything—he stole from Raymond's kitchen table on his way out this morning.

By the time Nolan finds the pill bottles and the envelope full of money, he's in such a sweat that he has to repeat the handy formula he learned in anger management: Relax. Stay calm. Take it easy. The plastic bottles feel good in his hands. Little vials of tranquillity. He's got maybe enough Vicodin and Xanax to last a couple of months if strict old Mr. Super Ego helps him keep things under control.

Then he counts the fifteen hundred dollars, the end product of those seventy hits of Ex. Not the ticket to Tahiti, not exactly the golden parachute that will let him down easy.

Nolan slips the money inside *The Way of the Warrior*, then stuffs everything back in his duffel. Probably it will be safe. Surely Bonnie raised her kids not to root through other people's belongings. Still, it seems like tempting fate to leave the bag in the middle of the room. He drags out enough stuff from under the bed to make space for the duffel. Computer keyboards, a printer. He piles them in a corner. What slobs.

One envelope turns out to contain a bunch of old tax returns.

On top is a 1992 1040 form on which Dr. Joel Kalen, physician, declared a hundred and sixteen grand from his medical practice and Bonnie Kalen, museum administrator, a more modest twenty-two thousand. What was Nolan doing that year? Laying carpet, maybe. Pulling in something around what Bonnie made. That scrap of arithmetic makes Nolan feel allied with Bonnie against the higher-earning Dr. Joel. So what if Nolan was *surviving* on that twenty-two thou, and Bonnie was spending her mad money on all those little fashion extras?

No point checking the other returns. Everyone cheats on their taxes, everyone gets away with it, everyone except poor bastards like Nolan's dad. Putting away the envelope, Nolan wants a little credit for respecting the Kalens' privacy.

He finds a box of folders from photo shops and for an instant lets himself dream that he's stumbled on a treasure trove of Dr. Joel's naked pictures of Bonnie. That would prove there was a God, and that God loved Nolan. He could probably jerk off and fall asleep. But having met Bonnie, Nolan doubts that such pictures exist.

The first sets of photos are, he knows right away, from the older kid's bar mitzvah. Nolan recalls a debate between Raymond and some bonehead who'd insisted that Jews get circumcised at thirteen, in public, at their bar mitzvahs. Raymond-the-expert said no, they were cut at birth by a rabbi who dried the foreskins to make a date-rape powder for elderly Jews to put in white Christian girls' drinks.

In the photos, everyone's shined up and groomed. Bonnie's wearing a navy blue suit with gold buttons. The tall guy with his arm around her must be Dr. Joel. How wrong the ARM cartoonists are, with their corny pictures of hunchbacked, hook-nosed, drooling trolls humping their money bags. The Jew you have to watch out for is the glossy overgrown boy, the Michael Eisners, the Steven Spielbergs, the former high school jocks like Dr. Joel, the chosen tribe destined from the cradle for some lucrative profession. At least that's what the old Nolan thought. The new Nolan tells himself: Look beyond the big nose and the fancy suit to the guy who loves his wife and kids on this proud occasion. Or anyway, the guy who was trying. It must have been around that time that Dr. Feelbad walked.

In some of the pictures, older relatives—grandparents, Nolan assumes—shrink from children's rough embraces. Most of the pictures show Bonnie and the doc and the younger kid grinning like maniacs, and the bar mitzvah boy scowling, as far from the others as he can get and still be in the same photo.

Next set of snapshots, same configuration: Mama Bear, Daddy Bear, Baby Bear clumped together, Sourpuss Bear on the side, all squinting into the camera, trying to look relaxed as they pose on a wharf surrounded by nautical tourist crap. The sticklike limbs of the kids angle out of their shorts and T-shirts. Here's Bonnie in a swimsuit. She's got a cute little body. The poor thing's lost a ton of weight since the old man left. On her face is a fake-exasperated smile with an edge of panic. Apparently she didn't want Dr. Shutterbug taking her picture.

With waning interest, Nolan flips through the packs of prints, watching everyone get progressively younger in a predictable series of Kodak moments: school plays, birthday parties, Thanksgivings, trips. Nolan can hardly stand this jolly time travel through the *Leave It to Beaver* life of the Kalen family. The part that really annoys him is: They take it all for granted. They think they don't have *enough!*

The Warrior gathers knowledge concerning his surroundings. At the very bottom of the box is Bonnie's wedding portrait. In her lacy white dress and veil, Bonnie just reaches Joel's shoulder. The darkly handsome Jewish prince stares out of the photo, while Bonnie is staring up at him. Worshipful and adoring. Nolan could have told them the marriage wouldn't last.

There seem to be no pictures beyond the kid's bar mitzvah, so that must have been when the show got canceled. Nolan loads the envelopes back into the box. He feels like he does after he's come and the porn tape is still running. He can't remember the last time he watched porn, certainly not on Raymond's couch with the kids running in and out. Just before he and Margaret split, she wouldn't let him turn off the TV while they were having sex. Mostly it was the nightly news. That should have sent him a message. Obviously, they had turned a corner in a road that led a long way back to those nights when Margaret would get home from work and she'd be halfway out of her uniform by the time she walked in the door.

Enough housework for one night! Nolan thinks he could sleep. His mind is still jacked up from the day, but his body is cashing it in. But wait a second. What's that sound? His chest tightens until he convinces himself: Raymond couldn't possibly know where he is.

The comfort is so shocking—total darkness, a bed to himself, clean sheets against his bare skin—that for some reason it takes him a while to decide if it feels good. Well, it does and it doesn't as he lies there, tense, determined to resist the seductive, treacherous noises of the house, the comfy nighttime creaks and sighs trying to sell him on that sweetness that the housefly thinks he's found, one second before his legs give way and he drowns in the jar of honey.

O<small>N A NORMAL MORNING</small>, Bonnie would tap on the boys' doors and begin the delicate task of prying them loose from their dreams. She starts with Max, who's easier. Her voice and a sliver of light are usually all it takes to persuade him to stretch out his arms. The hug is a promise that Max will be getting out of bed even as she moves on to Danny's room, where the sound of her voice will have the opposite effect. Danny will roll away from her, a mummy wedged in the corner. Bonnie hadn't liked it when he'd put his mattress on the floor. But at sixteen you're old enough to decide how you want to sleep, old enough so that a mother (these days!) knows how little can be asked, knows to be grateful (he's not mainlining heroin or shooting up his high school cafeteria!) when, every morning, her darling says, Would you shut *up?* Would you go a-*way?*

Bonnie feels her shoulders stiffen before she gets to Danny's door. At least there's no one else around—like Joel, for example—to accuse her of spoiling the boys and letting them bully her. What if Joel had wanted custody? What will happen when Joel finds out about their skinhead houseguest? These mornings, hard as they are, could have been—could still be—stolen from her. Bonnie knows how soon it will end. A few brief years, and the boys will be gone.

On a normal morning, she would yell from the kitchen, hurling empty threats at Danny until she's almost hoarse. No wonder the kid hates the sound of her voice. Anyway, it's all theater. Danny and Bonnie both know he will sleep until exactly ten minutes before the school bus comes, ten minutes of frantic racing around, looking for the homework that he will accuse her of throwing out. Until he grabs his coat in a rage and leaves just as the bus driver honks a final warning.

That's what Bonnie has to look forward to as she grimly soldiers on with her own morning, showers, dresses, brews coffee, finds *Max's* lost homework, the papers *she* needs to take to the office, whirling through her house in a dervishlike frenzy spiked by jolts of adrenaline whenever she wonders how long it's been since she tried to wake up Danny. Until at last she loses it and begins to scream.

But this isn't a normal morning. Bonnie will not yell at her children with a stranger in the house. How depressing that the presence of a neo-Nazi could make a person behave more like a civilized adult. But if that's how it is, so be it. It's one more benefit of Vincent's presence, of her having done what Meyer suggested. Now if only Vincent stays in his room until the boys leave for school. Bonnie puts on a longer skirt than she had planned on wearing.

She was proud of her kids last night. They handled the situation like grown-ups. But how will their maturity stand the test of seeing him this morning? Shielding them from the awkwardness of meeting a strange man at breakfast is one of the things that's kept her from dating since Joel left. Not that anyone's asked her, so it's theoretical. She did endure a few sad dinners with the lonely-guy friends of friends, plus one blind date with an entertainment lawyer who spent dinner describing, in detail, what twenty years of bulimia had done to his ex-wife's dental health.

Bonnie's been awake since five, fully present and alert for a three-hour dark night of the soul that began with a dream so disgusting that she can hardly stand to recall it. She dreamed she was having a party and went into the bathroom and saw that the guests had been urinating in the tub, leaving those little puddles that dogs (you hope it's dogs) leave on city streets. Stuck in one of the puddles was a pubic hair that, on closer inspection, turned out to be a micro Loch Ness monster with melancholy eyes and a tiny triangular head.

No need to wake up Dr. Freud. Bonnie knows what the dream means—her unconscious has found a way to punish her for being squeamish about Vincent sharing her children's bathroom—without the years of expensive psychotherapy that, at the end, Joel offered to pay for. Joel always claimed she was paranoid, but as it turned out, she wasn't.

In any case, they've made it through the night. Bonnie checks on the boys and is overjoyed to find them in their beds. It delights her when Danny says, "Get lost." Look for the hidden blessing: Vincent's presence has made her treasure the most difficult part of her day.

For once, Danny doesn't stay in bed until the very last minute but rather comes down early and stands in the kitchen doorway, glowering at her coffee cup and at Max's half-eaten corn muffin.

"Please tell me the Nazi's not still here," he says.

"As far as I know he is," says Bonnie. "Let's hope. That is, if you have any interest in your mom keeping her job."

"Are you insane?" says Danny. "Bring that creep home? Was this that sick bastard Meyer's idea?"

"Language," says Bonnie.

"*Was* it?" says Danny.

This might not be the most opportune moment to discuss the power balance between herself and Meyer. In the past, she's lectured the kids, perhaps unwisely, on the life of Meyer Maslow, on what a hero he is, and how lucky she is to be working for him. Meanwhile she knows that they think she's a spineless wimp who would jump off the Tappan Zee if Meyer told her to. Well, they're wrong. She stands her ground when it matters. Her first week at the foundation, Meyer asked if she would mind picking up his dry cleaning on her way back from lunch. It took all her courage to tell him that it wasn't her job. That same afternoon, she returned from lunch to find that he'd sent her flowers.

So it's not only Meyer teaching her things. It's a two-way street. Anyway, it's not about Meyer. How often do you get a chance to test yourself, to open your heart, to really put yourself out, by rescuing someone who needs your help?

Bonnie says, "It was also *my* idea. Sweetheart, the poor guy's homeless."

"That's what *I* said," Max pipes up.

"Fucking kiss-up!" Danny spits at his brother, making obscene kissing motions as he grabs his backpack and heads for the door.

"Bye. Love you," says Bonnie, forlornly.

Max watches his brother go, then says, "You know, Mom, there's lots of other homeless people we could take in. It doesn't have to be *this* guy . . ."

"Honey," says Bonnie. "You don't get to choose. It's not like adopting a puppy from the pound."

"I figured that, too." How could Max be four years younger and forty years more mature than his brother? Or his father, for that matter? Bonnie feels disloyal for comparing her kids. So what if one tries to make her life simple and the other one lives to make her suffer? Bonnie loves them both. It's just that Max is easy. Danny's more of a challenge, because he's so much more like her and consequently hates her for the qualities they share.

Max shrugs and squeezes Bonnie's shoulder. He's already running after his brother, thinking of some smart remark (doubtless at Bonnie's expense) that will make them friends again before Danny's bus comes, closely followed by Max's bus to the middle school that's only a two-minute walk from Danny's high school.

Vincent comes downstairs a few minutes after the boys leave. Was he awake and listening?

"Coffee?" says Bonnie. "How did you sleep?"

"Like a baby," Vincent says. The shy half smile, the slow appreciative way he sips his coffee, the friendly silence into which he lapses reassure Bonnie that this is not the homicidal maniac she pictured at five A.M. At the same time, she has the feeling that all his expressions and gestures are calculated to reassure her.

"I slept like a baby," Vincent says. "I woke up screaming every two hours."

The minute Bonnie relaxes, Vincent reminds her not to.

"Joke," Vincent says. "That's supposed to be funny. I slept great. I feel terrific."

"So I guess we should get ready to go."

"Say the word," says Vincent.

Outside, the street has been newly washed, and so, it appears, has the bright spring morning. Vincent and Bonnie get into the van.

"The dashboard light's still blinking," says Bonnie.

"Jap corporate greed," Vincent says. "They have it all worked out. It's their way of making sure you get it serviced more than you need to, and then they skim some cash off the top from the chain garages."

"Are American cars different?" Bonnie wishes he hadn't said *Jap*. "Different from Jap*anese?*"

"Don't kid yourself," says Vincent. "It's all Jap-owned."

Bonnie pulls out on the highway. Vaguely companionable and sleepy, like the rest of the zoned-out carpoolers around them, they ride in silence until the traffic slows and they pull up alongside a vintage Saab station wagon with Vermont plates and three rugrats swarming all over their parents.

"Child neglect," says Bonnie. "How could they not make their kids wear seat belts?"

Vincent says, "I've seen statistics proving that seat belts double your chance of dying in a wreck."

"Fasten yours, please," Bonnie says.

"I already did," says Vincent. "So did your kids get off to school okay?"

How nice of him to ask. "I guess so," Bonnie says. "After the daily psychodrama."

"Your kids think you're great," says Vincent.

"They do?" says Bonnie. So this is what Bonnie's come to. She's overjoyed because some Nazi burnout tells her that her kids like her. Of course they like her. They love her. But she can't help wanting to know how it looks from the outside. That's one of the many drawbacks of being a single parent. There's no one to consult. Not that she could have asked Joel, who always found a way to point out what a fabulous parent he was and how miserably Bonnie was failing. She let the kids walk all over her. She was not allowing them to turn into *men*.

"They admire you," Vincent says.

"Really?"

"Trust me on this." Could Vincent be conning her? Pushing her buttons? It takes a certain sensitivity to know where someone's buttons are.

"Where did you grow up?" Bonnie asks.

"The Catskills. Liberty, Swan Lake, around there."

"The Borscht Belt?" says Bonnie.

"The Bean Sprout Belt," Vincent says. "My mom was a sort of New Ager."

Bonnie hadn't expected that, but fine, she can factor it in.

"What did your father do?"

"Died," says Vincent.

"What?" says Bonnie.

"He was an electrician. And then he died."

"And your mom?"

"After he passed, she cooked for all these weird hippie religious joints, ashrams and temples and shit, in return for free board and meditation lessons."

"That's a lot of cooking," says Bonnie.

"Brown rice and stir-fry." Vincent shrugs. "Not as much as you'd think. I never went for the spiritual jive. I walked in the woods. I read comics."

"Your mom was ahead of her time."

"Actually, she was a couple of decades behind it. I guess you could say I was sort of preprogrammed to join ARM. I mean, I got used to hanging around with nut jobs."

"You were born to work for Brotherhood Watch." Bonnie laughs, too loudly. She doesn't think the foundation is full of nut jobs, though she can see how someone might.

Vincent smiles. "I guess you could say that, too."

Vincent's relaxed—for Vincent—as long as they're on the thruway, but as soon as they turn off the West Side Highway, Bonnie can feel the tension growing until, by the time they're walking from the parking lot to the office, his shoulders are raised like a prizefighter's, ready to fend off whoever comes out swinging.

"Don't be nervous," says Bonnie. "No one at the foundation bites."

"Life bites," Vincent says.

At reception, Anita Shu's good morning could hardly be frostier.

"Have we found Vincent office space?" Bonnie says.

"One-sixteen-B," says Anita.

Bonnie ushers Vincent to the cheerless empty workstation they keep for temps and volunteers. The gunmetal desk is bare except for a crumpled candy bar wrapper that adds to the desolation the way a tangle of tumbleweed makes the desert seem more desolate.

"Lovely." Bonnie grabs the candy wrapper.

"Don't worry about it," says Vincent.

"Will you be okay here?" The guy spent years in a hate group, and Bonnie's asking if he can survive half an hour at an empty desk? But when Vincent throws himself into the chair with a little boy's stagy bravado and grins and says, "Sure," she knows why she asked. She feels like she's dropping him off at day care. She should have told him to bring a book.

"Look, I've got a better idea. Why don't you wait in my office?" An invitation she regrets at once. There's nothing for him to do there, either, except look out the window—or go through her desk and files. Why does she keep suspecting him of wanting to rifle through her stuff?

So far everything—well, most things—indicate that Vincent Nolan is what he appears to be, that he means what he says. And yet she's chilled by the prospect of leaving him alone with the financial records of Brotherhood Watch. Suppose he's looking for evidence to bring his Nazi pals to prove that Jews *are* richer than the most delusional skinhead's dreams. Or at least that's how it might look on paper, to outsiders unaware of the foundation's staggering expenses, of how hard it has become to raise the capital, and of how much depends on the benefit dinner.

"Don't touch anything," Bonnie can't help saying. It's what she would tell her kids, and Vincent's grin conveys the fact that he knows that.

Leaving her door open, she heads for Meyer's office, where, just as she feared, Meyer and Roberta Dwyer have begun without her.

It shames Bonnie that her happiness depends on the speed with which Meyer detaches from Roberta and how glad he looks to see her. She's seen him look glad to see thousands of people he wasn't glad to see. She's proud that she is one of the few who evoke a genuine smile.

As always, it seems to take Roberta a moment to remember who Bonnie is, though they work together constantly and depend on one another. Bonnie needs Roberta to get publicity for the foundation, and though Roberta would rather have her expensively manicured fingernails pulled out, one by one, than admit it, without Bonnie there would be no money to pay the maintenance on her West Village co-op.

"Hi there," says Roberta.

"Oh, hi, Roberta!" The fear of sounding sullen makes Bonnie trill like Minnie Mouse.

"This recovering skinhead thing could be *dynamite*." Roberta turns thumbs up at Bonnie. It's not Roberta's fault that she's the older version of the high-school successes whose mission was to keep Bonnie off the cheerleading squad. But one of the perks of being so long past high school is the maturity that turns girls who despised one another into women who can cooperate and see one another's good points. Bonnie likes it that Roberta's bitchy, passive-aggressive pep-squad energy is deployed in the service of Brotherhood Watch. And no doubt Roberta thinks that Bonnie's nerdy sincerity is persuasive and reassuring to potential big-ticket donors.

"How did last night work out?" asks Meyer. "With our friend Mr. Nolan."

Does Roberta know that Bonnie was chosen to take Vincent

home? Vincent moving into her West Ninth Street doorman building is not an honor she wants.

"We survived," Bonnie replies. "He was perfectly well behaved."

"I meant to call you," Meyer says. "And I'm sorry. I fell asleep."

Meyer thought about calling her, with all he has on his mind! Of course, he should have called. Look whom he sent to stay at her house.

"And your sons?" says Meyer. "Danny and Max? How did they react?" So Meyer really is thoughtful. Bonnie wants to believe he cares. It impresses her that, with a major foundation to oversee, with the weight of the world on his shoulders, he takes time to worry about her boys. A lesser man in Meyer's place wouldn't remember their names.

"It wasn't exactly love at first sight. But they understood."

"Bonnie, if this is too much . . . ," says Meyer. "Irene couldn't believe it when I told her you'd offered to take Vincent home. She couldn't believe I let you do it. I thought she'd never forgive me—"

"We'll be fine." Bonnie knocks on Meyer's desk. "It will probably turn out to be a learning experience." Bonnie hates the phrase *learning experience*. So why is she using it now? Because she's lying, and she isn't. She wishes she could go back to her regular, more or less peaceful existence with her kids. But there's something interesting about life with the bizarro houseguest. Anyway, this is not the moment to express her doubts. It's time to give Meyer the breezy reassurance he wants.

"They're good boys," pronounces Meyer. Bonnie beams, though she's aware that Meyer hardly knows them. They *are* good boys. And Meyer knows that, just as he knew that Vincent wouldn't murder them in their beds. What was it that Vincent said? Danny and Max admire her.

"I'm sure they're great kids," says Roberta, dutifully. "Of course they get it. An idiot *child* can see how we can make this skinhead thing work."

"Vincent Nolan," says Bonnie. "The skinhead's name is Vincent Nolan."

"Got that. Vin-cent No-lan." Roberta draws out the syllables for as long as it takes to jot down his name in her Daily Reminder. "Beautiful. The first thing we need is a press release. We can take it from there."

"How soon can you get the release out?" Meyer asks.

"As soon as I get some information." Why is Roberta looking at Bonnie? Roberta is the experienced publicist who came to them via a circuitous route that snaked from the music business through the World Wildlife Fund. Bonnie and Roberta started working at the foundation around the same time. Early on, they'd gone out for lunch, an awkward occasion during which Roberta told Bonnie about her marriage to an Egyptian graduate student who disappeared after six months and divorced her two years later. Was it some kind of green-card scam? Roberta never said. Was she waiting for Bonnie to ask? They never had lunch together again, except on official occasions.

"What do you need?" says Bonnie. "Former ARM member comes to work with Brotherhood Watch."

"That's the headline," says Roberta. "Now give me some text. What turned this guy's head around? What made him come to *us?*"

"Maybe you should talk to him." Bonnie wishes she hadn't said that. What if Vincent prefers Roberta to Bonnie? What an inappropriate thought. Vincent's a hard-luck case trying to change—not a potential boyfriend. The fact that it took Bonnie so long to catch on about Joel and Lorraine has made her afraid that's she's missing all sorts of important clues to the most deceptively simple male-female exchanges. Once, during the months of couples counseling that Joel insisted they go through, Bonnie brought up how betrayed she felt by Joel's insistence that nothing was going on with Lorraine, that it was all in Bonnie's mind. At which point the therapist, Dr. Steinweiss, reminded her that they weren't there to deal with the past, but only with the future. This is about the boys, Joel said. And Dr. Steinweiss agreed.

Bonnie could tell Roberta what Vincent said yesterday in Meyer's office, about his experience at the rave. Roberta, being Roberta, will quickly figure out that Vincent's tale about his rock-concert revelation may not be the ideal anecdote for their demographic.

"Bonnie could work with him," Meyer says. "Find out what his story really is, and then put it in a form that the public will want to hear—"

"I'm having a thought," says Roberta. "Call me crazy, but . . . wouldn't it be amazing if Vincent could talk at the benefit dinner? And we could get some coverage, get mailings out while it's still possible to buy tickets. That could change the whole picture."

No one's going to correct her. It might not change the whole picture, but it's worth a try. And Roberta's not saying anything they haven't already thought.

Outside Meyer's window, the shadow of an airplane flickers over the buildings, a visual echo of the pall that's fallen over the room. That word, *tickets*, has transformed them into three girls without dates for the prom. Joel used to blame Bonnie when they had nowhere to go, no invitations for Labor Day or, God forbid, New Year's Eve. Bonnie weighs her reluctance to feel this way against her anxieties about what Vincent might do at such a dinner. Neither Meyer nor Roberta know that he says *Jap* and *Rican*. But for now, it's impossible to weigh the possible harm against the possible good. Anyhow, it's not Bonnie's decision. Meyer will decide.

"Bonnie, talk to our friend again," Meyer says. "You and Vincent work together. Get something down on paper for Roberta so she can send out a release."

"Sure, I can do that." And it's true. Bonnie loves taking on a challenge. Besides, she's the right person. She already knows more about Vincent than anyone at the office. Plus she knows what will interest the sort of partygoers who can buy tables and invite their twelve best friends to dinner. Maybe Vincent can give a speech without using *Jew* as a verb. Did he talk that way with his cousin? Bonnie would rather not know.

"It's not just about a dinner," Meyer says. "It's about the future. This is someone we can work with, a man whose cooperation may inspire us to devise new outreach programs. For now, we need to stay open to his potential. And to all the reasons why God has sent him to us."

Put that way, the job facing Bonnie sounds a lot more attractive than interrogating Vincent until he comes up with a more acceptable story than the one about the Ecstasy-addled rave.

"The sooner the better," Roberta says.

"Pronto," says Bonnie. "I promise."

Whatever Bonnie expects to see when she gets back to her office—Vincent going through her files—is not what she finds. He's standing at the window, staring out so fixedly that he doesn't move until Bonnie says, "Hello-o?"

"You know what's weird?" Vincent says. "No one down there knows me. Each one of those windows represents—what?—ten people, and each building has thousands and thousands of people inside, and thousands more on the streets, millions of people out there, and none of them, not *one* of them, knows that I exist."

Bonnie comes up behind him and gazes down at the city—the place that doesn't know Vincent. What a narcissist this guy is! And yet Bonnie's moved. His loneliness is so intense that it's all she can do not to cry out, "No one knows me, either!" But that wouldn't be true. Somewhere out there are friends, acquaintances, former colleagues, neighbors, landlords, doctors, dentists, the guys in the bodega where she buys coffee.

"I have a feeling. Just a bleep on the radar." Bonnie knows she sounds like Meyer. "But I have a feeling that soon lots of people will know who you are."

"You think so?" says Vincent.

"Trust me on this," says Bonnie.

Bonnie has the strangest thought: She's like Satan tempting Christ. Offering him the world. Looking down from . . . where? The Bible's not Bonnie's strong suit. Anyway, Bonnie's got it wrong. She's not offering Vincent a chance to trade his soul for worldly power. She's offering him a chance to change himself, and then to change what's down there.

Mrs. Graber writes on the blackboard, TALIBAN, in capital letters, then faces the class and says, "Okay, boys and girls, or should I say *men and women*, let's play a game. Everyone close his or her eyes. Now imagine all the girls in the room covered by black veils. Imagine that a new law has been passed. Woman can no longer drive."

Danny thinks: They can't drive anyway. As far as he's concerned, most of the girls in the room could be walking around in black plastic trash bags, and school would be a more beautiful place. Though if Chloe were wearing a trash bag, Danny couldn't have spent the first half of class idly wondering what would happen if he leaned forward and touched her tattoo. But didn't the article Mrs. Graber just read aloud say that Afghan girls could no longer go to school? Did she somehow miss that?

Last period, he and Chloe cut study hall and sneaked down to the riverbank and split a joint of high-grade Jamaican. Being stoned in school is an improvement on not being stoned in school, and not at all what you'd expect. It doesn't make you eat everything in the cafeteria, or get paranoid, or giggle and stumble around and crash into the lockers. Everything seems more interesting, as if every thought has a litter of thoughts that give birth to other thought-babies.

Danny squeezes his eyes shut and tries to imagine what it might be like if the Taliban took over Clairmont. Okay, his mom couldn't drive to work. Nor would Danny be taking Driver's Ed from Mrs. Limpovski, aka Mrs. Blimpovski, whose scary ass pastes you against the driver's side door. Mrs. Graber wouldn't be teaching this class.

Danny opens his eyes to let the lingering afterimage of Blimpovski's ass out of his head, and finds himself staring into the black hole of Mrs. Graber's stare. Linda Graber hates him. She hates all the boys. Her forehead gleams with sweat. No wonder. The classroom's broiling, and she's wearing a short-sleeved turtleneck, a variation on what she's worn every day for the past two weeks since she finally found out what every kid in school has known since Christmas. Someone had put up a Web site, grabermole.com, on which you could post school gossip and flame the teachers. On the homepage were photos of Mrs. Graber, with close-ups of the giant brown birthmarks all over her neck and chest.

The text underneath one photo said: "Enter today's contest! Name the continent that the splotch above resembles. (Hint: Australia!)" No one, at least not Danny's friends, knows who put it up and then took it down when the principal offered amnesty, if the site came down, to whoever did it. Danny thought it was cruel. Yet some part of him thinks that Linda Graber deserved it.

The geniuses who designed the site are probably not in World Civilizations, the class for the retards who can't get into AP American History. Two things Danny's grateful for: One, his mom doesn't seem to know there's an AP class, so two, she doesn't know Danny's not in it.

Mrs. Graber glares at Danny. Does she think he put up the Web site? He wishes he had the computer skills. But he wouldn't have done it. Linda Graber's moles aren't her fault, though plenty of other things are. If she weren't so mean, her skin wouldn't have gotten its own home page. No one has posted a photo of Mrs. Blimpovski's ass.

To escape Graber's cattle prod of a stare, Danny shuts his eyes again.

"Wake up," says Mrs. Graber. "Yoo-hoo. You over there. The living dead." Danny's chest contracts until he realizes she means the whole class. World Civilizations has run out of steam ever since they finished the textbook about how the nations of the world have contributed to world civilization. Danny remembers nothing except the potato famine and Marco Polo bringing back pasta from China. Which could be a problem, with finals coming up. In these last weeks of school, the kids—that is, the ones so dumb they don't realize there's no point kissing up to the teacher in a class like World Civilizations—are bringing in articles from the newspaper, about AIDS, or Africa, or, today, Afghanistan.

Graber waltzes over to Smitty, the most pitiful kid in the room.

"Mis-ter Smith," she says. "Seeing as how you haven't passed one test since the semester began, you might want to listen and make a few notes before we're looking at summer school." She sounds like the witch in *The Wizard of Oz*. She skips away from the vulcanized ruin that, seconds ago, was Smitty.

"Lights, please," says Mrs. Graber. Someone dims the light, and an image flashes on the wall: an Afghan woman in one of those shiny, pleated body bags.

Mrs. Graber reads aloud by the beam of the penlight that sometimes, when she feels naughty, she shines in kids' eyes. "Among the most controversial Taliban edicts is a law requiring non-Muslims to wear an identifying badge." Another click, and there's a shot of an old Jewish man in Germany with a yellow star sewn to his coat. In case one single person doesn't get where Linda Graber's going with this. Half the class is Jewish. They've known about yellow stars since birth. The rest caught up in eighth grade when they did Anne Frank. And yet it makes Danny self-conscious, as if it's his personal problem.

Maybe he shouldn't have smoked that joint. There *is* a downside to the slippery ease with which each thought leads to others, in this case to a memory from last night.

In the middle of the night, he'd gotten up to piss and found a copy of *Soldier of Fortune* on the bathroom floor. It might as well have been a turd floating in the toilet, or a copy of *Penthouse* with its pages stuck together. That's how grossed out Danny was by this evidence of Vincent Nolan's presence. Did this mean that the Nazi sat here and took a shit and read this? Or that he sat here and read it and jerked off? Which would have been more disgusting?

Danny sat on the edge of the tub and—suddenly nervous in his own bathroom—skimmed what turned out to be a weirdo fashion magazine, full of ads for boots and military gear, camping equipment, water canteens that these morons called "hydration systems." Fake army medals to pin on your fake camouflage fatigues. And then, of course, the gun ads. At first it gave Danny the creeps, but after a while he got into one particularly silvery semiautomatic rifle, Model 92b1. It seemed so light and streamlined, like an alien praying mantis. He paged past photos of covert operations in foreign countries, paused at a piece about a former U.S. diplomat turned South American drug lord, then moved on to an article about the Oklahoma City bombing, which, like several others in the issue, offered evidence proving that Tim McVeigh could not have acted alone. A second yellow rental van, something about a motel. Danny couldn't follow it. Maybe he'd been sleepy.

This morning, when he woke up, the magazine was gone. Max probably hadn't seen it, which made it seem like a private message from Vincent Nolan to Danny.

In the kitchen, he'd almost mentioned it when Mom and Max were complimenting themselves on how *good* they were to adopt a homeless guy. He'd wanted his mother to know what her new pal was reading, especially since she'd made such a point of his being a reader. It's hard to say what busting Vincent for having the magazine would have added to the information already provided by his tattoos. Well, how about this? The tattoos were about the past. He could have changed his mind since then. But he's reading the magazine *now*. Something told Danny to save the magazine for some occasion when he might need it.

"Danny?" Mrs. Graber's jackhammer voice shatters his private moment. "Are you with us? Are you ay-*lie-ive?*"

Why is she singling out Danny? He takes it back about weed never making you paranoid in school.

Danny and Mrs. Graber lock eyes. Total communication. She knows he hasn't been listening. He knows she's disappointed in him, and also in herself for once again failing to reach him. Everything is understood except, he hopes, how high he is. And why is she saying his name? She's reading from a list. Which means that there must be other names besides his.

"Danny, you are one of three students left who have not yet deigned to inform me about the topic of your final paper."

Deign this, Danny thinks. But wait. It's all coming back to him. Final. Paper. Topic. Pick an individual who has changed the course of twentieth-century history.

"Hitler." Why did Danny say that? Could it be because he's sharing a bathroom with the führer?

"That's quite a demanding subject," Mrs. Graber says. "Do you really think you want to take on such a challenging topic after having spent the whole year occupying that seat without giving any indication that you plan to do any work at all? Also you might think twice about spending your time studying a man who did so much harm, a man who was so evil—"

"Kiss my ass" slips out, like a burp.

"What was that?" Mrs. Graber doesn't need to raise her voice. No one's breathing.

"Nothing." Danny *has* to sound innocent. This could go so many ways.

Mrs. Graber hesitates. Does she want to make serious trouble? Does she hate Danny enough to start something that would mean *her* staying after school?

"So is Hitler okay?" asks Danny.

"Obviously," she says. The class is all so glad the tension's defused, they laugh, as if it's a joke. Mrs. Graber writes something— presumably "Hitler"—next to Danny's name.

Not a second too soon, the bell rings.

"Bring in your newspaper clippings," Mrs. Graber sings after them. The minute the classroom door opens, her voice sweetens into something approaching normal.

In the hall, Danny slows down until Chloe is trotting along beside him.

"That was tough," says Danny. "I mean, I was totally wasted—"

"Oh, were you?" One of the things he is learning from Chloe is never to admit, not even to your best friend, that you are not in control. "You must have been high. Picking Hitler—are you crazy? Everyone's doing Nelson Mandela. Every retard knows that's how you get a good grade in Linda Graber's class. You do Nelson Mandela. Or maybe Mother Teresa. Or Elie Wiesel."

Danny thinks his mom might know Elie Wiesel. Why didn't he pick him? "What did Mother Teresa ever do? I mean, compared to Hitler."

Two pigtails, frosted pink today, jiggle like antennae as Chloe rocks her pretty head back and forth to underline the sarcasm. "Because Mother Teresa represents the *values*"—she's imitating Linda Graber—"we've learned about in World Civilizations."

"Values?" says Danny. "Boring. Values is a girl thing."

"So what's a boy thing?" Chloe asks.

"Hitler," Danny says.

How desperately Meyer depends on his staff! How impossible life would be if these energetic, capable women were any less good at their jobs. Roberta has contacted the media and set up a press conference so that all Meyer has to do is show up in the foundation's Jean Moulin Conference Room at eleven-fifteen. And Bonnie has not only fed and housed their white-power poster boy, not only groomed him, sartorially and spiritually, not only worked with him, one-on-one, but has achieved near-miraculous progress. Meyer can see it when he passes Vincent in the hall. That squirrelly furtiveness is turning into something presentable and convincing.

Bonnie scares Meyer sometimes. There's something alarming about a person who will do anything you ask. The scary part is seeing how much you *will* ask. It's lucky that Bonnie found Brotherhood Watch, where she is among friends who would never abuse her generosity. Knowing that she is working to make the world a less hate-filled place has to be good for a wife and mother whose husband abandoned her for a woman who already killed two husbands. Meyer tries not to hear office gossip, but his staff tells Irene.

As he enters the conference room, Meyer's spirits sink. Huddling at one end of the long table are Roberta, Bonnie, Vincent Nolan, and a young woman in a smart black suit and a volcano of shiny black curls.

In other words, one reporter. Meyer hates it that he cares. But isn't everyone vain? Even Vincent Nolan, rocked back, one arm slung over his chair, as if the conference table were a flashy car he's driving. Did Bonnie buy him that shirt and tie? Meyer hopes she billed the foundation. But how could anyone, even Bonnie, have made his hair grow in so fast? He's already sprouted a reddish fuzz that softens the angry message delivered, just days ago, by his skull. Testosterone, thinks Meyer. God's hair tonic.

Roberta rises to greet him. "This is Colette Martinez, from the *New York Times*. Colette, Meyer Maslow. The *Times* asked if they could have a day's jump. Lead time on everyone else."

"Certainly," says Meyer. His mood improves slightly when the reporter, Colette, says in an awed voice, "It's a great honor to meet you." In fact, she's quite pretty. Exotic.

"It's a pleasure, Miss Martinez." Meyer gazes into her eyes.

Her laugh is like a gulp. "I don't want to misrepresent myself. Please don't get your hopes up. They've got me on page two in the Metro section." Since when do reporters require so much emotional support? Is this one waiting for a group hug?

"Ink is ink," says Roberta.

"We're delighted you're here," Bonnie says.

Bonnie looks well. Her skin has the pinkish sheen Irene gets from the dermatologist Meyer calls Doctor Three Hundred Dollars. Bonnie reminds him of a girlfriend he had when he first came to this country. Attractive enough, a certain waifish appeal. But the girl burst into tears after sex. Some men like that sort of thing. Some men like one-legged women. Irene used to make him laugh in bed. That seems so long ago now.

In theory, this conference is Roberta's show. But it's Bonnie who, with a prompting smile, signals that they should begin. The job *is* doing Bonnie good. It must be satisfying to accomplish what she's achieved with Vincent. Meyer wishes he had the time. How far he's come from those early years when each person he met seemed like a fallen angel crying out to be rescued! One heart at a time.

So let's start with this reporter's heart. Getting her on the foundation's side will translate into donors and enough hard currency to bribe whoever can spring the Iranian. In the long run, Meyer knows, the press can help him accomplish his Robin Hood mission, separating the rich from their money without the Merry Band, the muggings in Sherwood Forest.

Colette produces a tape recorder and notebook and coolly appraises Vincent and Meyer, then scribbles a few notes and says, "Maybe we should begin. The material I got from my editors said that Mr. Nolan has recently left a neo-Nazi hate group and has decided to work with Brotherhood Watch."

"Exactly," says Meyer, encouragingly.

"You're so prepared!" says Roberta.

"Well, obviously—" says Colette.

"You'd be surprised by some reporters I've met," persists Roberta.

Colette swivels to face Vincent, cocking her head like a boxer. Poor thing, she wasn't brought up to ask strangers personal questions.

"Let's go back a bit," she says. "I think our readers will want to know how you got involved with the Aryan Resistance Movement."

"Good question," says Vincent, with a bashful smile, above which he's making confident, steady eye contact with his interlocutor. The two of them could be alone in the room. It's second nature for Meyer to seduce the press. But he should be taking lessons.

Yesterday at the staff meeting Bonnie declined to say exactly what Vincent would tell the reporters today. She said that the more she and Vincent talked, layers were peeled away, and everything was turning out to have multiple reasons and explanations. Why he joined ARM, why he left. Basically, who the guy *is*.

"Vincent's intuitive," Bonnie had said. "He gets things. Even stuff about my kids. I think we ought to trust his instinct for what a particular reporter needs to hear and for what each situation requires."

"Basically," says Vincent, "it's all about the IRS."

"The IRS?" says Colette.

"Can I back up a little?"

"Please," says Colette. "Feel free."

"Well, when I was a kid, all I knew was that my dad had left my mom and then died, which put Mom and me in a tough situation. I got into trouble, kid stuff. I guess I wanted attention. Eventually, I pulled my act together. Sort of. Finished high school, got a job, another job. Girlfriends, whatever. Nothing seemed to work out. Pretty boring, huh?"

"Not at all." Colette's taking notes.

"I kind of lost touch with my family. And then things fell apart. I got fired. Split up with my girlfriend. I was broke and practically homeless. Then one day, I'm eating breakfast in this diner on Route 17, and my cousin Raymond walks in.

"It was strange. I hadn't seen the guy for, like, five years. I tell him my sad story, and he says it all makes sense, and I say, What do you mean, it makes sense, nothing makes sense. He says, What he never understood was how everyone in the family except me knew that my dad got reamed by the IRS for some bookkeeping screwup when he tried to start that pathetic electrical business. Some crazy IRS fucker came after him, some licensed U.S. government killer, loaded for bear. My dad lost everything and left us and shot himself in the mouth. He did it in my uncle Vern's—Raymond's dad's— garage. A real mess to clean up. Raymond's dad made Raymond's mom do it, even though it was *his* brother."

"Gosh, I'm sorry," Colette says.

"It's not your fault," says Vincent. "Not your fault and not your problem. I was three."

Colette can't help sneaking a glance at Meyer, and then at Bonnie, whose jaw has dropped. Has Bonnie never heard this? Somehow Meyer thinks not. Colette writes something, pauses, writes more. This is more realness than she bargained for when she left the newsroom this morning.

"Should I go on?" asks Vincent.

"Please. But I've got to tell you, I've only got three hundred words—"

"Unless it's a fabulous story," says Roberta.

"Even if," says Colette. "And it *is* a fabulous story. Even so . . ."

"Go on," Bonnie tells Vincent. "That's so awful about your dad."

"I still haven't got around to asking Mom why she never told me about how he died. But that's a whole other can of worms. Anyhow, I'm sitting there in the diner with Raymond, and by now I could pretty much care less about my eggs over easy, and Raymond is telling me, in this very weird, robotic voice, how it all fits together, what killed my dad and what's screwing me is basically the same, the United States government and the rich Jews who own every-thing and are using the Negroes as a weapon to destroy the white race. Right from the start, I had doubts. I mean, there were holes in his argument. Like, if black people are taking over the country, how come they're so poor, and why would the Jews go to all that trouble pretending the Holocaust happened?"

Vincent looks at Meyer, who nods—a little exchange that's not lost on anyone in the room. Colette scribbles frantically. Meyer wishes he could see what she is writing.

"Meanwhile, I'm sitting in the diner trying to process all this heavy shit. He's talking Waco and Ruby Ridge, and I'm still back on what he's told me about my dad. And I'm thinking, Well, Raymond may not have the *complete* explanation, but it *is* an explanation. Whereas I just always assumed it was all random pointless birdshit raining down on my head and—"

"And no one else's head." Colette finishes his sentence.

"Excuse me?" Vincent smiles.

"On your head and no one else's." Colette's a little flustered.

"My head and no one else's," Vincent says. "You get my point exactly."

Bonnie exhales, loudly. The woman hasn't taken a breath the

whole time Vincent's been speaking. Now she clasps her hands, as if she's just watched one of her sons perform in a school play. She's heard the kid rehearse, and now she's thrilled by how well he's done when it counts, in front of an audience. An audience of one—one woman touched, despite herself, by this overgrown working-class kid, this hard-luck, basically likable young man who never had a chance. But how many bad breaks does it take to turn you into a guy with SS tattoos? The idea is so *American*. If you've had a tough childhood, everything is forgiven. According to that logic, Meyer should be Genghis Khan.

"Anyhow, I tell Raymond, Great, so the federal government is selling us out. What can you do about it? Who gives a shit what *we* think? And then he gets this crazy light in his eyes and starts talking about how much one person can make a difference. Hitler, Jesus, he goes through the list. He's drinking gallons of coffee. And you know, the funny thing is that later, when I got ready to leave ARM, when I started reading Dr. Maslow's books, the weird thing was that Dr. Maslow said the exact same thing: One person can make a difference. The world can change, one heart at a time."

Is Vincent saying that the essence of Meyer's new book is the same crap some Nazi told him in an upstate greasy spoon? Don't fascists believe in changing the world a thousand minds at a time, and breaking the skulls around those minds that are slow or reluctant to change? Is Vincent making up this part? The only thing that's inarguable is that he's plugging Meyer's book.

"That's very impressive." Colette beams at Vincent, then bestows a sympathetic smile on Meyer, meant to be admiring, but somehow patronizing, he feels.

"It must be so wonderful for you, Dr. Maslow, to know that something you wrote converted someone, turned somebody around. I can't help wishing your books had been published sixty years ago. You know . . . before . . . the war. But I guess that's impossible."

It takes Meyer a few seconds to decide if she could possibly mean what he thinks she means. Is she saying that his book could have converted a *real* Nazi, could somehow have helped dismantle the German war machine? The woman is an idiot. She's probably the kind who thinks if she went to bed with Hitler and taught him about true love, *that* would have been the Final Solution.

Three forbidden words cross Meyer's mind: affirmative action candidate. Meyer repents on the spot. He monitors himself very closely to make sure he doesn't become like so many men he knows, men his age, successful, comfortable white males, Jews and non-Jews alike, members in good standing of the human rights community. Liberal on the surface, subtly racist underneath. Sometimes not so subtly. When Sol and his friends band together, defensively warding off the cholesterol-rich femininity of Minna's Sunday brunches, they think it's acceptable to tell jokes about women and blacks because they're also telling jokes about old Jewish men.

"You're kidding," Meyer tells Colette. "I would have had to write the books as a child. And what would I have written about?" Is Meyer overreacting? He'll hear about this later from Roberta and Bonnie.

"I didn't mean—" she says.

"Moreover, as you may know, Jews were forbidden to publish. So my books might have had trouble finding readers to convert."

"I'm sorry," says Colette. "Really. I—" An uncomfortable silence falls, from which Colette rescues them by turning back to Vincent. Their white-power hero. "Do you think you could say a little more about what made you change?"

"Can I say one thing first?" Vincent asks Colette.

"Please," says Colette. "Say whatever you want. It's a ninety-minute tape." What about the three-hundred-word limit?

"I was never into violence," Vincent says. "I won't say I didn't *know* guys who were. But whenever that stuff went down, I managed to be somewhere else. Disappeared. It's a trick you learn when you grow up in a tough situation."

What is Vincent fishing for? Some hint that Colette, too, grew up in a tough situation. Vincent's been in ARM too long. Colette's fifteen minutes out of Brown. Her father could be an orthopedic surgeon with an investment account that hardly registered the dent made by her college tuition. It's better that Vincent doesn't know. It might make him regress back into blaming minorities for his disenfranchisement. Better that Vincent not dwell on the fact that, though he's the one being interviewed, Colette earns way more than he does.

"The hate stuff was always a side issue for me. I came in through the other door. The government, the IRS. Waco. I won't pretend I was the most tolerant guy. I was pretty pissed at the world. And everybody's a racist deep inside. Don't you sometimes think that?"

Colette's not going to touch this with a ten-foot pole. Thank God. The same discussion goes on at practically every conference. The teenagers who come to the Pride and Prejudice camp spend half their time arguing about whether everyone is a racist. And the other half smoking marijuana. Probably everyone *is* a racist, Meyer thinks. But who cares what you are deep inside? What matters is what you *do*.

Vincent's saying, "I got into the anger *some*. And maybe because I wasn't raised that way, it felt kind of good, letting out all that rage. Having someone to blame always helps. Everybody knows that."

After a silence, Colette says, "So what made you change your mind?"

"His *heart*," says Meyer.

"Pardon me?" Colette has forgotten Meyer.

"The mind is easy to change. The heart is much more tricky. And our friend here has had a change of heart."

"Heart, then." Colette's feathers seem ruffled. Does she think Meyer's correcting her? He was just trying to take things to a higher level. And, to be honest, he has to admit he wants her attention. It's one thing to see Wiesel swarmed by paparazzi. Vincent Nolan grabbing the limelight is something else entirely.

"A change of heart," says Vincent. "It happened over time."

That's not what Vincent said last week. Did Bonnie persuade him to edit his story? That would be unlike her. More likely, she made him understand that the conversion started before the rave. It took longer than he realized.

"I never totally bought it," he says. "Not that I totally *didn't* buy it.

But there were always lots of little things helping me keep my head straight. Books I read. The Internet. Stuff I saw on TV. I never liked the music, which should have told me something. Luftwaffe marches played at top volume are not what you'd call swinging, and those hate bands like Iron Fist . . . who could listen to that?"

"What kind of music *do* you like?" says Colette.

"Al Green," says Vincent.

"I *love* Al Green," says Colette.

"Al Green changed my life," says Vincent. "One night, I was at my cousin's, everyone had gone to bed, I was listening to my Discman, playing this Al Green CD. *Love and Happiness*. That part where he says, 'Three o'clock in the morning'—"

"I love that part," says Colette.

"And Al Green, excuse me, is . . . ?" asks Meyer. Who is this man with the power to turn a *New York Times* reporter to jelly? Meyer quizzes Bonnie, then Roberta. The others are also gazing at Vincent with puppylike affection.

Bonnie comes to Meyer's rescue. "Al Green. I guess you'd have to hear him. He sang all these really sweet love songs, and now he's doing gospel. . . ." Bonnie's hands fall open. Explaining would take forever. And Meyer still wouldn't have a clue unless he heard Al Green, and probably not then. Meyer likes Beethoven and Stravinsky.

Well, the hell with all of them, sitting here on their fat protected American behinds, while his mother and father were being murdered, while he was sleeping in the woods and pleading with drunken peasants to let him live one more day. Meyer knows he's being unfair. Bonnie, Roberta, Vincent, Colette—they weren't born until after the war.

Still, why is Meyer wasting what little is left of his life watching children talk to children, listening to some punk kid hold forth on what music he likes? He thinks of Minna, in her hospital bed. He'll be there before long. Meanwhile, Meyer needs to remind himself why he's here: so he can afford to give the help that he himself had to plead for. There's an innocent man in jail in Iran. Meyer's got a foundation to run, bills to pay, work to do. He sighs. And Bonnie, bless her heart, leans across the table and fills Meyer's water glass as if all her love is pouring out to him from that sweating pitcher.

"Al Green—" prompts the reporter.

"So I was listening to Al Green. And I finally understood. That the stuff ARM says can't be true, because Al Green is, you know . . . African-American—"

Vincent's never used that term before. But he does now. Smoothly. He's practiced.

"Obviously." Colette rolls her eyes.

"Some of the guys in ARM used to say that after God created the white races, he had some dirt left over, so he made the mud people. It was late in the week. God was tired. He wasn't concentrating. But before he could catch his mistake, the mud races were up and running. And then other guys would say—and it would always start this huge argument—that God made blacks on the fifth day, when He made the beasts of the field, and not on the sixth day, when He created humans. There's also a school of thought that says the mud races were created by humans mating with animals. . . ."

Vincent's been doing well so far, but now he seems to have wandered off on some horrifying tangent. Next he'll be telling the reporter that the white men are the true Israelites whom God has commanded to save the world from Satan's Jewish children. Meyer shoots a quick look at Bonnie, who also seems concerned. Clearly, there's some more work to be done, a few more . . . experiments to be run, before they let this guy loose in a room with everyone who might ever give a nickel to Brotherhood Watch.

"But the bottom line," Vincent is saying, "is that when you hear a guy like Al Green, you know that can't be true. A guy like that, he has such a beautiful voice, you hear him, and you *know* he's been hand-picked by God."

"Do you believe in God?" Colette asks. Is all this going into those three hundred words on page two of the Metro section? That question could pin them here for hours while Vincent rambles on about his spiritual development.

Vincent turns to Meyer. "If this guy believes, *I* believe," he says.

"Because to me, he's like a . . . samurai hero. The other thing that turned me around was reading Dr. Maslow's books."

Colette writes this down, then turns to Meyer for comment. What is Meyer supposed to say? He's glad he saved the guy's life. If that's what they want to believe.

"It gives us hope," Meyer says. "All our work is based on our faith that humans can change. But sometimes even *we* have doubts. So it's encouraging to meet someone who has passed from dark into light and who wants to work for justice and freedom."

Just then, there's a knock at the door.

It's Colette who says, "Come in." She knows the knock is for her: a bearded guy with a chest full of cameras.

"Sorry," he says. "I didn't mean to interrupt. Are you almost finished?"

"We're finished," says Colette.

"I'm Jim Mason," says the photographer, giving the group a professional once-over. Who's someone, who's not, who's photogenic. Elie Wiesel isn't around at the moment. The guy will settle for whoever's here. He asks Meyer and Vincent, "Can I get a couple of shots of you guys together?"

"Uh . . . about the benefit dinner," Bonnie prompts Colette.

"Hold on," says Colette. "One last question. Mr. Nolan, I understand you plan to speak at the annual Brotherhood Watch Rights benefit gala."

"I am?" Vincent looks at Bonnie. He seems genuinely surprised. It's been several days since Meyer and Bonnie made the final decision. Could Vincent really not know? Meyer's used to being able to tell if someone is telling the truth. Not knowing gives him an unsettled feeling about the whole situation.

"I guess I am." Vincent grins shyly.

"We guess he is," says Meyer.

"And the dinner is where? And when?" Colette is just checking. Roberta has made sure she knows.

"The Temple of Dendur," Bonnie says. "The Metropolitan Museum of Art."

"June 11," says Roberta.

Colette notes this, then looks up.

"Timothy McVeigh's execution," she says. "That can't have been accidental."

Meyer thought the date sounded familiar. Some night for a party! Meyer glares at Roberta, who evades his gaze, then Bonnie, whose expression is so pained that Meyer can't allow himself the consolation of anger. It isn't anyone's fault. They changed the date of the execution. Meyer's got a lot on his mind. This is what he depends on his staff for.

Meyer says, "It wasn't an accident. There *are* no accidents. And what could be more appropriate?"

It's a bluff, but Meyer risks it. He must still be quick on his feet, or anyway, quick enough, because Colette is balancing on the edge of not knowing what he means and thinking she *should* know what he means. The balance tips toward *should* know.

"Nothing. I guess," Colette says. "Thank you all for your time."

A NY SECOND NOW, Bonnie will calm down and get on with her work, but it's been two hours since the press conference, and not a minute has passed without Bonnie thinking about it or, alternately, trying not to think about it. And not knowing what to think about it.

Evidently, Vincent's a natural. He had that *Times* reporter eating out of his hand. He's nearly as good as Meyer, even though he's just a beginner. And really, it's a miracle considering who the guy is and where he's come from. Given the right breaks, he could have been an ARM leader. But maybe if he had been, he wouldn't have come to them. Maybe he wouldn't have gone to that rave. Maybe he would have been home collecting the proceeds from the drugs being sold by foot soldiers like Cousin Raymond.

Since she's come to work for Meyer, Bonnie's become a student of—an expert on—personal charisma. And it's always impressive, even if you don't trust it. The impressive part is how well it works. What she doesn't trust is the part that can seem calculated and phony.

Once, on a family vacation, when the boys were small, they took a tour boat around Boston Harbor. Max found a bunch of worshipful teenage girls and had them enthralled with some tall story about his dad's experiences on a lion-hunting safari. Practically in tears, Danny kept saying to Bonnie and Joel, "But he's lying. He's *lying.*" When Meyer—and now Vincent—go to work on reporters, Bonnie understands how Danny must have felt.

Bonnie has heard Meyer repeat the same anecdotes so often that she can tell them herself, exactly like Meyer, word for word, pause for pause. But with Vincent, what's disturbed her is the story she'd never heard him tell. The one about his father's death. Why hadn't he told Bonnie? She'd given him plenty of room. Early in their acquaintance, she'd mentioned that she was an orphan. She'd told him about the death of her father in a freak auto accident on the FDR, almost eight years ago. And about how her mother had died, of a stroke, two years before that. Slumped forward on the kitchen table, at dinner with Bonnie's father.

Vincent had said that his father was dead and that his mother was remarried and living upstate. But he'd never mentioned suicide. And today he told a reporter, a *stranger.* Bonnie had caught herself wringing her hands when that little item slipped out. Is Bonnie feeling *competitive?* How bizarre is *that?*

It shouldn't bother her, really. Vincent's tragedy wowed Brenda Starr. And maybe it wouldn't have worked so well if he was repeating himself, telling a story that someone in the room already knew. Still, he couldn't have been saving it for an occasion like this. The guy may be good with reporters, but he's not a publicity genius. Or maybe he is. Some of the other stuff he said was not merely convincing, but beautiful. That part about Al Green being handpicked by God. You couldn't just make that up.

Bonnie cannot imagine knowing Vincent well enough to ask him how he could tell a reporter an important fact about his life that he never told her. It would seem as if she were complaining in a way that she wouldn't dare, not unless they were lovers, family members, dear friends, closer than what they are: coworkers and temporary roommates.

She leaves her office and strolls over to the cubicle where Vincent has been set up with his own computer. Most of the office computers feed into a bank of high-volume printers. But Vincent has his own cheap printer. It's like quarantine. Maybe the tech-support guys picked up on something about him and had a techie reflex: Keep him out of the system.

Vincent's job, such as it is, is to type everything he knows about ARM into a file on hate groups that the foundation is compiling. That was Meyer's idea. It never occurred to Meyer to ask if Vincent could type. Luckily, Bonnie discovered, he'd learned in junior high. And if he'd found the foundation on the Internet, he must know his way around a computer.

Now he's leaning over the keyboard, way too close to the screen. He could hurt his eyes. Could he need glasses?

"What are you writing?" Bonnie says.

Vincent jumps. His instinct is to cover the screen. After a beat he relaxes.

"Check it out," he says, vaulting out of his chair so Bonnie can get near the monitor.

Bonnie sits down and reads to herself:

"One hot-button topic in ARM is the Jewish monopoly of the media. There are guys who can recite long lists of names of the Jews who run TV stations and Hollywood studios and all the major newspapers. And the hard core not only knows the big Jews' names but also their home addresses."

"Interesting," Bonnie says. Big Jews? *All* the major newspapers? She looks at Vincent, longing to ask: How much of that did you—do you—believe? But it doesn't seem fair to make him explain himself anymore today after he's already spent so much time and energy explaining himself to a reporter. He doesn't have to work overtime just because Bonnie's curious. It's something Bonnie feels strongly about, respecting others' labor. It's why she's a generous tipper and would never leave her hotel room a mess for the maid to straighten up and—

"It was so boring," Vincent says.

"What was?" says Bonnie.

"They'd just sit there and repeat the list. Michael Eisner. Steven Spielberg. Brandon Tartikoff. Half those Hollywood guys were probably dead, and I'll bet another third weren't even Jewish."

Bonnie shivers. Those were somebody's *names*. Somebody's home addresses. Thank God she isn't one of those guys, on some maniac's hit list. Thank God she isn't married to one, living at that address. It's bad enough she's got an ARM renegade staying at her house, a human time bomb waiting for his former comrades to track him down and detonate his life. And hers.

After a silence she says, "You did a great job. Back there. With Lois Lane."

"I think she'll want to write about us," he says. "I mean, about the foundation." Bonnie stares into Vincent's eyes: two pools of perfect sincerity, as deep as she can see. Strangely, she feels as she sometimes does when she's working with Meyer, as if there's a gust of wind at their backs and they're sailing toward the horizon.

"Are your . . . eyes okay?" she says.

"Twenty-twenty," says Vincent. "Why?"

"I think you've been sitting too close to the screen."

"I'll sit farther back," Vincent says. "All right?"

Another silence, then Bonnie says, "It *is* okay about the benefit dinner, isn't it? I mean, about you giving a little speech? Three, four minutes. Nothing. I'm sorry you found out that way. We put you on the spot. I should have mentioned it sooner. I was getting around to it. For some reason, I wasn't aware Roberta had told the reporter."

Vincent says, "No problaymo. I can manage. Simple. I can stand up and thank the foundation for helping turn my life around. It's the least I can do."

"I'm sorry about your father," Bonnie says. "I don't think I knew that."

"I thought I told you," Vincent says. "Well, thanks. I was three. I didn't know him that well. What bothers me is that he did it in my aunt's garage. He knew my uncle would make her clean up. Why couldn't he have gone and done it in the woods somewhere?"

Bonnie takes a deep breath. What a thoughtful guy he is, under all that swagger. A smaller person would be fixated on what the death had done to *him*. "The poor guy probably wasn't thinking about that," she says.

"He should have been," says Vincent. "It was the last thing he had to think about. He could have had a plan."

Something about this gives Bonnie chills. Does Vincent have a plan? And where does she fit in? Meyer would say it's all God's plan. Bonnie wishes she believed in a plan. She sees it more like a wrestling match, with evil and chaos often winning. Against the forces of . . . what? Order and good. Bonnie and Meyer's side. And maybe Vincent's, too.

Bonnie says, "Is there anything else? Something important you haven't told me?"

Vincent knits his brow and pantomimes thinking, then smiles. "Nothing I can remember," he says. "I'll let you know if something comes to mind. It's a promise. Okay?"

T HE FREAKIER NOLAN'S LIFE GETS, the more certain he is there's a reason. An order and a plan. Every setback and obstacle, every test and trial, is a lesson steeling him for the harder tests to come. For example, his time at Raymond's taught him how to keep a low profile, to occupy the minimum room in the least physical space. Crashing at somebody else's place, the Warrior follows three rules: Do the dishes. Don't give advice. Don't leave your socks in the hall. You won't find *that* in the samurai book, which Nolan has stopped reading. Anyway, its rules don't apply to his current situation as a paid consultant to an international foundation, earning room and board and two hundred dollars a week for riding to work with Bonnie and telling her his life story and writing down everything he saw and heard while he was in ARM. In other words, doing nothing. He writes a lot about Raymond's Jewish media obsession. But he never uses Raymond's name.

It's a great job, but unfortunately most of Nolan's so-called salary goes to the city garage that he visits once a week, at lunch, so he can pay his parking fees and—being very careful that no one from the office sees him—take Raymond's truck for a spin. Because there is another rule that the Warrior needs to follow: Map out your escape route. Check the exits. Never sit with your back to the door.

Learning how to make himself scarce when Lucy blended her revolting health-smoothie breakfasts has turned out to be good preparation for dinnertime at Bonnie's, where it took about a week before the company manners wore off and everyone reverted to normal. First Danny reduces Bonnie almost to tears, then Max jumps in, working to cool her out while signaling his brother that he knows Mom is a loser.

Nolan feels sorry for Bonnie. But if she knew that, she'd feel worse. And her kids aren't so bad. Certainly they're better off than Nolan was at their age. So what if the older one has a semi-serious pot habit and the younger one's well on his way to growing up queer? Bratty Jewish kids, Raymond would say. The phrase gets Nolan nowhere. It took a certain effort at the start of that interview with the hot Spanish chick not to let himself think: the *Jew York Times*. But then he'd gotten into the groove. He'd leaned back in the arms of Al Green and let Al sing him through it.

The Warrior can eat Nolan's dust. Nolan's got it down to a science, calibrating his precise daily chemical requirements. Two beers at dinner, just to take the edge off. The *edge* of the edge off. Then he goes back to his room and takes half a Vicodin and reads till he passes out. He's careful. And it's working. It's been nice, hanging around the office, telling Bonnie his problems. It's like getting loaded at a bar, without the tequila and lime.

Sometimes he even thinks that Bonnie genuinely likes him. A few days ago he was telling her about the doughnut shop, showing her the scars on his hands from the boiling oil. Tears popped into Bonnie's eyes. He'd said it hadn't hurt that much, and Bonnie said that the sad thing was that a guy with such an excellent mind had to work at a job like that. Which makes her the first person since Nolan's mom to register the fact that he *has* a mind, excellent or not.

Getting along with Bonnie lubricates daily life. Everything is easier. Everything has to be easy. The hoops they're setting for

Nolan to jump are getting higher daily. The limbo stick he's bending under is dipping lower and lower.

Take, for instance, tonight's ordeal. This evening, after work, Nolan is going to a dinner party at Meyer Maslow's apartment.

Nolan knows it's his trial run. They're shaking out the kinks before they turn him loose on the rich and famous at this benefit that's got them so worked up. They should know he can do it. Bonnie and Meyer were in the room when he did that reporter. But the *Times* thing didn't go exactly as planned. They tried to keep it from Nolan, but he could hardly not notice when the whole office got suicidal because the *Times* piece finally came out, and—after all the trouble he went to with that journalist, there isn't a woman in the world who doesn't fall for Al Green—they only got one paragraph in the gossip column of the Metro section.

Which suited Nolan fine. Sure, it might have been a kick to see his face in the papers. But it's not the wisest idea to advertise his current coordinates. Not that Raymond and his friends read the *Times*. But Raymond knows guys who know guys who do. Let's say some yupster comes into the tire shop and mentions that he saw a photo of that guy who used to work here. Oh, yeah, says Raymond. Where was that? It would take Raymond about three mouse-clicks to find him.

So it was okay with Nolan that the other reporters scheduled to show up the next day must have seen the *Times* piece and picked up the scent of a dead story. And canceled—the second part of the tragedy, for which everyone blames Roberta. Nolan doesn't like Roberta, he doesn't *not* like Roberta. She's harmless. But one, she doesn't know jack shit about who he really is, and two, he suspects she'd make her granny pose nude in *Penthouse* if she thought there was something in it for her.

In the end, the *Times* piece worked. That postage stamp in the Metro section turned out to be enough to set off a ticket-buying frenzy and sell out the house. Nolan wishes he had a dollar for every time Bonnie said that New Yorkers must read every word of the paper with a magnifying glass. By now they've filled almost every table at their Temple of Dingbat Dinner. What would Raymond say if he knew that Nolan was preaching in a temple?

The press conference was the first he'd heard about his giving a speech at the benefit. It wasn't exactly fair. He could hardly say no in front of the reporter. He had to rise to the occasion. Since then, he's reassured everyone: He can do it with half his brain shot away. But why should they believe anything he says, considering what he used to be? As if they had the slightest idea what he used to be. Or what he is now.

Nolan doesn't blame Bonnie and Maslow for cooking up the brilliant scheme of taking him to the old man's for dinner to see how the pony runs the track. Though he is disappointed. What was all that smoke Bonnie was blowing up his ass about his excellent mind? Apparently not excellent enough to watch his manners at a table full of rich fat bastards.

Bonnie is Nolan's walker. His date for the evening. They're going to Meyer's together. They meet in the hall after Nolan's dash to the restroom to check his armpits, shirt, tie, hair. Hopeless! His shirt is soaked. His hair's sticking up in points. He hates the tie Bonnie bought him.

The elevator is crowded, so at least they don't have to talk. Nolan's gotten over his fear of catching contagious diseases as he rides up in the metal cage dangling over an air shaft. Strangely, after that first day, he's never seen Work-Out Dwarf. So maybe Nolan imagined him. Or maybe the dude was just visiting. Or maybe Nolan and the buff dwarf keep different hours.

Traffic's ground to standstill, but still Bonnie flops her fingers at some cabs that are already full. What sane driver would pick them up? One look at Bonnie and Nolan, and what two words go through your mind? Answer: lousy tippers.

The guys in ARM had a videotape, a collection of Danny Glover's appearances on talk shows to bitch about taxis not stopping because he was black. The ARM guys would watch, their jaws dropped, until somebody blew his stack. What was the guy complaining about? Pakistanis too stupid to tell a rich Negro actor from your garden-variety mugger? Most of the ARM guys had probably never ridden in a cab in their lives.

Nolan would rather not take a taxi. Things are going too well for him to get killed by some Korean for whom human life has no value. The old Nolan isn't entirely gone. Nolan still hears his voice, though now it's joined a chorus with Maslow and Bonnie singing the melody part. Every human life has value. And Raymond singing high harmony with the ARM position that the lives you value most are your family's and your own. Which is hard to argue with, no matter what Maslow says.

What does Nolan really think? Cover your own ass first. Then you can save other asses. Keep your nose clean. Watch your back. Survival of the fittest. Doubt it, and you're dead. Raymond's other favorite TV show was *Survivor.* He and his friends liked getting steamed about the fortunes being spent to prove ARM's point about your basic dog-eat-dog. The other thing they liked about *Survivor* was the way it showed the Jewish media making sure that no straight white man ever won. ARM believes that when push comes to shove, everybody cares about the lives of their own kind more than the lives of other races and creeds. That's how the species is, how it always was. It's never going to change. *Hardwired.* Raymond loved that phrase, which is why Nolan hates it.

"Maybe we should walk," Nolan says.

"I guess," Bonnie says. "It's a pretty evening. I left us plenty of time. We're way early, as the kids say."

The more agitated Bonnie gets, the more she mentions her kids. Not that Nolan blames her for being nervous, strolling across Manhattan for a sit-down with him and Meyer Maslow.

Nolan lets her set the pace. Early or not, they hurry, threading through the crowd. Bonnie's sad little ponytail flip-flops against her neck. Nolan drops back to watch. This morning she took forever to dress. They were late getting into the office. In her black suit and perky white blouse, she has, if you don't look too hard, a vaguely sexy, schoolgirl appeal. Bonnie's been looking foxy, at least compared to how she looked when Nolan first got here. Well, he's given her a project, a cause—and besides, it's spring. The early evening air is cool and sweet, bathing the streets in a tender blue carbon-monoxide haze.

The Vicodin Nolan took before he left the office hasn't quite kicked in. Taking it before dinner meant breaking his own rules. But hey, it's a special occasion. Any moment now he expects a chemical assist, a modest bump as the drug steps in and files down the evening's ragged edges.

As they turn onto Fifty-seventh Street, someone grazes Nolan's arm. An acid spurt of fury rises in his chest. He's learned to handle elevators, but crowded streets are still rough. It hasn't gotten much smoother since his first day in New York.

Nolan knows it's pure paranoia, but Raymond's everywhere. *Everywhere.* Lurking in every doorway. Floating up out of the oncoming mob, streaking past his peripheral vision. Is that him turning the corner?

The second time someone touches him, he wheels around. It's Bonnie. How did she get behind him? She was just ahead.

"Look!" Bonnie's holding his forearm. They hardly ever touch. They keep a careful buffer zone. Nolan wonders why they bother. Being touched by Bonnie is not like being touched by a girl. He also wonders why not. Because he's got a sweet deal going that he would hate to mess up by letting himself have even one fleeting sexual thought about Bonnie. Even if she's the only female around, even if he's living at her house, even if she likes him and probably hasn't gotten laid since the cardiologist left.

It's too much responsibility. Bonnie's a grown-up. She's got kids. But the thought *has* occurred to him. Big surprise. Nolan hasn't gotten laid since last year's Homeland Encampment.

Bonnie's fingers slide toward his wrist. They're practically holding hands. She nods toward a large window. Racks of black and white clothing dance like a chorus line of cartoon ghosts in an otherwise empty store.

"That used to be the Automat." Bonnie sounds like *she's* the one on drugs. "My dad used to take me there when we went to the museum. We'd put nickels in the slots and get apple pie. Gee, it's not so far from work. I hardly ever pass by here."

Bonnie's talking to herself. Her dad died in a car wreck. Her eyes fill with tears whenever she mentions him. It's the tragedy of Bonnie's life, along with the husband leaving. Are they supposed to stand here sobbing their heads off because so much time has passed since Daddy's little girl dropped a coin in the slot and *ca-chunk*, apple pie? What was Nolan doing then? Helping Mom make salad for three hundred religious fanatics.

But wait. What's this? What the hell is *this?* While Nolan's been time-traveling back to the Zen kitchen, a situation's developed here. A definite situation.

Their stillness in the swirling crowd has attracted the interest of some kind of . . . Negro street individual. He's too young to be so messed up, but the guy's been drinking, smoking crack, or whatever, and now he's invading their personal space. He's standing face-to-face with Bonnie. Close. Nolan should knock his head off. He comes up to Nolan's shoulder. Nolan could take him out. Anger management comes flooding back. Count to ten, take a breath. Think beyond the moment.

Beyond the moment is showing up at Maslow's apartment with some crackhead's blood all over his shirt. And the evening's going to be tricky enough without the adrenaline hangover. Why doesn't Bonnie shake him off? Hasn't she got any instincts? Is she waiting to hear what this bottom-feeder has to say?

It's a wonder she's not more tuned in to the irony of the situation: the racist thug watching a Negro invade *her space*—and doing nothing about it. Nolan's acting like the former-skinhead Martin Luther King. He's trying to key into that all-embracing love he remembers feeling at the rave, though by now the truth is, he doesn't recall the rave or that feeling so much as he remembers telling Maslow and Bonnie about it. Anyhow, he's not slamming the guy. Which is, after all, the real test. Bonnie and Maslow have it wrong. They think the test— tonight's dinner—is about making sure he won't use the wrong fork or blow his nose in his napkin.

The homeless guy gives Bonnie a long look, and now Bonnie's returning his stare. Very mongoose-cobra.

"You look fat-*tigued*," says the scumsucker.

And then to Nolan, "You better take her home, man. The lady looks fat-*tigued*."

After that brilliant diagnosis, Dr. Dirtbag laughs, displaying black holes where his teeth should be, then staggers off into the crowd. Nolan should have killed him. The color's drained from Bonnie's face. She does look fatigued. Three-quarters dead. She looks as if someone's slugged her. All because some wino gave her health and beauty advice?

"Do I look that tired?" Bonnie says.

Every day Bonnie must stare in the mirror and see some new wrinkle or splotch. Why didn't Nolan coldcock the bastard before he could open his mouth? If Raymond and his buddies were here, Nolan could never have let it go. It was exactly the kind of provocation they were always waiting and hoping for, and could never get to happen.

"I don't know where he got that. I swear to God, I was just thinking you looked great." In fact, Nolan *was* thinking something like that. Which makes him twice as furious at the homeless motherfucker.

"You were?" It's sad, how much Bonnie needs his approval. No wonder the husband left. It gets tough, propping someone up. Your own ass is heavy enough. Nolan knows that's how Margaret felt. She was carrying his dead weight. Margaret's not having said as much makes Nolan start missing her all over again.

"So help me," says Nolan. "Great." They pass a store window in which diamonds hang from gold chains worn by brown eggs in a carton.

"Tiffany's," says Bonnie.

Nolan says, "How are we doing?"

"Great," says Bonnie. "Four more blocks."

Four more blocks? Nolan needs more time. There are some details he meant to work out. The codeine must be kicking in. He's getting that drug nausea he hardly ever gets. Doctor, I have a feeling it's not what I ate for lunch. As long as he knows what it is, he can ride it out. Still, what a drag to show up at Maslow's, seasick and distracted.

"*Ola,* Jorge!" Bonnie greets Maslow's doorman. Nolan gets it. She's a regular. They spin through the revolving doors into the lobby full of monster floral arrangements pumping out funeral-parlor perfume. The elevator is broiling. All the oxygen's been sucked up by the elevator operator, a swarthy guy with a unibrow, dressed like an organ grinder's monkey. He nods, then stares ahead as he takes them up, politely ignoring Nolan's struggle not to puke on his shoes.

Bonnie says, "Oh, my God. I forgot to tell Irene! About your being allergic."

Her saying this in front of the Rican Jeeves is humiliating. What a pussy the guy must think Nolan is! Oh, dearie me! I'm allergic. Well, let the doormonkey go through a couple of trips to the hospital as *his* throat plays its little game, racing to constrict before the ER interns find the right syringe.

Bonnie says, "It's become second nature at home. I'm always careful, cooking. But I forgot to tell Irene. I will, as soon as I get there. They've got a terrific Indian chef. He can make you something. Meanwhile, not a bite till we get this straight. Stay away from the hors d'oeuvres."

Bonnie's acting like Nolan is one of her kids. And he might as well be. Nolan imagines he smells curry. It makes him want to vomit.

The doors open, and Bonnie and Nolan step into the apartment without the chance to collect themselves that a hall would have provided. The long road Nolan thinks he's traveled from Raymond's couch to Bonnie's house shrinks to a footstep along the route that's brought Maslow here from his hiding place on some pig farm. Well, the guy deserves the good life. Nolan admires Maslow. He's a real Napoleon, a little king, but you've got to give him credit. At this point, Maslow could be cruising on a yacht drinking mai tais and clipping coupons. Instead of which he's slaving away to get some foreigner out of jail. Nolan likes talking to

Maslow. He's always got something interesting to say, especially if you steer him away from the mystical baloney.

Nolan scans the room for Maslow, but his view is intercepted by a tuxedo holding a tray of wineglasses. White wine. Red wine. Sparkling water with lemon. At the moment, the wine won't mix with the drugs, though once the sickness disappears the wine could give him a boost.

Indecision makes Nolan spastic. He reaches toward the tray and—instantly *and* in slow motion—dumps a glass of red wine down his shirt. Immediate sobriety. The codeine wears off in a heartbeat. He checks the carpet. Nothing, thank God. His shirt took the entire hit. There's a wet grapey blotch on his chest, as if he's been shot. Why couldn't he have picked white wine if he was going to spill it? He might as well have clocked the sonofabitch who insulted Bonnie, and walked in with blood on his shirt.

"Oh, my," says Bonnie. She bought him that shirt. But at least she sticks by him and doesn't rush off into the party, which is what most women would do. Not that Nolan and the women he dated ever went to this kind of party.

The waiter oozes away, then oozes back with a napkin he pokes into Nolan's chest.

"Watch it," says Nolan. "Watch it, okay?" A tremor of aggression radiates into the room, creating the kind of atmospheric disturbance that, in any social gathering, can be counted on to pry the host loose from his guests.

Maslow sails out of the living room where he's been queening around with a half dozen people, all with drinks, pinkies extended. Maslow's wearing a dark blue silk shirt, open at the neck. Nolan's overdressed. He's been overdressed since he got to the city.

"Welcome, welcome." Maslow kisses Bonnie on both cheeks. He doesn't do that at the office. Home team rules apply. Nolan sticks out his hand in case Maslow plans to kiss *him*. Maslow takes in the scenario: waiter, spilled wine, splotch. By now their stall has lasted long enough so that even Mrs. Maslow comes over to see what's up. She starts with Bonnie: a one-cheek kiss.

"Bonnie, dear, it's been *way* too long."

"Hi, Irene," mumbles Bonnie.

"Irene," says Maslow. "Vincent. Irene Maslow, Vincent Nolan."

Has Vincent met Irene before? The codeine says maybe. What is it about drugs that make you think you know the person? Could the Maslows have a house in Woodstock? Did Vincent install her pool? Probably he met her clone, and a dozen more like her. Women who size you up so fast it's like they're scanning your bar code. Is Nolan worth paying attention to? Only if he comes in with the lowest bid for the chlorine, or if he's the former Nazi who helped sell all those tickets to the old man's benefit dinner.

Irene's sort of attractive. She's got that European Marlene Dietrich thing going. Part queen, part drag queen. Your vulnerable dominatrix. Sexy for an older woman.

"I've heard so much about you," she says, gracing Nolan with a smile rehearsed to take maximum advantage of the point to which her face has been tightened. All that money, all that pain, to make former beauties like Irene look like the dolls they played with as little girls.

"Don't believe everything you hear." Nolan shoots a tracer bullet of flirtation in Irene's direction, testing to see if anything lights up.

Irene does. "Why shouldn't I? Is there something else I should know?"

Time for Maslow to break up the love fest. "Irene, darling. What should we do? Vincent's had a disaster." Oh-ho-ho. Is that irony? Using a dramatic word to show that you think it's nothing. Well, it *isn't* nothing. It *is* a fucking disaster. Irene smiles again. This sophisticated couple has entertained enough to have seen worse go down. As the wife of a world leader, Irene's learned a sense of proportion. What's a little spilled wine compared to a starving Ethiopian village? In Meyer's office, there's a photo of Irene holding a skeletal baby, regarding it with the horror she must have meant to look like pity.

"Meyer, darling, why don't you find our guest a shirt?"

Nolan can't believe that in such a short time you can go from nearly getting kicked off your cousin's nubbly couch to standing in

Meyer Maslow's penthouse and hearing the great man tell his wife that the two of you can't possibly wear the same shirt size.

"Cashmere stretches, angel." Under a gauzy white shawl, Irene's fleshy shoulders shimmy with impatience. "Men," she says to Bonnie. "They can save whole populations, but they can't get the guest a shirt."

"So it does," says Maslow, tensely. "Stretches."

Maslow takes Vincent's elbow and steers him into the apartment. On the way he flashes Irene a semi-hostile look that she ignores and Nolan pretends not to see. Maslow guides him down the hall and into the massive bedroom where he and the wife do whatever they do, at their age, in a canopied king-size bed.

His closet is a whole room. Maslow hits a button, and a rack of clothes sways toward them. Maslow says, "What was I thinking? No sweaters in the closet. This closet is Irene's baby. But what should I tell her? Irene, darling, no thank you. I don't want you to help me keep my clothes neat. You have to choose your battles, in marriage as well as the world. So what if the cost of this closet could feed a whole Ethiopian village?"

Funny. Nolan was just thinking about that Ethiopian village. Every so often he still gets the feeling the old man's reading his mind. But if he could do that, wouldn't he know that the info about the closet is more than Nolan needs? Who cares how much the closet cost? Or whether Irene twists Meyer's arm every time he gets dressed?

Maslow walks over to some open shelves: a sweater mausoleum, each knit item in its own body bag. "My wife's a shopper, what can you do?" He pulls out a black jersey.

Is Nolan supposed to strip and change? Thanks, but no thanks, he'll pass. For one thing, he can't go through the tattoo soap opera again. Maslow points to the bathroom. Nolan slips inside. He gazes longingly at the medicine chest, but with Meyer waiting outside the door, he hasn't got time to read labels and decide how much he can borrow of Irene's supply of—he'd guess—Valium and Paxil. Unbuttoning his shirt, he jumps when Maslow calls, "Just leave it on the hamper." Which one is the hamper? Let's assume it's this straw basket. Nolan slips the black sweater over his head. A little tight, but whatever. Wearing it is like being stroked everywhere at once by an expensive call girl. Maybe that's what the rich do when they get too old to fuck. They put on five-hundred-dollar shirts and have sex with their cashmere sweaters.

Emerging to find Maslow gone, Nolan's rethinking the medicine chest when Maslow calls him from the next room. Maslow's study, a clubby affair, dark and manly and rich, has been decorated by the shopper wife in full-blown Ralph Lauren wet dream.

"Would you like a drink? I gather the red wine didn't work out." Maslow's got a private bar in his study. Good living!

"Actually," says Nolan, "a shot of tequila would be excellent." Excellent, though maybe not sensible. Nolan thinks he can risk it. He feels so taken care of, by Bonnie and now by Maslow. They're not going to let him drown in these shark-infested waters. And already Maslow's wife digs him. He'll have someone to talk to. A shot of tequila would take up the slack and may even locate the few grains of codeine still floating around his bloodstream.

"I'm sorry. I don't think we have tequila. . . ." Maslow's warm smile is maddening.

Nolan makes a buzzer sound. "Oops. Wrong answer." Of course they don't have tequila. Look around. The Jew does not drink. The Jew fears losing control. Not a useful thought right now. But thinking it lets off some pressure.

"How about Scotch?" Maslow says.

"That would be great." Nolan hates Scotch. But he gratefully gulps it down as Maslow walks him over to the window and they stand, shoulder to shoulder, watching a garbage barge inch up the East River.

Maslow says, "There's still so much we haven't had a chance to discuss." It sounds like something you'd say to a chick. Is Maslow making a pass? A bubble of nausea rises lazily up toward Nolan's throat. Could it be the codeine? Nolan prays it is.

"Not really," he agrees.

"It's been a crazy week," Maslow says. "I've been dealing with a very frustrating case. As you may know, an important cartoonist, a friend, has been arrested in Iran."

"That's awful," says Nolan. "I think I heard about that."

"I don't know how much we can do. So far no real progress. As usual there's nothing to do but make phone calls and hope for the best. Which consumes a lot of time. Plus . . ." Maslow falls silent, then says, "Have you read Dickens?"

That's exactly the sort of thing Nolan likes about Maslow. The old man would never assume that Nolan doesn't know how to read, or might not have read the classics. Or maybe Bonnie's told him about the Dostoyevsky she thought was so amazing.

"No," says Vincent. "Can't say I have. No, wait. That's not true. We did *Tale of Two Cities* in high school. I should go back and give it another try."

Something snags Nolan's attention—a light on the other side of the river. Could someone be signaling him? It's only the sun hitting a window.

"As I'm sure Bonnie's told you," Maslow says, "we really value your help."

In another lifetime, this would lead to the pink-slip conversation. We value your help, but unfortunately . . . But that's not happening here. The view is suddenly sickening. Nolan shuts his eyes. This is how he used to feel when he couldn't drive over bridges.

"Bonnie Kalen's a treasure," says Maslow. Nolan opens his eyes to find Maslow checking him for a reaction.

"She's a very nice person." Nolan is not having sex with her, if that's what's being asked. Or maybe that's not what's being asked. Bonnie *is* a nice person.

"I thought you and Bonnie did a terrific job with that reporter from the *Times*."

You and Bonnie? Did Bonnie say one word? That was Nolan working his nuts off. "Thanks. I kind of liked her."

"Don't. Don't ever *like* them."

"Reporters?" Nolan tries that first before they move on to Latin chicks and God knows what else Maslow means by *them.*

Maslow nods. "A bad idea. Don't like them and don't trust them. Bad mistakes have been made. Anyone would have thought that the woman was going to *join* Brotherhood Watch. Then she gets back to the office, and her editor comes back from lunch, and she cuts us down to a paragraph."

Nolan notes that Maslow's glass has emptied as quickly as his.

"Would you like another Scotch?" The Jew believes all goyim are drunks.

"No, thanks," Nolan says. There will be wine at dinner. Nolan's got to pace himself.

Maslow says, "There'll be wine with dinner."

So why don't they *go* to dinner? Let Nolan have another shot at picking a drink off a tray. But Maslow has something he wants to say. Nolan finds it amusing to have been plucked out of the party, singled out, and spirited off to Mr. Big's inner sanctum.

Maslow says, "I noticed that when you talked to the reporter, you didn't tell that story about the vision you had at the outdoor dance."

"Well, I've been realizing that story was just one thing among many things that happened. Part of a longer process."

"It's probably good you didn't tell it. I don't know why, just a feeling . . ." What is Maslow getting at? Is he trying to find out if deleting the part about the rave was Nolan's idea or Bonnie's? And why *didn't* Nolan tell it, seeing that it was the truth? It makes more sense than what he *did* say. There's no way that Al Green would have made *anyone* quit ARM. But the Spanish chick went for it. And somehow Nolan knew not to mention the rave. *Somehow?* Every time the rave comes up, Bonnie gets a pinched look. Hell, if you shock a lab rat enough, it learns which alley not to take.

"And yet . . . ," Maslow says. "When it comes time for you to speak to our friends at the gala, I almost wish there were *one* incident you could recall. One moment that stuck in your memory, when you changed, or knew you had changed. Let me put it this way. The Holocaust lasted for years. But when I wrote my books, I picked specific events. Particular moments. I edited. Understand?"

Nolan nods uncertainly. He'd planned to say just a few words. I'd like to thank World Brotherhood Watch for helping me change my life. Thank you. Smile. Applause. On and off. So what is Meyer telling him? What kind of public-speaking advice is he offering? Get up there and tell *stories?* Meyer tells enough stories for both of them put together. But Vincent can do it, if he has to. It's just a matter of finding the right story for the occasion. The rave's out. And the benefit crowd is not going to go for the Al Green moment. That's more of a woman thing, for a more intimate setting. Even though both of those stories are true, he needs another anecdote for his speech at the dinner.

"I'll think about it," says Nolan.

"Talk it over with Bonnie."

They go back to staring at the barge with such fascination, you'd think they were watching a car chase instead of a floating garbage dump that's made no visible progress since they started looking.

Maslow says, "Where did you grow up? After your father died. I can't remember if Bonnie said."

Nolan says, "We moved around a lot."

"I knew you would say that," says Maslow. "It's so American. Whenever Americans have trouble, that's what they say. We moved around a lot. As if a rootless childhood is the all-purpose excuse. Well, every Jew could say that. We've been moving around for two thousand years. And we accomplished plenty."

Hang on! Nolan doesn't appreciate Maslow using the word *American* as a negative. Nor does he like him holding up what the Jews *accomplished* compared to lazy American blamers and slackers—like Nolan—bitching about their childhoods.

"I wasn't saying it was an excuse. I said we moved around a lot."

"Sorry," says Maslow. "I didn't mean—"

"Two years was maximum for my mom and me. Right after my dad left, we pretty much hit the road. My mom got into all this spiritual stuff, which was okay, except that we had no money, and all the other seeker types at these places were rich, so she'd get these weird jobs in return for room and board. For a while she was making salad for three hundred monks at a Zen retreat—"

"Three meals a day?" says Maslow.

"Two," Nolan says. "No lunch."

"Is your mother still religious?"

"She's a chanting Buddhist. She chants. For winning lottery numbers."

"Does she win?" says Maslow.

"No, not really," Nolan laughs. "Sometimes twenty bucks."

"Marvelous," says Maslow.

Nolan wonders if he knows what a chanting Buddhist is.

"It's why we can work together," Maslow says. "I recognized that in you right away. The religious impulse."

"You mean I'm a fanatic," Nolan says.

"Not exactly. I don't think you're a fanatic. I don't think you ever were. You're too realistic for that. Too down-to-earth. Survival-oriented. Mostly, these days, people say *fanatic* when what they really mean is *idealist*. Though frankly, I'll take a fanatic over your average person. You know where you stand with fanatics. They don't say one thing and do another. Actually, very few people wind up working for us unless they *are* some kind of fanatic. Idealists, I should say."

"Including Bonnie?"

"Definitely Bonnie. Bonnie's on a mission. To be a good person and do the right thing. The foundation has been a godsend for her. I'll tell you something I've noticed. Almost everyone who works with us was raised in *some* religion. Roberta used to be a serious Catholic before she married an Egyptian."

"Roberta's married?"

"Divorced. Anita Shu grew up in one of those Korean Christian churches. Faith is a habit, developed young. It's not something you come to late. Once a person has a faith, he can change his religion, but you need to have that capacity—"

"Like fat cells," Vincent says.

"Fat cells?"

"I read that's why fat kids grow up into fat adults. They develop the cells for it."

"Faith cells," says Maslow. "Something like that. I like the concept. Fat cells. Faith cells. Listen, I'll bet if you went back and polled your friends in ARM, you'd probably find that most of them had some kind of religious training."

Sure. Let Maslow take that poll. ARM members don't think they're fanatics. They consider themselves the reasonable products of a coolheaded, logical analysis of American history and government.

"I'll think about it," Nolan says. "For the outreach program." Unlike Bonnie and Roberta, who seem focused on Vincent's speech at the dinner, Maslow has been talking in larger terms, about some kind of program aimed at guys like Nolan. I want to help you guys save guys like me from becoming guys like me. Nolan likes Maslow's thinking on that. It's a reason for keeping Nolan around after the benefit dinner.

"My thoughts exactly," says Maslow. "The outreach program. Meanwhile let me tell you something. That Iranian guy we're trying to save, he has a wife and kids. And they've started to torture him. Yesterday we heard that they might hang him as an example. And why?"

"Why?" asks Nolan, obediently.

"Because he refused to write a confession denouncing his wife, who had been arrested for not wearing a veil in the doorway of their own house. How wonderful it would be if God helps us free him in time to get here and also say a few words at the benefit dinner."

Nolan feels the stirrings of a sibling situation. Well, sure. Who's going to get more applause? A former neo-Nazi? Or some purple-dick hero who went to the Iranian slammer for defending his wife? Having the guy here would be *wonderful*. Over Nolan's dead body.

"If we save his life," Maslow says, "it will represent just a small part of our mission. Small, compared to feeding and clothing refugee populations. But we're always enlarging our scope. Which is why God sent you to us, to help us do something new. How great it would be if together we *could* find a way to reach young men like you, to redirect the energy that's gone into anger and hate, to set them working for the cause of brotherhood and freedom."

One reason Nolan picked up on Maslow's ideas so fast was that they were weirdly similar to the stuff you heard at the Homeland Encampment if you listened to the speakers ranting in the background while you were getting plastered and trying to get some white-supremacist nooky. That's what they're always saying: Bring our cause to the world. Reach out and show the way to one white man at a time.

Maslow must be dreaming if he thinks that ARM is a religion. It's a way that guys have found to explain to themselves why they're unemployed and broke, or working crappy jobs they hate. And broke. Pay them like you're paying Nolan for doing what Nolan's doing, and that's the end of ARM. Because, really, how good a gig is *this?* A salary, room, and board for talking to Bonnie and Meyer and the occasional reporter. Having fun with the computer. Writing some stuff about ARM. Surfing for porn sites. Putting in an appearance at the occasional dinner party. Drinking Scotch. Wearing cashmere. For the first time ever, Nolan feels that his luck might be improving.

All right! The codeine's checking back in. And the Scotch isn't half bad. No wonder it's the beverage of choice of your basic fat old bastard. Nolan feels terrific. A mysterious sense of well-being.

Hang on. What's Maslow talking about? Nolan's missed a link.

"—that is, if you *do* think we can change. That redemption and progress are possible. Or do you think it's hopeless? That we're born one way, and that's that. What do they say? Hardwired."

"I hate that expression," Nolan says. "Everyone changes. Look at me. Look at how I've changed."

"How you're *changing*," Maslow corrects him. "How far along you've come."

How would the old man know how far Nolan is? Far along on his way to what?

Maslow's smile smoothes over everything. "Peace through change. One heart at a time. That's why we're in business. I would have gone mad if I didn't believe that there was a reason I was saved when millions of others weren't. I would be a very unhappy man if I didn't believe that there was a plan."

Funny, that's what Nolan's been thinking ever since he left Raymond's. Everything has an order and a plan. Has Maslow been reading his mind again? Through the faint haze of drugs and alcohol, Nolan can see what Bonnie means when she talks about Maslow kicking things up to a higher level.

Maslow says, "I think we understand one another. Good. Now let's go enjoy a good dinner."

❧❧❧❧

If Meyer stays in his study a minute longer, Irene will go in there and shoot him, unless his skinhead friend has already done it for her. Which would make Meyer a martyr, and Irene a martyr's widow, her reward for all these years of being the wife of a saint.

"Prince of Peace Whacked by Wife." Let Roberta and Bonnie spin that! Lucky Meyer, surrounded by women who will take a bullet for him. Whereas here on the home front, the buck stops at Irene, the only person in the house who can make a decision. Babu may be a fabulous cook, but the poor guy's Untouchable origins surface at inconvenient times, like this morning, when the gravlax arrived with a fluorescent green patina. It was Irene who phoned Zabar's, Irene who complained to the florist about the arrangement that cost the earth and looked like a bouquet of toilet brushes.

That's partly why Meyer married her. Irene can manage a home with all the amenities of a five-star hotel, can see to details of physical survival so that her husband can concentrate on higher things—in Meyer's case, saving the world. That's partly what attracted him to Irene, the savvy Viennese who combines her grandparents' peasant shrewdness with her mother's knack for living as if she'd always had money, plus the foresight and common sense that enabled her father to get the family out of Vienna in time. What else did Meyer see in her? Sex. Beauty, which has mostly vanished, though Meyer claims not to think so. And the flattering appeal of Irene having left her millionaire husband for Meyer. Well, that's ancient history now. No one but Irene remembers.

So much work, this dinner for eight, for which she will get no credit. And how much should she get, really, for telling Babu what to cook, what plates to put on the table? It's not the same as saving an Iranian who's about to be tortured to death. Irene believes in Meyer's work. Her husband is a hero. She's proud to give her time, glad to surrender whole evenings to those benefits at which she sits next to some old geezer who thinks he's bought the great man's wife for the evening, purchased the right to tell her, in excruciating detail, every step along his road to success and fortune.

Social events have gotten harder since middle age stole the last consolation: the chance that the evening might at least provide the low-level hum of attraction. She understood when she married Meyer, twenty years ago, that a part of her life was ending. She would never have another lover. There was not a man in the world who could be trusted to keep quiet about having fucked the wife of an iconic world leader. Flirting, however, was harmless fun. It made the time go faster. Not that she fully appreciated it until one evening when she went out—who remembers exactly when, she was fifty, fifty-one—and it was gone. Vanished forever. Except in Europe, where men are less like teenage boys, and Irene is still in the running. Now an evening without that faint possibility seems endless. Unbearable.

The official reason for this dinner party, which Meyer, Roberta, and Bonnie dreamed up, is to see if this feral adult they dragged in from the woods can sit down and eat with human beings. And what if he can't? The lucky guy will probably get his own table at the gala. While, across the room, Irene will be pushing around her dried-out salmon and limp mesclun, shouting over the band and grinning at whatever deep-pockets Bonnie has sat her beside.

Who's here tonight? No one worth getting nervous about. Or excited, for that matter. Guinea pigs they can afford to offend if the Nazi runs amok. Sol and Minna, just out of the hospital. Roberta

Dwyer, whose job is on the line, though she doesn't know it, ever since the *Times* ran that insultingly tiny item. It was Roberta's responsibility to make sure that the paper *got* the story. But no one's replacing Roberta till the gala is over, and meanwhile she has to be here for Wolf Boy's shakeout cruise.

Irene's heart goes out to Roberta, and Bonnie, and an office full of women and men who have Meyer instead of a life. In fact, Irene feels so badly that she has invited someone for Roberta: Elliot Green, divorced for a couple of years. In any case, Meyer owes Elliot, whose law firm does a lot of pro bono work for the foundation. If nothing clicks with Roberta, at least Elliot will have been invited to a payback dinner.

Irene told everyone to come half an hour before Bonnie and the skinhead. Then she could get things settled before they have to deal with whatever craziness a Nazi dinner guest turns out to involve.

That extra half hour was a mistake. Within seconds, everyone knew that Roberta's lukewarm interest in Elliot was unreturned. Irene wondered how she, Irene, could have spent decades married to a man like Meyer without a bit of his goodness rubbing off on her. A decent person would never feel the competitive lift that Irene got from watching Roberta strike out. So what? It's not Irene's fault if the survival of the species depends on sexual competition. Not that Irene has done much—biologically—to help the species survive. By the time she married Meyer, she was almost forty. In those days a woman that age was considered way too old to have children. Now the streets are full of gray-heads pushing triplets in designer strollers. Irene's done her part, in other ways. Who knows how many lives have been saved because of her smiling and lip-reading at those noisy dinners?

No one's life will be altered by what transpires this evening. Roberta won't even wind up with a date. After they watched the high-speed drama of faint hope and rejection transpire between Roberta and Elliot, the others felt depleted, and the collective energy wilted, though Meyer tried to keep the group focused with news about the Iranian.

Then Bonnie and the skinhead showed up, and he spilled red

wine down his shirt, not a promising sign for a future of putting the squeeze on wealthy donors. Meyer took the guy off to change. Bonnie and Elliot said hello. They knew each other from work. Elliot showed even less interest in Bonnie than he'd shown in Roberta. Irene introduced Bonnie to Sol and Minna, whom she also already knew.

Bonnie said to Minna, "I'm so glad you're feeling better."

Minna, who Irene thinks has been behaving oddly since her illness, said, "Thanks. I'm surprised you knew I was ill. You must be very busy raising money for all Meyer's causes."

Bonnie seemed confused, then recovered and said, "Meyer was terribly worried."

Sol and Minna seemed thrilled to hear it. And that was it for conversation. Now, as they wait for Meyer's return, trying not to feel slighted by his absence, it's Irene's job to get the derailed chitchat back on track.

It's a relief when Bonnie says, "Irene, could I talk to you for a moment? Alone?"

Irene looks guiltily at the other guests. Maybe they will find it easier to relax without her around.

Whatever Bonnie has to say must be terribly private, or scandalous—Irene hopes—because Bonnie drags her across the room, all the way to the piano, on which Irene can't help admiring her piano shawl, an heirloom artifact from a tribe of nomadic Ethiopian Jews. A souvenir of their travels, a grateful gift to Meyer.

When the drinks tray comes by, Bonnie exchanges her empty glass for a full one with such a desperate lunge that the waiter is tipped off balance, and they nearly have the second casualty of the evening. Already Irene is prepared to agree to whatever Bonnie asks.

Irene's heart goes out to Bonnie, raising those two boys alone, though something in her reacts against a certain pride and vanity she senses beneath Bonnie's self-effacing exterior—pride in the nun's life she is leading, supposedly for her boys' sake, as well as the vanity with which she wears the mantle of goodness that she imagines has dropped on her just from working with Meyer. Meyer, who at this moment is being so good that he's wandered off with the Nazi and left Irene to deal with whatever Bonnie is apologizing for in advance. With her admirable but hopeless desire to *be* good, to *do* good, Bonnie reminds Irene of that ninny in *Middlemarch*, which they read in Irene's book group.

"This is all my fault," Bonnie is saying. "Blame it completely on me."

"What could be so bad?" says Irene. Bonnie also reminds her of a woman she met once, a pale girl who had turned out to be a former lover of Meyer's. When Irene asked Meyer how in the world he could have found the woman attractive, he'd said: Waifish. A certain waifish appeal. A quality Irene had never considered an ingredient in any recipe for attraction. Meanwhile, speaking of vanity . . . Irene could be wrong, but has Bonnie streaked her hair? When would Bonnie get the time? On her lunch break, maybe. And whom did she do it for? Not the skinhead. Or is it?

"This could be terrible," Bonnie says. "Vincent . . . For a former Nazi, Irene, the guy's got a lot of problems—"

"A problem getting a glass to his mouth."

Bonnie tries to laugh. "Irene," she says, "this is serious." Everything is, with Bonnie. Sex is probably serious, which is probably why her husband took off with the two-time-loser widow. Irene can never tell if, from behind her thick glasses, Bonnie is looking deeply into her eyes or trying, as Irene suspects, to figure out if Irene's had surgery since Bonnie saw her last.

What if Bonnie and her colleagues knew that it's Meyer who wants Irene to get the procedures? Not that he would admit it. In fact he makes fun of women (women like Irene!) running to expensive, miracle-working dermatologists. But she can read it in his face, in his exquisitely controlled distaste for each new wrinkle and pouch. And considering what other men do—presidents getting blow jobs from interns, respected surgeons chopping up their mistresses and dumping them out of helicopters—who could fault a prince of peace and a Holocaust hero for wanting to sleep with his own wife? Only minus the eye bags. Meanwhile, Irene's fate is to have everyone think she's had surgery, even though she hasn't—and won't as long as she thinks Meyer wants it.

"Irene!" A note of childish petulance has crept into Bonnie's voice. "Listen."

"I *am* listening, Bonnie."

"I forgot to tell you that Vincent is fatally allergic to nuts. All he has to do is eat something that's been in the same bowl with a peanut, and he winds up in the emergency room. If he makes it to the emergency room. Irene, he could *die*."

"Americans," says Irene. "Always allergic to something. In Europe there are no allergies." Irene's shock is disingenuous. And she knows how ungracious it sounds to have lived here for forty years and still be talking about *Americans*. Nowadays, Europeans have allergies, too. They also jog and don't smoke. In fact Irene is so aware of how common such allergic problems are that she usually asks her assistant to call and ask the guests' assistants what the guests can't eat. But ex-skinheads don't have assistants, and—incorrectly, as it turns out—Irene never imagined that one would have food allergies. A nightmare in the making. She and Meyer will have to personally escort the guy to the emergency room, and wait around on plastic chairs amid screaming gunshot victims.

Irene sighs. "It's in Europe now, too. Anyhow, I'm joking. The truth is, this happens so often that at this point I would sooner serve rat poison than a bowl of cocktail peanuts. Just to be safe, tell your friend to stay away from the hors d'oeuvres, and I will go and interrogate poor Babu about the main course."

"Oh, I feel so bad," Bonnie says.

"Don't," is all Irene can bear to reply.

"And dessert," prompts Bonnie.

"Of course, dessert," says Irene.

"Thank you. I appreciate this so much, Irene, I—" Bonnie is visibly relieved now that she has dumped her crisis in Irene's lap.

What's the Hindi word for allergy? Irene races into the kitchen and somehow locates a bag of walnuts and mimes eating a walnut and grabbing her throat and dying. Babu shakes his head no. No nuts in the dinner. But does he mean no walnuts? Or no nuts of any kind? Irene has done her best. If the guy has an attack, they'll deal with it when it happens.

When she returns to the living room, Meyer still isn't back. Everyone stands in a circle, staring into their drinks, except Minna, who can't drink, and who sinks down onto the sofa. Oh, good Lord, where is Meyer? What has Irene done to deserve this?

Irene has passed the point of irritation when Meyer emerges from his study, his skinhead friend in tow and looking rather handsome in Meyer's black cashmere sweater. She recalls a photo she saw once: Nixon shaking hands with Elvis. Not that Meyer looks anything like Nixon, nor does Nolan look like Elvis, though his eyes do have that unfocused, slightly druggy look. It's something about the two men's complicity, their having recognized one another. Both are holding drinks. This could be one of those evenings when someone gets totally smashed.

"Well, at last!" Irene says. "Meyer! We all thought you gentlemen had gone out for a drink!"

Nolan gives her a searching look. Does he wonder if she's serious, if that's something Meyer does, wander off from his parties and wind up at the corner bar? Or does he think she's remarking on *his* inebriation? What did Meyer give him? Doesn't he realize that she is just giving Meyer an ordinary, married-couple hard time?

"Of course, I am only kidding," she says. "Please. Come in. Let's sit down. Dinner's getting cold. *Meyer.*"

But Meyer makes them wait longer, makes them watch from across the room as he shows Vincent the Picasso drawings, the Degas sketches, the Redon watercolor—the private art tour most guests get the first time they visit Meyer's. Bonnie remembers when Meyer took her on the tour, soon after she came to Brotherhood Watch. She'd tried to be cool. She knew about art, probably more than Meyer did. She'd majored in art history. She'd had curatorial jobs.

She'd run the development program at the Clairmont Museum. Bonnie-the-professional noted that Meyer had good taste—or a good adviser. But Bonnie-the-human-being felt nearly incandescent, illuminated by the glow of Meyer Maslow's regard, dimmed only slightly by the strain of trying to make some halfway intelligent comment as they hovered in front of each work, as Meyer took time from his busy life to treat his new employee as if she were the only person in the room. Of course it's flattering to be seduced by a great man, a hero, and to know he's seducing you into helping him save the world. Besides which, the paintings and drawings are great. Bonnie never has time to look at art anymore. She hardly has time to miss it.

Vincent is nodding. How nervous must *he* be? Bonnie catches his anxiety like an airborne virus. She tries to read their body language, but it's as if she's not wearing her glasses. Meyer's pointing and talking. They both seem strangely relaxed under the circumstances—the circumstances being six pairs of eyes glaring at them, waiting to start dinner. Meyer's giving Vincent his moment. It's something Meyer does. At some point he'll make each person in the room feel chosen.

So why does Bonnie feel protective, worried on Vincent's behalf? Because tonight is an audition masquerading as dinner. Everyone—including her—is watching to see how he'll do in civilized society, if they can trust him to stand up at the benefit and not start talking about Ricans and the Jewish media and the federal government's plans to control its citizens via E-ZPass.

What right do Bonnie and Meyer and Irene and their friends have to judge him? Every right, in fact. While they have been working for human rights and world peace, Nolan was going to white-power jamborees and getting drunk and tattooed. But still, the poor guy might have dropped from Mars into Meyer and Irene's art-filled, intimidating apartment. Well, it's not a bad place to land. Bonnie hopes Vincent knows that.

Vincent can use the practice. It's only fair to let him paddle around in the calm shoals of a dinner party before tossing him into the rapids of the benefit gala. Already he's dumped wine down his shirt. No wonder he's on edge. She'd sensed it on the way here. He'd strutted down Fifty-seventh Street like a rooster scattering hens.

Something else is upsetting Bonnie. It takes her a while to track back to that guy on the street telling her she looked fatigued. That's what she's been thinking lately, whenever she looks in the mirror. It's why every piece of clothing she owns is, as of this morning, on her bedroom floor. Though maybe the guy was being aggressive instead of observant. No one tells you that you look tired unless they mean to hurt you and get away with it. Anyway, why is Bonnie concerned about the guy making her feel unattractive, instead of about the awful way he must have to live?

"Meyer can't resist showing off his collection." Irene's voice is pitched loud enough so that it's clear she's talking to Meyer.

Meyer says, "On the contrary, darling! It's not showing off. It would be so selfish to keep all this beauty to ourselves."

Vincent turns and blinks at them. Meyer's science project.

The guests stall at the dining room door, paralyzed by the gorgeousness of the table, until Irene points them toward their places with such forceful efficiency that she could be flinging them into their seats. Long ago, in that other life of giving parties with Joel, Bonnie went so far as to make seating plans in her head, but at the last moment she always gave up and told the guests to sit wherever they wanted. She was always so nervous, she always had a terrible time. But now she works out seating charts for dinners for five hundred. She has to remember who's feuding, who's single, who used to be married to whom. Seating potential donors next to their spouse's lover or a former business partner they're suing won't deliver that fat check for Brotherhood Watch.

Irene and Meyer sit at opposite ends of the long table. Bonnie and Minna flank Meyer; Irene surrounds herself with Vincent and Sol and exiles Elliot and Roberta to face off in the dead zone in the middle.

Bonnie's wineglass is full. She sips from it as the others shift in their chairs to establish the optimum distance from their neighbors. At the other end of the table, beyond the reach of Bonnie's guidance,

Vincent leans on his elbow toward Irene, as if he's trying to eavesdrop on the tight-lipped chat between Irene and Elliot Green. Irene seems displeased with Elliot, perhaps because of his lack of interest in the two single women. Irene loves to matchmake. It was thanks to her that Bonnie enjoyed those few hellish dates after Joel left.

Bonnie's a little afraid of Elliot, who, she feels certain, is fundamentally incapable of understanding who Vincent is or what he could do for the foundation. Bonnie knows how Elliot thinks: You can never be too careful. You see a skinhead coming down the street, you cross to the other side. She understands that Elliot and his law firm are a necessary part of the safety net that enables Meyer to walk his tightrope—speaking out, telling the truth, unafraid of the consequences. Let Elliot deal with the consequences! Bonnie's put in a lot of time on the phone with Elliot—for example, last summer, after the pot bust at the Pride and Prejudice camp. How could Meyer *like* Elliot? He's the anti-Meyer. Type A, so anal, so small-minded, always assuming that everyone has the basest, most selfish motives, always bringing everything down to his own scheming, conniving level. Bonnie should be grateful. Elliot works for them pro bono.

Elliot can never focus on Bonnie unless they have a problem to resolve. But he's certainly fixed on Irene. For one thing, she's married to the alpha male. Also, like many European women, Irene has a certain disputatious geisha quality that insists that every conversation be, simultaneously, a flirtation and a surrender.

Is Vincent drunk? When he and Meyer returned from their long break from the party, each was holding a drink. If he's a little high—like Bonnie right now—perhaps that's why he seems so wrapped up in what Irene's saying to Elliot. One thing Bonnie likes about alcohol is how it gives you patience, lets you concentrate, relax, and look at someone for as long as it takes. As long as it takes to what? To watch Irene blow off Elliot and turn toward Vincent.

Irene's smile shines on Vincent like one of those mirrors doctors used to wear on their heads. Perhaps Bonnie's thinking of doctors because a small, elderly Indian man in a white surgical jacket has just entered the room with a silver tray. It's Babu, the Maslows'

Harijan cook. Is this Bonnie's third or second glass? That she can't remember probably means she's had enough.

"Thank you, Babu," says Irene, taking both spoons and deftly helping herself to a tangle of dark, slippery ribbons. Bonnie will never be able to make the transfer so smoothly. She'll scatter slimy worms all over Babu's spotless scrubs. Irene puts one hand on Babu's arm, checks rapidly down the table, then, with a pat on the elbow, sends Babu on his way and returns to whatever fascinating thing Vincent is saying. Someone touches Bonnie's shoulder, and she spins around to find Babu and the platter.

Bonnie helps herself to the eel-like objects that, when they appear without mishap on her plate, turn out to be eggplant. The food has reanchored Bonnie to her end of the table, where now—dutifully, it's like punishment, how strange that she should feel that way—she struggles to catch up with Meyer and Minna in midconversation.

They're talking about the eggplant. Not a giant leap.

The ever-thoughtful Meyer shifts his posture to include Bonnie. "I'm afraid we can thank the horrors of the caste system for this marvelous *bhinji masala*. Our guardian angel, Babu, is a well-known activist for the scheduled castes—" He waits for some sign of recognition from Minna. "The Untouchables, as they used to say." Another beat. "You know, Gandhi called them Harijans. Children of God."

"Sorry," says Minna. "You know, Meyer, I think I may still be a little spacey from the anesthetic."

"By now, Babu has many dangerous enemies—not only in Hyderabad, but in Delhi and Bombay. And once we found out that he was also a brilliant cook . . . what can I tell you? It suddenly got much easier to get him a visa."

"I guess your Brahmin friends won't be eating here anymore. I gather they're not fond of eating food handled by Untouchables." Minna's spaciness has worn off, fast and with a vengeance. Why is she being unpleasant? Meyer visited her in the hospital.

"I suppose you're right," says Meyer, who so fears making cultural mistakes that he keeps a file of newspaper clippings documenting scandalous gaffes. Bush vomiting in the Japanese prime minister's lap. JFK telling the Germans, I am a jelly doughnut. The ill-advised marketing campaign that, literally translated into Tagalog, promised that a certain soda would bring their ancestors back from the dead. "Then our Brahmin friends will have to learn to overcome their prejudice."

"Good luck," says Minna.

"I love Indian food!" says Bonnie. In fact, her first bite of eggplant seems to be conspiring with the wine in her stomach.

"You know what I've noticed?" says Minna. "Every time Sol and I go out to an Indian restaurant, it's always full of Orthodox kids courting, on dates. I guess they can go there and feel safe and not have to worry about the prosciutto bits in the pasta."

Meyer says, "You know how they say that duck is Jewish pork? Well, curry is—"

"Instant heartburn," says Minna. What is Minna's problem? Bonnie always liked her. "I remember when Sol and I visited Cochin, and right in the middle of this Indian city, we turned a corner into the ghetto, and suddenly everyone looked exactly like my neighbors on the Upper West Side. And this marvelous little old man showed us around the synagogue, and Sol was speaking Yiddish to him. It was all so moving—"

The memory of her travels is reviving Minna. Bonnie wonders if Minna is as fully recovered as everyone wants to believe. Meyer listens and lets her shine, because he's singled out Minna as being in the most urgent need of his therapeutic attention.

Minna says, "They claim to have come over in King Solomon's times."

"Some say around the time of the Assyrian exile," Meyer corrects her. "The first documentation is a dispensation from the Malabar king, written on copper plates, in Tamil." How does Meyer know so much about the Cochin Jews?

A peal of laughter from Irene floats down the table, ending Meyer's disquisition. Blindsided by shame, Bonnie, Meyer, and

Minna stare into space. How stiff and serious they feel, with their dull, scholarly chat about the Malabar Jews, while, just a few seats down, Irene and Vincent are having so much fun.

"Oh, dear." Irene dabs at her eyes. "Vincent was just telling me the most hilarious stories about redneck cuisine!"

"Critter cuisine," says Vincent.

"Apparently," says Irene, "Vincent and his friends used to hunt squirrels, and they'd cook the *legs*—little squirrel drumettes—in the microwave oven. Have you ever heard anything more disgusting in your life?"

No one has, it seems.

"Grotesque," says Roberta. "Honestly."

"Free protein," Elliot says. God forbid anyone think that the foundation lawyer has been dining on gourmet delicacies while his manly brothers have been hunting the beasts of the forest.

"And apparently," Irene continues, "Vincent knows a recipe for cooking a trout on some engine part. Vincent?"

"The manifold." Vincent looks proud, the shy kid picked to star in the school play. "You wrap it in tinfoil and put it on the manifold and drive for, like, a hundred miles. Let's say, Manhattan to Kingston."

"Doesn't it smell?" Minna asks.

"Nah," says Vincent. "The smell burns off."

"Let's try it!" Irene says. "Too bad we don't have a car. Who does? Bonnie? What do you say?"

"I'd be afraid to try," Bonnie says. "My van's got a hundred and twenty five thousand miles on it, and it's not in the best shape already." So much for the general merriment. Bonnie never got the joke in the first place. And why has Vincent never made *her* laugh with amusing anecdotes about squirrel and trout? All he tells her are sad stories about the IRS, his breakup with his last girlfriend, Margaret, his time in ARM. The kind of stuff you'd tell your understanding older sister. Why should Bonnie care? And why has she gotten so possessive? Like after that press conference, when she was so upset that Vincent had told the reporter something he hadn't told her. She should be delighted that Irene is charmed. Bonnie should be trying to decide which rich woman of a certain age should sit beside Vincent at the gala.

Babu appears with a bottle of wine.

"Fill 'er up," says Bonnie.

What happened to the eggplant? Could Bonnie have eaten it all? While they were contemplating the challenge of cooking a trout on an engine, Babu has cleared their plates. And now he's returned, staggering under the weight of an enormous silver platter and a gargantuan fish.

"Oh, Irene!" cries Roberta. "What a magnificent creature."

"Moby Dick," says Vincent.

"Very good, Vincent," says Meyer.

Irene says, "Striped bass. Heart healthy. In honor of our dear Minna."

"To Minna!" Meyer raises his glass, and the others do the same—all, that is, except Bonnie, whose glass is empty. Babu replenishes her wine so that Bonnie can join in the toast and the vigorous gulping that follows.

"Where did you get such a lovely fish?" Minna calls down the table, as Irene addresses herself to the fish, struggling slightly to saw through its spine with the two serving spoons. If Irene's having trouble, how will Bonnie manage?

"Oh, I caught it myself," says Irene. "At Citarella. And then we got a car, and Babu cooked it on the engine."

"That would have been quite a trip," Vincent says. "New York to Tennessee."

Irene says, "Why would anyone want to go to Tennessee?"

That's where they hold the Homeland Encampment. But Bonnie would never say the two words that would destroy the positive effects of everyone's efforts to overlook Vincent's past. Vincent told her that the ARM convention was just an excuse to play drinking games and get laid. He said it wasn't so different from what college kids do at frat parties and football weekends. A neo-Nazi Cancún.

Except for the swastikas, Bonnie thought. And the pamphlets. The Internet site. The slime trails of hate.

"Why Tennessee?" says Meyer.

Meyer knows why Tennessee. He wants to see how Vincent handles this, what he finds to say. It makes Bonnie anxious to see Meyer playing guinea pig with Vincent. But it's what they're all doing tonight.

Bonnie looks at Vincent, who evades her gaze and leans toward Irene, almost with defiance, unless Bonnie's imagining it. How irritated Joel always was when Bonnie found him deep in conversation with some woman at a party. He'd keep on talking, leave her standing there like a demanding child, whining, Daddy, can we go ho-ome? And oh, the fights on the drive back. He was only *talking*. Was Bonnie saying he wasn't allowed to *talk* to another woman? As it happened, Bonnie never saw him talking to Lorraine. She heard them on the phone. Even now, she hardly sees Lorraine. Joel picks up the kids. Is Bonnie thinking all this because Vincent talked to Irene?

"Why would you go to Tennessee?" Vincent asks the table. "To buy legal fireworks!" Everyone laughs. Vincent's rockets and Catherine wheels have blown away the dark galaxy of the Homeland Encampment. He's saved himself, saved the moment, and in the process saved Bonnie, who would rather think about fireworks than about a white separatist convention. Or about Joel's bad behavior. Such thoughts keep Bonnie from relaxing and enjoying herself, like Irene.

Irene makes people feel better. Lucky to be alive. Whereas Bonnie makes them uncomfortable. I've drunk too much, Bonnie thinks.

"Fireworks!" says Irene. "If only we had some. We could set them off on the terrace!"

Bonnie's trying to picture this scene—Vincent kneeling, lighting the fuse, making the others stand back—when she becomes aware that Babu has appeared beside her with the fish. The bass stares at her dolefully, as if it knows it's missing huge ragged chunks of flesh. Bonnie can't make it whole again. She grabs the spoon and manages to tug a small portion of fish away from the carcass.

"Is that all you're having?" Meyer says.

Bonnie tries to say she's not hungry but for some reason can't speak. So she idiotically puffs out her cheeks and points to her stomach. Meyer helps himself to some fish, then turns back to Bonnie.

"So how are your sons?"

Meyer always asks after the boys, though sometimes she suspects that he could care less. How *are* the boys? Home alone, without her. She'd asked the kids if they wanted a babysitter. Danny pointed out that most kids his age *are* babysitters. He'd asked what she was afraid of. Did he really want to hear? Armed intruders, fire, flood. Leaking carbon monoxide.

Bonnie says, "Speaking of the boys, I think I'll call and check."

"Use the phone in my study," Meyer says. "You'll have more privacy."

"It doesn't have to be private," says Bonnie. But that's the phone Meyer offers, and Bonnie can hardly pull out her cellphone and call from the table. Standing up is a bad idea. Too late to fix it now. Bonnie lurches off. She notes that she's listing toward one side. But she's sober enough to remember that here, if you slam into the walls, a Degas comes crashing down.

Bonnie should be ashamed, helping arrange this dinner partly to see how Vincent behaves, and now she's the one who's loaded. She'll worry about that later. For now, she needs to find Meyer's study. But first a trip to the bathroom, where in the glare of shocking white light, she briefly forgets why she's there and looks in the mirror. A big mistake. What did that guy on the street say? The lady looks fatigued. And Bonnie's upset about that, instead of feeling good about the fact that Vincent stood there and let the guy say that without breaking his head. Vincent has changed already. He . . . Bonnie loses track. She must have drunk even more than she realized. She splashes cold water on her face, then stares in horror at Irene's inviolate white towels. She grabs a crumpled cloth from the top of the laundry hamper. Vincent's wine-stained shirt. She wipes her face, inhales. How has she reached the point of standing, drunk and dizzy, in Meyer Maslow's bathroom with her streaming face pressed into a Nazi's dirty shirt?

Bonnie walks into what appears to be Irene and Meyer's bed-
room. Meyer said his study. Bonnie's never been back here before.
There's a phone on the night table. Meyer didn't say not to use it.
Bonnie sits on the bed and dials.

The line's busy. Bonnie slams down the receiver. Is everything
okay? Probably Danny's online or talking to a friend. How can he
do that when she's trying to phone him? But of course, he doesn't
know that. She's getting call-waiting tomorrow.

Try again. Still busy. It can't be busy forever. She'll give it a
minute. For the moment, she can lie back and shut her eyes and
think.

Meyer is the first to notice how long Bonnie has been gone. He
gives her a few minutes, and when she doesn't reappear, sends some
freighted glances in Irene's direction. But Irene's so focused on Vincent that she ignores Meyer's signals until everyone has registered
Bonnie's absence.

"Irene, darling," says Meyer, "do we think you should go find Bonnie?"

"I'm sure she's fine. She's probably phoning her children." Irene
turns back to Vincent until the intensity between them lapses, and
she says, "Meyer. Where's Bonnie?"

Shouldn't Irene go find her, or Roberta or Minna, in case it's some
sort of bathroom thing, some female situation? Everyone's looking at
Meyer. Their sun. Their leader. Dad. The way that Irene plants her
elbow on the table and cups her chin in her hand is eloquently com-
municative. It means: Bonnie is Meyer's problem. He works with her,
he invited her, this dinner was their idea.

First he heads for the bathroom, imagining the grisly scenario
in which Bonnie is ill or drunk. He'll stand outside the bathroom
door, listening to her retch, and thinking: I have to work with this
woman tomorrow. This is why you should never mix business and
social life.

But the bathroom door is wide open. Bonnie isn't there. For a moment, Meyer is alarmed. Could she have gone home? Has she been acting strangely tonight? Meyer can't recall. He remembers being bored by a conversation with Minna about the Cochin Jews.

Then Meyer sees Bonnie asleep on his bed. Even from a distance, he can tell: snoozing. Not in danger. Curled up on her side. Should Meyer wake her or let her sleep? What if she won't get up? Where the hell is Irene? Meyer would rather be brokering a peace agreement between Arabs and Jews, he'd rather give a begging speech to five hundred New York bigwigs, he'd rather be speaking French on a crackly long-distance line with some sadistic Iranian prison warden, than deal with *this* in his own room, at the end of a long day. The last thing he's in the mood for is coping with the problem of his passed-out development director. There is no hidden blessing in this. It's a plain and simple pain in the ass. He wishes it weren't happening.

But what choice does Meyer have? Run to Irene, to Mommy? Meyer approaches the bed. He clears his throat, then coughs and coughs again, louder.

Bonnie's snoring lightly. Like a kid. Meyer stands above her, hoping she'll sense his presence. He can't bring himself to disturb her. Her knuckles are mashed into her cheek. Her glasses have slipped down her nose. Bizarrely, tears fill Meyer's eyes. He's becoming an old woman! Why didn't he and Irene have children? The question was settled so long ago that he's forgotten the answer. Back then, a woman of forty was old. God knows, they took enough chances. Irene never got pregnant. Both of them were busy. And everyone understood if a man with Meyer's history chose not to bring children into the world. No one ever asked him why. Doesn't Irene care?

Bonnie shifts in her sleep, rucking up her skirt and exposing a ragged ladder in her dark pantyhose. This hardworking, defenseless, admirable woman would do anything for him. How hard and lonely it must be, raising those sons alone. And now she's taken on Vincent. Meyer told her to, and she did it.

Watching Bonnie sleep, Meyer sees her willingness for what it is: the simple desire to please, to do good, to make everything better. Watching her, Meyer no longer feels nostalgic for the young man he once was, or even for the healthy, middle-aged version of himself who at least might have considered the sexual implications of a not-unattractive woman curled up on his pillow.

Meyer feels like a different person. Purified. Washed clean. It's as if he's come through to the other side, and instead of grief or regret, he can experience pure love for a fellow human being—the sympathy that, he'd begun to fear, he could only feel from a distance. Telescopic philanthropy. Compassion is something that waxes and wanes, like closeness in a marriage. When you lose it, you think it will never return. But it always comes back. So far.

He wants to cover Bonnie with a blanket. He wants to cherish and protect her. Whoever sent him the Dickens chapter could not have been more deluded. This welling up of love for Bonnie is what he longs to feel for the world. This is what God gives you in return for trying to be conscious and do the right thing.

This sense of grace doesn't falter, not even when Irene enters the room. How flushed and excited Irene looks! How much Meyer loves her. God bless Vincent for giving her the male attention she longs for. Meyer puts his arm around her. Irene leans lightly against him.

"Christ," says Irene. "She can't drive back to the suburbs like that. Vincent's going to have to drive. Unless you want the two of them staying in the guest room. And I'll tell you, Meyer, honestly, I'd rather jump out that window than have to face them tomorrow morning."

"We wouldn't want that," says Meyer. "Your jumping out the window. Anyway, Bonnie's got children. A babysitter, I'll bet. She probably needs to get back. And as for Vincent driving—"

"Fabulous," says Irene. "That simplifies things. Meyer, dear, give me the phone."

Watching Irene call car service and make arrangements for Bonnie and Vincent to be picked up and driven to Clairmont, Meyer feels nearly faint with gratitude and admiration. Maybe he's also drunk too much. It's been quite an evening.

Meyer follows Irene into the dining room. How smoothly they

work together, switching seats so Meyer can confer with Vincent. No need to tell Vincent that Bonnie's drunk. He can figure that out on his own. Meyer says that she isn't feeling well and that they have called car service.

"I could have driven her home," says Vincent.

Vincent has probably had as much as Bonnie. He just handles it better.

"That's all right," says Meyer. "These things happen. What can you do?"

By the time the doorman rings to say the car has arrived, Bonnie is up and walking. The other guests form a phalanx and, with quick social kisses, take Bonnie off their hands.

Meyer and Irene's relief is so intense that they hug each other, a joyous embrace observed by Babu, who has appeared at the dining room door and whose presence stops Meyer's hand in its instinctive migration toward Irene's ass. Irene detaches herself and heads toward the kitchen to oversee a few details, while Meyer goes off to wait for her over a brandy, in his study.

He places his palm in the impression that Bonnie left on the bedspread, then smoothes out the bed. He can't decide where he wants to be—in bed, in his favorite chair, drink, no drink, looking out the window. What he can't decide is how he wants Irene to find him.

They could be going on their first date, that's how jittery Meyer feels. Except that there was no first date. There was only that New York dinner party, not unlike the one tonight, except that, at the end of it, Irene got Meyer his coat and, with her millionaire husband standing not three feet away, told Meyer she wanted to see him again.

Some of that came back to him when they embraced in the hall. In addition, the pure love he had felt as he'd watched Bonnie sleep has focused, like a beam of light, on his wife and her body.

Meyer decides on his favorite chair. What book should he be reading? He checks in fiction, under *D*. Here's *Bleak House*. Could Irene have sent the chapter? Or could it have been Babu? Do they read Dickens in India? Meyer goes through the stack of books he plans to read. *IBM and the Jews*. Let Irene find him reading that, swirling a snifter of brandy. A successful, powerful, caring man . . .

As it turns out, a miscalculation. Meyer can tell at once that what Irene is seeing is not Dick Powell, Ronald Colman, the suave movie-hero husband. What she's seeing is some jerk who has been sitting on his fanny all the time she's been working with Babu, overseeing mountains of dishes and details while her lord and master relaxes.

"Irene, dear, would you like a drink?" How he wants her to say yes! If they can't be passionate young lovers again, at least they can be partners, fellow soldiers who have survived another skirmish, and who in the calm after the battle can enjoy a moment of peace.

"No, thanks," says Irene.

Irene slips into the second-best chair and consents to sit beside him in that companionable silence that takes decades to achieve. Somewhere, on Randall's Island, a window reflects the moon, and the light of the bridge is draped like a bright ribbon across the East River. How still and beautiful everything is, this lovely panorama paid for with so much suffering, so much hard work, and with the mysterious grace of God, who has given this to Meyer and not to so many others who suffered more and worked harder.

Irene says, "I'll bet you fifty dollars she'll be fucking him in two weeks. If she isn't already."

Meyer says, "Who are we talking about?"

"Bonnie and your Nazi. Did you see how she looked at him? And the way she was looking at *me*? She would have killed me if she could, just for talking to the guy."

Why is Irene doing this? Taking the best part of his evening— the swell of agreeable emotions he's had ever since he watched Bonnie sleep—and reducing it to bitchy gossip. But Irene's not doing anything to *him*. This is not about Meyer, as Irene so often says. She's just reporting an observation. *Is* something going on between Bonnie and Vincent? How could Meyer not have noticed? The same way Mrs. Jellyby doesn't hear her children falling downstairs and getting their heads stuck in railings.

Instantly Meyer's good mood is gone, all that love and empathy distilled to a puddle of ill-will. Is it envy? Envy of what? He doesn't want Bonnie. He wants that lost-forever world of romance, surprise, and adventure. Bonnie and Vincent are young and alive. Or, at any rate, younger.

He knows that Irene is feeling this too, perhaps more strongly than he is. She's depleted by the energy she's expended flirting with a man who is going home with Bonnie, a woman less attractive in every way except that she's twenty years younger. Once more he wants to take Irene's hand, but he fears that his sympathy might enrage her.

Anyway, who says that Irene is right about Bonnie and Vincent? Men assume that women have some ESP for romance and personal situations. Bonnie isn't stupid. She doesn't need to get involved with a man like Vincent Nolan. Even though he does have many excellent qualities. What was it he said this evening? Faith cells were like fat cells, you developed them when you were young. . . .

"Irene, darling, excuse me." Meyer goes into his study and finds the notebook in which he has been jotting phrases for his speech at the benefit dinner. He writes, "Faith cells—like fat cells." Then he leafs back through the book. He reads: "Moral bungee jump. The courage to change." This is Meyer's real work. This is what matters, not a trivial misunderstanding with his wife, or some possible hanky-panky between two colleagues on his staff.

By the time he goes back in the other room, Irene has gone to the bathroom, from which he hears the clinks of jars on porcelain, the buzz of her sonic toothbrush, the rush of water, and the sounds of her ritualistic preparations for sleep, the transfixed application of magic creams and time-reversing concoctions, useless and costing the earth.

A HUGE EXPLOSION RATTLES the house.

"What was *that?*" says Max.

"Thunder, idiot," says Danny. "What the hell do you think?" For Max's sake, impatience and insult are the best way to go. Keep it real, keep it normal.

"Thunder and lightning," Max says.

Rain stampedes the roof. Danny says, "It's a fucking hurricane. Mom would shit if she knew. How come she didn't tell us what to do if the house gets hit by lightning? Could you believe the crap she put us through before she'd let us stay alone? Telling us not to bleed to death if we, like, cut a bagel."

"Give her a break," says Max. "She keeps it pretty together."

Max is always defending Mom. But this time, Max is wrong. Mom should have it more together. She should be able to leave two competent teenagers home for one night without the major drama. Though she should have told them what to do in case of a tornado. Do they have a flashlight? Probably not. Making sure there's a flashlight is something fathers do. Something *other* fathers do.

That was thunder. But what was *that?* All night, Danny's been hearing strange noises, footsteps, slamming doors. Mom's turned him into a wimp. It's her fault that every floor creak makes his heart slam around in his chest.

He's actually considered the strategic advantages of being down in the basement in case the house does get hit by lightning or someone does break in. Mom kept saying: I know I can trust you guys. Well, she's right. She can trust Danny not to get high tonight. And he's glad he didn't. By now, he'd be so paranoid he'd be phoning the Clairmont police, which would only make him more paranoid. He'd have to flush the minuscule pot stash he keeps in an espresso can on a shelf in his bedroom behind his dictionary.

It's strange that his mom hasn't called. To interrogate whoever is stupid enough to pick up the phone. No, Max hasn't fallen down the stairs. Nobody's running a fever.

By the time Danny remembers his computer and runs up to his room to unplug it—a kid at his school had his hard disk fried by lightning—the thunder is down to a growl. And the rain's stopped. Excellent. Danny can go online. Which means that his mother can't call. Maybe this will make her spring for a dedicated phone line.

Danny's e-mail consists of three offers to sell him sleeping pills and enlarge his penis and a group message from Chloe that says: "Emergency! Any of you guys know anything about Nelson Mandela?"

Emergency? Pathetic! The paper's not due for ages, beside which it annoys him that Chloe's doing Nelson Mandela. Does that mean that she is going over to the other side, writing a paper guaranteed to get an A from Linda Graber? Chloe swore that wasn't why. She admires Nelson Mandela. So does Danny, actually—another reason not to write about him. Instead of which he's doing Hitler, an automatic D-minus.

Danny's ahead of schedule. He's already checked Hitler's biography out of the school library, at which point he discovered that Hitler's face on a book jacket was not something he wanted to flash as he walked down the hall to class. That's all he needs: the whole school calling him Hitler Boy. Even at home, where there's no one to see, the book feels embarrassing, somehow. Danny turns the front cover facedown.

If Danny takes the Hitler bio downstairs and reads it while he watches television, he'll be doing his schoolwork, minus the boredom. The boring book and the boring TV will cancel each other out. He logs off and heads down to Dad's room, where he finds Max.

"Wanna watch Howard Stern?" Max asks.

"Go for it." Danny stretches out on the couch and tosses the book on the rug.

Howard's talking to two identical twins: Gen and Jess. He's asking how often they have three-ways with guys. He asks if their breasts are identical. The women strip off their bikini tops, and four tiny digital fuzzballs dance on the screen.

Within seconds, Max is asleep. Howard Stern always puts him right out. Maybe he's too young for it. Maybe it makes him nervous.

Danny hears a noise and hits the mute button. Definitely a car. Definitely not his mom's car. Not pulling into the driveway. Stopping in front of the house.

Two male voices. Holy shit. *Not* his Mom and Vincent. Two men talking loudly as they approach the door.

Maybe it *is* the police. Maybe Danny should flush his stash. Or maybe it's two serial killers. Should he and Max hide somewhere or go out the back door? Some unfamiliar instinct makes Danny run up the stairs and fling open the front door.

A black Lincoln Town Car is parked at the end of the driveway, down which Mom is walking, propped up by Vincent and a uniformed driver. His mother is weaving unsteadily, dipping every so often. Totally hammered. That explains the Town Car. At least it's not still pouring. Why couldn't Vincent drive them home? How could Mom let this happen?

Danny knows plenty of kids whose parents are stone alcoholics. He's lucky. His dad hardly drinks, and he's never seen his mom plastered, or maybe just a couple of times right after his dad left. And she was good. You could hardly tell. She'd take the bourbon to her room. She'd be normal the next morning.

It's pitiful to watch Mom lurch up the front walk. But Danny can understand how she might have folded under the pressure of taking Vincent to dinner at Maslow's.

Danny's just so glad that it's them, and not cops or psycho killers.

Somehow Mom pulls her act together enough to sign the driver's receipt.

"Did it rain here?" she asks him. "It didn't, in the city." She's so wrecked she's asking the driver who came up with them.

Vincent says, "Thanks, man. Have a good evening. We can take it from here."

Danny thinks, Who's this *we?*

Danny's mom swoops toward him and crooks her arm around his neck. She's apparently sober enough to land a big gloppy kiss on his cheek, but not enough to notice when Danny wipes it off with the back of his hand.

"Is everything all right?" she asks.

"Fucking fantastic," he says.

"Language!" she says. "Where's Max?"

"Asleep, I guess."

"Honey, I'm so glad to *see* you!" she says.

"Whatever," Danny says.

Mom sways past him, heading for the stairs and, he hopes, her room. Danny goes down to the TV room, gets Max, and walks him up to his bed. Then he goes to his own room and lies down on top of his bed, unmade for two weeks, since the last time his Mom did the laundry.

Danny's jacked up. He'll never sleep. He should read the Hitler book. One page, and he'll be unconscious. But he left the book downstairs. He needs to go and get it.

From the hall, he hears the TV. Danny's sure he turned it off. It's not his mom, not Max. Which leaves Vincent. Nothing could be more annoying than dealing with Vincent right now. But Danny wants his book back. He doesn't want Vincent to touch it.

Downstairs, he finds Vincent lying on the couch, reading the Hitler book and watching *Nightline*. At least it's not Howard Stern. Vincent sits up and makes room for him on the couch.

"Floor's good," Danny says.

Danny sits cross-legged on the carpet like a guest in his own TV room—Dad's room—and watches thirty-second interviews with Oklahoma City bombing survivors and the victims' relatives. Three words flash onto the screen—*Vengeance or forgiveness*—over a shot of a weeping family laying flowers on a grave. Cut to commercial break.

"I thought you never watched TV," Danny says. "I thought that's what my mom said."

"When did she say that?"

"The first night you got here. I thought you were such a big reader."

"Man, I wish I were your age and could remember the stuff you remember. Anyhow, it's true. Look at me. What am I doing? Reading or watching TV?"

"Both," says Danny.

"Multitasking. I recommend it."

"But you *are* watching TV. Which means that you lied to my mother."

"Which you never do," says Vincent.

Danny refuses to go there. After a pause, he says, "What was up with Mom tonight? Is she okay, or what?" Is Danny asking this loser's opinion on his mother's sobriety and mental health?

"I don't blame her," Vincent says. "I would have done the same. Drunk myself blotto. I mean, I practically did do the same. Fortunately, I've done more serious drinking in my time. I've got calluses on my liver. It's got to have been rough on her, taking Godzilla to dinner at Meyer Maslow's."

"How did it go?" Danny's glad to be at least partly off the subject of Mom.

"Great, man. Really. Terrific. Maslow's wife was practically blowing me under the table. Jesus, what would your mom say if she knew I was saying stuff like that around you?"

Danny can't help laughing out loud. He's never liked Irene Maslow, or her light perfumy kisses. "Yuck. She's around ninety."

"Not exactly," Vincent says. "And she's got a certain . . . something. I guess it's invisible to a guy your age. You've got to take my word for it."

On TV, a woman is saying that it isn't fair. Tim McVeigh will die in less than two minutes, and she will have to deal with her loss for a lifetime.

"Actually, that's not true," Vincent says. "They're not telling us the truth about how long it takes to die from lethal injection. More like eight to ten minutes, and it isn't pretty. But does America want to hear that? No sir, it does not. Anyway, I have a better idea. After they kill the guy they should chop him in pieces and sell them, like they used to sell real estate on the moon. Or the bones of saints. Then everybody who wants a piece of him could have an *actual* piece. Wait. I take that back. You know what they should do? Auction the pieces on e-Bay."

Has Vincent got into Danny's stash? Danny says, "What would they do with the money?"

"I don't know," says Vincent. "Build a new Murragh Building memorial. Something better than those cheesy chairs. Or give the cash to the survivors."

"Creepy," Danny says.

"Speaking of creepy, how come you're reading *this?*"

Danny wants to say, Not because of you. "I have to write a paper. For school."

"They assign you to write about Hitler? What are you going to write?"

"I'll think of something," says Danny. "It's hard to come up with anything new. Or something that doesn't sound stupid. Like, I think it really sucks that the guy killed six million Jews."

On TV, a rescue worker is running through the parking lot with a bundled-up, bleeding baby.

"That is, if you believe that," Danny says. "Or are you one of those guys who claims that Auschwitz never happened?"

"Where did you hear about that?" Vincent says.

"My mom made me go to this two-week nerd camp. They told us all this stuff about hate groups."

Vincent looks over the top of the Hitler book. It's a freaky juxtaposition, Vincent's face growing out of Hitler's face. Vincent follows Danny's glance, and looks down at the cover and laughs.

"My man, do you really think that I would be working with Meyer Maslow and your mom if I thought that the Holocaust never happened? You think I'm busting my balls for the two hundred bills a week?"

Danny can almost hear his mom say: Don't answer a question with a question. "Two hundred bucks is money."

"Look," says Vincent. "Between you and me and the wall. I'll tell you something about Hitler. Put it in your paper. The guy was a flamer. All his staff was in love with him. Even the married guys. He never had normal relations with a woman. He didn't marry Eva Braun till the day they killed themselves. And you won't find that in the books. Supposedly, you can't prove it. The evidence died with him—"

How strange that Danny never saw that before. How stupid has he been? That weird little mustache, that high hoarse voice, that Woody Woodpecker jumping.

"Wait a minute," says Danny. "Back up. Let me get this straight. Are you saying that Hitler killed six million Jews because he was *gay?*"

Vincent taps the side of his head and lets his jaw go slack. "Excuse me? Did I say that? That's your conclusion, my man. Personally, I don't care what the guy did behind closed doors. I don't even want to think about what Hitler did or didn't do. In bed. My point was something else. My point was: all these guys I used to hang with . . . you couldn't even bring it up. They'd kick your ass if you hinted that Hitler was a little light in the loafers. Because they dug Hitler and hated fags. They couldn't handle the contradictions. That was their number-one problem. They couldn't deal with the gray areas. They couldn't get beyond the point where everything has to be black or white, one way or the other."

"*That* was their problem?" Danny says. "I thought their problem was they liked to beat up black people and Jews and torch synagogues and shit."

Vincent flinches. "They liked to *think* about it. Which was also their problem. They were always saying, Let's slug down a couple of brewskies and go beat up some fags. But in my experience, the brewskies were the issue. The fags were not the issue. Three forty-ouncers later, they'd have forgotten the fags and just be telling dirty jokes or passing out in front of the History Channel."

"The History Channel," says Danny. "How funny is that? Everyone calls it the All-Hitler Channel. You always wonder who watches that—"

"Think about it," says Vincent. "It always struck me as weird that they could hate homosexuals and worship this dude who was one. That was an inconsistency right there. And their whole thing was logic. You bought into one part of their program, and then the rest followed logically. So say if you mentioned that somebody in your family had income tax problems, that always led logically to the international Bolshevik Talmudist conspiracy. Let me ask you something. Do you believe in God?"

No one's asked Danny an annoying question like that since he was in second grade. Even Chloe, who can get metaphysical, tends to stick with the Buddhists and Hindus. Do you believe in enlightenment? What about reincarnation? Max always used to ask Danny: Who created the universe? Where do we go after we die? The universe created itself. We go in the ground, retard.

"Not really," Danny says. "I mean, not some guy with a white beard—"

"Is that your final answer?"

"I guess so," Danny says.

"Correct!" says Vincent. "Me, neither. It doesn't make sense. I do believe, however, that there is definitely a divine order and a plan. That things happen for a reason and a purpose, though we don't always know what it is. Still, to tell you the truth, it gives me the willies every time Maslow goes on about faith. Though I guess the guy has reason to believe. First, because it worked for him. And second, because, as he always says, how else can you explain it?"

Unbelievable, Danny thinks. The guy practically just got here, and already, he's quoting Meyer. Like Mom.

"You do know," says Vincent, "that there *are* two kinds of humans in the world. You understand that, don't you?"

Danny guesses, "People who believe in God and people who don't?"

"Wrong!" Vincent makes a buzzing sound. "The kind who run toward whatever dangerous shit is going down. And the kind who run away from it."

Danny knows which kind he is. He only hopes Vincent doesn't. Although tonight . . . he went *toward* the door when he heard the driver talking to Vincent. Before he even knew who it was. Maybe some hormone is kicking in. Testosterone, his mom says. He's heard her telling strangers that she lives in a testosterone-saturated atmosphere. It's some kind of pathetic boast. Danny doesn't appreciate her making jokes about his hormones. Especially when he secretly worries about not having enough.

Vincent tosses Danny the Hitler book. "You'll be needing this more than I do." He settles deeper in the couch. Is he hinting that Danny can leave?

"Nice room," Vincent says. "Comfortable. So this is where you guys disappear to every night after dinner?"

"This was my dad's room," Danny says.

"I figured that. That's why it's sort of like a DMZ between you and your mom. She doesn't come down here much."

"She never liked it. Not even when Dad was around. She has this thing against TV. In case you haven't noticed."

"So what's up with that? About your dad? How come they split up?"

Who does this guy think he is? Where does he get the nerve? Still, Danny can see how you might ask, how you might get curious. So what are Danny's options? One: Tell Vincent to stick it. Two: Pretend he doesn't know. Three: Be cool and answer, no big deal, it's a reasonable question. Four: Tell the truth and pimp your family nightmare to the skinhead outsider.

"I don't know," Danny says. "Some weirdness. My dad's been living with this ho."

"Ouch," Vincent says. "Something gave me that idea."

"Like what?" says Danny.

"Some vibe in the air," says Vincent. "So do you guys ever see him?"

"We see him a lot," Danny says.

"Meaning . . ."

"Sometimes alternate weekends. Except for those weekends when he's on call or he's got to be at the hospital. Which is fine with Mom. She'd basically rather we never spent any time with Dad and Lorraine the Ho. Lo the Ho. Who doesn't want us there, either."

"Right," says Vincent. "Lo the Ho. Does your dad know about me?"

"I don't know." Probably Danny should say yes. Yes, white supremacist dude, my dad knows who you are and where you live and everything about you and if you try anything funny, he'll come over and take you down.

It suddenly seems incredible that Danny *hasn't* told Dad. His dad would be seriously pissed at Mom, which Danny would sort of appreciate. He wouldn't mind some adult telling her, You can't do that. You don't just adopt a guy like that to live with you and your kids. Straight talk that she isn't about to hear from those cult freaks she works with. Guys like Meyer Maslow, getting their save-the-world rocks off. *Go* save the world. Let someone else do the laundry! Let your kids sleep on dirty sheets after you bring home a Nazi. Dad's not knowing about Vincent is one more thing that Danny holds against his father, though he understands that you can't blame someone for not knowing something no one will tell him.

Danny realizes he could do the wash. It isn't about the laundry. And why hasn't he told his dad? Because finally, when it comes down to it, Dad is not going to say: Danny, Max, I'll save you! Leave your mom and the Nazi and move in with me and Lorraine! And Danny's not in the mood for another disappointment.

Danny has been very clear on that score—on who Dad is and what he is willing to do—ever since he was a kid, long before the divorce. His dad was never the goofy but wise and loving father you saw on TV sitcoms. When Danny was little, and he'd have bad dreams and run to his parents' bed, he figured out pretty soon that his dad might grunt and make waking-up noises. But he needed his sleep.

Dad had heart patients to see the next day. He could kill someone if he was tired. Was it worth risking a sick person's life just to walk Danny to his room? It was Mom who walked him back. And now of course it's up to Danny to drag his own self to bed.

"I guess I'll be going to sleep," Danny says.

"Cool. Sweet dreams," says Vincent.

PART TWO

V INCENT YANKS AT HIS BOWTIE, calculating the odds that in one night, a collar could chafe through your neck and make your head fall off. Unlikely, but possible. Anything is possible. If only this didn't feel so much like the senior prom. Waiting for Bonnie to get dressed is a lot like sitting in Nadine Wozniak's living room, trying to convince her father that Vincent's plans for the evening didn't include getting Daddy's little precious pregnant.

Though actually, it's not the same. Vincent's older and wiser. And Bonnie's not going to pull the same stunt as his prom date, Nadine, who broke up with him in her dad's car on the way to the dance, choosing that moment to inform him that she'd only agreed to go with him to make her boyfriend, Tommy Hernandez, jealous. She'd already patched things up with Tommy, but still she and Vincent—they'd already rented and paid for the clothes—had to get through the hours ahead. Vincent eased the pain with megadoses of beer and Southern Comfort. Why has he not mentioned this all these weeks he's been telling Bonnie why a guy might join ARM? Why? Because the prom queen ditched him for a greaseball named Tommy Hernandez.

What's bringing all the good memories back is the rented tuxedo. But this baby is Hugo Boss, threads from another galaxy than the powder-blue piece of wide-lapeled shit that nearly bankrupted his mom. Last week, Bonnie accompanied him to the rental place to make sure they pulled out all the stops and got Mr. Nolan the very best. Luckily, Vincent thought ahead and refused to take off his long-sleeved shirt. It would have put a damper on the process if the old Jewish guy helping Vincent knew he was outfitting Mr. Waffen-SS.

Coming out of the dressing room, Vincent didn't need to look in the mirror. He could see his reflection in Bonnie's eyes. *Our man is looking good!*

Now he hears Bonnie's footsteps on the stairs—not Bonnie's normal footsteps, but the wobbly click-click of a woman on ridiculous high heels. He's going to have to monitor Bonnie's alcohol consumption if he doesn't want a replay of what happened at Maslow's. Vincent needs to watch it himself, at least until after he gets up and tells Mr. and Mrs. Deep Pockets why they need to empty their bank accounts all over World Brotherhood Watch.

Why *isn't* Vincent nervous? It's not like he does this every night, stands up and bullshits five hundred princes and princesses of the city. He has the strangest feeling, as if he's been waiting for this all his life. He hates to admit it, but the truth is, if he'd been one of those guys who ranted and raved onstage at the Homeland Encampment, he never would have gotten involved with ARM in the first place.

In her heels, Bonnie feels so tall she thinks she has to bow her head to clear the bottom stairs. She's wearing a silvery, tubelike thing with short sleeves and a high neck. Is Bonnie unaware that the whole point of an evening dress is to show a little skin? And why did Maslow spring for Vincent's tuxedo and not the fashion upgrade for Brotherhood Cinderella? Even if Meyer had insisted, Bonnie would never have gone shopping on the foundation's nickel, even though she probably knows the budget covers Maslow's Armani. Though actually, Vincent bets that Maslow pays for his clothes himself.

Even in her unsexy gown, Bonnie looks radiant and excited. Her blue eyes glitter prettily under the coke-bottle glasses. Bonnie is a major improvement over Nadine Wozniak mincing down the stairs of her parents' dump in Warwick, calculating the best way to tell Nolan the bad news about the boyfriend.

Vincent whistles as loud as he can. Bonnie blushes and bursts out laughing.

"Fox!" says Vincent.

"Right," says Bonnie. "I've had this dress forever—"

"Come on. You look great. Don't spoil it. Champagne?"

Bonnie looks confused.

"Joke," he says.

"Glad to hear it," Bonnie says. "We've both got to be *really* careful."

Vincent holds up his palm, swearing in. "Sobriety Central," he says.

Everything seems different tonight. Starting with Bonnie's face. Considering that it's the make-it-or-break-it, do-or-die night of the year, she seems unusually relaxed. The only thing Vincent can figure is: the kids aren't here. They're spending the night with their dad. Not that Bonnie especially likes them being at their father's. She keeps forgetting that she's already told Vincent how Joel and Lorraine always manage to upset the kids and hurt their feelings. The boys would never tell her that, but she *knows*. She keeps saying, "My ex-husband and his girlfriend give narcissism a bad name," and each time Vincent has to smile as if he's never heard it before.

But tonight Bonnie has no choice, she needs to concentrate, and knowing the boys are with their dad will be less distracting. In Vincent's humble opinion, she should leave them alone more often. Some adult responsibility might slow Danny's development into a slacker stoner, an obvious danger that Bonnie ignores while she fixates on the most unlikely disasters. How little she knows about them—about, say, how the older kid is scared of his own shadow. He'd probably feel braver if he laid off the weed for five minutes.

One weekend, when Bonnie and the kids were off at the Nanuet Mall, Vincent found Danny's stash—behind some books on his shelf—and rolled himself a thin joint and got so wasted he had to lie down. Where do today's kids get this stuff? Danny's dope was a million times stronger than anything Vincent knew about at his age.

"Are you all right?" asks Bonnie.

"Completely," answers Vincent to all the things Bonnie might mean.

In their fancy clothes, Bonnie and Vincent could be strangers. They look at each other, then fall silent.

Not a moment too soon, the doorbell rings.

"Great! The car," says Bonnie. "He's early. That's terrific."

Vincent opens the front door to find a plump, middle-aged Indian waiting on the steps. Bonnie comes up behind Vincent, but the guy's only got eyes for him. It's probably some Paki thing about not walking into a stranger's house and eyeballing his harem.

The driver says, "Good evening, Mr. Kalen."

What the hell's *wrong* with this camel jockey? Is this his first day on the job? Did he skip the introductory session of Elementary Town Car? Never assume two people have the same last name. Vincent and Bonnie exchange smiles and shrugs, so intimate and comfy that they *could* be a married couple.

Vincent counts to ten and runs through the anger management tips. There's no reason to revert back to all that racist ARM shit, just because his driver made a social mistake. So what if the guy thinks that Vincent and Bonnie are married and this is Vincent's house? It's a compliment, not an insult.

Maybe Vincent *is* nervous. That could be part of it, too. For one crazy moment, he'd considered telling tonight's crowd how he dunked Mrs. Browner in the pool, and how sorry he felt afterward. If they want to judge how much he's changed, that would give them a hint. But they would never understand. And the last thing he wants is that lawyer, Elliot what's-his-name, finding out that Vincent's got a record. Except that he doesn't have a record. The charges were dropped. Is there some way Elliot could find that out? Elliot has been looking for a way to bring Vincent down ever since that dinner at Meyer's when it was so plain that the old man's wife preferred Vincent. God knows what this benefit crowd thinks he did in ARM. It thrills them to imagine the worst. And Vincent's afraid they'll find out that he baptized a little old lady?

As they set off for the city, Vincent settles back and, despite the dirty look Ali Baba flashes him in the rearview mirror, rolls down the window. Lounging back in the cushiony seat, in his good tuxedo, wisps of semi-clean suburban air kissing his face, the long necklace of the Tappan Zee coming up in the windshield, Vincent feels like a king. He must be doing something right if he's progressed from Nadine Wozniak's father's car to his own rusted Ford truck to Margaret's UPS van to Raymond's Chevy pickup to this chauffeured town car.

"Are you sure you're all right?" asks Bonnie.

"I'm fine," says Vincent. "Honestly. You don't have to keep asking."

"I didn't ask," says Bonnie. "I mean, this is the first time I'm asking."

It isn't, but Vincent lets it pass. The calmer Bonnie is, the better the evening will go.

They speed across the Hudson and head south along the parkway, traveling against the stream of late-working commuters. No traffic in *their* direction. You children are *free*. In no time, they're in the city, sailing down the West Side Highway. How beautiful New York is at night. Vincent never sees it. Not counting that evening he rode back from Maslow's, afraid the whole time that Bonnie was going to get sick all over the car-service Lincoln. Right now there's nothing to worry about, nothing to look at besides the lights and the trees. How could Vincent not have noticed that the city is in blossom?

Because he's never driven—*been* driven—through Central Park on a warm spring evening in the back of a chauffeured car while all around him were flowering shrubs and trees and the twinkly fairy lights of some fairy restaurant. No one *he* knows would know this route or know that you *could* go in one end of the park and come out on the other side, exactly where you wanted. So how does this guy know, this driver who's probably been in the country all of ten minutes? Because it's his job. He had to learn. There is no conspiracy behind it.

It's funny how his improved circumstances have helped Vincent understand those poor bozos in ARM. Vincent's begun to realize that whenever those guys got anxious or noticed that life was unfair, they immediately started looking around for an ethnic group to blame. Well, Vincent isn't anxious just now, and for once the unfairness is working for him. He's doing *better* than his Paki friend at the wheel.

The ARM guys loved to read about themselves on the Internet. One night Raymond found a site that called the white-power movement "the last resort of the disenfranchised." For weeks afterward, you could count on getting a laugh if you said something like, Keep on doing that, buddy, and I'm gonna disenfranchise your ass. But those guys *are* disenfranchised, and for the moment Vincent isn't. He's the one being driven, the one in the tuxedo, the one who's been chosen to tell the richest, most important people in this beautiful city why they need to support an organization that's picked Vincent, out of all the world, to speak to them this evening.

Vincent rolls his windows up. No need to make the guy's job harder. He can afford to be charitable.

At last the car glides up to the curb in front of the Metropolitan Museum, in front of the monumental staircase over which someone has rolled an actual red carpet. Does the driver *get* it? The carpet is there for Vincent, who gallantly gives Bonnie his arm so they can play movie stars arriving for the Oscars. Who was that singer he just read about who turned down a chance to be an Oscar presenter because she was newly out of rehab and her agent said, Sorry, she'd love to, but right now she doesn't do stairs well? Just thinking about it is like getting a hate letter from the parallel universe of ODing on downers and taking dives in public. Earlier this evening, Vincent spent a good fifteen minutes staring at a Vicodin tab, that familiar white bullet of safety and positivity, cradled in his palm. Then he curled his fingers around it and put it back into the bottle, then took it out again and slipped it into his pocket, from which he will not remove it except in an emergency situation.

Tightening his hold on Bonnie's arm, Vincent feels her shaky high heels vibrating up through her bones. It seems important not to let Bonnie know that he's never been to the museum. The folks in charge make it easy for him. Strategically stationed guards point them in the right direction and keep them from wandering around and helping themselves to the priceless art treasures. Vincent and Bonnie head for a stone wall that turns out to be an Egyptian tomb. They pass cases filled with sculpture, jewelry, fragments of broken pots.

"Have you been here before?" Bonnie says.

"Yes," lies Vincent. It annoys him that she assumes he hasn't.

Everyone else has been here a million times. The penguin couples streaming in have seen this stuff so often that not one person pauses to check out the hippos, lions, and jackals, the pharaohs and their queens striding into the afterlife with metal poles rammed up their butts, the bizarre dollhouses, the slave boat and garden scenes, the creepy altars for worshipping what look like giant Q-tips, the massive sarcophagi that suddenly seem like inviting places in which to curl up and take a snooze. Everyone hurries through, rushing to get to the party. For all the looking at art they're doing, they could be changing trains in the subway.

"Comfy, huh?" Vincent points to a painted sarcophagus. "Nap-time, right?"

Bonnie stops and faces Vincent and puts one hand on each of his shoulders. It's not something she would ordinarily do, but this is a special evening. A lot is riding on how generous these merrymakers feel by the end of the night. Passing guests glance at them, but Bonnie doesn't seem to care.

"Time out," she tells him. "Relax."

"Come on," says Vincent. "I'm totally together. I just have to do one thing tonight. You'll be doing a million things. Like you always do."

Bonnie's face just melts for him, as Vincent knew it would. Otis Redding was only partly right about trying a little tenderness. Vincent knows from all those years of dealing with his mom that what women really want is for you to notice how hard they're working.

They continue into the next room, where everything's super-sized: mega-pharaohs, giant body parts, monumental sphinxes.

Bonnie says, "Do you know the sphinx's riddle?"

"What's that?"

"What walks on four legs in the morning, two legs at noon, and three legs in the evening?"

"A man," says Vincent.

He wishes Bonnie weren't surprised. He doesn't know how he knows. He just does. He knew it when it was a *Jeopardy* clue, when he was staying at Raymond's. The thought of Raymond settles around him like a poisonous fog rising from the pharaoh's tomb. As always, he expects to see Raymond around the next corner. Which proves that Vincent's insane. It's unlikely that Raymond would have forked over hundreds of bucks to attend the World Brotherhood Watch benefit dinner. And yet there's a precedent for it. John Wilkes Booth—who, ARM claims, was a Jew—bought a theater ticket.

The roar of the party, coming out to meet them, reminds Vincent of the archers yelling in samurai films as the arrows wing out of the fortress. But this isn't a battle. They're letting down the drawbridge, pulling back the golden rope and cheering him into their castle. He's the VIP guest with a seat at the head table, the white knight who gets to stand up and toast the king.

Bonnie takes his arm as they wade into the crowd. Her grip registers halfway between a friendly squeeze and a headlock. Following Bonnie around the room is like some schizo square dance, kiss kiss, chat chat, say a few words, spin off to the next group. Bonnie knows everyone, or almost everyone. Not the peasants who read the *Times* and called up and bought one ticket, but the ones who sprung for whole tables, the ones who might give serious money. She has to, it's her job. It puts food not only in her kids' mouths but in the mouths of innocent children tortured by evil dictators.

Vincent moves when Bonnie does, then pauses, nods, smiles. Mumbles hello. No one can hear a word. There's a band, four guys in dashikis singing and hopping up and down as if the floor is a hot griddle. No one's listening to them, they're just jacking up the noise. It doesn't matter what you do in this room full of people pretending to be laughing and talking. Once Vincent figures that out, he can relax and check out his surroundings.

The party is being held on the vast stone patio of an Egyptian temple. It's like being outdoors, but better. No weather, perfect lighting. One side of the room is a glass wall through which the sparkly illuminated trees in the park outside seem no more real than the clay ones in those dollhouses for the dead. In front of him is a reflecting pool, its floor thickly sprinkled with coins, perhaps a hint to the guests that money is about to be dislodged from their pockets.

Watching Bonnie is like watching a slalom champ who knows exactly when to turn, when to coast, when to switch direction. A special hug for everyone with a purse or checkbook. Bonnie guides Vincent up onto the platform near the temple itself, where—thank you, Jesus!—the drinks and the food are set out on tables. Vincent helps himself to a postage stamp of rare roast beef on a cracker, and then, with a longing look at the vodka, picks up a glass of white wine. For support he fingers the Vicodin in the fold of his pocket.

He braces himself for the disapproving glance from Bonnie, who begged him not to drink until after his speech. But a glass of wine isn't *drinking*, and anyway, Bonnie seems to have forgotten him as she crosses the room to whisper into the ear of some important old fart. Sorry. Vincent can't follow her there. Let's take a peek at the sculpture.

Presiding over this end of the pool is a row of giant cat women carved from polished black granite. Vincent remembers a scene from the original *Cat People*: the shadow of a maddened feline stalks a woman in a deserted swimming pool. But despite her sternness, her grim unfocused stare, this cat goddess seems so kindly that Vincent wants to crawl into her lap. What is it about these statues that keeps making him want to curl up inside them?

Pressing his back against the wall, Vincent watches the crowd, waiting to feel uncomfortable because he doesn't know anyone. But in fact it's strangely soothing, like being at the beach, as if the sea of people were an actual sea. He tries to hear the crowd noise as the roar of the ocean, to feel it rushing over him like a salt wind on his face.

But wait. He *knows* that woman. Long black curls, short black dress. Cute body. He'd know if she worked in the office. Could she be a temp? Or someone from his old life? Now she spots him too, and smiles, and heads straight for him, which gives him a minute, two minutes at most, to shake out his memory banks.

The woman puts out her hand and says, "I'm Colette Martinez. From the *New York Times*. I interviewed you. Remember?"

"Right," says Vincent. "Lois Lane." It was Bonnie who called her that.

"What does that make *you?*" Lois has had a couple of drinks, a couple up on Vincent. "Superman?"

"You come here often?" Vincent says.

Colette laughs. "I get in free." The fact that, in this crowd of thousand-dollar-a-platers, neither of them have laid out a penny sets off a small electric charge between them.

"I saw what you wrote about us," Vincent says.

"Sorry," Colette says. "I fought for five hundred words. I had to cut it. Something else was happening that day—"

"Don't be sorry," says Vincent. "*Something* worked. Look around. The place is packed. Anyway, I wasn't that crazy about having my picture in the paper."

"Why not? Everyone always wants to be in the *Times*."

"Shy, I guess." Vincent's not in the mood to explain about Raymond wanting him dead.

Colette snags two glasses of wine off a waiter's tray, and, surprised to find his own glass empty, Vincent takes one from her. She's not going anywhere. She's given up mingling for Vincent. It's sexy, their leaning against the wall, side by side, as if they're watching a movie.

"Are you nervous?" Colette says.

"About what?"

"About giving a speech tonight."

Vincent does a body check: brain, heart, stomach. At the moment, not a flutter. Why *isn't* he more nervous? For one thing, he and Bonnie have figured out approximately what he's going to say. They agreed it might be better to delete the part about the rave, though he'll end with the feeling he had on the Ex, of loving everyone and everything, wanting to embrace all God's children. Naturally, he won't mention the Ex. And he'll explain that the light shone on him slowly, a little more each day, like a beam of winter sunlight crossing the floor. He can't recall if he or Bonnie came up with that beam of winter sun.

Working with Bonnie has certainly made him more confident than he'd felt walking into Brotherhood Watch that first day and spitting out that ridiculous tongue twister: I want to help you guys save guys like me from becoming guys like me. He's glad Bonnie doesn't seem to remember, glad she didn't ask him to say something like that tonight.

Another waiter swoops down on them, this time with a tray of food. Eggy mush in pie-crust cups. He and Colette each pop one.

"Micro-quiche," Colette says. "It's amazing you're not nervous. I mean, I don't imagine you get up and talk in front of crowds like this every night."

"And your point is?" Fuck her. Is she trying to *make* him nervous?

"Plus I wouldn't imagine that these are exactly your people," says Colette.

Double fuck her. "Actually, I wouldn't imagine they're *your* people either."

Colette smiles sweetly up at him. "My father is the former governor of Puerto Rico."

You wouldn't expect a statement like that to work like a sexual come-on. But it's funny, how the most unlikely phrase can suddenly make it clear that he and Miss Governor-of-Puerto-Rico's-daughter could work something out, if they wanted.

Except that now, from across the room, Vincent sees Bonnie searching for him. Her face has that naked, terrified look you see on mothers yelling for lost toddlers. Does she think he's gotten stage fright and skipped? Doesn't she know him better than that? Vincent lets her sweat a minute before he catches her eye and saves her.

Bonnie stands on tiptoe and waves. But as she comes closer and sees he's with Colette, her expression changes from relief to . . . what? Who knows what she's registering on her female antennae. If Bonnie were anyone else, Vincent would swear that she looked jealous.

∘⊱∘⊱∘⊱∘⊱

Bonnie can't find Vincent anywhere. She searches the party, avoiding eye contact with people she should be chatting up, ignoring the sympathetic or irritated expressions of strangers who sense her panic. It's how she felt when the boys were little and they'd wander off in the supermarket. She used to imagine the grisly scenarios—the voice on the PA system, driving home without them—in such detail that sometimes she'd burst into tears when she finally found Danny and Max in the breakfast-cereal aisle.

That first day Vincent showed up at Brotherhood Watch, Meyer warned her he might disappear. Since then, she's worked so hard, given so much of herself. Even so, if he vanishes now, it won't matter how much she's done. It will still be her fault. Vincent *has* to be here.

Her day has been tough enough. First the *New York* magazine photographer canceled, then changed his mind, and she'd had to double-check to make sure there were going to be a few semi-celebrities present and willing to pose with Meyer. Which is Roberta's job. Bonnie called twice to confirm with the city councilman's wife. Welcome to Fundraisingland. Is *this* what Meyer meant by kicking things up to a higher level? Besides which, she dreads going to the Met, where it requires an effort not to think about being there with her father.

She'd made herself stay focused on the Iranian cartoonist, released from jail *this morning*—who could ask for better timing?—and presently en route to Paris with his wife and children. Another life saved by Brotherhood Watch. It's the least Bonnie can do to make a couple of phone calls and now nearly faint because she can't find Vincent.

When she finally spots him over by the wall, she relaxes, then tenses again. Vincent's holding a wineglass. Bonnie asked him not to drink. He's talking to Colette Martinez, the *Times* journalist who wasted their time and wrote one dinky paragraph. Why isn't she out doing her job, working the crowd, reporting?

If Bonnie didn't know better, she'd think that they were flirting. The former skinhead, the Latina reporter, both reasonably attractive. They make a handsome couple. Why wouldn't Colette flirt with him? Because Bonnie hasn't. For Vincent to live with her and the boys has meant ignoring the fact that Bonnie is a woman and Vincent is a man. A fact he's probably never noticed. Why would he? Bonnie's a middle-aged divorced mother of two—half a lifetime beyond whatever Vincent and the young woman from the *Times* may, or may not, be involved in. It knocks the wind right out of her. Bonnie can hardly stand it.

But why is Bonnie tormenting herself? Forty-one isn't ancient. Every day, women older than she is marry and have kids. Anyway, Bonnie reminds herself, her annoyance has nothing to do with whatever's transpiring between Vincent and the reporter. It's what a coach might feel if he saw his star athlete chatting up some girl right before a game. A player needs to concentrate. Anything else is distraction.

In twenty minutes, half an hour, depending on how long people take to find their tables and how long Meyer speaks, Vincent will have to get up and tell this terrifying crowd how he was converted from ARM to Brotherhood Watch. Bonnie has spoken to groups of donors, at conferences and board meetings. But she'd find this one difficult. How brave Vincent was to agree.

She and Roberta decided to schedule the speeches during dinner, instead of at the more usual time—before dessert—on the chance that some guests might have another engagement. And also (Bonnie's secret reason) because she thought that Vincent might be a more persuasive speaker before he'd had a chance to loosen up and enjoy the evening. But why is she worried about Vincent? He should be worried about *her.* The last time someone drank too much, it was Bonnie, at Meyer's. Vincent *is* worried about her. She sensed it earlier this evening. How tenderly they have begun to monitor each other's substance intake.

Bonnie needs to get Vincent and Meyer and start them moving toward their table. So why should she find it humiliating to bear down on Vincent and Colette and break up their tête-à-tête, like some prudish chaperone prying apart a prom couple humping on the dance floor?

Colette is wearing a tiny black dress, a square yard of sexy perfection, sculptural in its stylish neatness and obscene in its suggestion of how rapidly it could be shed. What made Bonnie think that she could get away with the gown she wore to Danny's bar mitzvah, a clingy outfit that's bunched in unflattering creases across her spreading hips?

"Colette," she says. "How nice to see you. I loved your little piece in the *Times.*"

"Sorry about the littleness," Colette says. That she can afford to be gracious has something to do with the fact that she's standing close to Vincent, and Bonnie isn't.

Bonnie turns to Vincent. "Showtime!" she says, stiffly.

"Wish me luck," Vincent tells Colette.

"Break a leg," she says.

"See you later," Vincent tells her.

"Nice to see you," repeats Bonnie. She takes Vincent's arm. It's shockingly pleasurable to feel a male bicep beneath a tuxedo. She practically drags Vincent along as she sets off in search of Meyer.

Spotting Irene, Bonnie takes a roundabout path to avoid her. Irene will be all over them, staking her territorial claim to the young man whose change of heart has made him the star of the evening. He's her boy. She sat next to him once at her apartment.

Vincent lets Bonnie lead him. This is her world, her work. Moved by his faith in her, Bonnie takes a brief but heartfelt vow not to let him down.

He says, "Don't say I never did anything for the foundation. I sweet-talked that Rican chick from the *New York Times* for a good half hour and then you came over and blew all my hard work. *Little article. Great.*"

For a moment, Bonnie forgets about Meyer and stops cold, struck by the conspiratorial intimacy of what Vincent has just said, by her certainty that he's lying about what was happening between him and Colette, and by a sudden dread that he'll use a word like *Rican* in his speech. Only Bonnie hears those words now. It's because he trusts her.

"Let's find Meyer," says Bonnie.

Meyer is hidden deep in the crowd. Bonnie feels like a soldier hacking her way through enemy jungle. Last week, straightening Max's room—a rare occurrence, but the mess had gotten so bad she couldn't open Max's door—she'd found a waterlogged copy of *Soldier of Fortune*. How had it gotten into the house? Did Max borrow it from Vincent? Or had he gone out and bought it because she'd invited a Nazi home?

"There he is." Vincent rarely uses Meyer's name. He still doesn't know what to call him.

How typical of Meyer that, in this mob of important people, he's managed to steal a moment with Sol and Minna. It's wonderful that he's so real, so unimpressed by status. On the other hand, he could be doing more to help Bonnie shake loose some donations. Bonnie makes a point of having Vincent in tow, as a signal that she's come to collect Meyer as well.

No one's going for it. Minna shifts over to make room for Vincent and to exclude Bonnie. "Vincent, how lovely to see you. We can't wait to hear what you have to say this evening."

"Me, too," says Vincent. "I mean, I'm still trying to figure out what I'm going to say." He's swaggering, thinks Bonnie. Or at least she hopes so. Why didn't Bonnie insist that Vincent go over his speech, word by word? What possessed her to trust him when he said he didn't want to ruin it by overpreparing? Vincent said he could do it, and she'd believed him because the two of them have persuaded themselves and each other that he can just get up and *be* his reconstructed, authentic, decent self.

Even Meyer asked her to look over some notes. It was pretty much what she'd expected. The kindness of strangers. Forgive but not forget. Plus some new experiments: the moral bungee jump, and something about . . . faith cells? Bonnie's often wanted to warn him against repeating himself. Almost everyone in the room has heard his act before. Maybe that's why ticket sales were slow at first. But Meyer knows what he's doing. These are his people, his crowd. Vincent may seduce *New York Times* reporters, but Meyer makes miracles happen.

Sol asks Meyer, "Did you watch the evening news?"

"I was getting dressed," Meyer says. "What fresh horror did I miss?"

"The McVeigh execution," Minna pipes up.

"Was that today?" Meyer slaps his forehead so hard, Bonnie winces. "My God, how could I have missed it? What was I doing? Fastening my cufflinks? Bonnie, why didn't you tell me?"

Bonnie, why didn't you tell me? Bonnie's spent weeks trying to second-guess the dietary and social needs of five hundred people, and at the same time grooming Vincent, coaching him to appeal to the guests. Even now she's struggling to help Meyer and Vincent to their table . . . and Meyer's criticizing her for not making sure he watched the McVeigh execution?

How much can you ask from one person? But once again, Meyer's right. Bonnie should have set up a TV for the office staff, the way she sometimes does for broadcasts of critical government hearings.

"Man, how did I miss that?" There's grief in Vincent's voice.

"How *could* we?" Meyer asks Vincent.

How could Bonnie have been so shortsighted, concentrating on this dinner, which is only about money, donations, a budget, while a human being was being put to death today, in their very own country? But why was it up to Bonnie—out of everyone in the office—to remember that today was the day on which McVeigh was slated to die?

"I'm ashamed of us all." Meyer voices Bonnie's thoughts.

"Please. You were busy," says Sol.

"What did they say on the news?" Meyer asks.

"It was filthy," Sol says. "They spliced together interviews with all these journalists who'd watched it. One sound bite per talking head, one face flashing after another. One reporter said: He stopped breathing. Another said: His pulse quit. Another said: The end was peaceful. How the hell did *they* know how peaceful the end was?"

Minna says, "Sol, sweetheart, you've got to relax. The guy was responsible for the deaths of hundreds of innocent people. I'm not saying I support—"

"All right, enough," Meyer says. "Excuse me, Minna, Sol. Bonnie will never speak to me again if I don't go quietly."

"Go ahead," says Sol.

"Good luck," says Minna. "There'll be a brunch on the first Sunday after we get back from the Cape."

"Before that, I hope," says Meyer. And he and Bonnie and Vincent are gone.

"Do you have my notes?" asks Meyer.

"*You* do." Bonnie's sure she gave them to him, after she photocopied them, enlarged so he won't have to wear his glasses. Steering the two men through the crowd feels like taking her boys to the dentist. Bonnie finds Meyer and Vincent's place cards and gets them seated before she takes her seat beside the empty chair in which Larry Ticknor—the real estate magnate whose wife, Laura, is one of Brotherhood Watch's most generous supporters—will sit between Bonnie and Irene.

Roberta is the first to show up. She kisses Bonnie and Meyer, then does an awkward dodge in front of Vincent and winds up shaking his hand. Relations between them, always cool, got chillier when the *Times* piece ran small. Did Roberta blame *him?*

Roberta asks Bonnie, "Did the *Times* send anyone? I can't figure out who's here."

"Colette Martinez," says Bonnie.

"Too bad," says Roberta. "But what can you do? I guess it's become her story." It cheers Bonnie to be discussing Colette as a public relations issue instead of as a pretty girl who monopolized Vincent's attention.

Irene has found Laura and Larry Ticknor and is steering them over. The Ticknors are an attractive couple, approximately Bonnie's age, but so much richer that it's as if they're much older. Irene, Laura, and Larry are all wearing expensive, severe black suits. The three of them are fashion holograms, sculpturally snipped by the A-team of hairstylists and designers. Bonnie feels like a bag lady. But what she's wearing is not the point. The point is for Larry and Laura to fund more food drops and phone calls to Iran, and buy less Calvin Klein.

"Oh, Irene!" says Roberta. "You look fabulous!"

"Hello, Roberta," says Irene.

Roberta extends her hand halfway between Larry and Laura Ticknor. "I'm Roberta Dwyer. Publicity."

Larry shakes Roberta's hand. His wife blows off Roberta and looks around in the panic that Bonnie has often seen in the eyes of celebrities when they find themselves stranded in a crowd of unknowns and are suddenly terrified that some ordinary citizen is about to waste their precious time. How relieved they are to spot someone equally famous, or, failing that, someone who knows how famous they are and will treat them accordingly. For now, Laura will settle for Bonnie's relatively familiar face.

"Laura," says Bonnie. "Welcome."

Bonnie guides Laura around the table. First Meyer rises, then Vincent. Laura likes being placed between the two stars of the evening. Brotherhood Watch is her charity, and her annual donation is sort of a love-gift-slash-reparations-payment from the compulsively unfaithful Larry. Bonnie hopes that Laura will bring a lot of her philanthropic friends on board for this worthy cause that she was the first to "discover." Across the table, Larry sits down next to Irene with as much wriggly pleasure as if he were snuggling between her breasts, which—bared tonight by her low-cut suit—are remarkably firm and unblemished for a woman Irene's age.

The seating plan is a huge success. Everyone jumps right into the evening. Irene's chatting up Larry Ticknor with an expertise distilled from generations of Viennese flirtatiousness. Vincent's focused on Laura, using whatever magic he seems to have always had, or to have developed in the last few weeks, the charm that worked such wonders on Irene and Colette. Roberta Dwyer has no one to talk to, Bonnie notices with guilty satisfaction. Meyer is staring into the middle distance, probably—or so Bonnie hopes—going over his speech, which Vincent should also be doing, an even better use of his time right now than talking to Laura Ticknor.

Bonnie glances at Meyer, who flashes her his warmest smile. Meyer understands how hard she works, how much more she wishes she could do. That's why he has chosen her from this crowd of beautiful people, selected her to fix with that steady beam of gratitude and friendship. So much of this—the guests, the room, the food, all the countless details that will make the evening a failure or a success—is Bonnie's doing. And Meyer understands that. Getting paid to feel this way is more than Bonnie could ask for.

She almost wishes that Joel were here to see what she has accomplished. But he would find a way to spoil it. How she used to hate those summer fund-raisers for the Clairmont Museum, on the sweeping riverfront lawn of somebody's gorgeous mansion, attended by her rich neighbors who had come to show off their picture hats and filmy garden dresses—and without the slightest intention of donating money. Afterward, Joel would point out how she'd spent the afternoon futilely kissing morons' asses to get them to finance the purchase of bad nineteenth-century prints. The meanest part was that Joel knew he was saying what Bonnie thought. Joel was a cardiologist. What *he* did was important.

But no one, not even Joel, could say that the foundation's work doesn't matter. Bonnie helps make it possible. And Meyer Maslow knows that.

Her private communion with Meyer ends. His gaze returns to the ozone, but Bonnie knows that he is fully present, simultaneously lost in thought and exquisitely attentive. He will know when it's right for him to stand and walk to the podium and start speak-

ing, without fanfare or introduction. Having no introduction was
Meyer's idea. This crowd knows who he is. What could anyone say
about him that they haven't heard? It was also Meyer's idea to end
his speech by introducing Vincent. How humble of Meyer to volunteer to be the opening act instead of the main attraction.

Bonnie surrenders to the pleasure of the moment, which feels almost like that oddly relaxed interlude that comes when you're early
for a lunch date and are waiting for a friend. Let the crowd produce
those rising swells of anticipation, of false or real excitement punctu-
ated by laughter. Let the others decide which person, on which side,
to talk to and try to hear, and when to address the problem of the
mesclun salad. Bonnie hopes they eat their salad. She knows how
much it costs. She has the figures, broken down, on her desk at the
office.

At the edge of her peripheral vision, Bonnie sees Irene watching
Meyer.

Finally Meyer rises, and the room goes still. It's as if everyone
who has been pretending to converse and eat their greens has really
been focused on him. He walks up onstage and takes his place at
the podium between the stone pillars guarding the entrance to the
temple. In his elegant black tuxedo, he looks like a temple priest,
like a chiseled gleaming knife blade of purity and moral courage.
Electricity seems to pulse in shimmering circles around him.

The hush deepens as Meyer leans toward the mike.

"Thank you," says Meyer. "Thank you all for taking time from
your impossibly busy lives to vote with your presence, your body
and soul, for what Brotherhood Watch is doing.

"My friends, what can I tell you about us that you don't know?
Probably I should talk about the Iranian journalist, the crusading
cartoonist and the loving husband and father who just today—
today!—was freed from the jail in which he was imprisoned and tortured."

Meyer pauses for a round of applause.

"Freed, my friends, because of what Brotherhood Watch was able
to do on his behalf! In honor of this great event, we have decided to

award our Iranian brother Cambiz Khosthami—in absentia—the brand-new annual Laura Ticknor Prize for Courage in Journalism, which we are giving tonight for the very first time."

Meyer is a genius. The crowd is up on its feet. Meyer points out Laura Ticknor. The crowd turns toward her and claps harder. Laura puts her hand to her heart. Getting Laura to increase her support will be like taking candy from a baby.

Meyer waits for the applause to die down. "Tonight I make you a promise. Next year at this time, Cambiz Khosthami will be here with us to accept his award in person."

The room cheers this vision of a handsome Iranian with his beautiful wife and children, the whole family gratefully acknowledging the gift of nothing less than a man's life, which he owes the men and women applauding themselves and him. Bonnie stands and claps, too, but now she is fending off a faint pinprick of unease. Whose idea was the Laura Ticknor Prize? Did Meyer come up with it himself? Shouldn't Bonnie have been the first to know, or was she left out of the loop?

"Should I describe the shipments of medicines, the rivers of vaccines and antibiotics, that Brotherhood Watch has sent streaming around the world? The children's lives saved, the victims of genocide resettled? Or perhaps I should update you on our successful conferences, the important and moving dialogues between Palestinians and Israelis, Chechens and Russians, Bosnian Muslims and Serbs, the atmosphere of love and trust that we have been able to establish, and that has allowed representatives of these embattled groups to speak from their hearts and even to become friends?"

Meyer pauses and the crowd cheers for . . . what? A dream that almost seems possible over mesclun salad and good white wine. World peace and understanding. Who doesn't want that? And it's Bonnie who gets to spend her life to try and make it happen.

"Or maybe I should mention the summer programs for high school kids—"

Bonnie wishes he wouldn't mention that. Somebody in the crowd must know about last summer's pot bust.

"—programs that bring young people together with their first foreigner or even, in some cases, their first hyphenated American." The first hyphenated American? The crowd gasps. Where have these kids been living? On Mars? Somewhere in the . . . Midwest?

"These children spend two weeks together at a remote location and come away with a new understanding of their own feelings about *the other*, and more importantly, with the truth about who those others really are. The reason I don't need to tell you any more is that you may soon be able to see for yourselves. Tonight, it is my pleasure to announce that PBS has expressed some interest in funding a documentary about our annual Pride and Prejudice camp."

Annual Pride and Prejudice camp? Documentary? When did this happen? And what is "some interest"? Bonnie takes off her glasses, then puts them on again. Roberta is smiling, taking credit. Where was Bonnie while this was going on? Closeted with her neo-Nazi while Roberta was negotiating with a major network? Well, not exactly major. But PBS isn't *nothing*. Fine. Roberta's doing her job—at last! A film can only help Brotherhood Watch, provided, of course, that no one gets wind of their legal trouble and *60 Minutes* gets involved. What a story that would be. Teenage drug use at the high-minded foundation retreat. But if the film goes well and gets aired, Bonnie's job will be easier. Sure, I'd be happy to donate. I saw your group on TV.

"But—" Meyer pauses for effect. "Human rights cannot exist without human responsibilities. Human rights requires from each of us what Kierkegaard called the leap of faith, a leap as brave as jumping out of an airplane. A moral bungee jump."

The audience, not the bravest crowd in the world, adores this image of themselves. Moral bungee jumpers. Engaging in extreme sports. So what if their daring leaps involve their telephones and checkbooks? Supporting something like Brotherhood Watch is a gesture, a gamble. They're gambling on human goodness and the future of the race. The collective enthusiasm works like a dose of Viagra. The guests rise to their feet.

Bonnie looks at Vincent. Meyer's hypnotic speech has briefly mesmerized her into forgetting that Vincent is on next. Talk about a hard act to follow! What is Vincent supposed to do after Meyer's fireworks? It's possible that he could get up there and panic and start mumbling into his shirt. He could slip and say something racist. *Rican. Jap.* If Vincent blows it, he could undo some of the great work Meyer is accomplishing right now. The last thing they want the crowd wondering is how much money the foundation has wasted on some redneck's semi-successful moral reclamation.

Vincent's so focused on Meyer that he doesn't notice Bonnie looking at him. She's trying to be objective, searching for a trace of a smirk, of irony or disdain. But all she sees in Vincent's face is admiration and affection. He loves Meyer and the foundation as much as Bonnie does. Who could help it? And that love will guide Vincent through whatever he has to do and say. Vincent takes a sip of wine and a bite of salad without taking his eyes off Meyer.

"Each leap stretches us, like exercise. As our friends in science would say, it blasts new neural pathways. Just as they are proving that in childhood we form fat cells in which to store body fat, so our souls grow faith cells, repositories of trust and belief. It's one more reason to proceed, one heart at a time, man by man, woman by woman, child by child. Human being by human being. Another reason to stop blaming others and go out and do it ourselves—"

Meyer pauses, and the crowd applauds this do-it-yourself approach to saving the world. Meyer stops the applause with one hand. He's playing the room like an orchestra, shaping every note. "If I had to pick one word for what we do, for what we try to do, what we *want* to do . . . that one word would be—"another pause, everyone's guessing—"that one word would be . . . *change.* Spiritual and political change.

"The person I want to introduce now is a man who *has* changed. A prodigal son returned to the fold of love after wandering in the desert of prejudice and hate. To meet this young man is to understand that we cannot spend all our time preaching to the choir. He is the living embodiment of what we must do—reach those who don't think as we do, those who think in ways we may fear and despise. We must learn about them, they must learn about us. And we will all be transformed.

"Vincent Nolan is a living example of the human capacity to change from one kind of person into another. Within the last weeks I have had the privilege of seeing a man who has lived among the political descendants of those who killed my family and so wanted to kill *me* that I spent my childhood in hiding. And I have seen this man changed, as so few of *them* were changed. I've seen his eyes opened, his path diverted from the way of hate to the road of love. Ladies and gentlemen, new friends and old, let me present to you . . . Vincent Nolan!"

Each time the audience leaps to its feet, standing gets easier. Everyone's craning and twisting for a peep at Vincent, who rises along with the rest but seems otherwise unaware that the commotion is for him. His face has a distant, mournful look. . . .

Does Meyer mean Vincent to come join him? Bonnie can't tell, and Vincent doesn't seem to think so. The two men are communicating in a code she will never break. The audience sits down again, and Meyer forges ahead.

"During the short time that Vincent has been with Brotherhood Watch, he has changed from a member of the American Rights Movement, also known as the Aryan Resistance Movement, into a believer in our mission. Those of us who have always refused to accept the idea that some part of man is evil, that our behavior is predetermined, *hardwired*, those who refuse to believe that there is something genetic, some product of race or gender, that makes us good or bad, those of us who stubbornly hang on to the faith that men and women can be changed for the better . . . even *we* sometimes wonder if such change can really occur."

Meyer pauses to let this sink in. The crowd responds with gentle applause. They've wondered about this themselves. They would like nothing better than to hear that every sick bastard can turn into Mother Teresa.

"Our hope is that our new friend and colleague can work with us to design an outreach program to help us find and change other young men like himself. And now, my friends, the living proof. I give you . . . a changed man. Vincent Nolan."

As if to fortify himself, Vincent takes another quick bite of salad. He stops and gives Bonnie a slightly wild look, and then goes up to join Meyer.

Together on the podium, Meyer and Vincent embrace for as long as the flashbulbs keep popping, as long as it takes for every eye to water over this image of the elderly but still potent Holocaust survivor and the young white-power punk, changed by love and knowledge into dear friends who love one another.

Only now does Bonnie take a bite of salad, of baby greens drizzled with olive oil and balsamic. Something crunchy underneath. Bonnie peers under an arugula shard, refusing at first to believe the horrendous evidence of her senses. Then, half-rocketing out of her seat, she looks over at Vincent's plate. Unless there's been a miracle, Vincent has eaten nuts.

It's as if *she's* the allergic one. Her heart speeds up, her throat swells. What is she supposed to do now? Shut down the proceedings? Charge up to the podium and make sure Vincent's okay? Drag him off to a doctor? She would, if he were her child.

Bonnie told the caterers to be aware that many of the guests had allergies. And she should have warned Vincent to be extra careful, just in case. She should have gotten one of those syringes filled with what they prescribe for kids allergic to peanuts and bee stings. She should have carried it everywhere, but there never seemed to be any need. Vincent was always so conscious, and so—until now—was she. Until the worst possible moment, which is when and why it happened. This is no time to blame herself. The question is: What now?

Why not give it a minute or two? Maybe he didn't eat any nuts. Maybe they're not the kind he's allergic to. Given Vincent's past, and the strangely haphazard way he seems to have learned crucial facts about his own life, there's always a chance that he isn't really allergic at all. In any case, she's got to trust him. He'll stop if he's feeling ill. Maybe it happens slowly, slowly enough for him to give his speech. If anything seems even slightly off, she'll intervene, and that will be that.

Meanwhile, why endanger everything they've worked so hard to create? Of course, she won't let things get to the point at which Vincent's health may be at risk. None of this is worth that, not one penny of the money that Meyer and Vincent will bring in from this evening. She'll watch Vincent, and Vincent will signal her if something's wrong. He will know how bad it is.

Vincent knows how bad it is: about as bad as it can get. It's hard to think of much worse than chomping down on that second bite of salad and getting a mouthful of nuts seconds before he has to step up to the Egyptian temple and talk to five hundred strangers. Not just chewing but swallowing the poison he's masticated to help it disperse through his body. And why has this happened? Because Bonnie, Maslow, and their warped little crew have disabled his instincts. They've removed the batteries from his survival smoke alarm. From the standpoint of mind control, this is worse than anything that happened to him in ARM. They've disconnected the reflexes that normally would have made him spit the half-eaten nuts all over Irene and Laura Ticknor's black suits and hair helmets.

Maybe it won't be so bad. Maybe he's outgrown his allergies. He's read where that can happen. It's probably been fifteen years since his last attack. So let's see how this plays out. And hell, if he's going to get sick, he might as well do it in front of the maximum number of Jewish doctors. The combined brains and income in the room will get him to the ER and the epinephrine shot a whole lot faster than if he was on his own.

So this crowd has to *want* to save his life. Which gives Vincent a few minutes to convince them that they can't live without him. Besides which, he wants to do this. He wants to be the man. And he'll be damned before he lets some allergy make him blow his big chance.

The chance to do what, exactly? The chance to be the Brotherhood Watch flavor of the month? As soon as Maslow mentioned the Iranian who would be here next year to accept his award, Vincent knew his days were numbered. A year is all he's got before the new kid on the block rolls into town.

Then why take the risk? Because Maslow and Bonnie care about him? Because he wants their . . . love? Or could it be that Vincent has finally sold *himself* on that scam he came up with that first day? I want to help you guys save guys like me from becoming guys like me.

All the time Maslow's hugging him, Vincent's fighting the urge to spill his personal catastrophe into Maslow's ear. Look, I'm about to die up here. Man, you've got to save me. But Maslow could never hear him above the noise of the crowd, and anyway, Vincent would rather die than show the whole world what a wimp he is, crying to Daddy.

Maslow leaves. Vincent is on his own. How alone he feels! The first symptom of anaphylactic shock is a sense of impending doom. Goddamn right there's a sense of doom. Because you're dead, and you know it.

What would the Warrior do now? Identify the enemy. Vincent has been there. Done that. His enemy is salad. He stands between the pillars looking out at the crowd. He touches the stone on either side, the graffiti and the hieroglyphics. If only he were Samson and could pull this clam shack down. He feels a mild scratchiness in his throat, that first knock-knock of . . . fuck it. He'll go down screaming.

He leans into the microphone, wrestles the head from its stand. He's thinking: Elvis. He says in Elvis's honeyed tones, "Let me tell you how it happened."

That gets the room's attention: the promise of a story. Just like Maslow suggested. It's better than what they expected—five minutes of platitudes and two minutes of begging. The challenge is to wrap it up before his throat swells shut.

"It was early in the spring. I was living with my cousin." Vincent wishes he hadn't said that last word. But there's no way to tell this without it. "At the time, I belonged to a group that, I realize now, fed on the fears and insecurities of hard-luck schmos like myself."

The crowd laughs, a little uneasily. Do they think he's doing stand-up? Just because he called himself a schmo doesn't make him Woody fucking Allen.

"Sometimes, on weekends, my cousin"—Vincent can't say his name—"my cousin would take me on these field trips, little lessons to teach me who to hate and why I should hate them."

Just saying *hate* in this crowd creates a buzz. These people don't want to hear about anything but love. But if it weren't for hate they wouldn't be here, so hate should get some credit. And in fact, the word turns them on. It's hot. It's so taboo. No one they know would tell anyone why they should *hate* someone else.

"Not that he would admit that. He said it was all about *love*. You had to know who your enemies were before you could love your own race. We'd go to synagogues. We'd park outside till the Jews came out of services. My cousin would tell me to look at their cars. To count the Lexuses and Lincoln Navigators."

Vincent pauses and waits for the shudder. That's *their* cars he's talking about. And they're right to respond that way. Vincent's not making this up. Raymond used to do that. Vincent went along. After all, he was staying on Raymond's couch. He had to be polite. And now he's being punished. His nose is starting to feel stuffed up. Every second that passes is a second less to find that epinephrine shot.

"And so maybe six weeks ago, my cousin asked me to come for a ride in his truck." Vincent thinks of the pickup, still stashed in the city garage. Trusty old friend. He exercised it and paid its board just a few days ago. He might need it if Raymond shows up. *When* Raymond shows up. How cheated Raymond and his buddies will feel to learn that Vincent died at the benefit dinner before they got a chance to work him over. The sense of doom is deepening. His palms are beginning to itch.

The first time it happened, he was eight; they were living in some hippie ashram. He and his mom wound up in the Middletown ER after his mom grabbed him away from the honcho guru pervert who said that all that Vincent needed was a coffee enema and some fresh-squeezed carrot juice. For the first time ever, Vincent was glad to see a fully loaded hypodermic coming at him. He'd like to see one right about now. His chest is feeling tight.

"We drove out to the country, to these giant greenhouses in the middle of a field. My cousin parked his truck. He said, 'Look. A Korean owns all that.'"

Vincent lets this seep in. Besides, he needs a break.

"'Come on,' said my cousin. 'Check it out.' There was no one around. Light was streaming in through what looked like white parachute silk onto these tables covered with rows of boxes filled with earth, all perfectly neat and labeled. In each one was a tiny sprig, a green wisp of something being born."

Vincent's got the crowd now, and not a minute too soon. His pulse races, then slows again. He's getting that sinus headache.

"What I wish I could tell you is how beautiful it was in the early spring wind, the clear white light. Those rows of flats, the moist dark soil, those tiny shoots of green stretching for what seemed like acres. My cousin said, 'Some Korean . . .' And he used a word I won't repeat in this company." He feels the crowd's disappointment. All right. "Korean motherfucker." He waits for the shocked, orgasmic gasp. "But that's not what *I* was thinking. I was thinking that it didn't matter who *owned* all this beauty, just so long as it was there. I didn't care what race the guy was, what country he had come from. And I kept thinking that the whole scene was like watching a beam of winter sunlight cross the floor."

Where's Bonnie? Is she listening? Did she notice he got it right?

"Just then a Korean guy appears and asks what we want. He looks at me and my cousin. He knows who we are."

Vincent feels as if someone's pinching his nostrils. He's underwater, drowning. Hang in there. Just a few seconds more. He's almost got to the punch line.

"I smiled at the Korean guy. I told him he had a nice place. And I told my cousin, 'Let's go, man. Let's leave the guy in peace.'"

Peace. How sweet that word sounds, how desperately Nolan wants it. Who wouldn't want to see the lion lying down with the lamb, everyone friendly with everyone else, every kid with plenty to eat, no reason to get stressed or upset, no reason to get excited. World peace. What a concept. He can go for that. Though right at the moment, what he wants more than anything is a nap. Ten minutes, a nod-out, a brief trip to somewhere quiet where there's no crowd cheering and clapping.

He no longer cares that they're cheering for *him*, that he's pulled it off, he's done it. He wishes that they'd all just shut up and let him rest, let him slink off and find a place where there's oxygen he can breathe, where there's any air at all.

It's getting really tight in here. He can hear himself wheezing, but the sound seems to come from a distance. Someone else is choking. Meanwhile, he needs to shut his eyes and lie down in the nice warm sun. . . .

A delicious heaviness spreads throughout his body. This is better than falling asleep. This is better than coming. Only dimly curious now, he wonders if he is dying, and if the bright light he sees is the light at the end of the tunnel.

⚭⚭⚭

Meyer watches Vincent take deep breaths to support the long sentences of his description of the Korean greenhouse. Meyer no longer thinks: My golem. He thinks: My prodigal son. How honest and touching his story is, how deeply the crowd is moved by this simple expression of how a man can come to see the rightness and *goodness* of compassion and love. Meyer's proud of Vincent's grace, of his sincerity and authenticity. And proud of himself for not minding—for enjoying—the fact that Vincent is upstaging him, that his speech is surpassing Meyer's meditation on faith cells and bungee jumps.

This must be how parents feel, or are supposed to feel. But until now Meyer never understood how you could experience another person's triumph as sweeter than your own. Like Vincent, Meyer has come a long way in just a few weeks. He's transcended the petty jealousy he felt at Vincent's first press conference.

So maybe Meyer's not paying the right kind of attention. Or maybe it just starts slowly, a ragged catch in Vincent's voice, two syllables switched, a pause before a tough word. Then a barely perceptible skip, a slight alteration in rhythm.

Vincent could still ruin everything. What if he's drunk and starts slurring? What if he rambles on? Why didn't Meyer warn Bonnie to monitor him more closely? Because Bonnie is so defensive when anyone mentions Vincent. Millions in donations lost because Meyer didn't want to hurt Bonnie's feelings!

Still, no matter what happens, Meyer can't lose sight of who Vincent is. A guy who is really trying, who desperately wants to change. Sure, he wants to save his own skin. But that's human nature. And if skin-saving were his only motive, there's plenty he could be doing short of putting on a monkey suit and addressing hundreds of sleek New York sharks waiting for him to go under so they can start the feeding frenzy. Which is human nature, too, or anyway their nature. Vincent's under the gun here. Meyer needs to keep that in mind. If the guy takes an extra drink, they'll have to understand.

As the crowd begins to applaud, Vincent grabs the podium. His mouth goes slack. He turns his head. His eyelids flutter. It happens in slow motion. His slumping and falling takes forever. The microphone crashes to the ground. A woman screams. People rush to the front, surrounding Vincent, who disappears beneath the swarm of helpers and rubberneckers.

Someone cries, "Medical emergency! The man needs a doctor." Medical emergency? Meyer feels the first stirrings of the guilt that will later haunt him for having suspected that Vincent was drunk.

The circle of onlookers parts to let Meyer through. Vincent is lying on his back, in that rag-doll sprawl that awaits even the most dignified on the other side of consciousness. His face looks ashen. Is he dead? He can't be. What senseless pride Meyer used to take in having seen more dead bodies than anyone he knew. Not long ago he boasted to Sol about having seen a hanging. What sort of badge of honor was that? The fewer corpses you see, the better.

Crouching over Vincent, administering CPR, is Larry Ticknor himself. Their biggest donor—or so they hope—is kneeling beside Vincent with one hand under his neck, his mouth on Vincent's mouth. From a fund-raising standpoint, is this a blessing or a disaster? Meyer can't think about that now. All that matters is that Vincent survives. And now Meyer is really frightened.

Meyer closes his eyes and prays in a way that he hasn't for a long time. It's a prayer without words, without thought, more physical than cerebral. It's as if every cell in his body has lined up to pour all its energy into the hope that everything might still be all right, into willing this crisis to pass without tragedy or disaster. Whom is Meyer praying to? A God he takes for granted sometimes, but whom he remembers only now, when someone he cares about is lying sprawled on the floor. Meyer will give anything, anything he has, just to see Vincent wake up.

Meyer's moment of transport passes, leaving him slightly drained as he looks around to see if anything has changed in the brief interval during which the force of his prayer nearly lifted his soul from his body.

Larry Ticknor is still bent over Vincent. Larry knows what he's doing. Maybe that's how he got so rich—by being a proactive, take-charge guy. But surely that's a naive, old-country idea about wealth. Now what rich people do best is delegate responsibility. Pedro, would you mind administering CPR to that gentleman on the floor? Not just on the floor—onstage. In the Temple of Dendur, and in full sight of the crowd, still more of whom are gathering around Vincent's fallen body to get nearer the eye of the storm, to play out some ancient drama: the murder of Julius Caesar, the sudden death of a pharaoh.

A pale man in a suit pushes through the crowd, saying something Meyer can't hear, magic words that make people scatter. Is he a doctor, the house detective, a medical technician?

Someone says: He's the caterer. And he's talking to Bonnie, who's helping him reach Vincent. Bonnie sinks on her knees beside

Vincent. Her face is grim and determined. She's become Mother Courage.

The caterer rips open a yellow package and extracts a syringe and taps it with the panache of a junkie. Insulin? Is Vincent diabetic? How could Meyer not have known?

The caterer plunges the syringe through Vincent's tuxedo and into his leg.

Seconds pass. A minute.

Vincent's eyelids fly open, then close again.

Meyer hears a voice over his shoulder, muttering, "Idiots! The guy's allergic to nuts! Meyer, I thought you *knew* that. Remember the giant headache we had when he came to our house? Did he eat that salad? Who signed off on the menu? Was your staff asleep?"

Meyer reaches back and squeezes Irene's hand. He's not ready to turn around and look at her. He's still feeling wrung out.

"Well," Irene is saying, "by now the syringe is probably standard catering equipment. If you're going to serve nuts these days, you'd better pack the needle right along with the champagne glasses. It would be professional suicide not to."

Vincent is moaning and thrashing around. It's not at all like in the movies when someone blacks out and then bobs gently toward consciousness. As Vincent lies there, convulsing, surrounded by a crowd, the whole configuration reminds Meyer of that silly TV show with the beefy Australian guy wrestling crocodiles into submission.

Eventually, the twitching stops. Vincent opens his eyes again, and this time they stay open.

His first words are, "The salad."

"I know that," says Bonnie. "I know what happened. I'm so sorry. It's my fault."

Vincent smiles at Bonnie, who smiles back. Meyer wonders if Irene might be right about their being . . . involved. Well, why not? Let them find some comfort. Everybody's lonely. Who cares about Bonnie and Vincent's private life? All that counts is that he is breathing. Alive. Meyer's prayer has been answered.

Irene says, "Meyer, wake up! Elliot's here."

Well, naturally, here's Elliot, reducing Meyer's spiritual flights to the swill of liability law. Elliot, who, according to Irene, took an instant dislike to Vincent that night they came for dinner.

Meyer knows they need Elliot. In the litigious culture they live in, everyone is either liable, or suing everyone else. But still, Meyer can't stand him, or rather can't stand the world in which they need guys like him.

"Elliot," says Meyer. "What a night."

Elliot laughs, knowing and superior, as if he were the father and everyone else his idiot child. "Meyer, tell me . . . for such a brilliant man—what were you people *thinking*, signing up this loose cannon? Wait till his buddies from ARM show up. You think they enjoy the spectacle of some race traitor getting famous by publicly blowing them off? Rejecting everything those lunatics stand for? Wait till they find the office, or Bonnie's house. Have you got *that* kind of insurance?"

How could Elliot understand what Meyer has gone through, or what he believes? All Elliot knows is writing letters that make people want to throw up. That's what gives Elliot pleasure, going mano a mano with other pricks who enjoy the same thing. No wonder people tell lawyer jokes.

Meyer covers his eyes. Here he is, raising money for tolerance and love—and the next minute he's thinking of demeaning jokes about an entire profession. He can't even feel compassion for a decent person like Elliot, a guy who works for them for free.

Telescopic philanthropy. Maybe Elliot sent the chapter. *Bleak House* is about lawyers. Elliot might have read it.

"Is something the matter?" Elliot says.

"I was thinking," Meyer says. "God is our insurance."

"Do me a favor," Elliot says. "Spare me the cabalistic bullshit."

Waiting for his dad to drive up, Danny wonders if Mom went over the plan with Dad as often and as annoyingly as she did with him and Max. If they had a dollar for every time Mom said, "Your dad will be waiting, he'll pick you guys up at four-thirty sharp, in front of Max's school," he and Max could take car service into the city and save Dad the trouble. And after all that, Dad *isn't* waiting.

Dad is always late. That's what Danny tells himself to keep from thinking that he and Max will stand here all afternoon, and their father will never show up. Either Dad lost track of the time, or he was in a car wreck.

"He's always late." Max sounds as if he's trying not to think the same thing Danny's trying not to think. Also Max likes saying stuff about Dad—he's always late, he's this, he's that—as if Dad is still a part of their lives and Max still knows things about him. For the first year after the divorce, Dad was around a lot, but since he and Lorraine got their own apartment, he's been gently pulling away, as if he were a Band-Aid and they were a cut that might bleed. Gently? They never see him. He calls maybe twice a week. He and Mom take care of business. Max gets on the phone if Dad asks. Danny motions Mom to say he's not home.

But Danny loves his father. The proof is how relieved he is when Dad finally pulls up in front of the school. Danny couldn't stand the thought that something might have happened to him. Isn't that how you know you love someone? That's what Mom seems to think.

As always, Danny's feelings about his father are not just confused, but contradictory. At first, it's like a physical rush: he's just so glad to see him. Until he remembers why he shouldn't be glad. Being around his father has begun to make him feel as if he is a convict on death row and his dad is the court-assigned lawyer who strolls into his cell and says, "Let me tell you about *my* problems." Maybe Dad was always that way, and Danny never noticed. For a few months after Dad left, they made Danny see a therapist. Once Danny told the guy that he'd had a dream about being menaced by an evil six-foot teddy bear, and the therapist asked if the teddy bear reminded him of his father. Danny quit on the spot, not because the therapist was lame, which he was, but because the giant stuffed toy in his dream was exactly like Dad.

"Whoa," says Max. "Crocodile Hunter. When did Safari Man get that?"

Dad's grinning at them from behind the wheel of a brand-new silver Lincoln Navigator. If only he had shown up on time, when the other kids were around.

The Lincoln has got to be Lorraine's idea. His dad would never have gotten a vehicle like that on his own. But so what? Danny loves it. Max loves it. They race toward the car and collide at the passenger door. Max must be on drugs if he thinks he's riding up front. As Danny jumps in the front seat, Max grabs the door and stands there so Danny can't close it without slamming it on his brother's fingers.

"Let go," says Danny. "Move it." This is so humiliating. He's sixteen, a high school junior, and he and his brother are arguing like babies. They hardly ever fight anymore. So why are they doing it now? It's how they acted when they were younger, when Dad was around. It's as if they're reminding him what it was like. For all Dad knows, they never stopped fighting.

"You guys can trade off later," says Dad. Max gets in the backseat.

Dad reaches over and musses Danny's hair. Danny stiffens and pulls away and instantly regrets it. Actually, what he longs to do is something really embarrassing, like leaning his head on Dad's shoulder. His dad shrugs, then reaches back and squeezes Max's knee.

Danny sneaks a look at Dad. His face looks ruddy, sunburned. He's lost a little weight. Maybe Lorraine's got him working out. Maybe it's not true that she killed her last two husbands. The last time Danny saw them, all she talked about was Dad's upscale gym membership. How long ago was that? Right around Danny's birthday. Dad came over to help Mom with some tax stuff.

"You guys look great." Dad pauses, waiting for them to say that he looks great, too.

"You do, too," Max says.

"I've been going to the gym. Pretty regularly."

"That's great, Dad," says Max.

There's a silence. Then Dad asks, "So what's new with you guys?" It's not much, but it's more than Danny can remember Dad saying the whole time he lived with them. They mostly watched TV together. Now that Dad lives with Lorraine, he wants to have *conversations.*

Danny throws Max a keep-your-mouth-shut look in the rearview mirror, a look so extreme and threatening that even Max can't miss it.

Last night was one of those times when Danny was struck, all over again, by the weirdness of his domestic situation: Danny and Max and Mom and their roommate, the former Nazi. Mostly now it just seems normal. Danny and Vincent can even talk—for example, about the Hitler paper that Danny's supposedly writing, and which he *is* working on, if only in his head. But every so often it gets to him, and last night was one of those times, maybe because Mom and Vincent were so freaked about tonight's benefit dinner.

Last night's take-out Chinese meal had begun with the usual

annoying drama of Mom making sure that Buddha Wok, where they speak about ten words of English, knew to leave out all the stuff Vincent's allergic to. No one spoke during dinner until Danny couldn't help it, he had to see what would happen if he said, "Call me crazy, or is the tension thick in here?"

Mom said, "Danny, give me a break. Tomorrow's benefit is really important. Are you *sure* you guys don't want to come? We could find two more seats. Are you positive you'll be okay at your dad's? You've got my cellphone number. Call me anytime, no matter what. Dad will be waiting at four-thirty sharp in front of Max's school."

Later, Danny said to Max, "In case you haven't figured this out . . . I wouldn't mention Vincent to Dad."

Max never took his eyes off *America's Most Wanted.* Danny thought he hadn't heard. Then he said, "You don't need to tell me."

Even so, Danny is glad he did. It would drive him over the edge to hear Dad say what he says every time he's mad at Mom. "I thought your mother was a smart woman. That's why I married her in the first place." Lately, Danny's come to think that what Dad means is that he didn't marry Mom because she was pretty.

"What's new?" Dad repeats. "What's shakin'?"

If Mom used a word like *shakin'* they'd punish her with silence.

"Nothing," Danny says.

"Nothing. Really," Max says.

"How's school?" Dad asks.

"Good," says Danny.

"Good," says Max.

"Why does this conversation feel like déjà vu? You know what a déjà vu is, don't you guys?"

"Jesus Christ," says Danny.

Max says, "So what about you, Dad?"

"Lots of news," Dad says. "Lots of big news."

"Yeah? Like what?" Max is trying to sound casual.

"I promised Lorraine I'd wait so we could tell you together."

Danny checks the mirror again. Even Max is smart enough not

to like the sound of that. Dad and Lorraine are getting married. They're going to court to fight for custody. They're having a baby. They're moving to California. It can't be anything good.

As they merge onto the East Side Drive, some guy in a green BMW pulls around them, honking. Max gives him the finger, though the guy's already too far ahead to see.

"Cut it out, Max," says Dad. "I guess I was going too slow. The guy was pissed because I wasn't going fast enough." Danny thinks of Vincent describing the anger management class where he learned to do tricky stuff like deep breathing and counting to ten. Danny has never wanted to ask why Vincent had to take the class. Anyway, anger management was never Dad's problem. Dad's problem was too *much* anger management. *Not* getting angry, making excuses for drivers who cut him off in traffic, and then taking it out on his family, criticizing and nagging Danny and Max and Mom. It used to bother Danny, but now he feels oddly cheerful to be in the car with Dad acting so Dadlike.

They exit the highway, and before Danny's had a chance to see the city, to feel the chemical rush of the crowd, the cars and shops and taxis, Dad scoots into the basement garage of the corny highrise where he lives with Lorraine—that mammoth penile column rising forty stories over the East River, a whole building full of middle-aged doctors starting second families.

"Good afternoon, Dr. Kalen," says the garage attendant just before he speeds off in Dad's new Navigator.

"Good afternoon, Doctor," says the doorman, as does the elevator operator who whisks them up in the mirrored car.

Unlocking the door, Dad sings out, "We're ho-ome?" in a high, unnatural voice. *We're* home? It's not Danny and Max's home.

"Oh, hi, guys," calls Lorraine. "Be out in half a sec."

"Ho ho ho," Danny says to Max. But now that they're here, they can't afford to think *Lo the Ho*. In person, it's like there's another Lorraine they have to be polite to.

Danny whispers to Max, "Bite the bullet. It's only for one night."

Would Lorraine always dress in black if she knew that everyone

called her the Black Widow? Tonight she's squeezed into some kind
of cat suit and a man's tuxedo jacket. Danny has the feeling that
Lorraine's supposed to be hot for her age, but if so, it's lost on him.
She's trying to be super-chic, but she looks like she threw on some
tired crap that's been in her closet since the seventies. Shoulder
pads? Get *out* of here. Her hair sticks up in yellow spikes. A pair of
reading glasses hangs from a silver chain around her neck. Lorraine
and Dad are *not* having a baby. Lorraine's too old, and anyway, she
wouldn't appreciate the weight gain.

Lorraine grabs Danny's shoulders and kisses him on both
cheeks, then does the same thing to Max. All of Lorraine's gestures
have a pushy, in-your-face confidence that Danny finds obnoxious.
Even so, he can see how his dad might have been attracted to that
kind of person after all those years with Mom. Whenever Dad was
around, Mom acted ten times as wimpy and neurotic as she did
when he wasn't there.

"Boys," Lorraine says. "You look great. My God, you've gotten
so tall." Are they meant to say thank you? Max looks at Danny, who
lowers his eyes and shrugs.

"Well, then," says Lorraine. "Come in."

Max and Danny brush past her into the living room, from which
they can see practically all the way up to Clairmont. No matter how
often they've been here—and it hasn't been all that often—Danny
has never gotten used to how the view sucks the air from his lungs.

By the time Danny and Max turn around, their dad has left
them with Lorraine.

The dining room table is set for ten. Are Dad and Lorraine having
a party? The one night his kids are staying over, Dad invites all his
boring friends over so he and Lorraine won't be alone with the fact
that Dad once had a whole other family. Maybe the dinner's tomorrow
night, and Lorraine the compulsive maniac has set the table early.

Lorraine sees Danny looking and says, "We're celebrating."

"Cool," says Danny. "What?"

"I *told* your dad we could do it some other night. I thought you
guys might want to have some"—she raises her fingers and makes

little hooks around the words—"'quality time.' But he insisted, and you know, *I* think he wants to show you off to our friends. He's so proud of you both. Well! You guys probably want to relax. There's a TV in the guest room. You could chill in there till the fun starts."

The one night they get to spend with Dad, and Lorraine is telling them to go chill. But it's better than standing here trying to think of something to say to Lorraine. Mom would never have kids over and send them off to watch TV in the guest room. Where has Dad gone? And what *are* they celebrating?

In any case, chilling is the last thing Danny wants to do on his one night in the city.

"We were thinking we could go out for a while. Mom gave us money for sneakers." Around Lorraine, Danny makes sure to mention Mom as frequently as possible.

"What a terrific idea," Lorraine says. "And I'll bet your dad would love to go with you. In fact, I'll bet he'd love to *buy* you both sneakers. So just be patient, okay? Your father has some phone calls to make. To check up on all the patients he canceled so he could pick you guys up. I'll send him in to get you, all right? Give him a couple of minutes."

Danny weighs the possibility that he could let Dad pay for the sneakers and keep the money Mom gave them against the certainty that he'll feel compelled to give the money back to her. Then he measures the chance that it might be fun to go with Dad against the likelihood that it would be more fun to go alone with Max, and then against the odds that Dad will just forget about the whole thing. In the end, it's too confusing. All he can do is shrug.

"You guys know where the guest bathroom is, right?" Lorraine says.

Lo the Ho, thinks Danny. Black Widow.

"Sure," says Max. Lorraine hightails it to the kitchen. Isn't Stepmom supposed to ask if they're hungry or thirsty? Stopping by the bathroom, Danny blows his nose in one of Lorraine's monogrammed guest towels, then refolds it and puts it back on the rack.

By the time he reaches the guest room, Max is sprawled on the bottom bunk, on top of the *Star Wars* bedspread. Lorraine and Dad made a big deal of decorating the room especially for them with bunk beds and spaceship sheets.

"What kind of crap are you watching?" Danny asks, rhetorically. It's *Chandler*. A half dozen punk and Goth kids—tattooed, pierced, dyed hair—are sitting, hunched and snarling, in Chandler's leather chairs. Apparently, the poor bastards have pissed off their parents so bad that they've all been sent away to a scary Marine-style boot camp. The fat dude in the safari hat is the camp director, and the kids are alternately sobbing and abjectly kissing his ass.

"What I want to know," Chandler says, "is how you kids feel you've changed for the better." What a moron Chandler is! If those losers have changed for the better, Danny would hate to see what they used to be.

"I guess we're lucky," Max says.

"*I* might be," says Danny. "But *your* luck just ran out. That's my bed. Get up to the top bunk, or I'll get Mom and Dad to send you away to one of those boot camps."

"They would never," Max says.

"Dream on," says Danny. "I've been around them longer than you have. I know what they're capable of. Lorraine would send *your* ass there in a minute."

They keep waiting for Dad to come in and take them out to buy sneakers. Maybe Lorraine never told him. And it's weirdly depressing that they don't feel comfortable enough to go find him.

Chandler ends, and they watch a couple repeat episodes of *The Real World* that they've already seen. Danny and Max are arguing over what to watch next when Lorraine knocks on the door.

"Come have some Coke and potato chips," she sings out.

"That's okay," says Danny. "We're watching something."

But Max is already out the door, and Danny follows, just for a change of scene.

Coke and potato chips turns out to be Lorraine's lying code phrase for a house full of grown-ups sipping drinks, admiring the view, making boring conversation. Danny and Max stick together and edge into the living room like Top Cops busting a crack house.

"Danny," shouts Dad. "Max. Hey, guys! Come in and say hello."

With his arms around their shoulders, Dad introduces them to a dozen strangers. At least Dad had the decency to acquire brand-new friends to match his brand-new life. It would be even worse if these were people Danny knew from before. The friend they used to see most was his Dad's partner Jeffrey. Now Jeffrey's dead. Lorraine killed him. And Dad is with Lorraine.

Some of these new friends look as if they never knew that Dad *had* kids, but are trying to pretend that they knew, or maybe that they knew and forgot. Danny shakes their hands only when it can't be avoided.

"Everybody sit down," Lorraine says. "Believe it or not, I did place cards!"

"How ambitious!" somebody says.

Danny would rather stand all night than poke around searching for his name with everybody watching. He waits till everyone sits, then takes his seat across from Max with Dad between them at the end of the table. They're in the guest-of-honor chairs, so maybe it's true about Dad being proud of them. Then again, maybe Dad feels guilty about how rarely he sees them. Or maybe Lorraine wanted to put them the maximum distance from her.

Danny decides to go with the "Dad is proud" explanation. Despite himself, he's flattered, so that it takes him a while to notice that Dad isn't talking to him or Max, but leaning around to exchange hospital gossip with a bald, fat doctor. This one got a substantial raise, that one's being sued, that one's screwing the ER nurse. Hello-o? Has Dad forgotten that Danny and Max are here?

What would Vincent do in this situation? What is Danny looking for? Etiquette tips from a Nazi? Weirdly, thinking of Vincent makes Danny feel more in control. He likes it that he and his mom and brother are living with a guy who would probably scare the shit out of Dad and Lorraine and their friends. If Vincent were in this situation, he would probably do exactly what Danny's doing: sitting quietly, being polite, trying not to be noticed.

Lorraine taps her wineglass with a spoon.

"People!" she says. "People? I'd like you to meet Consuela. She'll be our server tonight."

Consuela isn't their server! Danny and Max have been here when she's come to clean the apartment. But if Dad's new friends have never met Danny and Max, fat chance they know Consuela.

The guests applaud Consuela, embarrassing her and themselves. Though maybe what they're applauding is the platter she's carrying and the gross slab of meat.

Dad's fat, bald friend says, "It takes balls to serve red meat these days."

"That's Lorraine for you," Dad says proudly.

Consuela circles the table, stopping at each guest and trying not to seem impatient with the ones who have trouble serving themselves. Danny's dreading his turn. It's like playing baseball and coming up to bat. But he concentrates, and it's not too bad. Home run is a thick slice of roast beef on his plate and no stains on the tablecloth.

At last Consuela reaches Dad, who's telling his friend a story. Apparently, the surgical floor was in a tizzy because the relatives of a recently diseased patient got hold of the patient's chart and were asking about every test and pill and procedure during his three months on life support.

"So they get to the page where the resident has written GORK in big block letters." About half of the guests laugh knowingly. "That's hospital-speak for God Only Knows," Dad explains to Danny and Max.

"God Only *Really* Knows," his fat friend corrects him. Danny hates this story.

"Right," says Dad. "God Only Really Knows." Meanwhile Consuela's still standing there. How could Dad not notice?

"And the family's asking what that means, and I say, off the top of my head, 'Oh, it's short for Gravity Oxygen Reduced Potassium.'"

The same guests who knew what it meant in the first place burst out laughing, while some of the others—Danny included—are beginning to stare at Consuela so maybe Dad will get the hint.

"Joel, dear," says Lorraine. "Do help out Consuela, won't you?"

Dad turns and nearly crashes into the platter. "Oh, I'm so sorry," he tells Consuela. He helps himself to a million pounds of meat, then looks down the table at Lorraine.

"Lorraine humanizes me," he says.

Max makes the classic gagging sign, so subtly that only Danny sees.

They're up to the dessert course—some kind of molded pink pudding that tastes like watermelon with chocolate chips—when Lorraine clinks her glass again.

"Hey, everyone?" she says. "People? Joel and I have an announcement."

Danny looks at Max. This is what they've been afraid of.

"Joel and I are getting married," says Lorraine. Everybody cheers and whistles as if they all thought marriage was the greatest thing on earth, as if Danny and Max weren't living proof of how often it doesn't work out.

"In August. But wait!" Lorraine holds up her hand. "That's not all."

She pauses and grins at Dad, who grins, like an idiot, back.

"Joel and I are adopting. A little baby from Bulgaria! A darling girl named Nina. Ten months old, an orphan, no health problems that we know of."

"That we *know* of," says Dad.

Lorraine raises her penciled-on eyebrows. "I would have shown you all the videotape we got from the agency. But it seemed a little awkward. So I got a great idea. I've e-mailed everyone her picture. Baby Nina will be on your computers by the time you get home!"

Everybody asks at once: How does it work, what needs to be done, when will the baby arrive?

"We're having her FedExed," says Dad.

Under the laughter, Max hisses to Danny, "A Bulgarian?"

"Whatever," Danny says.

"A *Bulgarian?*" repeats Max.

"What's the difference?" says Danny. "Retard."

Now it's Dad's turn to clink his glass. "And the best news of all," he says, "is that Lorraine's writing a book about the adoption. So we can write the whole thing off as a business expense."

Everyone laughs again, nervously. Dad's joke has fallen flat. His jokes always did. They used to tease him about it. Once more, Max and Danny exchange looks. These people don't know Dad. Still, it's not the smartest thing to say that the new Bulgarian baby is a tax write-off. Danny wonders if Dad ever says that about him and Max. How much child support does Dad pay? Among the things Danny knows his parents learned in counseling was not to complain, in front of them, about how the other spouse handles money.

"Jesus, Joel," says Lorraine.

"Joking," says Dad. "I was joking. Where's your sense of humor?"

"A tax-deductible baby," Lorraine asks the guests. "Is that supposed to be funny?"

Strangely, everyone laughs harder. Which must be the right thing to do, because it defuses the tension between Dad and Lorraine. They're all relieved to turn back to Lorraine and resume asking questions and not listening to the the the answers. Dad says to his bald friend, "It's basically Lorraine's idea. I mean, I've already got kids." And he wraps both arms around the back of Max and Danny's chairs.

The friend says, "I assume that you and Lorraine have been trying to have your own." Are Danny and Max invisible? Do these guys really want to talk about *trying* to have kids around the kids the guy already has? "No one wants to admit it, but thirty-four's the cut-off. After that the odds gets tougher."

Dad says, "It's been hard on Lorraine." And now Danny understands why his dad is so proud, why he's making such a big deal of having fathered two kids. He wants to make it clear that whatever fertility problem they've been having—whatever glitch has forced them to go to Bulgaria to buy a kid—is not his fault. It's not that he's proud of Danny and Max. He's proud of himself. Of his sperm count.

After that, Danny zones out. He knows he's free to absent himself just as long as he physically sits there. More talk, more stupid laughter, then everybody gets up to go home. A few women kiss Danny. They've gotten to be such good friends that shaking hands isn't enough. Max stays at the table: a clever way to keep from having to kiss anyone.

Danny's thinking how brilliant Max is for figuring this out when suddenly he realizes that Max is crying. Fat tears wobble down his brother's cheeks. Dad and Lorraine are standing at the front door. See you soon. You're welcome. Exchanging that one last banality while Max is sobbing his eyes out.

Danny puts his arm around him. "Hey, man, what's the matter?"

Max's mumble is unintelligible.

"I can't understand what you're saying!" Danny is instantly frantic. He needs to hear what's bothering Max before Dad and Lorraine come in and make everything worse.

Max takes a rattling breath and tries again. This time, Danny makes out two words: *Bulgaria. Dracula.*

It would be hilarious if it weren't so sad. Max is totally freaked out about their new vampire baby sister.

"No, man," Danny says gently, trying not to sound impatient, trying not to lecture him the way he normally would. "That's Transylvania. This is Bulgaria. Different country completely."

That should solve Max's problem. But of course, it doesn't. Max starts crying again, pausing every so often to take heavy liquid gulps. Because Max's problem isn't Dracula, it isn't even Baby Nina. Naturally, Max and Danny understand that the baby is bad news. Dad will have even less room and time for them than he does now, especially when he figures out that the kid is more than a tax deduction. Does the baby get the guest room? The *Star Wars* sheets? Where will Danny and Max sleep?

But even that, bad as it is, isn't what's troubling Max. He's crying about what their lives were and what their lives are now, and how much worse everything is, how they've completely lost Dad. They can hardly remember before the divorce. What's bothering Max is that their old life will never come back again, and there's no way they can change that. They keep wanting to see Dad, but when they do, he's not the guy they imagined.

Danny's nearly bawling too by the time Dad and Lorraine return. He can't believe how long it takes them to notice that something's wrong with Max. But why should Danny be surprised? They know what's important. The farty self-congratulation. *That was such a nice party. I thought so. Didn't you, darling? Everybody was so happy for us. Everybody enjoyed it.*

Finally, Dad says, "Max! Hey, guy? What's up?"

Max has lost the power of speech. Tears keep welling up. His silence and total . . . *limpness* make it scarier, less like watching someone cry than like watching someone bleed. What if he never stops crying? Nobody cries forever. It's like hiccuping, when you think it might go on and on.

Just as Danny predicted, Dad and Lorraine make it worse. They're all over Max. It's like a scene from *ER*, the crack team of doctors and nurses flinging themselves on the gurney. Sir, where does it hurt? Can you tell us what's wrong? Dad could probably think of a dozen reasons without even trying, starting with the new marriage and the Bulgarian baby. Dad is a cardiologist. Max's heart is broken.

Max stops crying, then starts again. After a while, Lorraine says, "Joel, darling. Isn't there anything you could give the poor child? Something to calm him down. You can't just let the kid suffer."

Dad says, "Excuse me, but I'm not drugging my kid just because you're sick of hearing him cry."

"It's not *me*," says Lorraine. "Look at him."

"He'll be okay," says Dad. "Give him a chance. It's been a stressful time for everyone."

"What's been stressful?" says Lorraine. "If this has been so stressful for you, we can call it all off. The wedding, the adoption. I wouldn't want to make your life *stressful*."

A volley of sobs from Max ends the conversation. For Max, this is way out of control. Kids wind up in mental hospitals for less. Danny imagines visiting his little brother in a middle-school version of *One Flew over the Cuckoo's Nest*. In an institutional room, smelling of sour milk, Max is playing checkers with some elderly zombie.

"I'm calling Mom," says Danny. But when has their mother ever been helpful in a crunch? Though sometimes, when someone in the family was upset, Mom would get so hysterical that whoever had been crying or fighting stopped cold and watched Mom spin out. *That* always seemed to help. "I can reach her on her cell-phone."

"I don't know if that's a good idea," says Dad.

"I don't know, either," says Lorraine. "You know how she worries about you guys."

That settles it. Danny's calling, just to let Lorraine know he's on to her. She doesn't care about Max, and certainly not about how much Mom worries. At least Mom is a good person, working to make the world a better place. And what does Lorraine do? Buys a baby so she can write a book and make a ton of money.

"Call her," says Max. "Please."

"Use the phone in the kitchen," Lorraine says. "It's mobile. Bring it in here."

Danny goes into the kitchen and dials. The phone rings twice, three times. Probably they're at the dinner, someone's giving a speech, his mom's got the phone turned off. On the fourth ring she picks up.

"Hello?" she says. "Danny! What's wrong?" For a moment Danny can't decide whether he's happy to hear her voice or annoyed because she's jumped to the conclusion that something's wrong. Maybe he's just calling to say hello. Hi, how's the dinner going?

"Max is crying," says Danny.

"Oh, my God, is he hurt?"

"No, but he's been crying for sort of a long time."

"But he's not hurt?"

"No, Mom, he's not hurt."

"How long is 'sort of long'?" says Mom.

"Fifteen minutes."

"Fifteen minutes? Max has been crying for *fifteen minutes?* What did Dad say to him? Did Lorraine hurt his feelings?"

"It wasn't Dad. Or Lorraine. Exactly."

"Did you and Max have a fight?"

"No, nothing like that. I think he's sad or something."

"Oh, dear God," says Mom.

Danny's walking into the living room, bringing Max and Mom closer. Bringing him Mom. Danny hears sounds in the background behind his mother. Police sirens, crackly announcements over loudspeakers. It doesn't sound like a benefit dinner.

"Where *are* you?" Danny asks.

"Nowhere special."

"Nowhere special? What's all that noise in the background? Where *are* you?"

"In the emergency room. But don't worry. Everything's fine."

"What the fuck? How fine could you be if you're in the emergency room? Mom, are you okay?"

"Language," says Mom. "Vincent had an allergy attack. In the middle of his speech. I guess he'd eaten nuts. Obviously, my fault. I wasn't paying attention. But a lot was going on—"

"Seriously?" says Danny.

"Can you believe it? Is that insane, or what?"

"Insane," says Danny. "Way insane."

"What a night," says Bonnie.

Danny smiles. There's something about his mom's tone that reminds him of their best times together, the way his mom sometimes acts as if everything is a ridiculous joke they're sharing. Just the two of them. Then Dad catches Danny's eye and melts the smile off his face. Danny makes himself focus. In the emergency room?

"Is he okay?" says Danny. Now Dad's really giving him major eyeball. Even Max has stopped crying and is listening in. How bad could Max's crying fit have been if he can turn it off like that? Danny feels stupid for having called Mom, but it's too late. Mom's talking about how great Vincent was, what a hero, how he kept going and finished his speech even though he could have died.

"So is he okay?" repeats Danny.

"Is *who* okay?" says Dad. Danny decides to ignore him.

Right on cue, Max starts bawling again, loud enough so Mom can hear.

"Fine. Vincent's fine," says Mom. "Let me talk to Max." Danny passes the phone to his brother, who sighs and takes it as if he's doing them a favor.

Is Mom asking Max what his problem is? *Please* don't let him bring up the marriage and the Bulgarian baby! Max is listening, still sniffling, but no longer looking so bug-eyed and wild.

"Where is she?" Dad asks Danny.

Danny wishes he could tell him. Or to be more exact, he wishes that his dad were someone whom he *could* tell. She's in the emergency room with our Nazi roommate. How great it would feel to tell that other, imaginary father about Vincent staying with them, and about the strangest thing, which is that Danny is starting to *like* him. Danny can talk to Vincent. As opposed to Dad.

"On her way home," Danny says.

"Car service, I hope?" Dad says. "She's such a lousy driver."

"Now, now," says Lorraine.

"Yeah. Car service," Danny says.

Max is handing the phone to him.

"Danny?" says Mom. "Get Max to a quiet room. Take off his shoes. Let him lie down. Sit next to him. Stroke his forehead. Is there a TV? Let him watch TV. I'm depending on you, okay?"

"I think I can do that," Danny says. "Not the forehead part."

"Danny, I love you so much," Mom says.

"I love you too, Mom," he says.

"Call me in ten minutes," says Mom.

"No," Danny says. "There's no point, Mom."

"Okay . . . but if you need to. Call me, Danny. Promise?"

"I promise," Danny says. And somehow they get through their good-byes without too many more warnings or interrogations.

"What did your mother say?" asks Dad.

Danny repeats Mom's directions.

"Brilliant." Is Dad relieved or sarcastic? Both. Dad likes it when anyone has a plan, even if it's Mom. It's strange that Mom should suddenly be the take-charge one. She must be like that at work. She raises all that money. Lorraine seems to have lots of plans. All Dad has to do is agree.

Danny hustles Max into the guest room, puts him on the lower bunk bed, and takes off his shoes. "Man," he says. "Your feet stink." Then says, "Guess where Mom was."

"Where? The dinner, right?"

"The emergency room."

That shocks Max out of his crybaby mood. "What's wrong? Is Mom okay?"

"She's fine," says Danny. "It's Vincent. He had some kind of allergy attack, some peanut thing, right in the middle of dinner."

Max blinks and sits up, and Danny has the pleasure of watching his brother's bright, crisp expression neaten up the blurry mess of his meltdown.

"Is Vincent okay?" Max says.

"Mom says he's fine," answers Danny. "He finished his speech even though he was practically dying."

"In the middle of the dinner?" Max actually smiles. "No way. That is *awesome*."

Tⁿᴇ ᴍɪɴᴜᴛᴇ Bᴏɴɴɪᴇ sᴘᴏᴛs Elliot Green among the on-lookers watching Vincent regain consciousness in her arms, she knows she can count on a visit to the emer-gency room. For liability reasons. Bonnie wonders what Elliot is whispering to Meyer. Could he be suggesting that Vincent is going to sue them?

Meyer comes over to Bonnie and says, "Let's take Vincent to Lenox Hill. Elliot thinks it's a good idea."

"Fine," says Bonnie. In fact, she's relieved. She wants a nice young intern to promise that some delayed reaction won't kick in eight hours from now—in *her* house—and kill Vincent in his sleep.

Vincent gingerly sits up. Careful, everyone move back, give the guy some air. Bonnie could, in theory, get off the floor. But whatever message her brain is trying to send to her feet is returning unan-swered. Maybe her legs have fallen asleep, maybe she's still wobbly. Maybe she was even more scared than she knew. For a moment she thinks *she* might pass out and really make everyone's evening.

There's no question but that the Ticknors' car will lead the shiny black convoy that streaks away from the museum, diagonals across Fifth Avenue, and veers east toward the hospital. Larry won't hear of anything else. The hero who gave Vincent mouth to mouth is not about to walk out at intermission.

Laura Ticknor rides up front with the driver, and Larry gets in back, where he and Bonnie sandwich Vincent between them. Bonnie's trying not to think about what all this might mean for the foundation. The only thing that counts is that Vincent is okay. And yet she can't help noting that the Ticknors' hands-on involvement augurs well for the future. How could they *not* support an organization after they've saved its poster boy's life?

"Don't I get dessert?" Vincent says. Everyone chuckles madly.

"Forget it," says Bonnie. "The way things have been going tonight, it's probably pecan pie."

"I'm sorry," says Vincent. "I fucked up."

The Ticknors will have to understand that Vincent wouldn't be saying *fuck* if he hadn't just passed out. Among the brain cells he must have lost are the ones that modulate self-presentation. At first, Bonnie mistook Vincent's adaptable chameleon quality for sneakiness, but that was before she realized that he simply wants things to go well. As she does. Anyway, why should Bonnie care if Vincent says *fuck* around the Ticknors?

"The caterers fucked up," says Larry. "That's who fucked up."

Finally, Bonnie gets it. Vincent's a movie star. Larry Ticknor is trying to speak the star's own language. Vincent's not just some white-supremacist creep, not just some upstate loser. He's a serious guy who nearly died in order to finish his speech. How much more could he have done to prove the strength of his convictions, the sincerity of his conversion? It was brave in every way, and Larry Ticknor knows that.

"It's my fault," Bonnie says. "I should have double-checked the menu. I'm sure I told the caterers, but—"

"Turn left," Laura tells the driver.

"Got it," the driver says.

"Oh, why am I telling *you*, Enrique? We've done this route a million times." Laura turns to explain to Vincent and Bonnie. "Our son is extremely accident-prone. It's part of the ADD."

"How old are your kids?" says Bonnie.

"Jake is thirteen, almost fourteen," says Laura. "And Brooklyn is six. Do you have children?"

"Two boys," Bonnie says. "Twelve and sixteen." She and Laura Ticknor are bonding over their children! The boys she's left with their self-centered, insensitive father who can be depended on to hurt their feelings, however accidentally. Not to mention Black Widow Lorraine. Bonnie has abandoned her kids so she can pimp them to Laura Ticknor.

"Bonnie's got great kids," Vincent says. So he *hasn't* damaged his brain. Or at least he can still use the part that knows how impressed Laura will be that he's not only noticed Bonnie's kids but, after all he's been through tonight, is being nice about them. How surprising that, as a male presence, Vincent has turned out to be so much more useful than Joel. Every time Joel helped the kids with their homework, it ended with shouting and tears. But Vincent has told her that he had a talk with Danny about a paper he's writing for school. A paper about Hitler. You'd think Danny would have had enough Hitler, first with Meyer and now Vincent. At least Bonnie's kids know who Hitler was, as opposed to those lame-brain high school students who, she read in a recent survey, think that the Holocaust is some kind of Jewish holiday.

They stop in front of the ER entrance, and within seconds Meyer's car screeches up to the curb. Back at the museum they'd done some triage to keep the delegation manageable. Roberta Dwyer and Elliot Green were dissuaded from tagging along. As is, they have enough people to fill a small waiting room.

Larry Ticknor isn't embarrassed by the size of the entourage. Quite the opposite, actually. He pauses and waits for his posse to collect and provide the wind in his sails as he grabs Vincent's elbow and swoops through the sliding doors.

The whole scene comes at Bonnie too fast for her to register more than a few quick impressions. The waiting area's not terribly crowded. No one seems badly hurt. Here and there, someone's pressing a neon-blue ice pack to some body part.

The population is more diverse than Bonnie would have expected. An African woman in a batik dress and a matching turban is breast-feeding her baby, while, a few seats away, an Asian family huddles for a whispered conference. The young man at the admissions desk wears a white coat and tie, wire-rimmed glasses, and a set of dreadlocks that seem calculated to stay just within the limits of a hospital dress code. Bonnie wonders what Vincent thinks about finding himself in this multiculti health-care situation.

Their group forms a protective squadron flanking Larry and Vincent as Larry leans across the desk and says, "I'm Larry Ticknor. And this is my friend Vincent Nolan. Vincent had an allergic episode while speaking at the Brotherhood Watch benefit dinner. And we'd feel a lot more comfortable if a doctor could take a look."

The reception clerk appraises Vincent, then takes off his glasses and rubs the bridge of his nose. How difficult it must be to work out here on the front line, deciding, hour after hour, precisely how much trouble each new arrival is in. Not much, it seems, in Vincent's case, or anyway not enough to disrupt the smoothness with which the clerk hands Larry a clipboard and says, "Fill these out, okay?"

Larry fill these out? Horrified, Larry looks at his friends. It's one thing to give CPR, to swap spits with a former Nazi, but it's quite another to be asked to fill out a questionnaire. He has assistants—an entire staff—paid to deal with crap like this!

"I'm Larry Ticknor," he repeats. Is this not ringing a *bell?* Doesn't the kid understand that the Ticknors have generously rewarded the hospital for their competence and efficiency during their son Jake's numerous ER visits?

"Of course, Mr. Ticknor," says the clerk, without a hint of impatience, without a trace of *I don't care who you are.* Well, maybe just the faintest trace. "But somebody needs to fill out the form. That's where we generally start from."

Bonnie was wrong. The kid is steamed. That *generally* is a tip-off.

Laura says, "Let it go, Larry. This might be one of those times when it's better not to throw your weight around and just pretend to be a normal civilian."

"Fine," says Larry. "Whatever. You field this one, Laura." He passes the clipboard to Laura, who hands it on to Bonnie. ER hot potato. Fishing around for her pen, Bonnie says, "Why doesn't everybody sit down?"

"There's a pen attached right there." The clerk is thrilled that he's going to be dealing with Bonnie instead of Larry or Laura.

Larry shepherds the others to an empty row, in which they arrange themselves facing the desk. Vincent's saved the seat beside him for Bonnie, a gesture that pleases her until she recalls: she's got to sit next to him. She's filling out his forms. Address, phone number, date of birth. It should be easy, but she's distracted by the hospital noises, bells, voices on the PA, sirens.

"Health insurance?" she asks, without hope.

"I doubt it," Vincent says. "Was I covered at the tire place? That wouldn't be good anymore, anyhow. It's been a while. I don't remember."

Of course he doesn't have health insurance. Bonnie should have thought of that weeks ago and looked into the Brotherhood Watch plan, which covers her and the kids. How much Bonnie takes for granted! She wonders, as she so often does: How do people manage? People like Vincent. For all she knows, one ER visit could cost hundreds of dollars. Thousands. If they're willing to see him at all unless he has insurance. Isn't there a law that says that the ER has to accept you? Bonnie takes out her wallet and finds the card from the foundation's health plan. She brings the clerk the forms, together with her card.

"He's on this same plan," she says. "He hasn't got his card with him."

The clerk types the information into the computer. Bonnie's heart is racing.

"Sorry. His name's not coming up."

"Believe me," says Bonnie. "He's on it. I know. I'll check at the office. I'll call our provider tomorrow."

Is it that word *provider?* Or is it, more likely, that he senses Bonnie's desperation? He knows Bonnie's lying. He types a while longer. "Here's the number to call," he says. "First thing tomorrow morning. All right?"

"The minute I wake up," says Bonnie. "Thank you thank you thank you." *Now* he hears her desperation. And now he gives Bonnie a long look: another sort of triage. Are she and Vincent a couple? Oddly, Bonnie likes the idea. What flatters her is not being mistaken for Vincent's wife so much as a stranger thinking that she *could* be with a good-looking younger man whose rich friends have whisked him to the emergency room in a fleet of town cars.

Bonnie's cellphone rings.

"Hello?" Bonnie says. "Danny? What's wrong?" The familiar horror scenario streams through her mind, modified to fit the current situation, which tonight involves Joel's apartment. Fifty stories up. She's never been there, but several times, she's been on the phone with Joel, and he's launched into a dreamy, ecstatic description of his million-dollar view. His million-point-two-dollar view.

Bonnie's already praying her way through the usual list. Don't let it be this, don't let it be that. She always knew that it would be something she never even imagined.

"Max is crying," says Danny.

Bonnie says, "Oh, my God, is he hurt?"

He isn't. If no one is in danger or pain, Bonnie can handle it. Still, Max must be awfully upset if Danny's worried enough to call. Bonnie asks Joel to take the boys for one night, and he can't even manage that!

"Where *are* you?" Danny asks.

"In the emergency room. But don't worry. Everything's fine."

"What the fuck? How fine could you be if you're in the emergency room? Mom, are you okay?"

Bonnie's haste to reassure him is delayed by a second of guilty pleasure at how concerned he sounds. She leans into the phone, turning her back on Vincent and the others.

"Language," says Bonnie. Somehow, telling Danny about Vincent's mishap convinces her that everything *is* going to be fine. An allergy attack in the middle of the gala dinner sounds like a bad joke. "How insane is that?"

"Insane," says Danny. "Way insane."

"What a night," says Bonnie.

"Is he okay?" says Danny. What a good human being Danny is, filled with sympathy and fellow feeling. He cares about Vincent. He wishes him well. Bonnie can tell from his voice.

"Vincent was great. He was a hero. He kept going and finished his speech even though he could have died."

"Is he okay?" repeats Danny.

Bonnie hears Max sobbing in the background.

"Fine," Bonnie says. "Vincent's fine. Let me talk to Max."

Max gulps hello, then starts crying again. Even so, Bonnie finds the sound of his voice comforting. He's alive and unhurt. Physically, at least.

"Honey," she says, "you'll feel better. I promise. Tomorrow night, we'll be home, you'll be sleeping in your own bed. Just find a nice quiet place to lie down. Get Danny to come with you. Let me talk to him a minute more. Okay? Bye, sweetheart. I love you."

Bonnie tells Danny to help Max find somewhere to rest. Let him watch TV.

"Danny, I love you so much," she says.

"I love you too, Mom," he says.

As soon as the line goes dead, Bonnie's overcome with regret for not having gone over tomorrow's arrangements. For not having reminded Joel that he's taking them to school in the morning. Let them think she's neurotic. Better safe than sorry. Max has been crying for fifteen minutes. Bonnie should drop everything and rush over there right now!

Coming out of her crouch with the phone, she sees the desk clerk watching her.

"Kids," says Bonnie, flapping her hand.

"What can you do?" says the clerk.

Bonnie wonders if he assumes that they're the kids she has with Vincent, the husband allegedly covered by her medical insurance.

"You'll let us know, right?" she tells the clerk. "I mean, when it's our turn."

"There's six of you," he says. "I'm not about to forget you."

Bonnie returns to her seat beside Vincent, who says, "Who called?"

"That was Danny," says Bonnie. "Max is having some kind of meltdown."

"Max?" says Vincent. "What kind of meltdown?"

"Crying," says Bonnie. "He won't stop."

"He'll stop," says Vincent. "Don't worry. Max is a stand-up guy."

Bonnie smiles, and Vincent smiles back. They're talking about her child's character. So why should this feel like flirtation? Having someone to talk to about her child is sexy, though maybe only a woman would think that. It's been so long since Bonnie flirted with anyone, she no longer knows what it feels like. Maybe the basic procedure was changed during the years she was married. Is she flirting with Vincent in a hospital waiting room? What could be less romantic? But it *is* romantic. That's why they set TV shows in emergency rooms. In any case, Bonnie's only dimly aware of her surroundings. It's as if the edges have melted away, and the only sharp image is Vincent. Which *is* what flirtation feels like. Bonnie remembers now. The fantasy—the impossible part—is that Vincent is flirting with *her.* Wake up. She's Bonnie. Flabby arms. Single mother of two.

Vincent says, "How bad did it look at the dinner? Did you think I was dying?"

"No," says Bonnie. "Not really. I mean yes. I was terrified." Well, of course, she was alarmed. Vincent passed out onstage. He's her friend. She thinks she can say that by now. Obviously, she was worried. Her friend was in trouble. Vincent knows her well enough to know that everything scares her. So why does Bonnie feel as if she's made a major confession? She can never tell him that she knew he'd eaten nuts and didn't try to save him. But what would he have wanted her to do? Run onstage and drag him off?

Could she possibly have the tiniest crush on Vincent? That's the last thing Bonnie needs. Which is probably why her subconscious, which must have known about this for some time, has decided to withhold the information until this supremely inconvenient moment. Why now? She'd thought he was going to die. Vincent's an astonishing guy. He gave a great speech tonight. He put his survival on the line for a cause that represents the opposite of everything he once stood for. Everybody admires him. He's the one Larry Ticknor wants to impress. *New York Times* reporters cozy up to him. And he talks to her about her kids. Why shouldn't Bonnie notice?

"Hey!" Vincent's waving his hand in front of her face. "Are you okay?" He's turned toward her as far as the plastic bucket seats will allow. And suddenly Bonnie's acutely aware of his knees, her knees, his hands, her hands, aware that she's forgotten everything—the chance that someone might be calling Vincent's name, the Ticknors, Meyer and Irene—that she needs to remember.

"I'm fine." Bonnie can't look at him. She's too busy worrying about the fact that the air-conditioning is raising ugly bumps on her arms. "I guess I was scared. Did *you* think you were going to die?"

"I *was* dying," says Vincent. "But I had to outrun it. Make it wait till I finished. I had the speech all worked out in my head. I wanted to get through it. Like staying awake when you're driving and you're really tired. You can do it if you need to. Listen. I want to get the tattoos removed. Do you think I could ask the doctor about that laser thing?"

Does Vincent mean the ER doctor? He's hardly the person to ask about laser tattoo removal, but Vincent—their feral child—doesn't know that. All he knows is that he's going to see a doctor. How tenderly Bonnie feels toward him, how protective, how moved, and also how proud of herself that he wants the tattoos gone. She feels that it has something to do with her. Of course, Meyer is part of it, too. But she can't help thinking that some affection for her has contributed to

Vincent's desire to get the signs of his former life blasted off his body. *Affection.* The word soothes Bonnie. That's all it is, or will be.

"You *do?*" Bonnie's shocked by the sound of her voice: tentative, pliant, girlish. Some balance between them has see-sawed and come to rest in a different place.

How long has the nurse been calling Vincent's name?

"Vincent?" Irene says. "Are you alive?"

Vincent and Bonnie jump up.

ᘯᙓᘯᙓ

"You must be exhausted," Bonnie says. "I can hardly see to unlock the door."

Vincent *should* be wasted. It's four o'clock in the morning, and he's certainly had one action-packed hell of a night. But something, maybe the epinephrine shot, has left him so wired that his visit to the emergency room and the long ride home have failed to slow him down.

Vincent and Bonnie linger in the front hall like guests waiting for someone to ask them in and tell them what to do. Vincent's in no rush to scurry off to his room and get a front-row seat for the instant replay of the evening's high spots.

It's Bonnie's house. Let her decide. Bonnie heads for the kitchen. Vincent follows, a moment later.

"Can I get you something?" Bonnie asks. "A cup of tea? A glass of water?"

Vincent says, "That would be great. I mean, I'll have some water."

Vincent lives here. He gets his own water. This is not their normal m.o. But sure. She's being Nurse Bonnie. She probably feels guilty. Did she know there were nuts in the salad? Bonnie's not his mom. Vincent's been on his own for years. He never expected Margaret to monitor what he ate. Not that Margaret was likely to add crushed macadamias to the KFC Big Bucket, or to the burgers and take-out cole slaw she served on special occasions. Margaret made him wash the dishes, which was fine, especially after that once she came up behind him at the sink and pressed her hips against him. That was soon after they met. The whole time they were together, he kept hoping it would happen again. He'd get hard just thinking about it. What exactly did Margaret get tired of? Was it really that he wasn't going anywhere? Margaret should have seen him tonight.

"Flat or fizzy?" Bonnie asks.

"Plain. Whatever," says Vincent.

Water, for Vincent, comes from the tap. But now he defers to Bonnie and her two-dollar bottle of Italian bubbles.

Bonnie's crouching in front of the refrigerator, reaching back for a bottle, when suddenly she looks up and back over her shoulder at Vincent and gives him a funny smile. And somehow Vincent knows. He knows. He could fuck Bonnie if he wants to.

Where is *this* thought coming from? To be honest, it's not the first time. Lately, he's been acutely aware of Bonnie's . . . physical plant. Like tonight, at the emergency room, when his name was called, and he and Bonnie stood up at once, and her hip brushed against his. It's hardly a surprise that a near-death experience—and the joy of finding yourself still alive—might leave a guy feeling horny. Vincent has got to be careful. This is not just about sex.

Bonnie fills the glass and brings it to him. Their eyes lock for a beat too long. So it's not his imagination. She hands him the glass of water, and then, as she stands in front of him for a good while after she should have moved, it's perfectly clear. It's obvious. It can't be anything else. Something is definitely happening here, whether Bonnie knows it or not.

In theory, Vincent could allow this state of suspended sexual buzz to continue for a while, at least until he figures out what to do about it. But sad experience has taught him that in most cases, it's now or never. There's a moment of possibility, and once it's gone, you can never get back there.

Vincent puts the water down on the counter. Bonnie's still standing in front of him. She hasn't moved.

Bonnie takes off her glasses.

Vincent leans down, and they kiss. In a way, he's just being a gentleman. But it feels great to kiss Bonnie. It would feel good to kiss anyone. Any*thing*. His lips have practically atrophied from months of underuse.

The kiss lasts long enough for Vincent to start thinking and pull back, catch his breath. Get his bearings.

Bonnie's face is morphing in front of his eyes into a giant question mark. Does he want to fuck her? Definitely. But maybe it's the epinephrine, or maybe he's really changed. Maybe that science experiment they're running on him has worked. Maybe he's grown up, or learned to think, or figured out that there are situations in which it's not a great idea to be led around by his dick.

Now, for example, he needs to weigh how good it might feel to go to bed with Bonnie against the probable consequences, which are: wrecking his whole new life. Sex with Bonnie would be the opposite of casual sex. There would be repercussions. Complications. Someone would get hurt.

Vincent's barely handling what he's got to handle already. Bonnie needs to cut him some slack. It's four in the morning. He nearly died. He's not in the greatest shape to begin a . . . romance. Let's take it slow. See what develops.

But already it's gone too far. Whatever happens now will cost them.

He puts his hand on Bonnie's shoulder. He kisses her lightly on the lips, then draws back again, more in control this time, and says, "I don't know how to say this. But this isn't my most shining hour. I should probably pack it in, get some rest . . ." He smiles. "If you want, tomorrow we can start again where we left off tonight."

No sensible person could argue with that. He's leaving the door open. No one could get their feelings hurt, not even a woman. He said they'd continue tomorrow. Does that sound like a definite no? They have all night to think, and tomorrow they can look at things in the clear light of day.

Bonnie puts her glasses back on. Is she disappointed? Embarrassed? Relieved? He can't tell. If he doesn't know that, he doesn't know her well enough to fuck her. Where did *that* thought come from? It's something a chick would think. All this time, he's pretended to change, and now it seems he has. Be careful what goofy expressions you make, your face could freeze that way.

Bonnie's left her body. Her face is a total blank. Bonnie the Woman has disappeared, and Bonnie the Mom takes over.

"How *are* you feeling?" Bonnie asks.

"Fine," says Vincent. "Tired."

"Me, too. We should probably get some sleep." Bonnie kisses his forehead, as if she's saying good night to her kids. So it's over. It's not over. It happened, and whatever happens now cannot erase or change that.

Bonnie says, "All right, then. I guess I should go to bed. What a night. You've really been through something. Did anybody bother to tell you that your speech was brilliant?"

"Was it?" says Vincent. "Thanks."

"Well, if you're sure you don't need anything . . . Promise you'll wake me up if you start not feeling well." Then without looking at him, Bonnie says, "Do you think I should try calling the kids? Maybe just to check in? They've had a tough night, too. Poor Max—"

"It's late," says Vincent. "Probably everybody's asleep. I'm sure the boys are okay."

"Okay. Good night, then," Bonnie says.

"See you tomorrow," says Vincent.

"Sleep as long as you like. I told them we'd be coming into the office late. And if you're not feeling well . . ."

"I'll be fine," says Vincent. "Good night."

Vincent waits till Bonnie leaves the kitchen. Then he turns out the light.

As he passes Danny's door, he considers a light raid on the kid's stash. Fainting must have softened his brain. How can he even *consider* getting high and winding up twice as paranoid? He needs to go the opposite way, down instead of up.

He's still got that Vicodin he put in his pocket before he went out. But it's a Xanax moment, ten milligrams at least. He locks his door, then drags his duffel bag out from under the bed and brushes it off. That's how long he's been here: the dust balls are growing dust balls. How much longer can he get away with this? Eventually, they'll call his bluff and send him packing. But what exactly *is* his bluff? Vincent can no longer tell. These peace and love types have gotten to him. He no longer knows who he is.

The weather is bound to get volatile if this . . . thing with Bonnie goes any further. It's going to change the climate. And not for the better. Well, fine, he never imagined that it would last forever, his sweet second chance in the spare room of some soccer mom's house. A sitting duck for Raymond and his friends to find and fuck with.

Vincent gropes in his bag, the ritual check required to set his mind at ease. There's always that hit of panic before he finds the money and the pills. He's been careful lately, not taking one every night, partly because he hasn't felt the need, and partly because he's afraid of running out. He's made a dent in his Vicodin stash, but he's still got most of the Xanax. How can he find a writing doc with Bonnie all over him, twenty-four/seven?

He thought about asking the fourteen-year-old Pakistani chick playing ER doctor. But he couldn't think of a reason why an allergic reaction would indicate an immediate need for painkillers or antianxiety medication. Doctor, do you have anything for those times when I'm afraid I'll pass out again? It might have worked. It might not have. He couldn't, with Bonnie watching. Should he have said he'd hit his head? That would have meant X-rays and tests. If he gets his tattoos lasered away, will they give him pills? He wants them off, regardless. They sent the message they needed to send, and now he no longer needs their services. In fact, he finds them embarrassing and unhelpful in his new life.

His mind is in full lab-rat mode, bouncing off blind alleys. If he takes a pill, at least he won't have to worry about his supply. Or worry about anything: one advantage of self-medication. He puts a pill on his tongue and chews, alarmed to note that its texture has gotten crumbly.

He removes his shoes and lies on the bed to wait for the Xanax to pull up the blankets and tuck him in. Instead of which he finds himself in some snit about wrinkling the rented tux. The rental joint would enjoy sticking Bonnie and the foundation with a hefty surcharge.

Vincent gets up, strips down to his shorts, lies down again, gets up, goes over to the light switch, and decides to leave the light on for a few minutes more.

Anything to avoid that inevitable moment of lying alone in the dark, with no distractions, no buffer between his brain and the fact that he didn't fuck Bonnie. He no longer recognizes himself. Who has he turned into? Some creep who would pass up the first free sex he's been offered in a year. Though it wasn't exactly free sex. Free sex is like free lunch. And this would be even more costly than most. Bonnie—his boss, hostess, caretaker, mom, there's no word for what she is. You don't screw that up just for sex. *Just* for sex? *Anything* for sex. That's what most guys think. But Vincent's no longer most guys. He's become the kind of jerk who *would* work for Brotherhood Watch, some worried, cautious loser, concerned about *consequences*. He's become the male Bonnie.

Maybe Vincent is being smart. Or stupid. Fucking Bonnie would have felt good, it might have improved his situation. Cemented his position. Sex would have changed the power balance. They could have followed wherever it led. Now he might never know what it would have been like. What the hell was he scared of?

Bonnie took off her glasses. She offered. He turned her down. From now on, it's up to him. She's not going out on the same limb twice. But Vincent can't imagine when in the daily routine of their lives—breakfast, car ride, office, car ride, dinner with Bonnie's kids—he can bring the subject back to sex.

Vincent nearly died tonight. No wonder he's confused. Why is he being hard on himself? He should be glad he's alive.

He thinks he can hold that thought long enough to lower his blood pressure some. For good measure, he takes another pill. The effect begins in seconds. The confidence, the calm. Lights out, head on pillow. He waits for the sweet oblivion, the nighty-night of anesthesia so sweet he doesn't feel it come on.

⊷⊶⊷⊶

It's important to brush your teeth, to follow your normal bedtime routine. Even when you're in hell. Especially when you're in hell. If Bonnie doesn't brush her teeth, she'll be even more depressed and consumed with self-loathing than she is already. Okay, as long as she does it without looking in the mirror. But finally she can't help giving in to the masochistic urge to take a good look at the woman who just threw herself at Vincent.

There's a dark blotch growing on her temple, and that crease beneath her eye is deepening. How drawn and homely Bonnie looks. *The lady looks fatigued.* That woman in the mirror tried to *seduce* someone? By taking off her *glasses?* It was like that cliché scene in a screwball comedy when the schoolmarm loses her spectacles and turns out to be a bombshell hiding behind those unmistakable semaphores of excessive female intelligence. *Why, Miss Blah Blah, you look lovely without your specs. Why did I never notice?* But Bonnie without her glasses is just Bonnie, but more myopic. Was she pretending to rest her eyes? What was that gesture supposed to mean? Hold me, kiss me, you big lug. Her intention was explicit. That was Bonnie's bungee jump. Not what Meyer meant.

Or maybe it was what Meyer meant. Bonnie was giving herself. Why should she feel humiliated? She was being open. Generous. Free. Vincent probably hasn't had sex in a long time. It was nice of her to offer. Is Bonnie trying to convince herself that's what happened? What did happen?

Something happened *to* her. An out-of-body moment during which she begged a guy ten years younger . . . Anyway, she hardly *begged.* All she did was take off her glasses. How foolish of the women of her generation to claim that women should have the right to be the aggressor. They should have shut up and let the culture protect them from what Bonnie is feeling now: the aftermath of rejection.

Bonnie puts on her long granny nightgown and climbs into bed. Every nerve cell is firing. There's not a chance she can sleep. Which gives her many hours to review the evening. Starting with Vincent's nearly dying, and the fact that it was her fault. No wonder he wouldn't come near her. He was probably still weak. And selfish Bonnie was obsessed with her pitiful dreams of romance. Who did she think they were going to be? Spencer Tracy and Katharine Hepburn?

The hours of the night drag by. This too shall pass. This too shall pass. Repeating that is the only way she can keep from bursting into tears. In the morning what happened tonight won't seem quite so painful, and in a few weeks it will seem even less shameful, until finally, though it may take years, it will become another humorous story about her life. The time the Nazi turned her down. Wasn't that a riot?

There had been guys in college who couldn't wait to get Bonnie into bed—until she agreed, and they lost interest. Or they would go through the motions, getting sex out of the way, or else it might be over in one shockingly brief moment. One way or another, it would often involve the acquisition of some new information about the other person, information she would rather not have had, and which she could never have imagined during the enchanted prelude of fantasy and attraction. It was better that Vincent turned her down than expose them both to the prospect of some humiliating failure!

Nothing like that happened with Joel. Everything had proceeded so naturally and smoothly that she could afford to be smug with friends whose boyfriends used that vile word, *commitment*, as if marriage were a jail term or a stay in the mental ward.

She'd met Joel in the microfilm room of the Forty-second Street Library. She was working for the Historical Society, which had sent her to track down the demolition date of a vintage Irish saloon for a caption under a photo in an upcoming exhibition. In his last year of medical school, Joel was taking an elective. Something to do with ethics. His assignment was to seek out the latest coverage of the euthanasia debate. Though they were sitting next to each other, so intent were they on their separate projects that they might never have met had Bonnie been able to thread the microfilm machine. Was there a gentleman in the house? Joel rushed right over.

Amused by the funny contrast in the subjects they were researching (the Blarney Stone on Tenth Avenue versus mercy killing in the Netherlands), they were unaware that this was a sign of what they would later see as the difference in the importance of what they did for a living. Nor did Joel's willingness to thread the microfilm for Bonnie give any indication of how he would someday mutter and fume when Bonnie failed to grasp the advanced features of some overcomplicated appliance. And why didn't she take it as a warning that he was researching his professional right to play God? Bonnie has to be careful of men with godlike ambitions. First Joel, then Meyer, though Meyer is nothing like Joel. Vincent has no desire to run the world. Or *her* world. Maybe that's what had made her feel brave enough to take off her glasses.

On the afternoon she and Joel met, they went out to lunch, which lasted through dinner. Neither of them touched their food. Eventually they wound up in Joel's dormitory room, an airless metal closet overlooking the Hudson. What they did on the lumpy single bed, while the hornetlike helicopters buzzed outside the window, seemed even more amazing in that sterile, monastic setting.

Within six months, she was pregnant. She certainly hadn't planned on it, but was happy when she found out. Joel was delighted. Just before he disappeared into residency and internship, he insisted that they sit down together while he showed her that it would be cost effective, cost *essential*, for her to quit her job. His minimal resident's salary, sky-high child care . . . How could Bonnie have held her ground against those columns of figures marching down the page?

She loved Joel once, she knows that. And there were moments of bliss. Sometimes, even on the most hellish family vacations, with both kids fighting, Danny sulking, Joel driving badly and exploding for no reason, she would feel her spirits soaring, lifted by an updraft of pure contentment.

She can't let herself think about that. It's too slippery a slope. What she mostly pretends, even to herself, is that her marriage was like a birthmark that turned malignant and had to be excised. It protects her from facing the painful truth that she will never get back those years. That was love, youth, her children's childhood, a time that will never return. And somehow, by leaving her, Joel has taken all that with him.

If only she could get some sleep. It's going to be a rocky morning, dealing with the fallout from last night's dinner. That's what Bonnie *should* be thinking about, the serious part of her life, raising money for Brotherhood Watch. Instead of which she's fixated on some . . . romantic rejection.

Can Bonnie take tomorrow off? Wake up in the morning and disappear, see a movie, go to the mall. Be home in time for the boys. The boys. That's how distracted she is, she's forgotten her kids. One of whom has spent the evening crying his poor little eyes out. It's too late to call. If something were wrong, Bonnie would have heard. Bonnie thinks that, over and over, until it puts her to sleep.

Bonnie's woken by the ringing phone. Where is she, and what's wrong?

Maybe it's Danny calling to say that Max hasn't stopped crying. That Joel has dropped them off at Grand Central, with a dollar between them. Joel was always lazy about the kids, though he used to cloak it in the guise of not wanting to spoil them. Unlike controlling, overprotective Bonnie, damaging and unmanning her sons by asking where they were going and how they planned to get home.

Bonnie grabs for the phone.

"Did I wake you?" Roberta says. "How are you, honey? How's Vincent?"

"I was awake," lies Bonnie. *Honey?* "But I think Vincent's asleep."
She often wonders how Roberta envisions Bonnie's domestic arrangements. Maybe Roberta imagines that every night Bonnie tears off her
glasses and falls into Vincent's arms. Bonnie likes the virtuous, sexless
sound of *I think he's asleep.* As opposed to: I *know* he's asleep. He's lying
here beside me.

"How *is* Vincent?" Roberta asks. "He gave us quite a scare."

"Roberta," says Bonnie. "What's up?"

Roberta says, "I gather you haven't seen this morning's *Post.*"

The first four pages are all Tim McVeigh, and then comes the
full page on Vincent. Maybe the press turnout at the benefit was
better than Bonnie realized, or maybe it all started with Colette
Martinez, whose byline, says Roberta, heads a long piece on the
front page of the *Times* Metro section.

"It's amazing," Roberta says. "I got in to the office this morning
at nine, and there were twelve messages on my machine. The
phone's been ringing off the hook. Newspapers, magazines. Some
feelers from TV. Everyone just *loves* it that Vincent died. Almost
died."

A lavalike blob of anger ascends from Bonnie's toes to her forehead. "He didn't die. He was never *dead.*"

"I said *almost* died. The bottom line is, five hundred movers and
shakers saw the guy go under. They all went home and told their
friends, and their friends told *their* friends, about the reformed Nazi
collapsing. From a *peanut* allergy. Bonnie, dear, don't you get it? It's
the kind of story people *love.* Life and death and courage. A noble
cause. A life turned around. A changed man. Et cetera. Bonnie, Barbara Walters's people called, just to test the waters. Do you know what
this could mean for the foundation?"

"So what are you saying?" asks Bonnie.

"I just wanted to make sure you guys are coming in today. I could
use a little support, fielding all these calls. Plus it would be great to
have some input on this, to ask Vincent what he's willing to do, what
he feels capable of."

"I should think last night proved that Vincent is capable of doing whatever he wants. Whatever we need."

"Bonnie, do me a favor. Wake the guy up."

"Roberta, my God. He almost died. Shouldn't we let him sleep?"

"Sure. Let him sleep. *Then* wake him up. Come in soon. Okay?"

"I'll do what I can." Bonnie's glad that Roberta has no idea what she's asking. How different this conversation would be if Roberta knew what happened last night in the kitchen. Or maybe it wouldn't be different at all. Roberta is doing business. She wants to keep her job. What does she care if Bonnie made a pass at Vincent?

Roberta says, "Do you want to talk to Meyer?"

"Do I need to?" says Bonnie. "Why?"

"Because he's over the moon. Several talk shows have suggested tie-ins to his new book. You know how modest Meyer is. He would never consider using this for his personal purposes. But even a saint can't help realizing what this could do for book sales."

Bonnie rubs the back of her neck. "All right, Roberta. I'll wake Vincent up. We'll be in soon. See you later."

D ANNY LEANS ACROSS DAD'S KITCHEN counter in a way meant to communicate his unhappiness so plainly that not even Dad can ignore it. Well, Danny *isn't* happy. Someone might as well know. It was two in the morning before Max quit sniffling and fell asleep. Danny was afraid to sleep for fear that Dad would wake up and forget they were there and tool off to his office. Danny would sooner hitchhike than ask Lo the Ho to drive them to school.

In fact, Dad is trying so hard to be paternal that he's bought a box of some disgusting cereal he must think they like. Or maybe Lorraine bought it. The sentiment is touching, but frankly, Danny wouldn't eat that candy-colored toxic crap, not if he were starving. If he were a better person, like Max, he'd tell Dad he'd love a bowl. Maybe Max *likes* that cereal. Mom would never buy it. It's sad that Dad is using cereal to win a contest he's still having, in his head, with Mom.

When Max says, "Sure, Dad, that would be great," it takes the pressure off Danny. No one eating Dad's cereal would be so pitiful that Danny would feel obliged to try some. This way he gets a chance to watch Dad take forever to open the box and then spill pink and green and yellow hearts all over the kitchen counter.

Max still seems depressed from last night. He'll snap out of it sooner or later. But even as they're leaving the apartment, getting into the Navigator, Max's bad mood hangs on. He doesn't protest when Danny grabs the front seat, though it's Max's turn to ride shotgun. The ease with which he rolls over is scary in itself.

Heading up the FDR, Dad says, "This is great. Man, I'm really enjoying taking you guys to school. We're going to do this more. I just wish it were easier. I had to cancel five patients."

Does Dad think that Danny and Max care how many people are getting heart attacks so he can floor the Navigator in the fifteen-second breaks between being stuck in traffic? Dad's boasting about his success. How many poor bastards are breathing their last because Dr. Kalen is driving his kids to Clairmont. Does he think that's going to make his sons love him more? Or love him at all? Pathetic!

Danny wants to ask about the Bulgarian baby. But that might set Max off. No one needs the little dude coming unglued again. The pressure builds in Danny's head until finally he can't stand it. He needs to hear Dad say that the baby and the marriage are just perverted fantasies dreamed up by the ho he lives with.

Danny glances back at Max, who is staring into space, so out of it that he probably won't hear Danny ask, "Was all that stuff true?"

"Was what true?"

"You know, about the Bulgarian kid, and you and Lorraine getting married."

"Sonofabitch," says his dad. "Did you see that bastard cut me off?" Then after a silence so long that Danny is afraid he might have to repeat the question, Dad says, "I guess. What can you do? You know how women are."

What is Danny supposed to know about women? Or men? Or about how you could leave your wife and kids and shack up with some bimbo who already killed two husbands and is about to adopt a baby she doesn't want so she can write a best-seller?

"Of course we're concerned," says Dad. "Those kids often have serious health problems. But we've got the best agency, and Lorraine knows somebody who knows somebody in the embassy in Sofia, so we have a pretty good shot at getting an infant who's in reasonably good shape. And she'll be one lucky kid. She gets to have a good life instead of suffering in some hellhole institution."

Danny can't argue with that. But is Dad talking to himself? Does he think Danny's a medical buddy with whom he can discuss Bulgarian pediatrics? When is he going to ask his sons how *they* like the idea of a brand-new baby sister and evil stepmom Lorraine? But why should Dad have to consult them? They're only children. *His* children.

Danny wishes he could tell his dad about Vincent. Not for advice or support. But just to let another grown-up know what Mom is doing. That is, a grown-up who doesn't work for Brotherhood Watch and won't obey Meyer Manson's every command. But maybe in his dad's brain-damaged state, he would think it was *nice*, that bringing home a Nazi was the Mom equivalent of a Bulgarian adoption. Which, in a way, it is.

What Danny could never explain to Dad is that he's starting to like Vincent. The guy's funny. He pays attention. The few times they watched *Jeopardy*, he'd kicked Max and Danny's asses. It's fun to watch him get steamed about the evening news and about how the media fucks with your brain and exploits the trashy popular taste for blood and gore. What's that expression he uses? If it bleeds, it leads. He talks to them more than Dad did. Danny could never tell Dad that, not unless he wants Vincent *out of his house this minute*.

But the truth is, it would be hard to get Dad that worked up. Probably Mom could *marry* Vincent, and Dad wouldn't care that much. Anyway, Mom's not going to marry Vincent.

Eventually Dad sighs and says, "There's no way you can understand. Not as long as you kids think you're immortal. Which I hope you do. Maybe when you're as old as me—"

"You're not old, Dad," Danny says.

"When you're as old as me, you'll look back and understand

why your dad had to do what he did. I love you guys, you know that, but your mom . . . her worries, her fears . . . I felt like I had one foot in the grave and the other on a banana peel.

"Like for example, I love this car. I know you probably think it's some middle-aged jerk-off fantasy. But it makes me happy. And when you get older, happiness isn't that easy. You know what your mom would have said. She would have told me, a million times, the horrifying statistics about how you wipe out the occupants of every car you graze in every fender bender.

"I know all that. I don't want to know it. I don't want to hear your mom's voice. And I don't want to think it might be my voice! And I *know* it's not Lorraine's voice. I love you guys, you've got to believe that. You're the number one thing in my life. But trust me, I'll be more useful to you if I can stay alive."

Danny can only stare ahead, paralyzed by the embarrassment of hearing his dad say "middle-aged jerk-off fantasy." Otherwise, he only understood part of whatever Dad meant. If he's so scared of dying, why is he living with the Black Widow? Someone who will make him die sooner. Danny doesn't want Dad to die. Danny would rather not think about that, because it gets in the way of his feeling angry at him. Is Dad saying that when Danny gets older and "understands" why Dad split, then it will be okay for him to ditch *his* wife and kids? Danny hates it that Dad mentioned how much Mom worries. He lost the right to talk about that when he quit being part of the family.

Meanwhile, for all Dad's fear of dying, it's Vincent who almost died. Vincent who wound up in the emergency room. Danny hopes that Vincent's okay. Mom would have told him if he weren't. Meanwhile Dad seems to be speaking. Probably something about himself. Danny doesn't have to listen too hard. He'll figure it out, or he won't.

For the first time ever, he's glad when they get to school.

THE FIRST VOICE MEYER HEARS in the morning is Irene's, saying, "Don't you think you should phone and see if the poor man survived?"

Hauling himself from a deep sleep, he can feel Irene's impatience coating him like the aerosol spray she insists Babu use for frying. The fights she's had with that poor man over clarified butter!

All the way home in the car last night, Irene had criticized Meyer, his staff, and especially Bonnie, who should have been watching Vincent instead of massaging the Ticknors' egos. And where was Meyer? Irene wanted to know. Showing off, rattling on about bungee jumps and faith cells. Did Meyer *care* if the guy lived?

Meyer had prayed for Vincent. But he couldn't tell Irene that without making himself sound smarmy and pious. The main thing is that Vincent survived. And that Meyer's speech and Vincent's bravery will do wonders for the foundation.

Meanwhile, Irene has been asking about their plans for Vincent's future. How will they dispose of him when he stops being useful? How far they have come from the time when, after an event like last night's, Irene couldn't stop telling Meyer how brilliant he was—instead of remarking, casually, on how impressive Vincent had been. When did Irene become Vincent's champion and protector? Since their dinner party, when Vincent flirted with her. Meyer doesn't blame Irene, but it's demoralizing, all the same: the chasm between what matters to Meyer and what's important to his wife.

"I'm sure he's fine," says Meyer wearily. "Bonnie would have called me."

How could Meyer *not* have phoned? He *is* becoming a monster.

Irene says, "Don't you think it's strange that you'll make a million calls to get a guy sprung from jail halfway around the globe, and here's this guy who's been working for you, and you're not even concerned?"

"I am concerned. I'm very concerned."

"Concerned!" says Irene. "Just not enough to pick up the phone. Meyer Maslow, the second in line for sainthood after Nelson Mandela, can't bother reaching out to see if his protégé made it through the night, just like that first night you stashed the guy at Bonnie's and didn't—"

"I'm sorry, I should have called."

"You should have," Irene says.

"I guess no man's a hero to his valet." Meyer gets out of bed.

"I hate it when you say that," Irene calls after him.

"I hate when you say 'reach out,'" Meyer says, shutting the bathroom door.

By the time he gets out of the shower, Irene has left the bedroom. How long does she want to drag this out?

Meyer could leave the house without seeing her, which would terrify Irene, who has a superstitious fear of physical separation or of falling asleep in the midst of an argument. Suppose one of them was hit by a car, and the other survived knowing the other died angry? Which proves that Irene still loves him. But does he love Irene?

He finds her in the breakfast room. He kisses the top of her head. Irene turns, grateful and radiant.

"Call me, please," she says.

Walking into the office, Meyer registers a barometric change. The receptionist, the pretty Asian girl whose name he always forgets, has turned back into the person she was when she first came to work here, when the sight of Meyer filled her eyes with droplets of admiration. After a while that dewiness dried up to the point at which she hardly bothered to say hello if she was answering a call. But now her voice catches as she says, "Good morning, Mr. Maslow."

"Good morning . . . ," says Meyer, not chancing a guess. Something with an A. Anita?

People sing out from their offices, *Meyer Meyer Meyer.* Everybody's calling his name, like some magical incantation. The dinner must have gone well. He knew his speech went over. He could feel the audience with him. Maybe they went home and thought about the faith cells and the moral bungee jump. And Vincent's unfortunate near-disaster provided a living lesson on the dangers and the glories of faith, and of letting yourself be changed.

Already, a huge stack of messages has piled up on Meyer's desk. People are probably calling to compliment him on his speech. He's trying to remember who Colette Martinez is when the door flies open, and Roberta bursts in.

"You're here! Do you know what's happening?"

When Roberta tells him that the reporters have been phoning about Vincent's allergy attack, Meyer can't help it. His heart sinks. The fuss is not about him or his speech but about . . . peanuts. Maybe *Meyer* should almost have died. He's closer to death than Vincent. But Meyer's old, which would mean that his death would be less dramatic and sexy. Odds are that it will not take place on-stage in front of an audience but in some lonely, frightening hospital bed, like Minna's.

"Are we on the same page here?" Roberta asks. "Everybody wants a piece of this. Vincent's skinhead past, his near-death experience. Personal growth. Human change. Turning your life around, nearly dying, surviving to do more. Everybody's fighting for an exclusive. A month ago, I couldn't get two paragraphs on the second page of the Metro section. Do you think I didn't *notice* how upset everybody was? Do you think I didn't *know* that my job was on the line? And this morning I get a call from Barbara Walters's people. Do you know what this means for your book?"

Meyer wishes that Roberta hadn't attempted this cheap appeal to his literary vanity. The subject is a sore one. No one needs to tell Meyer that *One Heart at a Time* has failed to sell as well as his previous books. He pretends it doesn't matter, that his real work is not about that. Only Irene has suggested, humiliatingly, that Meyer ask his publisher why they're not doing more. Does Irene think that Nelson Mandela does bookstore readings and tours? Yet now, just hearing that the book might do well is having a positive effect. For the first time since he finished *One Heart at a Time*, Meyer can imagine writing again, perhaps something combining last night's speech with the story of his experience with Vincent.

"All right, forget that," Roberta says. "Forget your book for a minute. Let's look at what this means for the foundation. Because face it, Meyer, not all of this is going to be about Vincent's close call. What gives this story meaning is the work we're doing, how much *more* we could do. Bonnie's got to get on board with this. We have to come up with a strategy for converting all this free publicity into wads of development money."

Roberta's right. It would be nice not to have to worry about what will happen to the foundation in the economic downturn everyone's predicting. When no one has a dime to spend on international human rights, Brotherhood Watch will have a comfort margin. Every interview, every TV spot, will translate into the rescue of innocent human beings. This is not about Meyer or Vincent. This is something higher. If the moral bungee jump that God wants Meyer to make requires being interviewed by Barbara Walters, so be it. Meyer will jump.

Roberta leaves. She'll be back. And now the electricity sparking all over the office begins to affect even Meyer. It's all he can do not to run down the hall and ask Roberta who's called now, who said what. He buzzes the receptionist and asks her to let him know when Vincent and Bonnie arrive.

Still holding the phone, Meyer reads through the messages on his desk. Larry Ticknor called, will call back. Minna called—congratulations on last night's speech—wants to know, did you get Dickens chapter?

Meyer puts down the message slip. So it was Minna who sent him the Mrs. Jellyby passage. Was it intended to be cruel, or merely to amuse him? Why does Meyer feel so sure that it wasn't meant well? Why else was it sent anonymously? But if Minna had wanted to hurt him, why was she calling now to say she'd done it? He visited her in the hospital! What did he do to offend her? Maybe illness has unhinged her. He remembers her acting strangely at dinner at his house, something about the Cochin Jews that he can't recall but which makes his stomach flutter. His queasiness intensifies as he thinks back to this morning. How irritated Irene was with him for not calling to ask about Vincent. So many good things are happening. Why should he feel so uneasy? The combined weight of Irene's annoyance and Minna's mysterious anger presses, like a knuckle, on the center of his chest.

The pressure doesn't let up until Bonnie and Vincent finally walk into his office. If only Irene and Minna could look into his heart. Meyer cares about Bonnie and Vincent. He's delighted to see them!

"How are you feeling?" Meyer says.

"Okay," says Vincent. "Tired."

Bonnie must be tired, too. Her eyes look sad, almost furtive. So it's partly to lift her spirits that Meyer says, "Have you heard the news? Hollywood's calling, I gather."

Bonnie has heard. Vincent hasn't. Bonnie hasn't told Vincent about the media onslaught, which means she must have found a way to sneak him past Roberta. Vincent's had a hard night. He's probably still fragile.

Meyer aims for the simple and direct. "Vincent, my friend, are you ready for this? You're about to become famous."

Vincent pales.

"What's wrong?" Meyer says. "Are you *sure* you're all right?"

"I'm fine," says Vincent. "Really. I'm fine. That's great. Let's get to work."

O N THE WAY HOME FROM SCHOOL, Danny spends fifteen minutes in the cracker aisle of the convenience store, choosing the perfect corn chip to get him through the hours of torture he's doomed to spend at his computer, writing his entire Hitler paper, which is due tomorrow.

This morning in World Civilizations class, he'd almost stopped being friends with Chloe. How could anyone, even a girl, not only write her paper on Nelson Mandela but hand it into Linda Graber a whole day early! Chloe did him a favor. Her turning in her paper inspired Mrs. Graber to give the class a pep talk on the importance of revising and proofreading. Revising? Proofreading? Whom was Graber kidding? All Danny heard were those three little words: paper due tomorrow.

Danny will be lucky to get the paper written at all, which is why he fortifies himself with the perfect mix of salty and sweet, two gigantic bags of chips and—after a stall between the orange soda and cola, a deliberation based on his estimation of the energy-giving potential of caffeine versus massive doses of Red Dye #2—the two-liter Pepsi.

The long sleepless night he spent at Dad's and the hellish car ride this morning have done nothing for Danny's mood or for his powers of concentration. And now he's got to write five pages on how Hitler changed the world. How about: The guy started World War II and killed six million Jews. Whom is Danny blaming here? Picking Hitler was his idea.

Briefly Danny considers writing something about Vincent. How Hitler's influence still hangs on, how he won't die, how he's like the Tom Cruise character in *Interview with the Vampire*. Because though most people know Hitler was evil, there are still guys, like the maniacs in ARM, who think he had some good ideas. That would take no research at all. Danny could just write it. But it's supposed to be about Hitler, not Danny's skinhead roommate. And Danny's not about to tell the whole school about his unusual home life.

Vincent claims he never liked Hitler. He also says the guy was gay. Maybe Danny should look into that. Is it a well-known fact? How gay was that mustache? Is that a homophobic thought? It's crucial that Mrs. Graber not think so. And Danny *isn't* homophobic, though he knows kids who are. Those kids will probably think that Danny's gay just for writing the paper. Danny's sure he isn't gay. Just because he hasn't had sex with a girl doesn't mean anything. He'd have sex in a minute if Chloe would do it with him. But it's so hard to tell about girls, and by now it's too late to ask the other guys, all of whom are pretending to already know everything about sex. Danny wonders how you start, how you know when a girl wants to. He can't think about that now. He needs to concentrate on Hitler.

At least he has the house to himself for a few hours. Max has a study date with some kid from his class—another fact that Mom drilled into Danny's brain yesterday before they left for Dad's. Danny hopes Max is okay, that he's gotten over whatever was wrong with him last night and this morning.

Danny goes to his room, sits down at the computer, and Googles "Hitler homosexuality." Over two thousand sites come up. Bingo. He's in business.

The first link takes him to some professor in Italy who's discovered a secret archive in Rome about the boys Hitler paid to go to bed with him when he was a student in Munich. Plus the men he murdered because they knew about it. On another site, a Chicago psychiatrist has written about how Hitler went to the greatest extremes in human history to prove that he was straight. From the lonely, low-tech look of these sites, Danny can safely assume that the question of Hitler's gayness is not the hottest topic in cyberspace. He could do something original. This paper could be fun.

After visiting a dozen sites, Danny writes his first sentence: "Since the end of the war, people have been trying to understand Adolf Hitler. Some people have said he was crazy. Others say he was evil. Still others believe he was a fanatical genius who believed that he was leading his people into a better life."

Danny stops. It's not too early in the paper to let Mrs. Graber know where he stands. "The six million innocent Jews murdered in Hitler's death camps are six million reasons to conclude that he was a monster. Not to mention the gypsies, and the Poles, and gay people.

"Now new evidence from an archive in Rome suggests that Hitler was gay and wanted to hide it, or else that he was secretly gay and wanted to be straight."

All right! This is a walk in the park. Now all he has to do is tease out the facts of Hitler's life and stop every so often to monitor Hitler's gay activity. He's almost gotten to the good part, the night of the long knives. He says it aloud a couple of times. *The night of the long knives.*

Just then, he hears the door slam. Mom and Vincent are back. They've picked up Max on their way home. So that's the end of his peaceful moment alone with Hitler and his boyfriends. Danny's surprised to discover that he's written almost three pages. All he has left to do is add some stuff about Himmler, whom the Web sites say was Hitler's main squeeze, and then a little about Albert Speer, whom Adolf supposedly had a crush on . . . and then about the death camps, just to make it clear that Danny isn't an idiot who believes that the important thing about Hitler was who he went to bed with. Or didn't. If the point of the paper is how the guy changed the world, ultimately that had nothing to do with his being in, or out of, the closet.

If Danny doesn't go downstairs soon, his mom is going to hunt him down and be annoyingly happy to find him at his desk. She'll noodle his head and look over his shoulder and read as much of his paper as she can before he pushes her away. Nothing could be less helpful than watching Mom rack her brain for a tactful way to tell him his paper sucks. That will make it harder to finish. If his mother hates it, what will Mrs. Graber think? With his quiz grades and low marks for classroom participation, he needs a B to pass. A wave of unease washes over him. He should be doing Nelson Mandela.

Anyhow, it's break time. What's happening down in the kitchen?

Vincent and Mom are at the table, drinking beer from bottles. Mom never liked beer before. Something feels different, some tension in the air that wasn't there yesterday. Is this about Vincent's allergy attack? Is Vincent pissed at Mom for nearly letting him die? Come on, it wasn't Mom's fault. Danny puts his arm around Mom's shoulders and gives her a two-second squeeze. Mom leans into his elbow so hard that Danny has to prop her up with his other hand so he can pry himself loose.

Then Mom says, "Danny, is Max okay? He seemed a little groggy when we picked him up today. He came home and went straight to sleep. Did Daddy give him something to calm him down?"

Is *Max* okay? Why doesn't she ask about Danny, whom Dad and Lorraine left to deal with his brother? But it's darling baby Max who gets all the attention.

"He's just sleepy," Danny says. "I don't think he got much rest. It was a weird night."

"Weird how?" says Mom. But Danny's not about to explain. Let her chew on that *weird.* Instead he turns to Vincent and says, "Hey, I hear you almost died."

He's glad that Vincent didn't die. What a grim scene this would be. Would they have to arrange his funeral? Would they invite his Nazi friends?

"Yeah," says Vincent. "Code blue, for sure. I was right on the edge."

"So what was it like?" Danny says. "Did you see all your dead relatives and a white corridor lined with bright lights?"

Vincent gives him a long look as if he's checking to see if he's high. Danny flashes him right back: No. At least Vincent knows enough to wonder if he is stoned. In that way, he knows Danny better than his parents.

"No red carpet, no welcoming committee," says Vincent. "But I did hear them unzipping the body bag."

"You're kidding, right?" says Danny.

Mom laughs out loud. Normally, a remark like that would earn Vincent a disapproving look, and she would say something like: Vincent, please. Don't be disgusting. As if he and Max were babies she had to protect from Vincent's crudeness. Something really *has* changed. For some reason it makes Danny mad. It's as if Mom and Vincent know something he doesn't. Has his mom no loyalty? Siding with Vincent against him. What makes him think anyone's taking sides? What *happened* at that dinner?

"So, Mom," Danny says. "Has Dad told you the good news?"

"Good news?" Mom's instantly nervous. Be *very* nervous. For once she's got a right.

"He and Lorraine are getting married and adopting a kid from Bulgaria. A girl." He can't believe he's socking her with this, in front of Vincent, before she's had dinner, before she's been home for fifteen minutes. Maybe spending the night at his father's, with Dad and Lo the Ho, has somehow rubbed off on him and made him a meaner person.

He shouldn't have said anything. Or at least not now. But he has, and his punishment is to watch Mom's face do that subtle cringe and recoil you wouldn't even notice unless you knew her. Danny wants to hug her. He wants to say he's sorry. But he can't say the one thing that would help, which is that it isn't true.

Danny waits for her to roll her eyes and say: How typical of your dad. How *silly* and *self-involved*, words she used all the time before the divorce counselor made her stop.

Instead, Mom smiles and says, "How sweet of them. Just think. Somewhere there's a Bulgarian baby who doesn't even have a clue that she's about to get lucky."

A FEW DAYS LATER, Bonnie dials Joel's number, hangs up,
then picks up the phone again as she calculates the odds
that Joel will answer. She's got a one-in-three chance.
There's always the possibility that he and Lorraine won't be home,
in which case she'll have to listen to the first bars of "Kind of Blue,"
which Bonnie always loved until Lorraine turned it into her chic
answering-machine message, with Miles Davis as Lorraine's side-
man, playing backup for the perfect assurance with which Lorraine
croons, "Joel and I aren't home right now."

The other possibility is that Lorraine will pick up. The one useful thing Bonnie learned in couples counseling was to stop hanging
up when that happened, and to speak civilly to the woman who
stole her husband. That, too, was about the children, as Joel and
Dr. Steinweiss so often pointed out. Bonnie couldn't help feeling
that Joel and the psychologist he'd hired were allied against her, except for a few times, when the therapist said something so jargon-
laden and predictable—*I'm hearing a little hostility here*—that Bonnie
and Joel looked at each other and rolled their eyes and laughed.
Those were the cruelest moments. That sudden feeling of close-

ness, of sharing a secret from this stranger, almost tricked them into wondering why they didn't give up this charade and get back together where they belonged.

"Hi, Bonnie, how are you?" Joel says.

"Fine. And you?"

"Fine. Okay. I guess."

That "I guess" is an invitation that Bonnie declines. She's practicing her own private anger management program. Breathe, count to ten. If she starts off by blaming Joel and Lorraine for having made Max unhappy, she will destroy any chance—however slim—that Joel might help her find out what's troubling her son. *Their* son.

"Actually," she says, "I'm worried about Max. He hasn't seemed . . . himself since he got back from staying with you and Lorraine. What happened? What set him off? What . . ." *What did you and Lorraine do to him?*

Joel sighs deeply, and in that sigh Bonnie hears the reasons why she knew, before she called, that she probably shouldn't bother. Joel is not an intuitive or reflective person. He will not be able to tell her anything about her child that she couldn't have figured out on her own. She remembers how glad she used to feel that she wasn't one of Joel's patients. Suppose she'd asked him if she would survive, and he'd sighed like that?

"How much did the boys tell you?" Joel's testing the waters.

"Oh, my God," says Bonnie. "I forgot to congratulate you about all your good news. That's wonderful about you and Lorraine getting married. And that lucky Romanian baby!"

"Bulgarian," says Joel. "And that's very generous of you to say so."

Bonnie feels like they're back in the therapist's office, being instructed to compliment the other person whenever someone seemed to be making a particular effort. *Joel, why don't you tell Bonnie what you liked about what she just said?* It hurt Bonnie that Joel took to therapy-speak like a duck to water. Who *was* this person she'd been married to, the father of her children? But she never blamed Joel, really. He was suffering, too. She understood that, though technically it was his fault for choosing Lorraine over her.

Another sigh. Then Joel says, "To tell you the truth, it's a little much. Everything's happening so fast. So much of it seems, frankly, out of my control . . ."

Is he saying that Lorraine has hijacked him? Bonnie could have told him that would happen. But it's more than that, she knows. Joel lives in a high-functioning trance from which he awakes every so often, shocked to see where life has brought him. Once she and Joel loved each other. Bonnie needs to keep that in mind.

Joel says, "You want to hear something ironic? Sometimes, these days, I feel like you."

"Meaning what?"

"I don't know. I'm worried all the time."

"Thanks a lot," says Bonnie. Joel once claimed he was leaving her to get out from under her anxieties. But how can she be annoyed now? There's grief in Joel's voice. He'll never be happy. He has no gift for happiness of even the simplest sort. According to the boys, he's driving a Lincoln Navigator. And that still doesn't do it. He can't help it, that's who he is. Bonnie resolves to remember that and to be more sympathetic.

"It's not just that," says Joel. "Not just the high anxiety. Listen. When Lorraine first brought it up, about adopting the baby, believe it or not, I found myself wondering, What would Bonnie do? I knew you would have said yes. Which is partly why I *did* say yes. *I* would have said no. Because I know the problems involved. Health issues, heredity, poverty. God only knows what you're getting. It was all so much easier when we had our own kids!"

Bonnie doesn't remember anything about it being easy. In fact it still isn't easy. Which is why she's calling. Bonnie is working hard to see this from Joel's point of view. That's what Meyer would suggest. What would Meyer see in Joel? A guy living with a woman he doesn't love in a highrise apartment. A guy about to adopt a child whose mother will be Lorraine.

"Come on, it's always a crapshoot," she says. "What kind of kid you'll get. Even when it's your own child, all kinds of stuff can happen." Which is not exactly what Joel means. But any consolation will help. Comfort, even empty comfort, isn't Lorraine's style.

"I guess you're right," says Joel. In the past, Bonnie could always cheer him up with the most banal reassurance. Is she supposed to despise him for that? It made her feel protective.

"So what *did* happen with Max?" she says.

"I think all the changes were too much for him, too. But I think he'll be fine."

No matter how little Joel actually knows, it's a relief to hear that. And it's an achievement for Joel not to hint that something will go seriously wrong with the kids, and that it will be Bonnie's fault.

"How was the benefit?" Joel asks. Bonnie's surprised he knows about it, until she remembers: That's why the kids stayed at his house.

"A huge success, I think," is all she can say. If she mentions Vincent and his speech, it will lead to so much that she would rather not reveal.

Bonnie has been banking—correctly, it seems—on the likelihood that Lorraine would never lower herself to read *People* magazine. Because there is an article in the most recent issue that makes it clear that Vincent is living with Bonnie and the kids. It even has a corny shot of them making pasta in the kitchen. They never cook together, but the photographer insisted. Joel will never see it unless Lorraine brings it home. The magazines in his waiting room all have titles like *Healthy Heart*.

Bonnie's omitting an important detail, but she's telling the truth. The benefit dinner *was* a success. A mood of excitement and optimism suffuses the whole office. Bonnie wishes she could be like Meyer and her coworkers, full of faith in the future. She wants everything to go smoothly but cannot shake off the suspicion that something will go wrong. Suddenly, Bonnie feels tired. The energy draining from her leaves a void that fills with unwelcome images of herself standing in front of Vincent and taking off her glasses.

Joel says, "It's so great you're doing what you're doing. With the foundation and whatever. I'm really proud. What an . . . admirable job."

"Thanks," says Bonnie. "Talk to you soon. Give Lorraine my congratulations."

PART THREE

R AYMOND'S AFRAID TO CLOSE HIS eyes because when he
does, he can look back through his eyeballs and see the
viscous puddle of blood forming in the creases of his
brain, the massive stroke he's about to have from the G-force of his
rage, the boiling steam valve he could release by blowing up at
Lucy. But that would mean admitting that a grown man, married,
the father of two, is so tapped out that his head is imploding because his old lady spent three bucks on *People* magazine.

He's better off not mentioning it. Lucy works as hard as he
does, maybe harder. It's not like she's screwing other guys. Or running up credit card debt. Or blowing their money—*what* money?—
on the slots in Atlantic City. She just wants to read a magazine in
which fat-cat Jews write about other fat-cat Jews and sell it to hardworking white Christian women who don't know any better.

Raymond would never have seen the magazine, he would never
have had the time, if he hadn't called in sick to the tire place. It's not a
lie, exactly, but it depends how you mean *sick*. He's got a wicked hangover. Last night, he and his buddies tied one on for poor Tim
McVeigh, who couldn't have one frigging beer, not even with his last
meal. Which the poor bastard hardly got to enjoy, what with those

animal-rights PETA freaks mounting a vicious publicity campaign to make sure that his last meal would be vegetarian. According to them, he'd shed enough blood already. Even the government had to admit that was cruel and unusual punishment. By those rules—kill someone, and you're looking at tofu—not one of those Washington bastards would ever see another steak. And what did McVeigh eat? Two pints of mint chocolate chip ice cream. What a giant fuck-you that was, the all-dessert last meal. The thought is almost too pitiful for Raymond to endure.

Just to give the guy some respect, Raymond and his friends had started off their private memorial service by reciting that poem McVeigh liked. "I am the master of my fate . . ." And things got rolling from there.

Now Raymond's reward is that he's missing a day of work and giving up the overtime that he and Lucy so desperately need, which they wouldn't need so desperately if his bloodsucking cousin hadn't stolen his truck and his money and his prescription medication. And the latest issue of *Soldier of Fortune*, which Raymond hadn't read, and which Vincent never liked anyway. So that was just pure meanness, which hurt. And this was after Raymond and Lucy took the sick puppy into their home and cared for him like a son.

Raymond wouldn't be worried about the cost of a lousy copy of *People* magazine if he'd given the go-ahead to Eitan and Avi, the Israelis he bought the Ex from. If he'd let them, they would have found Vincent by now, and gotten their money back. At first, Raymond had felt uneasy about doing business with Jews. But Eitan and Avi didn't seem like Jews. They were hard-asses. They'd been in the military. They'd wanted to go after Vincent. Teach the guy a lesson. So did Raymond's brothers in ARM. It's their money, too. But Raymond said no thank you. He'll handle it himself.

Vincent is family. How would it look if Raymond went to the mat for the white race and green-lighted a pair of Israelis to whack his own first cousin? It's lucky for Vincent that the two Jews care more about money than about justice or retribution. They were reasonable about the terms on which Raymond agreed to pay them back, payments added to the monthly nut for the replacement truck.

Raymond *will* find Vincent, when he gets the time, which right now is in short supply, what with working double shifts to repay the money and make payments on a truck that runs worse than the one Vincent stole. Raymond doesn't know what he'll do when he sees Vincent again. Maybe he *will* wind up killing him. He'll just have to go with his gut.

Raymond can thank his mother for this. Watching out for Vincent was one of the laundry list of promises that Raymond's mom extracted from him on her deathbed. Who would have thought that a dying woman would remember the nephew whom everyone in the family spoiled because his tree-hugging hippie mother had been stupid enough to marry a loser who'd let the Infernal Revenue Service jack him around until he blew his brains out?

Right now, while Raymond is stressing over the cost of a magazine, Vincent is probably in Florida. That was something he used to say: *Maybe I should go down to Disney World and put on a Goofy suit and let toddlers fuck with my head.* Talk about hiding in plain sight. What a brilliant cover. Raymond can't see himself hightailing it down to Orlando and roughing up every pervert in a dog nose and floppy ears. Raymond always knew that Vincent was one flaky son of a bitch. But somehow he never would have predicted that the guy would clean him out and split without having the simple decency to say thank you or even good-bye.

Last night's gathering began with solemn toasts to McVeigh and to the Murragh Building victims, innocent casualties of the war that the federal government—working in collusion with the United Nations, NATO, the Council on Foreign Relations, Mossad—is waging against its own God-fearing white citizens. At some point it was decided that each of the guys would drink one shot of vodka for each martyr killed at Waco. The last thing Raymond remembers is going out to the backyard. One of the guys wrote the names of Janet Reno, Bill Clinton, Michael Eisner, and Steven Spielberg on Post-its they stuck on beer cans and shot at with Raymond's deer-hunting rifle until a neighbor phoned the cops. By then they were too shitfaced to see. It's a miracle no one got shot.

Raymond holds the magazine at arm's length. You never know who handled these things, how many people picked their nose and . . . Which is why, if you've got the bucks, a subscription is preferable to buying these rags on the newsstand. He shudders and drops the magazine and has to fight off a lurch of nausea before he can open it again.

Okay, let's see how many Jews have pushed their way to the top and hogged a hundred and fifty percent of national press attention. Here's Billy Joel and Jerry Seinfeld partying in the Hamptons. And there's Jennifer Aniston. Does she think that nose job fools anyone? And Al Gore. Raymond has it on good authority that Gore is part negroid, like Bill Clinton and Rosalind Carter. All these mud-race slimeballs sucking down the caviar and champagne while white guys like Raymond are blowing a blood vessel because their old ladies spent good money to read what some Zionist press agent wants them to believe.

The hangover isn't helping. Another swell of nausea almost makes Raymond quit, but he gives the magazine one more look, and this time . . . Hey, what's this? *What is this?* What the *fuck* is this?

Raymond's so shocked to see someone he knows staring up at him from the page that it takes him a few seconds to figure out who it is. Even then it's a strange sensation. Probably because he's been thinking about Vincent, it's almost as if he hallucinated him, imagined him into the magazine. It must be a bad dream. Because here's Vincent standing on some kind of stage with his arm around a little old Jew under the headline: "A Changed Man. Former Skinhead Finds Brotherhood with Holocaust Survivor."

"In Trouble" says the line above that. *In trouble* is putting it mildly. Where does Vincent get the nerve to show his face? Does he think that Raymond will see his photo and think, Oh, how *nice* for Cousin Vince! How *lovely* that someone in the family has finally hit the big time!

Vincent must have thought that Raymond was making it up

about the mud people and the Jews helping themselves to what belongs to the white man. He must have thought that everything Raymond holds sacred, everything ARM stands for, is some scam that every sleazy race traitor can exploit for fame and fortune when he sells out his white brothers and goes over to the side with more cash and clout. And not just his white brothers. How about the cousin who took him in, who picked him up and dusted him off and gave him something to believe in?

Raymond reads a sentence or two of the article, then has to stop and fight the urge to puke. And that's how it goes from there: Read, stop, almost puke, read, stop, almost puke.

Somehow in the middle of this, Raymond gets the picture:

Vincent sought those fuckers *out*. He went there straight from Raymond's, after making off with his drugs. Which must come in handy. You'd need a shitload of Xanax and Vicodin to stand there with that old Jew's arm around you and smile for the camera. You'd have to be pretty tranked to hang out with that shyster cult leader, to watch him convincing people that he wants to save the world and meanwhile raking in the chips, minus a cut for Israel.

Vincent's become a part of that. He's pitching in, doing his best to keep the circle jerk going. Meanwhile Moron is so screwed up he eats nuts at the fancy dinner and has to be rushed to the emergency room. Raymond remembers the family picnics turned to shit, the mad dashes to the hospital because Allergy Boy got into the Pee Bee and Jay and was turning blue while the adults fought over who was sober enough to drive.

Dumbo had an allergy attack. That's their idea of *in trouble?* Raymond should show them what *in trouble* really means. He turns the page and there, sure enough, is the standard *People* shot of the losers in the kitchen. Laughing and whooping it up. That's how "In Trouble" always ends, with that kitchen scene, everybody feeling better now, or at least in remission. Usually it's some bald chick cooking for her friends.

But now it's Vincent yukking it up at the stove with the middle-aged soccer mom grinning so tightly you can practically hear her face rip. Obviously, Vincent's fucking her. Women always liked Vincent, who always managed to seem so *surprised* that they did. The phony bastard's probably telling that same story about that Polish broad who ditched him at the senior prom. What is Vincent pretending to cook? Raymond would like to know. He lived with Raymond and Lucy for years and never lifted a finger.

This is why Raymond wasn't in more of a hurry to track Vincent down. He knew something like this would happen. Obviously, not *this*. He never expected an article in a national magazine. But he knew that help would come his way, some piece of information. Vincent would reveal himself, not because of who Vincent is, but because some force in the universe believes in justice and retribution and facing up to the evil you've done.

Sometimes Raymond sees ARM that way, as an agent of payback, a crusade against the powers that could make a guy like Vincent's father kill himself, that would murder Randy Weaver's wife and those babies at Waco, that would throw hardworking white citizens out of their jobs and fill them with mud people just so rich Jews can prosper and thrive.

It's as if Vincent is reaching out through the media and punching Raymond in the nose. Is Raymond supposed to roll over and let his cousin abuse his family's hospitality? Vincent must have felt guilty to have made himself so easy to find. He might as well have phoned Raymond and given him his address. Brotherhood Watch must have a Web site. It's probably listed in the phone book.

But is that the way to go? Raymond doesn't want to tip Vincent off. As if Raymond knew what he'd be tipping him off *about*. Is Raymond planning to kill him? Somehow he thinks not. Something is called for, that's for sure. He wishes he knew what it was.

Has Lucy read the magazine? Did she see the article while she was standing in line at the supermarket? Is that why she bought it? If the answer to any of these questions is yes, it's doubly important for Raymond to act. If Lucy knows, everyone knows. Everyone is watching.

H ERE'S HOW ON TOP OF IT VINCENT IS: he wakes up a half hour early so the Vicodin can kick in before breakfast. Everything has happened so fast in the week since the benefit dinner, everything is spinning so far out of control that it has begun to seem smart to self-medicate lightly just to get up in the morning. His drug stash is diminishing at an alarming rate. All this time, he's been so good, saving for the future. But now he needs that spongy buffer between himself and the swirling confusion around him.

Dealing with Bonnie has become a serious tactical challenge. Ever since that . . . misunderstanding in the kitchen, that night when Bonnie hit on him, if that's what she was doing, ever since that kiss, it's as if there's a conversation going on under their normal conversation, as if they're talking about a love affair they aren't even having. It's almost as if they're breaking up, except they were never together.

Bonnie even looks different. When she talks to him, her face takes on a peculiar expression, as if she wants to ask him something, or as if she's stifling a burp. What secret code is she communicating in? What does she want to happen? By the time they get back from the city,

Bonnie's kids are in the basement watching TV, so the chances of Vincent and Bonnie working their way back to that kiss are slim, unless they stop at the Motel 6 on the way home. Which seems highly unlikely. They're careful not to brush elbows as they sit in the car.

Vincent thinks about this at night. It makes it hard to sleep. Which also has been taking its toll on his Xanax supply. He thinks about fucking Bonnie, even though he knows that it's probably the fastest route back to homelessness.

He's got enough problems at work. Every day he's shooting the breeze with some grizzled newsroom vet or boy-genius reporter. Or he's struggling to stay focused as he repeats himself on the phone with some NPR station in East Kalamazoo.

On the day after the benefit, when Vincent was still spacey from passing out, he and Bonnie and Meyer and Roberta had a meeting. Roberta explained that Vincent was now, officially, Mr. Changed Man. A man who'd nearly died transforming himself into a moral hero. Personal growth is what everyone wants. This was talk-show material. People need inspiration, hope.

Roberta stared at Vincent as she'd explained how big this could be. Vincent felt like a character in an action comic who drinks some radioactive goop and grows ten times normal size. The magic drug was a walnut. Not a peanut. The newspapers got it wrong. Another media lie.

As Roberta yakked on, Bonnie kept shooting him worried looks, until at last she'd said, "Are you sure you want to do this?" Vincent knew she was on his side, yet he found her concern annoying. As if he needed Bonnie to tell him what Roberta was doing: packaging him, commodifying him. *A Changed Man* was his brand name.

Vincent's options are limited. Let's say he says, Sorry, he'd rather keep a low profile. Next day, he walks into Bonnie's house, and it's like Goldilocks: Who is this Iranian family sleeping in my bed? So Vincent has to play ball, or else his new best friends at Brotherhood Watch will find a reason to cut him loose. If he screws this up, they'll find something about him that they don't like, or that isn't useful. And what then? Vincent was never serious about going to work as Goofy at Disney World. He isn't ready to blow this scene. To say bye-bye to Bonnie and Maslow.

Meanwhile, with every interview Vincent gives, every time his face appears in the paper, he puts his ass further out on the line. It's just a matter of time till Raymond not only knows where Vincent is but can no longer resist the understandable urge to come see him. Vincent's luck can't hold. After all this publicity about the hero who has turned his back on ARM's demented racist ways, every leader and grunt in the movement probably wants him dead. But they'll give Raymond the privilege. It's part of their Teutonic feudal-code-of-honor bullshit.

For the first time in a while, Vincent has been reading *The Way of the Warrior*, not so much for what it says but to get in touch with his former self—the edgy, paranoid, nowhere man who walked into Brotherhood Watch and imagined that the receptionist was someone to contend with. The Warrior makes a plan. So what plan would the Warrior make now? This is not as simple as ditching Raymond's truck, finding the foundation office, offering his services, seeing what happens next. Vincent has *seen* what happens next. But what's next after this?

The only control Vincent has is to make his own daily schedule, parallel to the agenda that everyone else is making for him, that Roberta has all mapped out by the time he gets to work. At two— are you listening, Vincent?—there's a telephone interview with Cleveland public radio about how it feels to change from a bigoted pig into a selfless human rights crusader.

His private schedule involves the wake-up Vicodin, two beers at lunch, then the evening Xanax, and as much time alone—quality face time with himself—as he can manage without making Bonnie suspect that something's wrong. Space, psychic and physical space, is the number-one essential.

Sometimes in the early evenings he walks around Clairmont, past the neatly coiffed front yards, the pretty white houses, the pretty white children playing on the swing sets made from organic redwood guaranteed uncontaminated by pesticides or preservatives.

It's a whole other planet, a planet he used to despise. But he doesn't have the time or energy for that kind of hatred now. Plus it's harder to hate these yuppie moms and dads now that Vincent's more famous than they are. Why should Vincent envy their gas barbecues and hammocks? He's soothed by the sight of the families, the kids, their kittens and puppies.

Perhaps it's because he knows this can't last. He's balancing on a knife blade, dodging bullet after bullet. And now one has his name on it.

Ever since the dinner Roberta kept saying that he was going to be on TV, which would mean—which would *ensure*—that he was dead meat. There was no way that the ARM guys wouldn't see whatever program he appears on. Vincent was secretly relieved when Barbara Walters's people never called back and Oprah didn't bite.

Then one day he came into the office, and Roberta was practically frothing at the mouth. She body-blocked them in the hall. "Bonnie! Vincent! Have you heard?"

"Heard what?" Vincent knows that Bonnie dislikes Roberta, though she would never admit it. He assumes it's some chick thing. Maybe it's competition. Bonnie can get competitive. It's one of the many things that Bonnie doesn't—doesn't want to—know about herself.

"It's all set up," Roberta said. "And confirmed. Vincent and Meyer are going to appear on *Chandler*! I pitched it to them again, and I think it helped that the other show they did with that neo-Nazi and the Wiesenthal Foundation got fabulous ratings. Apparently everyone saw it. And they understand that this is even better. I mean, as we know, Vincent nearly *died*. Vincent, aren't you thrilled?"

"Great," was all Vincent could mumble. *Chandler* was Raymond's favorite show. So now Raymond will get to watch America's most overpaid Negro ask Vincent how he could have hated innocent men and women of color. *Men and women like me.* He'll ask Vincent why he changed, how he turned his life around.

"Vincent?" said Bonnie. "Are you all right?"

"Maybe he's nervous," said Roberta. "I wouldn't blame him. This is a really big break."

So it's just a matter of waiting for the other shoe to drop and, until that happens, tinkering with his dosage so he doesn't flinch when he hears the second Doc Marten hitting the floor. With his skull underneath it. The bedtime Xanax is no longer enough. Changed circumstances require that he chase the pill with a shot of vodka.

Before dinner, after he's had his drink, and maybe another pill, depending on his nerves, he sits in the chair at the end of the garden and stares into the hedges. There's not much to look at, but it gives him a sense of peace. He stays there while Bonnie cooks, until she calls him and he goes into the house. By then he's usually feeling mellow enough to deal with her and the boys, though, he hopes, not so mellow that they'll wonder what he's on. Danny's usually pretty mellow himself. He handed in his Hitler paper, he proudly announced to Vincent. So now he can just stay loaded. Mealtimes tend to be peaceful. Bonnie keeps her distance. Max still seems slightly down in the mouth ever since that night at Doctor Dad's. Though whenever Bonnie asks Vincent if Max seems depressed, Vincent says no, he doesn't. He says, Probably Max is tired from all the growing he's doing.

On one such placid evening, Vincent is sitting at the bottom of the garden, feeling himself slip pleasantly into that cottony state in which he knows it's pointless to worry. He might as well enjoy this perfectly lovely, comfortable moment. A pink glow hovers over the river. Dinner's on its way. There's nothing to do but sit here with a drink in his hand and watch some tiny aphids nibble a leaf that's probably deadly poison. Built-in population control, biologically engineered to produce a steady die-out in the aphid population.

Vincent can feel the footsteps coming up behind him, muffled by the thick grass. Lately he's become attuned to the faintest whispers and stirrings. Just in case it's somebody with mayhem on his mind. He wheels around. It's Bonnie.

Vincent wishes she didn't look so apologetic. "The boys and I are going out for pizza. Do you want to come?"

"No, that's okay." Vincent watches her face fall. Bonnie needs to lighten up. This is not about rejection. He'd rather not spoil his high.

"Can you bring me back a couple of slices?" It's the right thing to ask. Bonnie's softened by this evidence that he still needs her to take care of him.

"Any preference?" she says.

"No," he says. "Whatever."

"Okay," says Bonnie. "See you soon."

"Thanks," Vincent calls after her. Beautiful! After this, he'll be left alone, even after they return. No one's going to force him to come inside and eat pizza. But it takes a while to grope his way back toward that unrattled state he was in before Bonnie disturbed him. Gradually, it steals over him. He finds a bug to focus on.

Inside the house, the phone rings.

Why doesn't the machine pick up? Has Bonnie turned it off? Suppose it's Bonnie stuck on the road between here and the pizza place. Her van's been making weird noises, but Vincent hasn't had the heart to point that out. He was afraid she'd take it as a personal criticism. He should have mentioned it. Because now, if she's stuck, it will be his fault, and he'll have to deal with that. He might as well start now. But what if it's the dad on the phone? Vincent will say he got the wrong number, and then when the doc calls back, he won't pick up. It's probably some telemarketer. Easy enough to tell them to fuck off. As long as it's not Bonnie.

He hauls himself up and trots toward the house. The phone stops ringing. Thank God. He goes back to his chair, but seconds later the phone begins again, and this time he's back there fast enough to get it on the third ring.

"Hello?" says Vincent.

Silence. Someone's there. It is not a wrong number. The caller hasn't hung up. Someone's waiting for him to say hello again. "Hello?" He can feel the menace thrumming at the other end of the line.

It's Raymond. Vincent knows it. He doesn't want to say Raymond's name. Doesn't want to, doesn't have to. Even so, it's as if they're having a meaningful discussion. The silence is Raymond telling him that he knows where he is. He knows what Vincent did, and why, though maybe not *exactly* why. He knows things that Vincent has never seen fit to mention to the people he lives and works with. This is the real conversation, a talk that Vincent has never stopped having. It's amazing how much you can say without having to say one word.

I T'S ALMOST FIVE, and Bonnie can't summon the energy for yet
another conversation with Roberta. So she ignores the phone
light—it can't be the kids, they use her cell—as she surfs the
net for information on anaphylactic shock. She searches "fainting"
for some reference to the aftereffects of losing consciousness,
symptoms that linger and worsen. She skims a few dozen sites,
none of which mention anything remotely relevant. What *are* Vincent's symptoms? A spacey remove, an indefinable . . . not-there-
ness. That could be anything, including a reaction to the pressures of
his new visibility. Meetings with Roberta, interviews, reporters. What
resources does Vincent have left for a casual chat with Bonnie?

At least Max seems to have recovered from his traumatic
evening at Joel's and returned to his cheerful self. Which leaves
Bonnie free to worry about Vincent's mental health.

Some mornings Vincent falls asleep in the car on the way to the
office, and in the evenings, when he retreats to his chair at the bottom of the yard, Bonnie has to yell to get him to come to dinner.
Or else she goes down and finds him with his head tipped back and
his eyes closed.

Bonnie knows he's been drinking some, but not enough to explain his behavior. Could he be on drugs? He's too quick, too conscious. He's so cogent and functional when he *does* wake up, so fully present with everyone—everyone except Bonnie. If he were high, she would know it, though of course she's heard stories about kids who had heavy habits and their parents never suspected.

Maybe the distance she feels between them is the aftermath of the humiliation of taking off her glasses. Maybe Vincent's embarrassed by some guy thing that makes him see the incident as a challenge to his manhood. A challenge he failed. Or maybe she's flattering herself to think that whatever's wrong with Vincent has any connection to her.

In any case, what matters now are not the dynamics between them but what he's doing for Brotherhood Watch. He's getting mail, fan letters, invitations to charity dinners and society parties. His interview requests outnumber Meyer's, though Meyer is often called on for a photo op or a sound bite on the subject of Vincent's transformation. Meyer always says how proud he is and how much hope it gives him to see how Vincent has changed.

Bonnie's dance card has filled up, too. Donors she's pursued since she came to Brotherhood Watch have been phoning and making lunch dates. Tomorrow, she's having lunch with Laura Ticknor, who has been hinting that she has all sorts of fresh contacts, new donors, and willing volunteers to bring into the fold. For the first time it seems possible that, this year, the foundation will actually meet its budget and break even.

Bonnie can't take credit, but she's proud of her part in changing Vincent from a calculating opportunist trying only to survive into a guy who would nearly die for Brotherhood Watch. So what if Vincent wouldn't get out of bed this morning and yelled to Bonnie through his closed bedroom door? He'd said he wasn't feeling well. Could he take the day off? He'd sounded exactly like her kids, faking illness to get out of school. But in fact he's been working so hard, he deserves a break. After phoning Roberta to make sure he had no interviews today, Bonnie said he could stay home and rest.

Just this once. It felt wickedly pleasurable to lie to Roberta and say she thought that Vincent might have a touch of the flu.

Obviously concerned, Roberta urged Bonnie to make sure that Vincent took care of himself. Everything around the office has revolved around Meyer and Vincent's upcoming appearance on *Chandler.* Roberta wants to be sure that the dog and pony are ready to do their act.

Bonnie turns from the computer, resigned to answering the blinking phone. What does Roberta want now?

"Hello?"

No reply. She hears traffic noise.

"Hello?"

Someone's there. Something's happening here. Bonnie doesn't like it. She goes for the worst scenario first: One of her kids is trying to reach her, and he can't get through, or worse, he's been kidnapped and has escaped and is trying to call. Vincent's ARM friends are resurfacing. She can't let herself think that now. In fact she hangs up and does such an excellent job of repression that when the phone rings ten minutes later, it never occurs to her that the same person might call again.

"Hello?"

Another silence. More traffic noise.

Bonnie hears a siren. It takes a disconcertingly long time to figure out the sound's coming simultaneously from over the phone and outside the window. Could the caller be nearby? She's seen this scene in a million films; it's always just before the car bomb goes off.

"Who is this?" Bonnie says. "Who's calling?"

The only thing that slows her free-fall descent into paranoia is the possibility that the call might be for someone else. Why would anyone phone Bonnie and let the line go dead? But when she checks with the front desk, Anita says the caller, a man, asked specifically for her. Both times he'd mumbled his name, and Anita put him through because she thought it sounded like the name of one of their donors.

Bonnie's first impulse—to lock her door and turn off her phone—wars against her second impulse, which is to go home and lock the doors and turn off the phone. It's after five. She's been here since nine. She has every right to leave and try to beat the worst of the Tappan Zee traffic.

Probably she should tell Meyer and Roberta that she's going. But she doesn't feel like being seen breezing out while they're still hard at work.

She's glad the elevator is crowded, that it's not just her and the lone obvious candidate for Mr. Mystery Caller. On the street, she spots a dozen guys who could be her phone friend. She keeps looking over her shoulder. How can you tell if you're being followed when everyone's walking in the same direction?

By the time she gets to the garage, she's so jittery that she considers asking the attendant to walk her to her car. But how would she explain it? Excuse me, I hate to bother you, but some pervert breathed into the phone.

Bonnie finds the van, drives down the ramp, inches out into traffic, all of which requires so much concentration that she forgets the crank calls, or whatever they were—maybe just wrong numbers—until the blinking light on her dashboard reminds her of the blinking phone, and then makes her forget it again because, as she heads toward the West Side Highway, the dashboard light seems to be flashing faster.

Maybe she's imagining it. The light's been going on intermittently since that first day she drove Vincent home. He'd said she had a thousand miles to go before she had to take it seriously. But the light on her dashboard doesn't seem to know that.

By the time she's driven through Riverdale, there's an ominous groaning, a tug of resistance every time she hits the gas. Then a disturbing clicking begins, several miles south of the bridge. Wouldn't you know this would happen on the one day Vincent isn't with her? Which is probably why it's happening, just to punish Bonnie, who feels the same obscure guilt she feels when she lets her kids cut school. If she'd been tougher on Vincent this morning and made him go to work, he'd be here to help her.

Meanwhile, what should Bonnie do? Pull over and call for help?

Every time she puts on her blinker, the sound stops and she thinks she can make it home. How wonderful it would be to limp all the way to her driveway and cope with this from the comfort of her living room instead of some gas station in Yonkers. The van bides its time, it waits till she's on to the approach to the bridge—no exit!—and then starts making noises that mean business.

Bonnie prays, Just let me make it across the bridge. There are no atheists with car trouble on the Tappan Zee. She bargains with the god of breakdowns to give her ten more miles, in return for which she'll do the right thing, she'll stop at JZ's garage on the way home. JZ knows her. He knows the car. He'll be able to take one look at it and tell her how bad things are. Why didn't she do this when the light started blinking? Why don't people rush to the doctor with that first cough or skipped heartbeat? Because she'd hoped it would go away. Because she'd been busy.

The car god hears her prayer. The noise doesn't get any louder, though that funny tug of resistance seems to be growing more pronounced. But even that gives her enough slack to cross the bridge and head north on 9W until she reaches the garage. It's a miracle she's gotten here, and a double blessing that, by the time she pulls into JZ's lot, the garage is still open and the sound is so loud that it summons JZ and his helper and eliminates the small talk they might otherwise have felt obliged to make.

She's known JZ, Jimmy Zagarella, ever since they moved up here. Bonnie always hated how Joel acted around Jimmy, as if they were close buddies, two guys into large engines. Once, when Bonnie needed to reach Joel, who was stopping by the garage, she called and asked for him by name, and Jimmy said, Uhh . . . what's the guy driving? That's how close they were. Jimmy figured out about the divorce. It didn't take a genius to make the logical deduction when Joel disappeared and suddenly it was Bonnie bringing in the van for its annual inspection. Sometimes Bonnie sees Jimmy at the middle school. He's got a son in Max's class. Jimmy's wife ditched him years ago, left him with two kids. He's been doing a marvelous job. He's Clairmont's model single parent.

Now the noises coming from under the hood make Jimmy grin and shake his head in awe and admiration. "Wow," he says. "When did *that* start?" Bonnie smiles back. It's an oddly congenial moment as Jimmy and Bonnie bond over how terrible her car sounds.

"It just started," Bonnie lies.

"Out of nowhere?" asks Jimmy.

"Well, there *was* this blinking light. I should have brought it in sooner—"

"I figured that," says Jimmy. How grateful Bonnie is to have reached this sweet, safe harbor where she can hand her troubles over to Jimmy. "The main thing is that you're not stuck on the bridge."

That's exactly what Bonnie thinks. How well Jimmy knows her. If Bonnie was determined to form some inappropriate and unrequited romantic attachment, why couldn't she have picked a nice guy, a single dad like Jimmy, instead of a former Nazi she works with at the office? If she'd hit on Jimmy, he would have turned her down, too. Where is Bonnie going with this? This is about her *car*.

"What's wrong with it?" Appalled to hear her question trail off in a whine, Bonnie tries to recast her whiny neediness as jaunty and ironic. "How much damage are we looking at?" She's trying to sound like a guy, when what she'd really like to do is burst into tears. How will she get to work? She absolutely cannot miss her lunch date tomorrow with Laura Ticknor! Wednesday is *The Chandler Show*. What if the van can't be fixed?

She can't afford a new vehicle like, for example, the obscene, gas-guzzling eco-criminal wet dream that Joel's apparently driving. The thought of Joel cruising around in that while she's nearly breaking down in the middle of the Tappan Zee is so maddening that it nearly undoes her resolve to be more sympathetic, the promise that she made to herself the last time she and Joel talked on the phone.

"Let's take a look," says Jimmy. Does he really mean *let's*? Is he suggesting that Bonnie watch over his shoulder like Joel used to? As if Joel knew jack about cars. Bonnie stands—close but not too close—behind Jimmy as he pokes around under the hood. Jimmy's attractive, around Bonnie's age, smallish, wiry, well built. And such a good father. Why has Bonnie never noticed? God help her, she's turned into a sex maniac, fantasizing romance with every guy she meets. But shouldn't she be grateful? Doesn't this signal the return of some faint promptings from the life force that she'd assumed was gone forever?

"What do you think it is?" Bonnie hears herself whining again.

"Serious things, not-so-serious things. It's hard to say right this minute."

"What are the not-so-serious things?"

"Spark plug. The fan could be hitting its housing."

"And the serious things?"

"I don't know. A wheel bearing. Bonnie, do me a favor. Go wait in the office, okay? Let me check it out."

"Okay, sure." Bonnie's face is hot with shame. You'd think, from the way she feels now, that she'd grabbed Jimmy's ass. Nothing happened to make Jimmy think that she was interested. Vincent's the guy it happened with. Bonnie took off her glasses.

The "office"—two chairs, a table—smells of motor oil and cigarettes. Bonnie eyes the coffeepot, the packets of creamer and sugar. She'd be awake all night. Plus she doesn't have the hand-eye coordination required to pour and tap and stir. She drops into a chair, flips through the magazines, discarding the ones with Tim McVeigh's face on the cover. She opens *House Proud* and reads about five women and their kitchens getting simultaneous beauty makeovers. She pages through a feature entitled "The 10 Most Important Things You Should Know About Your Child's Food Allergies." What malevolent spirit sent that helpful essay her way? She studies every word, then picks up a teen magazine and opens to "How Do You Know If He Likes You?" *Guys are easier to figure out than most girls realize.* She flings it down, and so it goes until she's worked her way through the stack in which each publication conveys a precisely targeted smart bomb of shame, curiosity, and horror.

She feels the same vague anxiety she associates with the doctor's office. So when Jimmy reappears, her apprehension spikes just as it does when the doctor enters with his nose in her chart.

Jimmy smiles. "Which do you want first, the good news or the bad news?"

"The good news." Bonnie really wants the bad news first but wants to seem like the sort of person who asks for the good news first.

"The good news is that it's the fan belt. Like I said. Remember?"

Excellent. Fan belt sounds fixable. But what about the bad news?

"Now for the *really* good news," Jimmy says. "I can fix it for you by tomorrow afternoon."

"Okay, so what's the bad news?"

"You've got to pick it up before two," Jimmy says. "I'm closing early. For the weekend. Sean's got a dirt bike meet all the way up in Cooperstown. We've got to leave Friday afternoon and stay over Friday night."

This isn't bad news. Bonnie's car can be fixed soon, and from the sound of Jimmy's voice, she guesses it won't be too expensive. She'll have to leave work early, or better yet, take the day off and get the car. What's wrong with this picture? Lunch with Laura Ticknor. *That's* the bad news. Bonnie can't reschedule. With Laura Ticknor's social life, that might mean a delay of three months, by which point they will have lost whatever momentum they picked up at the benefit dinner. Good-bye new donors, farewell celebrity volunteers. Vincent will have almost died for nothing.

Why should she go through this so that Jimmy's son can ride a dangerous dirt bike too fast around a track? Can't Jimmy's helper stay late enough to exchange Bonnie's car keys for money?

"Can't you leave the car and the key for me till I get home from work tomorrow night? And I'll get you a check."

Jimmy says, "We're not supposed to let this get out. But a car was stolen from the lot two weeks ago. So we're being extra careful."

"Hey, I've got an idea," Bonnie says. "There's this guy I work with, I could send him to pick up the car tomorrow. And I'll call you and send you a check. Or I could give it to him. But how will I know how much it is?"

"I'll trust you for it," says Jimmy.

HOW LONG HAS MEYER BEEN ASLEEP? Long enough for the light to have changed. The sky above the city has taken on a dusty lavender color, a color for which, he seems to recall, there was a Hungarian word. But he can't remember it, and maybe there never was one, just an illusion left over from the dream state he'd slipped into at his desk. Has he missed anything? Probably. So much is happening every minute. The TV show coming up, and all the hullabaloo about Vincent . . .

Every light on his phone is blinking. He rings Bonnie and gets her voice mail. Meyer calls the front desk. Has everyone gone home? He looks at his watch. It's seven. No wonder they're gone. How could he have slept so long? Why didn't anyone wake him? Didn't anyone care enough to see if he was alive?

Meyer leaves his office and wanders down the halls lined with empty cubicles. How melancholy and alone he feels, like an abandoned child. On the morning of the day he came home from school to find that his mother had been taken away by the Germans, they'd had a fight because he'd refused to wear the scratchy new scarf she'd made him. The scarf was there. She wasn't. Only then did he put it on. A lifetime later, he can still feel the coarse wool around his neck.

Why think that now? Because he's alone in the office? Because the elderly baby can't be left on his own? Meyer's being hard on himself. He's not a pampered infant. His work is important. He just freed an innocent man from jail, halfway around the world. Meyer made some phone calls. He called in a couple of favors. But no one wants to hear about that. They all want to know about Vincent.

Why should Meyer be surprised that Vincent's story should be easier to market? It's new. They're tired of Meyer's song and dance. The Holocaust is over. Please, no more Hitler, no more ovens, no more filthy, skeletal half-dead Jews in striped pajamas. It's time to move on. Enough with the Hungarian kid who had unspeakable things done to him and survived. Let's concentrate on this younger, handsomer model who once had a couple of racist thoughts and later changed his mind.

What has it all added up to? How much time does Meyer have left? And what will he do with that time? Sit in this office, make calls. No one cares. No one buys his books.

Meyer needs to snap out of it. He probably has plans for the evening, something Irene arranged. Some museum opening, opera, ballet. Why can't Meyer remember? Because he never knows. When he gets home, Irene will give him the evening's assignment, tell him when and where he will be playing Meyer Maslow.

In any case, he needs to go. He hurries back to his office to grab his briefcase and keys. Isn't there a security guard? It shames him that he doesn't know how to lock up his own place of business. Every grocer can do that.

The light on his phone blinks again. Obviously, it's Irene, asking where he is, scolding him for being late. He dreads the sound of her voice. But there's nothing to be gained by making Irene worry.

"Hello," says Meyer.

There's a silence. Then a man says, "Ah need to talk to Vincent."

The tone is low and menacing, and the southern drawl sounds even more threatening because it seems fake.

"Who is this?" Meyer asks.

"Who wants to know?" says the voice.

"This is Meyer Maslow."

"This is Meyer Maslow." The man imitates him, several registers higher. "Vincent Nolan will know who I am."

"He's not here," says Meyer.

"Tell him I called." The line goes dead. Meyer stands there with the phone to his ear, listening to the silence.

Meyer has enough instinct left to know that the guy isn't kidding. The guy means Vincent harm. That sixth sense that enabled him to read a person's true intentions must still be functioning. There's no ESP required. Just common sense, and anyway, Vincent said as much that first day. The guys in ARM were after him. That's why he needed to stay at Bonnie's. And now at last they've found him.

Meyer knew something like this would happen. But he chose to ignore it, because Vincent was useful to him. That's how low Meyer has sunk. He's put someone else's life in danger. And for what? To publicize his book? No, it's not about that. It's to support the foundation.

Meanwhile Vincent's a sitting duck. That's what Meyer and Bonnie have made him. They've bred the instinct out of him: the impulse to take off running. Meyer recognized that reflex. That's why he made Bonnie watch him. To change Vincent that way, to denature him, is like handling a baby bird, like domesticating a wild beast and setting it loose in the forest.

The phone lights again. Meyer picks up.

"Hello?" he says. "Hello?"

"Meyer," Irene says. "Where are you? Do you have any i-dee-a?"

G ETTING HIGH WAS A HUGE MISTAKE. Danny's got to stop
it. He promises himself that he'll cut down as soon as
school is over. He knows it's a promise he only makes at
the very worst moments, like now, when Mrs. Graber is looming
over his desk, asking him to look at his schedule and see what period he has free to meet with her and Mr. Armstrong. That's the assistant principal. And Mrs. Graber doesn't sound friendly. The pot
is giving her voice a kind of echoey reverb. Danny takes out his
schedule. There's no way he can pretend not to have the next two
periods free. Doesn't Graber have to teach? This must be important if Linda Graber's blowing off a class for a conference about
whatever Danny supposedly did.

"Next period then," Mrs. Graber says. "We'll expect you in
David Armstrong's office."

"Can I ask what this is about?" Danny hates the wimpy sound of
his voice. The whole class is watching. He'll never live this down.
Can I ask what this is about? will dog him all the way to next year's
graduation. Anyway, he doesn't have to ask. He already knows.

"I think you know," Mrs. Graber says.

"My Hitler paper?" Danny says.

"Good guess, Danny," says Graber.

But there's nothing wrong with his paper. It was a fairly straight-forward biography of Hitler plus some information about how he might have been gay. Which he put in to make it more interesting. He was trying to say something new.

"What's the problem?" Danny stalls. Mrs. Graber's supposed to tell him together with the assistant principal. But she can hardly wait. She's dying to break the news herself.

"Frankly, Danny, there was some concern that your paper might be . . . homophobic."

Homophobic? Danny wasn't saying that being gay meant you were Hitler, or that Hitler was Hitler because he was gay, or that all gay guys are like Hitler. How could Graber and Armstrong get it so wrong? Armstrong's famously touchy about this, being as how he *is* gay, the only out administrator in the Lower Hudson Valley system. Ever since Armstrong came to the school, they've had a week of sensitivity training every fall, five days of nonstop embarrassment, of making the few black and Hispanic kids want to kill themselves on the spot as the homeroom teachers read from a script that lists the nasty prejudices you might have about other races. The teach-ers ask the kids who believe it to raise their hands. No kid is that stupid. A school joke is that Armstrong's initials, DGA, stand for Definitely Gay Astronaut. He *could* be the first gay astronaut. He looks like one. He's got an astronaut name.

Next period. Let's get it over with. At least Graber won't expect him to listen as she drones on for the rest of class. He's too busy trying to remember exactly what he said in his paper. He knows Mrs. Graber won't call on him because today, even if it's obvious that he hasn't done the reading, it's no fun for her. She can't get him in trouble. He's al-ready in trouble.

As soon as the bell rings, Danny hurries out, then hangs back. The last thing he wants is to get to Armstrong's office early and stand around making small talk until Graber shows up. Taking baby steps to the second floor, he gets there just as Mrs. Graber walks in.

She sits down beside Armstrong's desk. There's no chair for Danny. But he never expected this to be a friendly social occasion. For a moment they pretend he's not there, allowing him to observe their perfect mutual understanding. They've already had a talk about him. The thought gives him the shivers.

David Armstrong is the one person in the whole school most likely to hate his essay. Because he's one of those gay guys who thinks he has to be super straight. Maybe Linda Graber is gay, too. Just because she's married . . . Whether anyone is gay or not has nothing to do with this. What matters is what Danny meant to say, and what he said, in his paper.

"Hello, Danny," Armstrong says. Have they actually met? They've said hello as they passed in the hall. Armstrong says hello to everyone and pretends he knows you. He probably thinks he *does* know you because you say hello. He probably thinks that's what knowing you *is*.

Stepping forward to shake his hand, Armstrong's doing his slightly hunched, pigeon-toed school-administrator walk, like the wild ostriches Danny saw last week on Discovery Channel. Armstrong's hand feels cool and soft.

"Hi," says Danny. "Hey, Mrs. Graber."

Graber rolls her eyes and sighs.

Mr. Armstrong says, "As we suppose you can imagine . . ." Who is this *we?* And *what* can Danny imagine? By suggesting he can imagine something, Armstrong's suggesting that Danny already knows something, which proves that he's guilty. "Mrs. Graber and I are terribly upset about the paper you turned in for World Civilizations."

Graber and Armstrong both sound like astronauts' names. Houston, we've got a problem.

"What was wrong with my paper?" *As I suppose you can imagine.*

"We feel . . . Mrs. Graber and I both feel that it's extremely homophobic of you to say that homosexuality or even the fear of his own homosexuality can turn a man into history's most evil mass murderer."

That's what Danny was afraid they *thought* he said. Except that he *didn't* say that. He never said that was why Hitler did what he did. He just said maybe Hitler was gay. *And* he was evil. Neither thing *caused* the other. They've completely misread him.

Ultimately, why should he care? Who are Armstrong and Graber? Two losers who work in his school. Still can't get past the fact that someone thinks he meant and said something he didn't mean or say. It throws him so off balance that now he isn't sure what he *did* mean and *did* say. Maybe he didn't say it clearly. Is there a way to explain? Danny's afraid there isn't, that he'll never change their minds. His only choice is to fall back on what's in his heart, what he believes. Which is that being gay doesn't mean you want to kill six million Jews, nor that all gay people are murderers. He's tired. He wants to sit down. What he really wants is to punch someone. It's so frustrating. A teen cliché. *Nobody understands me.*

"That's not what I meant," says Danny. "I never said that Hitler did what he did because he was a closeted gay. I never said that all gays are capable of doing what Hitler did. I said that Hitler had a lot of problems. And one of them was maybe sexual . . ."

It's as if he hasn't spoken, as if he's moving his lips. Testing, testing, has someone turned off the audio? Graber and Armstrong don't blink. Danny wishes he weren't stoned. It's making this twice as scary. Danny will never get high again. Not ever, as long as he lives.

Armstrong runs a hand through his blond bristles and leans across his desk. His pink face shines at Danny like those interrogation lamps you see in movies about Nazis. Best not to think of those films now. Danny has to stay clear.

"We so want our students to understand that the most valuable thing we can teach them, even more important than what they learn in class, is a sense of community, of inclusiveness and tolerance, of live and let live."

"I know that." Danny ought to. He's certainly heard it enough.

"And to believe or say anything counter to that is . . . well, it's a re-al problem for the community. Danny, I'll be straight with you. It's like a knife in our hearts."

The most important thing is not to crack up because David

Armstrong said he wanted to be *straight* with him. Danny didn't write what they say he wrote. And what if he did? What about *his* freedom of speech? His First Amendment rights? Where were Graber and Armstrong last year when they took American History, and Mr. Hellenschmidt, one of the only cool teachers, made sure that even the slowest kids understood what the Constitution guaranteed.

"So what happens now?" asks Danny.

Armstrong and Graber look at him, surprised and a little stung. They want to torture him longer, and Danny's ruined their fun.

"We need to think it over and discuss it amongst ourselves," says Mr. Armstrong. "We need to consider your case." So they *are* going to torture him more. Starting with the disgusting idea of them *discussing his case.*

"And until then?" Danny's been a cringing wreck ever since Linda Graber stood over his desk. What would happen if he needed to fight a real enemy—let's say, the Nazis? He fears cowardice above all things. He fears he's the kind who runs away from danger instead of the kind who runs toward it. He fears he's inherited it from his mom. It's in his DNA code.

Graber and Armstrong exchange looks. They've got this all worked out. Why don't they say it in unison, like cartoon chipmunks? Why does Mrs. Graber defer to Mr. Armstrong? Because he's the *man.*

"Let's start with a temporary suspension," he says.

"Fine. Let's start with that." Danny likes the feeling of saying it, so he says it again. "Let's start with that." The second time may have been a mistake. Anyway, it's his exit line. Danny is up and out of the office.

Testosterone is the wind in his sails! It carries him past Armstrong's secretary and straight toward the door, toward the sunlight and warm air. Let the hall monitors stop him. Danny is following orders.

Outside, it's a beautiful day. Only lunatics would be rotting in school, wasting their time in class. Danny decides to go home and figure out what he needs to do next. The thought of home leads directly to Mom, who will not be pleased by the suspension. But Danny will show her his paper. She'll understand what Danny was saying, and she'll take his side. Despite how often Danny wishes his mom were different, he's glad she's the way she is.

It all feels unaccountably fantastic, the charitable thoughts about his mom, the residual high combined with the pleasant weather, the beautiful streets of Clairmont. Every flowering tree is in bloom. Too bad for those puppies stuck in school beneath the fluorescent lights. For all that Danny complains about Clairmont, that it's boring, there's nothing to do, today he has to admit that it's a great place to live. Not that he'll be here long. He's got college after next year. Oops. Temporary suspension. Which ultimately won't matter. It's in the school's interests for him to get into college. They'll downplay this little glitch. And the truth is, Danny is Mr. Tolerance. *That's* in his DNA code. Just look at where his mother works. If worst comes to worst, Mom can get Maslow to write a letter testifying to Danny's brotherly love credentials.

Danny rounds his corner. Something's going on. More cars than usual are parked on his street. Maybe there's something at the church. Maybe somebody's selling their house and is having the realtors in.

The parking thins near his house. The bad house on the good block. Danny used to get annoyed when his parents said that, as if living in the neighborhood dump was something to boast about. But Danny's come to like the fact that his house is the real house, as opposed to all the pretentious fantasy houses, the Scarlett O'Hara, the Mount Vernon, the Addams Family mansion. Danny's still slightly wasted. That was good weed Chloe had.

How happy he is to see his house. It's how he's been feeling about his mom. His house, his mother, he loves them. Nothing like a chat with Armstrong and Graber to make you appreciate what you've got. He wishes Mom were home now. He could tell her what happened. She'd be upset at first, but then she'd read his paper. . . .

There's a pickup truck in his driveway. Is Mom having work done on the house? Danny doubts it. She would have told him. A million times. She would have spent days reminding him that someone was going to be there, someone it was safe to let in, as opposed to all the serial killers trying to break down the front door. She would have given him a detailed description of the electrician or plumber: mug shot, license number, psychological profile.

Maybe some creep is casing the house. Maybe Mom's worst fantasy has come true. Or maybe it's just some guy who's decided to take a nap in Danny's driveway, or trawl for neighborhood kids to molest. In any case, it's not what Danny wants to deal with at the moment.

Danny considers pretending that there's no guy and no truck in his driveway. He could walk around the block, cut across the neighbor's yard, sneak in the back way. Lock the door, keep the curtains pulled. That's what the weed is suggesting. The problem is that Danny can't forget that conversation with Vincent about the people who run away from trouble and the ones who run toward it. Danny's a guy from the first group who wants to belong to the second. And the truck in his driveway is definitely a test.

There's no way he can sneak inside with that guy sitting there. Since Dad's gone, Danny's the man of the house. So he's got to do something besides what he would love to do—which is to keep going.

It takes all the nerve Danny has to walk up to the truck. He pulls himself up to his full height and tries to swagger like a cop giving a ticket. Which is *not* what he wants to look like, a cop handing out a ticket, unless he wants his head blown off by whoever is sitting in the rusted, twenty-year-old pickup. The other end of the line from what Dad was driving. Danny can see his blood and brains splashed all over the driveway, his little brother finding him when he comes home from school. And calling Mom. Poor Mom!

This is what bravery is. Bravery has nothing to do with giving Armstrong and Graber attitude. It serves Danny right for even imagining *that* took courage. His punishment for even thinking that is to come home and face the real thing. What happened in school was foreplay. The nightmare is beginning.

Danny approaches the driver's-side window. He's investing so much energy in trying not to look scared that it keeps him from getting as nervous as he otherwise would. That is, until he looks in the truck and sees a butt-ugly, scowling, bald guy. There's a funny indentation around his forehead, as if he's got permanent hat hair without hair or a hat. He's also missing a couple of teeth. Where did they get this creep? Call central casting, get me a redneck. But wait. It gets worse. A redneck Nazi. Danny can't help but notice the swastika tattooed on the back of the guy's right hand.

Which absolutely takes guts. Unlike Vincent, who's got his tattoos higher up on his arms so he can hide them, this guy wants it in your face. There's no going back for this dude without laser surgery. Vincent was always hedging his bets. Danny sees that now.

The guy is here for Vincent. Anything else is too coincidental. Adopt a skinhead, and surprise! Another one comes along. Danny knew this would happen. His mom mentioned it the very first night Vincent came home with her. And then somehow Danny forgot.

Isn't Danny supposed to talk first? Say something weak like, Excuse me. Can I help you?

The guy looks Danny in the eye for a long time, very dramatic and stagey.

Finally he says, "Hey, kid. Tell me something. You live here?"

Danny would laugh if his legs didn't feel like rubber. Once again he wishes he'd never smoked that joint. Should he admit he lives here? In case the guy is planning to come back and rob and kill him and Mom and Max? Or maybe he means to do it right now. Is there some way to communicate that his parents are home, or better yet, the high school football team just happens to be here right now? But why would the football team hang out at Danny's?

"Yeah." A simple statement of fact.

"Who else lives here?" says the guy.

They might as well bump chests, lock horns. There's no point to this conversation. The guy knows Vincent lives with them. Danny's hands are shaking.

"Why do you want to know?" Danny says. All right! This is

more like it. This beats telling Graber and Armstrong to take their suspension and shove it.

"Census," says the guy.

"Yeah? Census my ass." Danny's heart starts to pound.

The guy reaches for the door handle.

"Watch your language," he says. "Who lives here is all I asked."

"My mom, my brother, and me." Danny regrets it instantly. Couldn't he have invented a father? Oh, and my dad, the professional wrestler. The head of the FBI.

"And who else?" repeats the guy.

"Nobody." Who is Danny kidding? This psycho's not cruising the neighborhood for a house to rob.

"Nobody," he repeats. He smiles and shakes his head. What a joke. Then he says, "You little shit, you're lucky I've got kids myself. Otherwise you could get hurt."

Danny's relieved. It sounds like the guy isn't going to kill him. At the same time, he's vaguely insulted. He reminds this guy of his *kids?* Imagine being this guy's kid. Would you have your own tiny swastika tats? Do they make stick-on tattoos for babies? Danny's had a bitch of a day. First they threaten him at school, and then he goes home and gets threatened by a guy parked in his own driveway. First he takes shit for writing about Hitler, and then Hitler's number one fan shows up at his house.

"All right," says the guy. "Let's cut the crap. Tell Nolan I know where he's at."

"Who should I tell him stopped by?" Danny asks.

The guy gives him another stagey look and does a phony double take. He's pretending to decide whether to break Danny's jaw or just answer his question. He decides not to punch him out. He'd already decided. He considers his answer.

"Who should you tell him stopped by? The Big Bad Wolf," he says.

So far Vincent's day off has been everything he'd hoped for. Seven-point-five on a scale of ten. The situation with Bonnie's van couldn't have worked out better. He was genuinely sorry that he hadn't been there for her when it died. But at least it wasn't some hairy breakdown that left Bonnie stranded. She got the vehicle to the garage. And her needing him to pick it up is the icing on the cake. He gets another day off to recover. Already he's so rested that he feels capable of going into the office tomorrow and dealing with Roberta and having the same conversation with a dozen different boring reporters. Except that tomorrow's Saturday. He's still got the weekend.

He even feels up for going on *Chandler*, which he'd been edgy about. It's got to be easier than the benefit dinner, since presumably he won't be dying of allergic shock on a major network. Though Chandler's people would probably think it was great TV. Don't eat *anything* they give you in the studio. It wouldn't be beyond the bastards to slip him a wad of peanut butter. And if his being on *Chandler* helps Raymond track him down . . . There's no way he can control that. Let the chips fall where they may.

Meanwhile a day of R and R is just the thing, especially a day on which Vincent's doing it right: deciding against the Vicodin first thing in the morning just to show himself that he can, one skinny joint from the kid's stash, then a stroll through the neighborhood, which has never looked so good, climaxing with a tuna fish sandwich at the Clairmont Creamery, a place that would have put him uptight not so long ago. Now he can simply occupy a booth and pass for your average Joe. Not that he *is* your average Joe. No, sir. Not by a long shot.

His outing takes an hour or so. More than enough fresh air. He walks home—sun shining, air warm, neighborhood in bloom—and lets himself into the silent house, then lies down for a nap. When he wakes up, he decides—as a present to himself, a reward for being so good—that he'll borrow one more bud from Danny. In a way, it's humiliating, stealing weed from a child. And it shoves Vincent's nose in the fact that this isn't his home. He's been here almost three months, and he still hasn't made a lousy pot connection. Probably the guys at the mailroom at work would know where he could get some, but that wouldn't be smart. His brotherhood honeymoon would dead-end after the first tiny drug bust. Quick! Get me the Iranian! We're cutting the Nazi loose.

It took Vincent about a minute to find the kid's pot. On the bookshelf, in a coffee can, behind the *Abridged Oxford English Dictionary*, probably a bar mitzvah present. Danny thinks it will be safe there because no one would dream that he would ever look at a book like that. Kids forget that everyone used to be a kid. Everyone grew up hiding their stash at the back of the shelves or the bottom of the closet.

The Warrior never steals more than one joint's worth at a time. It's a new rule Vincent's made up, and it seems to work. No getting greedy. The kid doesn't suspect. He assumes he could have smoked that much. God knows how he's paying for it. Vincent hopes he isn't dealing.

Vincent's got the bud in his hand and is replacing the can when he hears the door open and wheels around to see Danny watching him. Which puts Vincent in an awkward position: standing on the bed holding a marijuana bud, balancing the coffee can and the abridged *OED*. The kid looks pale and shaken. But somehow Vincent senses that whatever is bothering Danny has nothing to do with him. It's something he brought into the room.

"Sor-ree," Vincent says.

Then he doesn't know why, he can't help it, he bursts out laughing. And Danny, who looks poised on the edge between pure what-are-you-doing-messing-with-my-shit? territorial rage and just as pure surprise, opts for the third choice: laughter. The strain melts from his face, and his color pinks up from chalk to something approaching normal.

For a while they're both cracking up. They can't even look at each other. Then they exchange quick glances, shrug, and start laughing again. Vincent's laugh is one part surprise, one part relief, one part embarrassment, one part what-the-hell. This could so easily have gone another way. The kid could have decided to make Vincent's life difficult. But what could he do? Report him to the cops? Tell Mom he caught Vincent helping himself to his drugs? He'll have to bite the bullet.

Vincent says, "You want me to put this bud back? Just say the word."

Danny says, "Nah, keep it. Now that you've gone to the trouble."

Vincent replaces the can and the book. This should not be happening. Bonnie trusts him to be a role model. How does it look for a cultural hero to be stealing drugs from a kid? How would it look to the charity donors, to Laura and Larry Ticknor? To the readers of *People*?

Vincent owes it to the kid to act like an adult, since there are so few around him. From Danny and Max's point of view, the dad is a total zero. Thanks to the doc's middle-class, midlife, walking nervous breakdown, he's more immature than they are.

"Hey, man, I'm glad it's you," Danny says. "I heard the noise in here and—"

Once again, the kid looks freaked. Like he did when he walked in the room. And Vincent feels even more certain that it's not about catching him with his hand in the cookie jar. Vincent decides to play it cool. The kid will tell him when he's ready.

"Who did you think it was?" Vincent's been getting along with the kid. And now the situation they're in—Vincent and Danny busting each other—is what you might call a bonding experience.

"No one. I don't know." Danny leaves the room to avoid watching Vincent hop down from the bed.

Vincent finds him in the kitchen, grimly working his way through a bag of potato chips.

"Aren't you home early?"

"How come you're home?" Danny says. "How come you're home at all?"

"Didn't your mom tell you not to answer a question with a question? I needed a day to catch up. I have to pick up the van from the garage."

"She's letting you drive the van?"

"As I understand it," Vincent says, "the lady had no choice."

"Whatever. Want some chips?"

Vincent doesn't. A heap of them came with his tuna fish sandwich. But he takes a big handful, which seems only sociable, the friendly thing to do with a kid who's just found you dipping into his stash.

Vincent and Danny eat their chips, until, at the same moment, they notice how loudly they're crunching, and laugh again.

"Crispy," says Danny.

"Right." Vincent wonders if the kid's high. "Want to come with me to pick up your mom's car?"

"I still can't believe she's letting you drive the van."

"Why wouldn't she?" says Vincent. Once, Bonnie might have hesitated to turn over the car keys to the Nazi houseguest. But that's not what Vincent is anymore. He's Brotherhood Watch's new hero. To say nothing of the fact that he's a guy who, not long ago, Bonnie seemed ready to have sex with. Would you want to sleep with a guy you wouldn't let drive your car? Actually, lots of women would. Women are insane.

"Maybe your mom trusts me. Maybe she's figured out I'm a better driver than she is. Maybe I've been driving since I was fifteen, and I've never had an accident except hitting a couple deer."

"Fine," says Danny. "Just don't tell her you drove *me* anywhere."

"I got that," Vincent says. "Believe me. Without your having to tell me."

"We'd never hear the end of it," Danny says. "She doesn't want me getting in a car with anyone but her. But she won't admit that. She talks about our family situation not working unless we all know where everybody is every minute of the day. It's like Soviet Russia around here—"

"Give your mom some slack, okay?" Poor Bonnie. Not a minute goes by when she's not worrying about her kids, and they think that makes her Stalin.

Danny says, "Actually . . . you know what? Earlier, I was thinking I'm glad she's my mom. Because I'm pretty sure she's going to be on my side about this nightmare at school."

"What nightmare at school?"

"They hated my Hitler paper." Is that why Danny is so upset? He must take this school stuff seriously. He seems more fried than you'd expect just because a teacher didn't like his paper.

"What happened? Wait, don't tell me. They don't want you *thinking* about Hitler."

"They don't want me thinking about gay people," said Danny. "They think saying Hitler might have been gay is an insult to gay people."

"The fact that he was human is an insult to the human race," Vincent says.

"That was sort of my point," Danny says.

"Tell it to the judge," Vincent says. "Hey, I know. I've been there. I put in some hard time in various principals' offices. Well, there's nothing you can do. We better go get the car. The garage guy's closing early so he can take his kid to a dirt-bike meet."

Danny and Vincent hit the street like a pair of TV detectives tear-ing out of the station house after a break in the case. Vincent wonders about the people—moms with strollers, nannies, senior citizens—they pass on the way to the garage. Do they assume he's a regular guy and Danny is his son? Unless everyone in town knows everything. Vincent has no way of telling. They might know Danny's whole history, and everything about Vincent. No reason to get paranoid. Just earlier, he was on this same block with zero paranoia. It's the kid who seems paranoid. He keeps looking back over his shoulder.

They pass the church where the billboard says: HONOR YOUR MOTHER.

"Honor *your* mother," Vincent says to no one in particular.

"They mean Mother Earth," says Danny.

"When did they change it from the last message? The Tomb Is Empty. Maybe they should combine it. Your Mother's Tomb Is Empty."

"This town sucks," Danny says. "It's a dump. Some days it *looks* pretty, like today. But underneath—"

"Enjoy it while you can," says Vincent. "It might take you twenty years to be able to afford a house in a dump like this." It might take the kid his whole life, but Vincent decides not to mention downward mobility. No reason to depress them both on this lovely afternoon. Not that the kid would listen to him or know what he's talking about. Whatever's going on at school is all the future he can imagine.

Neither speaks again till they get to JZ's. Vincent sees Bonnie's car on the lot, looking fixed and ready to go. He feels a rush of tender emotions for the van, as if it's a toddler he's picking up from nursery school.

Vincent likes JZ right away. He's a good-natured, hardworking stiff just trying to get along and keep his garage afloat. He hasn't got time to wonder why Vincent's picking up the car for Bonnie, if he's some kind of servant or assistant or gigolo, or what.

"I'm here to get Bonnie Kalen's car."

"Right. So she said." JZ believes Vincent. No ID check, no

searches, no long looks. Vincent would prefer to think that this is about clear communication rather than about this guy being so eager to leave on the trip with his kid that he'll hand over Bonnie's van to the first deadbeat who claims to know her.

Anyway, Danny's presence gives Vincent credibility. Having him along makes things more familial. Vincent's a friend of the family, a friend helping out a friend. That's partly why he asked the kid to come along in the first place.

JZ gives Vincent the keys. The van starts up right away. Minus the warning light on the dashboard and the noise from under the hood.

"Beautiful," Vincent calls to JZ, who nods. He knows what he's doing.

"She'll call you. She'll bring in the check," Vincent says.

"Whenever," says JZ.

"I hope your kid wins the race," says Danny.

"Thanks. I'll tell him. Catch you later." JZ goes back toward the office.

"What do you say we try it out?" Vincent asks Danny. "Take it for a spin. A test run. See how she's driving. We wouldn't want your mom breaking down again in traffic."

"We wouldn't want that," Danny agrees. "Just like we wouldn't want her knowing we did this."

"No reason for her to know," Vincent says. "It'll just make her nervous for nothing. Hey, are you okay? You look a little spooked."

"No, I'm fine," says Danny.

Vincent eases the minivan out onto the streets of Clairmont. The bliss of being behind the wheel is almost hallucinatory. It's freedom. It's like the day he got his license. That was when his mom was making salad at the Zen monastery. The dishwasher, Ronnie, taught Vincent to drive in the monastery van. He took him for the road test both times. He even let him kidnap the van after he passed on his second try. Vincent was raised to steal cars! It's not his fault he stole Raymond's. That's the way he should be thinking in preparation for *Chandler*. Nothing was ever his fault. He's been through a lot. He suffered. Some pervert at those meditation camps was always grabbing his ass.

Current Check-Outs summary for VENEMAN,
     Thu Apr 21 16:20:45 PDT 2016

BARCODE: 31111023404252
TITLE: A changed man : a novel / Francin
DUE DATE: May 12 2016
STATUS:

But Vincent got over his problems. He was able to move on and change.

Vincent's enjoying the chance to imagine that this is *his* van, *his* life, *his* laid-back drive with *his* kid on the spring afternoon he's taken off early from work, kicking back for a few hours before he heads home, where the missus is cooking dinner. Vincent can go two ways with this. He can wallow in self-pity because his real life isn't like this. Or he can enjoy this moment of dropping into that life and not having to deal with the tedious parts, the mortgage, the taxes, the homework. He's already doing the homework. He might as well have fun.

Vincent rolls down his window. So does the kid. The air streaming in feels terrific. They're silent, but Vincent senses that the kid has something to say.

Finally, Danny says, "Did you hear about the Bulgarian baby?"

"Is that the first line of a joke? Is that what you guys are telling now? Bulgarian baby jokes?"

"Right. A joke. I wish. Did you hear that Dad and Lorraine are adopting a Bulgarian baby?"

"I was there when you told your mom, remember? Very diplomatic."

The thought makes Vincent want to gag. That is so like those middle-class idiots, adopting a designer Bulgarian baby when there are millions of perfectly healthy American kids, white kids, without homes. To say nothing of the fact that the guy already has two kids, one of whom is getting stoned daily and no one seems to notice.

Vincent feels a familiar vibe emanating from Danny. It reminds him of how the atmosphere got when some chick was about to cry, and there was nothing he could do. Vincent's glad he never had kids. Women are hard enough.

Vincent says, "Can I ask you something?"

"Sure," says Danny. "As long as I don't have to answer."

"When your mom and dad split up, was there a big custody battle?"

"No," Danny says. "My dad signed some papers. The lawyers met. It took about five minutes."

Not exactly what Vincent imagined: the cardiologist rolling over. Maybe the doc feels guilty. So here comes the Bulgarian baby.

Vincent drives for a while. Scales of sunlight bounce off the Hudson and give the air a silvery gleam. The road curves through a patch of forest. The kid loves it. Who wouldn't? Vincent feels Danny shedding some of the tightness he brought back from school. But he's still hiding something. He's got something to say. And he wants to say it before the drive is through. Go ahead. Spit it out. Vincent's all ears. To be here for the little pip-squeak is the least he can do.

Finally Danny says, "Today when I got home from school, there was this guy parked in the driveway."

"What kind of guy?" says Vincent. Very calm, very cool.

"Pickup truck," says Danny.

"And?"

"Swastika on his right hand." So that's what's been bugging the kid. Everything becomes clear. Vincent's got to give him credit for not blurting it out the minute he walked in the house. Where was Vincent when all this was going down? Inside, taking a nap.

"Got the picture," says Vincent. "What did he want?" What a stupid question. Raymond wants Vincent dead.

"He said to tell you he knows where you are."

"Obviously," says Vincent.

"Is this guy going to kick your ass?" says Danny.

"He could try." Vincent likes the unperturbed, Clint Eastwood–like way he sounds.

"Does that scare you?" Danny asks. Talk about stupid questions. Does Danny think Vincent's looking forward to getting his ass kicked? *Anybody* would be scared knowing there's somebody out there who wants to hurt you, somebody sneaking around so you'll never know when he'll jump out of the bushes. Sure, he's scared. Danny knows about being scared. Danny knows it better than anyone.

Vincent checks his rearview mirror. Not a car on the road as far back as he can see. He would have noticed if they were being followed, especially by a pickup. Raymond was in their driveway. While Vincent slept in the house. Vincent wonders if this is how Maslow felt, dodging one bullet after another.

"Shit," says Vincent.

"You said it," says Danny.

The Warrior does not admit to fear in the presence of a child who is looking for a model of adult male behavior. Bonnie would say that Vincent was wrong, that men should admit they're scared. Let Bonnie see how useful it is to admit it when Raymond shows up. I'm scared. Please don't hurt me. Why is Vincent having a conversation in his head with Bonnie?

"What the hell. It was bound to happen. The past has a way of catching up."

Vincent can tell that Danny's impressed. He doesn't think it's macho bullshit. He thinks Vincent is being brave. He thinks Vincent is a guy who runs toward danger instead of away. Which must mean Vincent *is* that guy. And what does Vincent get out of this? A second chance to die for World Brotherhood Watch.

"Why is he after you?" Danny says.

"They don't like people to leave the fold," Vincent says. "It makes them feel rejected. No one likes anyone to leave. That's why everything is so much harder to get out of than get into. Marriage, for example. Anything involving another human being. Any kind of organization. It's like one of those joke Mexican finger traps. You can put your finger in, but you can't get it out. Like some giant roach motel."

"Life's a roach motel," says Danny. "Man, how true is that? So what now? Do they still want you in their organization? After you've left, and done the stuff you've done, I'd think they wouldn't trust you."

"Who said anything about their wanting me back? That's not how they operate. There was this guy in Wyoming ARM who never really believed it all in the first place, but he needed a place to stay, and he sort of got with the program. . . ." Vincent's embroidering now. He's talking about himself. He knows nothing about the

Wyoming guy, except the next part, which is true. "Anyway, five, six, guys came after him, and they sat him down and talked to him about how he'd screwed up. It's what they refer to as putting someone in the hot seat. And then—" He pauses a beat, for emphasis. "Then they cut off three of his toes. Nice, huh?"

"Gross. But I don't get it," Danny says. "If you've stopped thinking the way they think, why don't they cut you loose and forget it?"

The strangest sensation comes over Vincent, the urge to tell someone, anyone. This kid would be perfect. He's an innocent. He's got no power. He wants to hear the truth. It will feel great to say it. Vincent wants that clean five minutes of having everything off his chest. This must be the reason Catholics line up in church every Sunday morning.

Vincent says, "You know how earlier this afternoon you caught me in your room and we laughed and let it go because I was just borrowing one marijuana bud? Remember?"

"Yeah, I remember. That was an hour ago."

"I took some stuff from my cousin. And let's just say it was a little more than one bud."

"Got it," says Danny. "What did you take?"

"A truck. Some money." No need to mention the drugs. It's not that Vincent feels especially guilty or embarrassed about the medication. He just doesn't want to be the first person to introduce the kid to the wonderful world of pills, even though half his friends are probably abusing Ritalin.

Danny thinks for a minute, then says, "What happened to the truck?"

"Broke down on the way to the city," says Vincent. "My luck. I had to ditch it and take the bus." He doesn't like lying to the kid, but on the other hand, hearing that Vincent is keeping his escape route open might not be the best thing for Danny's already wobbly sense of security and well-being. How would it look if first the dad and then Vincent just, one day, took a hike? What kind of model would that be of adult male behavior?

"How much money?" Danny says.

"What?"

"How much did you take?"

"Let's just say it was more than one bud." Vincent laughs. "It was a bad move. I see that now. I shouldn't have done it, okay?"

Danny considers this for a while. Runs through the implications. But it's too much for him to process. He doesn't ask again how much money. The kid's had a hard day. They both have.

"Shouldn't we go home?" Danny says.

"Definitely," says Vincent.

WELCOME. You're the first to arrive. Would you care to go to your table?"

Rendered speechless by the beauty of the reception-ist, a smoldering gypsy in a pigeon-colored suit, Bonnie nods and is ushered past Scopello's famous Wall of Fish, a cascading cornucopia of ice lit by the atrium skylight and studded with fat pink snappers, iridescent flounder, lobsters the size of lap dogs. Everyone's come to eat fish with shiny eyes, and though the cost of lunch will be over the top for Brotherhood Watch, Bonnie's betting that just being here will make Laura Ticknor feel happy and generous.

Bonnie stops and stares at the Wall of Fish, as she is meant to. The receptionist is used to it. She pauses a few feet ahead. Calamari will be least likely to break the bank. Bonnie can't waste the money they should be using to buy vaccines or free prisoners and spend it on sixty-dollar-a-pound wild Patagonian sea bass. But maybe Laura will. The important thing is to focus and not be distracted by the thought of Vincent picking up her van.

Why should it bother Bonnie if a guy who drives better than she does goes ten blocks in a Toyota with a hundred and twenty-five thou-sand miles on it? If you can trust someone to speak at the Brotherhood

Watch benefit dinner, if you can take off your glasses and . . . well, you can trust him to get your vehicle from the garage. Bonnie wishes she'd told Vincent to go straight home. He probably will, on his own. She just wishes she'd made it clear. Would that have insulted him? She can't always tell. She can never tell what Vincent thinks is going on between them. Bonnie never offers to let him drive the car. How emasculating is *that?* No wonder the guy wouldn't fuck her even when she practically asked. What the hell. It's her van. Vincent is her houseguest.

Of course, it's at that moment, when Bonnie is thinking the thought least likely to arrange her features in a confident expression, that tidy, stylish Laura Ticknor sweeps into the room. Where did Laura learn to tie her cashmere sweater in that perfect capelet, both arms lying flat without a bulge or twist? Where does she get her hair streaked? How sloppy Bonnie feels, even though she dressed with such special care that her best high heels are viciously mashing her toes together. She crosses her legs and feels her pressed-down thigh spreading across her chair.

Laura too pauses by the Wall of Fish, and only now does Bonnie realize that the fish display is not just restaurant design but interactive performance art. Everybody watches everybody else checking out the fish. Were there people observing her search for the squid? Laura takes it all in and, crisp and precise, with her hands slightly out at her sides, like a cross between a little girl and a fifties film star, she swings around and follows the receptionist to Bonnie's table.

Bonnie half rises as she and Laura blow kisses at each other.

"Hi, sweetie, how are you?" Laura says.

The *sweetie* means nothing. From the minute Bonnie met Laura, Laura—she has the money, she calls the shots—has acted as if they were old friends. Complaints about her husband and kids, girl-talk about hair and shoes. It's also semi-ironic, as if intimacy is a joke. Laura and Bonnie will never know each other any better than they do now, or than they did when they met. It was then that Laura said that Brotherhood Watch was Larry's bribe for her ignoring the bulimic

intern he was currently poking. Women like Laura challenge Bonnie
to be especially open and sympathetic. Nonjudgmental. Sure, Laura is
worth a fortune. But she's in pain, like everyone else. Her husband
doesn't love her. She supports good causes, instead of just going shopping. Though probably she shops plenty.

"Great to see you," Bonnie says.

"Great to see *you*," says Laura.

"You're looking great," says Bonnie.

"Please," says Laura. "Let's not talk about it. Jake turns fourteen
next week."

Bonnie vaguely recalls some gossip about the lavish Jacob Ticknor
bar mitzvah. Forty kids to a Knicks game. Then the Tavern on the
Green for the evening. She feels a jolt of possessiveness, as if she and
young Jake Ticknor are competitors for Larry and Laura's money.

"You *do*," says Bonnie. "You look fabulous."

Laura twists slightly to gaze back at the restaurant—should Bonnie
have gotten up and offered her the seat with the view?—and says, "It's
funny that they think this is authentic Sicilian. Larry and I were just *in*
Sicily, and I guess there were restaurants like this. There was one place
in Palermo where we paid New York prices, but the joints where you
got the really fresh fish always had a TV blaring up in one corner."

Bonnie looks around the room, as if in search of a TV. But the
expense-account customers lit by flashes of atrium sun aren't paying
for a television to compete with the deals they're making. Is Laura
suggesting that this place is inauthentic? Bonnie should have listened
to the instinct that told her it was obscene to raise money for Brotherhood Watch over portions of fish that traveled first class by jet from
Tierra del Fuego.

"Excuse me, ladies. Can I get you a drink?" The waiter, like the
receptionist, is movie-star Mediterranean.

"Water," says Bonnie. "Tap water." Then she thinks better of it,
and asks Laura, "Would you like a real drink?"

"Do you have La Planeta chardonnay?" Laura asks the waiter.

"Only by the bottle."

"Then open a bottle and bring us two glasses." Laura fixes the waiter with a smile of such serene command that it hardly matters she's just arrived and is already ordering off the menu. Laura will give the foundation money. The question is, how much?

"It's this terrific wine made by these Sicilian aristocrats who took the family fortune and planted it in grapes," Laura explains.

The wine appears in seconds. It's as if they're drinking sunlight. A golden aura surrounds them. Bonnie must have been mad to think she could get through this on water.

Bonnie says, "So . . . where did you go in Sicily?"

"We based ourselves in Taormina. Everyone warned us against the San Domenico hotel, but we really liked it."

"Oh," says Bonnie. "How great."

The waiter brings them menus they know better than to open. You order from the Wall of Fish. You order it baked or broiled.

"I'll have the calamari," Bonnie says.

"With the tomato-anise foam?" says the waiter.

"Sure," says Bonnie.

"Baked or broiled?" says the waiter.

"Umm. Broiled," says Bonnie.

Laura says, "I'll have the Patagonian sea bass."

"An excellent choice. Baked or broiled."

"What do *you* suggest?" Laura asks the waiter.

"Today? Baked."

"Baked it is," says Laura. "And could I also have the coulis on the side?"

"Certainly. Would you like to pick out your fish?" Why didn't he ask Bonnie if she wanted to choose her squid?

"No thanks. I'll trust you." Again Laura directs a beam of brilliant cosmetic dentistry at the bedazzled waiter. Then she says to Bonnie, "Larry would insist on going over there and prodding every one of those poor bastard dead fish till their eyes pop."

Bonnie says, "So you've eaten here before."

Laura watches the waiter go. Then she says, "Don't answer if this is too personal. But do you ever get sentimental about your divorce? Do you ever wish that you and your husband were still together?"

Bonnie can hardly speak. Did she tell Laura about her divorce? Could Laura's presumption of intimacy have lured her into confessing? In which case, what did Bonnie say?

"I don't know," says Bonnie.

"Well, don't. Don't romanticize marriage." Laura sips her wine and smiles conspiratorially over the glass at Bonnie.

Finally Laura says, "That was some dinner. Scary."

Bonnie knows which scary dinner Laura means. But she's not ready to talk about it. She needs another few minutes of Laura rattling on about Larry's character flaws. How long does it take to harvest squid and bass from the Wall of Fish and cook it?

"Scary," Laura repeats.

"It *was* scary," Bonnie says. "Watching Vincent go down. Not knowing if he was going to pull through . . ."

"I never thought he would die," Laura says. "Maybe that's just the way I am. An optimist. Despite everything. My therapist says that's my problem."

"He *could* have died," says Bonnie, defensively. It's a medical fact. She needs to put some spin on this, the sooner and harder the better. "The gratifying thing is how people have taken to him, how they've *got* his story. The most hard-boiled reporters, media vets— even they have been deeply moved. Because Vincent knew what was happening and risked his life to finish his speech."

Bonnie's taking a gamble here. She's telling Laura that the foundation is currently hot. Super-hot. Perhaps she's making Laura feel competitive with all the newcomers glomming on to Brotherhood Watch. Laura got there first. But it might be good for Laura to feel a twinge of competition.

Laura says, "So is the guy living with you?"

"In my house," says Bonnie. "With me and my kids—my sons."

"I meant *living* living. Are you sleeping with him?"

"No!" says Bonnie, as if she's been pinched. "God, no! Why do you ask?" What has Laura intuited? Bonnie longs to find out. The strange thing is how pleased she is to think that Laura might have picked up some sign of romance. Bonnie wants it to be true, even though it isn't. Unless it *is* true. You'd think Bonnie would know. Anyway, whatever may have been happening on the night of the dinner definitely stopped happening after that night.

"No reason," says Laura. "Curious. Maybe it's just my fantasy about the divorced and single getting a lot of action."

"So far we're just good friends. Sometimes we stay up talking all night. He's a really interesting guy. He's had a difficult life. It's amazing, how much he's changed." If Laura wants a romantic fantasy, Bonnie will give her one: that charged moment of pure potential, when you're "good friends" with a man, and anything might happen. The last thing Laura wants is for Bonnie to confess that they are days past the point at which Bonnie took off her glasses and Vincent turned her down.

"I'm sure he's had a doozy of a life." Laura widens her eyes unnervingly.

Maybe it would feel terrific, spilling it all out to Laura. Bonnie hasn't told anyone about her feelings for Vincent. It horrifies her that she doesn't have one friend she can call and ask what it means when a guy acts a certain way. She used to have plenty of friends. All those years with Joel, then the kids. Somehow she lost touch.

Laura Ticknor is not that friend, not the forgiving soul with whom Bonnie can share the secrets of her heart. It would be a terrible error to indulge in the luxury of confessing to Laura, who would make her pay for it with fake pity and real contempt. The buck would stop, like the check for lunch, at the foundation. Bonnie's glad she has the common sense to keep from soliciting advice about the fact that Vincent apparently doesn't want to have sex with her.

"Don't ask me," says Laura, as if she's read Bonnie's mind. "I have zero experience. I've been married fifteen long years. And I've been faithful to Larry. If you can believe it. That's the tragedy of my life."

"I believe it," says Bonnie. How will they progress from this to the question of how much Laura might give Brotherhood Watch? "So tell me: What is Jake interested in?" A safe enough question that usually works. Women love talking about their kids. Bonnie hopes Laura doesn't ask about her kids. What are their interests? TV? Bonnie promises herself she'll spend more time with them. They'll go somewhere this weekend.

Unfortunately, she's missed Laura's reply, and so can only smile, hoping that Laura hasn't said her son was into Ecstasy and Internet porn.

God must be on Bonnie's side. The waiter brings their food.

Bonnie should have known that the calamari would be a mistake. Probably one reason it's so cheap is the social challenge it offers, sawing through those squirmy legs and rubbery bodies without spraying tomato foam all over the table. You could pick the tiny squid up in your hands if you were having lunch with a close friend. But not with Laura Ticknor.

Laura touches her fish with a fork and it flakes into perfect bite-sized chunks of pearlescent flesh.

"How's your sea bass?" asks Bonnie.

"Heaven," says Laura.

They eat for a while, Laura savoring her bass, Bonnie battling her squidlets. Laura picks up her fork and, gently waving the chunk of bass speared on the tines, punctuates the interior conversation she seems to be having before she repeats it aloud.

"It *is* amazing," she says. "Here's this guy who could have gone in any direction, who falls into the hands of these lowlife racists and gets brainwashed into buying their party line. And then he spends a few months with you guys, and he's a changed man. A new, improved, model human being. I don't know what you and Meyer did with the guy, what kind of magic you worked, but basically, Meyer's right. You can take one guy, one woman, one Israeli, one Palestinian, one heart at a time. You really can make a difference. Or at least you can try. Which is what you guys are doing, trying to make a difference. And you never see that. Courage, generosity. You never see anyone thinking about anything besides their own miserable selfish self!"

Bonnie lifts her wineglass. Laura nods, accepting the tribute. The fork completes its arc to her mouth. Laura chews and swallows.

"This is so great." She means the bass. For this golden moment, in Laura's mind, the greatness of the fish melds seamlessly with the greatness of the foundation. If you've got money, you can have both. And why not? Why not feed your body and your spirit? And someone else's body and spirit. Bonnie dreads becoming the kind of puritan who believes it's wrong to spend your money on delicious, costly fish. On the other hand she does believe—and it's what she's doing here—that for every dollar you spend on fish, you should spend a hundred on your fellow humans.

"It's worth it," says Laura. "Worth anything." Laura's off the subject of fish and back on the foundation. "That's why I want to support it. What better way to use Larry's money? Whatever project Meyer was talking about, that outreach thing, for other guys like Vincent. Not that I would imagine there *are* many guys like Vincent. But hey, it worked once. Let's try it again."

"Let me tell you what we need," says Bonnie, mindful of what she's learned: the rich can be insulted if you ask for a sum that seems too low. Bonnie and Laura put their heads together, two friends, coconspirators whispering over the subject of money, tax credits, and budgets, as if they were having the girl chat that Bonnie imagined earlier. But this is so much better. This was worth holding out for.

Bonnie can't believe she's managed to get from there to here. *Here* being Laura Ticknor's offer to donate three hundred thousand dollars over a period of three years to finance the One Heart at a Time program.

"Will you ladies be having dessert?"

"I'll have the cannoli," Bonnie says.

"Make that two," says Laura.

When the check comes, Laura says, "Please. This one's on me."

Outside the restaurant, Bonnie kisses Laura good-bye, smacky kisses on both cheeks, a warm hug at the end. Bonnie practically runs down the street. She can't wait to get to the office and tell Meyer what happened. She rehearses several different ways: Guess what happened, guess what happened with Laura Ticknor, guess how much Laura Ticknor is giving us for the One Heart program. Which is how she decides to phrase it as she walks into Meyer's office.

Meyer gives her a strangely blank look. An alarmingly blank look. The man is over seventy. Anything could have happened.

"How much?" asks Meyer.

"Three hundred thousand," says Bonnie "Over three years." Suddenly, it sounds like less than it did at lunch.

"Excellent." Meyer's thoughts have already moved on to something else. "Bonnie. Help me out. Remind me. Who was in the office that first day Vincent came in?"

"The three of us," says Bonnie. "You, me, and Vincent. Why?"

"The most upsetting thing happened today. According to Roberta, someone from *Chandler* called to ask if Vincent could wear a short-sleeved shirt. They seem to know about his tattoos. Roberta explained that Vincent was sensitive about the tattoos. It was part of how much he had changed. At this point he prefers to keep them covered, and being asked to display them on TV would hardly put him in a mood to show Chandler's audience the changed man they want to see. The woman from the show said she understood. Then she said it was her impression that I also had a tattoo, from the camp. She said what exciting TV it would be if we both showed our tattoos. Compared them."

"That's disgusting!" says Bonnie. "I mean, doing it on TV." Though of course, not in private. She remembers it as a powerfully moving moment. "I mean, it was really wonderful that first day Vincent came into the office. . . ."

Meyer is beyond flattery, which isn't Bonnie's intention. "Roberta talked them out of it. She mentioned my wariness about cheapening the Holocaust. Cheapening the Holocaust. Those three words always do the trick. Later I began to wonder if Roberta told the TV people that something like that had happened in my office. And I wondered if she'd been there. Or if someone told *her*."

"I don't think I told anybody," says Bonnie, immediately guilty. She remembers telling her kids. Could she have told Roberta? She can't remember whom she told, and yet her shame is so intense, it's as if she sold the story to the *National Enquirer.* She *didn't* tell Roberta. Chandler's people guessed, and guessed right.

By now she can't recall what had seemed so important about Laura Ticknor's pledge. She has to be patient and wait until this *Chandler* thing blows over. She knows that Meyer is concerned about appearing on the show. But why should a hero like Meyer be worried about TV? This too will pass. The TV show will be over and forgotten, but Laura's donation will keep the One Heart program alive for years to come. Maybe Vincent can help run it.

These days, just thinking about Vincent can make Bonnie feel unsettled, as if she's left the house and forgotten to turn off the stove. Today it's not just the familiar nagging of general unease, the residual embarrassment from the night of the benefit dinner. Vincent is picking up her van. He should be home already. Did she tell him where the garage is? It's probably fine. Knock on wood. He's a guy. He can get there on instruments, flying on male radar. Should she invent some excuse to call? Would he think she was checking up?

"Bonnie, where are you going?" Meyer says.

"I need to get home," says Bonnie.

BONNIE KNOWS IT'S the second day in a row she's left work early, but she feels that Meyer's lukewarm response to her success with Laura has given her license to take off. And she has to make sure that things have gone smoothly with Vincent and her van.

The train ride home is pure pleasure, and Bob, her favorite taxi driver, is waiting at the Clairmont station. On the way to her house they have an enjoyable chat about this spring's spectacular bloom. As the cab rounds the corner onto her block, Bonnie spots her van in the driveway. Vincent has made it. The car is fixed. Everything has worked out.

Better yet, she finds Vincent and both boys downstairs, watching *Chandler*. Has Bonnie ever seen the show? Oddly, she can't remember. It's important to check it out. It's a professional obligation. She's not wasting time. She's doing work-related research. Some time ago, Roberta asked Chandler's people to send over a tape of the show with the former skinhead who went to work with the Wiesenthal Foundation. Bonnie's eager to see it, as if it might explain everything, or *some*thing. But whenever Bonnie asks, it's never a good time for Roberta, who seems to feel that the tape is in her sacred trust and can only be viewed in her presence.

Bonnie should watch *Chandler* now, just to see what it's like. Sitting down would be a commitment, so she lingers in the doorway of what used to be Joel's room, the space he claimed as his own and bequeathed to the kids in his ongoing campaign to make them love him more.

The program's about orthodonture. A row of teenagers sit in brown leather club chairs and take turns describing what wrecks they used to be, while photos flash onto the screen—"before" shots of the same kids with disfiguring underbites and buck teeth. Each story is worse than the last, until one girl breaks down as she describes how her undershot jaw drove her to drink and drugs and prostitution. Now their teeth are white and straight, and the kids are happy, doing well in school. College bound.

"Hey, Vincent, man," says Max. "Maybe you can get them to fix your teeth before you go on the show."

"Nothing's wrong with my teeth," Vincent says.

"Maybe you can get them to fix what's wrong with your head, Max," says Danny.

Poor Max, thinks Bonnie. He was just trying to make them laugh.

Max says, "Nothing's wrong with my—"

"Shut up and listen," says Danny.

Chandler is telling the audience how sometimes a simple physical change can work miracles. Bonnie thinks the guy should be jailed for using these kids like circus animals. Still, she's got to admit they look better with their new teeth.

"Hey, guys, how is everyone?" Bonnie chirps.

"Fine," says Max. Danny's got the remote. He hits it, and the image changes to a giant iguana swallowing a smaller lizard. The bottom half of the little lizard's body thrashes between its predator's jaws.

"Hi, Bonnie," says Vincent, politely. He too is fixated on the screen.

"Gross," says Max. "This is like one of those gross dinosaur movies."

"*Jurassic Park,*" says Danny.

"This is real," says Vincent. "That's just special effects."

"I realize that," says Danny.

"How's the car?" asks Bonnie.

Vincent, who's lying on the couch, turns to look at Bonnie. She thinks he's smiling, but she can't tell. It's dark in the basement. The only light comes from the TV.

"Great," says Vincent. "Like new."

The sated lizard lumbers off the screen, and now a Crocodile Dundee type in a safari suit, carrying a pole and a net, whispers as he creeps up on some hapless creature napping in the mud.

"Everything's fixed?" says Bonnie.

"Totally. As far as I could tell. I only drove it from the garage to here." Vincent and the boys turn back to the TV.

"How was school?" asks Bonnie.

Not a word.

"School? How was school?"

"It was okay," says Danny.

"Was that so hard?" says Bonnie. Which usually makes them roll their eyes and smile. But right now they're beyond that, spirited off on safari in giant reptile land. Okay. Bonnie can live with this. She's had a productive day at work, and there's been no disaster at home. What else could she ask for? To come home and find her kids *reading?*

"What about dinner?" Bonnie persists, annoying even herself. "Are you guys going to be hungry?" She'll keep this up as long as she has to.

"Can we talk about this later?" Danny says.

Bonnie goes upstairs and wanders into the kitchen just as the phone starts ringing. Four times in the past week the silent breather has called Bonnie at home. Obviously, it's disturbing. Bonnie knows perfectly well that it could be Vincent's former buddies from ARM, coming—after all this time—to get him. But her response has been to hope that the caller will tire of harassing them and give up. Too much else is happening right now, there's too much else going on. Bonnie doesn't have the time to wait on hold for two hours so the phone company can tell her there's nothing they can do.

Meanwhile, she'll let the machine answer. She hears her professional voice, "Hi, you've reached the Kalens. Leave a message after the beep." Thank God she was never one of those mothers who let the children record their cute baby-talk greetings. She'd hate to hear their sweet voices, and then the hostile silence that will signal the breather's presence, and for which she braces herself now as a man says:

"Hi. This is David Armstrong? I'm the assistant principal at Clairmont High School? I'm trying to reach Mrs. Kalen. Er, Bonnie Kalen—"

It's five-thirty on a Friday evening. No one from school would be trying to reach her now unless Danny was being expelled, or if he'd been exposed to some deadly disease. But then the nurse would be calling.

Bonnie picks up. "Oh, hi," she says. "I was just walking in the door."

"I'm so glad you're there," says Armstrong. "Is this an okay time to talk?"

"Okay as any." Bonnie wants and doesn't want to hear what he's got to say.

"I know we've met—" says the assistant principal.

"Of course," says Bonnie. If what he means by *met* is Bonnie's having seen him speak at PTA meetings.

"I imagine you're just as upset as we are about what happened today with Danny."

If Bonnie admits she doesn't know what he means, what kind of mother will she look like? But if she pretends to know, Armstrong will call her bluff. "What happened? I mean, I just walked in. I haven't seen Danny yet." Which is, literally speaking, true. It was dark in the basement.

"Danny wrote a paper that some of us found disturbing."

"What paper?" Bonnie's stalling for time. She knows.

"Danny's paper about Hitler."

"Oh, that paper," says Bonnie. Has he turned it in already? How could she not have read it? She should have kept in closer touch, checked to find out how he was doing. Vincent talked about it with him. She's been so proud of herself for what she accomplished with Laura Ticknor. And all hell's broken loose for her child, and he didn't tell her.

"I'm sorry to inform you," Armstrong continues, "that Danny's received a temporary suspension as an interim measure until we decide what further action to take."

"Are you kidding?" says Bonnie.

"I'm afraid not," the assistant principal says.

"Wait a minute. Let me get this straight. You've suspended my son because he wrote a paper about Hitler?"

"Mrs. Kalen, believe me, there were serious problems with the paper. Which we'd be happy to discuss with you—"

"*What* problems?" Bonnie hears her voice get shrill, but there's nothing she can do. It's pure maternal instinct singing out those high notes.

"We felt that his paper had elements that were, shall we say, homophobic."

"Homophobic?" says Bonnie. "*What* elements? What are you talking about? I read Danny's paper, and I thought it was brilliant!" Bonnie's taking a chance here. In fact, she's outright lying. But she's following her heart. She knows her son. She trusts him. Danny would never have written anything that was bigoted. Or would he? If something like that happened, it could only be her fault for neglecting him, or bringing a Nazi home. "And what do you mean, you *suspended* him? What about his right to a fair hearing? What about the First Amendment? What about—"

"Mrs. Kalen," says Armstrong. "Please. You've got to calm down. I'm sure something can be worked out."

"Worked out? What do you mean, *worked out?*"

There's a long silence. Then Armstrong says, "I'm sure we could reach some arrangement. Because actually, the truth is . . . I know this may sound a little strange, but Danny's situation is not the main reason I'm calling."

That isn't the main reason he's calling? Danny's been suspended, and *that's not why the guy called?*

"Excuse me, Mr. Armstrong—"

"Please. Call me Dave."

Dave? "Dave. I'm confused. Then why *did* you call?"

"We've got a bit of a problem here at the school, as you may be aware."

Bonnie isn't aware. If she doesn't know that her son has been suspended, she isn't going to be aware of the bit of a problem they're having at school.

"Well, as I'm sure you know, our graduation speaker was supposed to be Brad De Vito."

The name is intended to ring a bell it isn't ringing for Bonnie. Armstrong's sigh conveys his opinion that her not recognizing Brad De Vito's name is almost as bad as her being unaware that her kid is in trouble. It's probably sufficient cause to make Armstrong call social services. And she'd rather not have her domestic situation scrutinized at the moment. What happened to the woman who today, at lunch at Scopello, talked one of New York's richest women out of a good chunk of change? That woman has slipped into the phone booth and reemerged as her true self: an irresponsible, clueless mother.

"Our state prosecutor. Former state prosecutor. You know. *Brad De Vito.*" Armstrong clears his throat. "The guy who just got indicted in that child porn Internet sting."

"Oh, that's right. I *do* know." Can he tell Bonnie doesn't? If she lied about having read Danny's paper, she might as well keep lying.

"Brad was a local boy, a Clairmont High graduate. He was scheduled to speak this year at our high school graduation. But in light of the current . . . um . . . seeing as his court case is now pending . . . Well, the fact of the matter is, we've found ourselves without a speaker. Graduation wouldn't be graduation without someone to set the tone. Our seniors will be so disappointed. We've already pushed the ceremony up two weeks. Well into summer vacation.

"And then this afternoon—unfortunately, just after we sent Danny home—someone brought me a copy of *People* magazine. That marvelous article about the foundation and you and . . . I'm so embarrassed. I should have known about the wonderful things that a Clairmont parent was doing. But gee, I'm so busy. It's so hard to keep up. . . . It was pointed out to me that you're Danny's mom. And we want to tell you how terrific we think it is. What you're doing, and everything you and Meyer Maslow stand for."

"Thanks," Bonnie says. How amazing, the power of the media, the ability of fame to transform her from Neglecto Mom into a celebrity hero.

"And we were tossing some ideas around this afternoon, and some of us wondered if you might consider filling in as our graduation speaker. We realize you must be terribly busy, but . . ."

So this is why the call wasn't about Danny *exactly*.

"I'm sure it would be wonderful for Danny to have his mother address the school community. It's so important to our seniors. I'm sure that next year, when Danny graduates, you'll see how much it matters."

Next year. When Danny graduates. That's the deal-maker, right there. Armstrong's laying his cards on the table. A little civilized blackmail. All right. She gets it. She *gets* it.

"Gosh," says Bonnie. "Sure!" Only after she's agreed does she begin to wonder how Danny will like his mom giving a speech at school. And what kind of speech could she give? Bonnie doesn't much like talking to groups. Part of the torture of those garden-party benefits for the Clairmont Museum was flushing the party-goers out of their spots on the beautiful green lawn and making them listen to her thanks for the donations they hadn't given. But after a few times, it wasn't that hard—surprisingly, for an anxious person like herself. She got up and said what she had to say. That was for etchings of steamboats. And this is about Danny's future. Armstrong has essentially guaranteed that when they get around to deciding on Danny's case, they won't be able to bring themselves to expel the graduation speaker's son. Talking at graduation will be easier and less complicated than what she really should be doing: arguing with them about Danny's paper.

"That's great!" says Armstrong. "Honestly, I'm delighted!"

"I'm delighted, too." Bonnie can't stop lying. Suddenly light-headed, she leans against the kitchen counter.

"Hello? Mrs. Kalen? Bonnie? Are you still there?"

"I was wondering what I could say . . . what could be . . . useful . . ."

"Just talk about what you do," Armstrong says. "And more important, *why* you do it. And maybe about the sorts of ideals we all associate with Meyer Maslow."

"Sure," says Bonnie. "I can do that."

Armstrong says, "There's one more thing I want to ask. And you should tell me right away if you think it's a bad idea. But we were wondering if Mr. Nolan could come with you and say a few words, too."

It takes Bonnie a while to remember that Mr. Nolan means Vincent. It takes her even longer to figure out what Armstrong is asking. There's no time left to consider her answer.

"Sure. He'd do a terrific job." Actually, he would. Bonnie imagines herself and Vincent doing a kind of road show, going from school to school, showing kids what can happen to you, and how you can change if you want to. Which will eventually mean more attention for Brotherhood Watch and more great things they can accomplish. This could be the first phase of the One Heart program. If that isn't outreach, what is? It will be helpful for Vincent to have the experience of talking to kids whose lives he *can* help turn around. Not that the Clairmont High senior class includes that many future Nazis. But this is what Bonnie has always hoped, and what Vincent promised that first day. I want to help you guys save guys like me from becoming guys like me.

"That would be fine," says Bonnie. "That's a wonderful idea. By the way, did you know that Vincent and Meyer Maslow are going to be on *Chandler* this week?"

"On *Chandler?* Really?" says Armstrong. "Oh, my Lord, that's terrific. I'll tell all the folks here at school."

"All right, then . . . Unless there's anything else," says Bonnie.

"We'll talk next week," says Armstrong. "And meanwhile, thank you. Thank you again."

"Thank *you*," says Bonnie. "I'm looking forward to it."

Bonnie hangs up just as Vincent walks into the kitchen. Is Bonnie imagining it, or does he look relieved to find that she has finished a conversation? Has he also been unnerved by the silent breather?

"Who was on the phone?" asks Vincent, getting a beer from the refrigerator in a way that's meant to seem relaxed. In fact, he's a nervous wreck. Vincent's gaze tracks toward the kitchen window and out over the driveway.

"Danny's school," says Bonnie. "Danny's assistant principal."

"Don't tell me," says Vincent. "They hated his Hitler paper."

"How do you know?" Bonnie can't conceal her surprise and— well, jealousy, really. Her son is telling Vincent things that he doesn't tell her. At the same time she's grateful that Danny is confiding in anyone at all, that he's got a male presence in the house, someone he can talk to in the absence of a father with any interest in the hard work of raising a son.

"Danny told me," says Vincent. "Poor kid. I think he was pretty freaked out."

"What did he say?" Bonnie will ask Danny to print out a copy of the paper and give it to her *tonight*.

"Not much. I think those morons at school decided that writing about Hitler means he *is* Hitler. Or wants to be. So how hard are they going to make this?"

"It's not as bad as it could have been. They've offered us a plea bargain." How funny, that *us* should mean Bonnie and Danny and Vincent.

"Time off for time served?"

"Not exactly. They'll go easy on Danny if you and I give a speech at their high school graduation."

"You and me? Graduation? You're kidding."

"That's the deal," says Bonnie. "And what makes it harder is, Danny's probably going to be there."

"We can do that," says Vincent.

In the silence that falls, they look at each other from across the kitchen. Bonnie likes the sounds of that *we*. Sexy. Conspiratorial. Well, okay. Here they go again. Maybe. The power of that one word draws them back toward wherever they were—or wherever she imagined they were—the night of the benefit dinner. But where is Bonnie going with this? Her son's assistant principal suggested that she and Vincent speak at graduation—not that they have sex! Bonnie's not heading back down that road.

"Guess what happened today? I had lunch with Laura Ticknor."

"That woman from the benefit?" Vincent says. "The one with all the money?"

"Bravo," says Bonnie. "I got her to pledge three hundred grand."

Vincent pumps his arm in the air. "Excellent!" he says. The difference between Vincent's response and Meyer's is not lost on Bonnie. At least Vincent's not obsessed with his upcoming TV appearance.

Bonnie says, "And you know what? The lunch was all about you. Really, it was all about what happened at the dinner, and what you did, and what happened later." She means his nearly dying. Don't let him think what happened later refers to what happened here in the kitchen.

"It's not about me," Vincent says. "It's about the foundation. About that Iranian guy. And all the amazing things we can do with Laura Ticknor's money."

THE LINE IS A PROBLEM FOR RAYMOND. Is he really supposed to fall in with these mongrelized mutants loitering out on the street, begging to watch some eggplant dandy chat with Cousin Vincent? How grateful is Raymond supposed to *be* for this public disgrace, the chance to join the other race traitors waiting to see Chandler, to be herded into the studio with the mud-race crowd, rubbing up against them and catching all their diseases?

Raymond should be an invited guest, like one of those experts they get to gas about global warming and the Middle East and Tim McVeigh. Raymond's field of expertise is ARM and Vincent Nolan. They should have sent him a ticket. In fact, the tickets were free. Raymond called and ordered his as soon as Lucy told him that his cousin was going to be on *Chandler*. He probably should have brought Lucy. At least he'd have someone to talk to. Raymond and Lucy should both be here as special guests of Chandler.

But there were plenty of reasons he didn't bring Lucy, most obviously the fact that he doesn't have a clue about what he's going to do when he finally sees Vincent. He knows what he plans *not* to do. He's not going to come out swinging, which is what the Jewish media expects from guys like Raymond. Certainly that's the media's line on the white-power movement, ever since all those years ago, when the Aryan brothers went off on Geraldo Rivera. Raymond won't play into their hands. He'll stay focused and say what he has to say about ARM in general and Vincent in particular.

Raymond's glad that Lucy isn't here to see him wait in line like some jerk taking directions from the hot tamale in the *Chandler* T-shirt who thinks a pair of headphones clipped to her woolly head makes her superior to the white men she's bossing around. But of course, *señorita!* Your wish is my command! He often fears that Lucy will stop being on his side, stop believing what he believes, as soon as she figures out how he stands in relation to all the people who don't need to work their nuts off, twenty-four/seven. Lucy might split, like Vincent did. Any smart person would.

Raymond hasn't been in Manhattan for five, six years. It wasn't all that easy to drive into the city, which seems ten times more crowded, noisy, polluted, and crime-ridden than it was the last time he was here. He deserves the Purple Heart just for finding a parking garage, and for getting here by eleven, like they said. The taping starts at noon.

And where is Vincent now? Backstage with his head tilted back and his mouth open, sucking down the streams of champagne and scarfing the caviar that gorgeous chicks in spangled swimsuits keep bringing out for the guests. Which, when you get right down to it, is the truth about Vincent. He sold out the white race for pricier booze and food.

Raymond should get *paid* to be on this show. He should get compensated for the hours he has put in, the days he's taken off from work to moonlight as Vincent's stalker and the agent of retribution by which a traitor will be brought to justice. Tracking down Vincent has become Raymond's second job. Those trips to the pay phones to call Vincent's new family were fun, like being a kid again, making crank calls to strangers just to screw with their heads. Still, there were the phone bills, the coins wasted on broken machines, plus the sick day he had to take in order to stake out that house in Clairmont and give that kid the message. He'd wanted to tell the kid that Vincent stole his truck and money and medication, but he couldn't predict how that would play. Some kids might think it was cool. That's how kids are being raised these days. With no morals to speak of. When the truth is, regardless of what you might think about Raymond and ARM, doing something like that is wrong. People should know about it.

It was better not to act hastily, better to have waited for this chance to tell a national audience that their so-called hero is a punk shithead thief. Raymond wishes, as he often has, that his little band of ARM brothers had, just once, put their asses on the line, that they'd at least seen how it felt to fuck somebody up badly. Found some Paki working late at the convenience mart and whaled on him. Whaled on him good. Maybe they would have enjoyed it. Who knows? It would have been a *bonding* experience. Vincent would have got into it. Raymond always felt that if you told Vincent, Kick this scum, Vincent would have kicked. Vincent, not Raymond, is the one who got sent to anger management, the one who dumped that old lady into the swimming pool. Now Vincent is famous for having ditched his supposedly violent pals and gone to work for peace and love. But it was always Vincent who was the real loose cannon.

Let's say they'd all lost it one night when the Paki convenience-store clerk told them to please not handle the petrified doughnut if they weren't going to buy it. Let's say Vincent was into it, just like everyone else. That would have given Raymond a little something extra to offer the *Chandler* audience. But Chandler's people would never let Raymond tell the truth. It might interfere with Chandler telling white Americans how to live and what to think and how to turn their kids into homosexuals and abortionists.

Raymond lets his gaze mosey down the line of *Chandler* ticket holders, the fat Rican teen, the welfare mothers with zip to do but take their snot-nosed kids to TV shows for the free air-conditioning, plus the unenlightened white citizens who, under the illusion that this is wholesome family entertainment, are helping the darker races climb up on the white man's back. Raymond's been working on an article for the ARM Web site about how the Jews control the media. Just the facts, the list of CEOs, who works where, and what they do. He's written seven pages, and he's going strong. So he should have known better than to imagine that the Zionist media moguls are going to give him free airtime.

Raymond needs to locate the *Chandler* robot in the T-shirt and earphones who knows what today's show is about and will grasp the potential of Raymond's contribution. In which case there's a good chance that Raymond might be let in early and get the semi-VP treatment, if not the full monty Vincent's getting. Isn't today's program about changing Raymond into Vincent? That's why Chandler needs them both. Together they form a walking, talking Before and After.

Raymond's body decides for him. He's jumping out of his skin. He would rather get his ego whomped and his ass kicked around the block than stand here one more second. He susses out the station employee most likely to be persuaded, a Jewish kid, real hustler, his hair brilliantined in spikes, as if every brain cell is discharging an idea so hot it's making his hair stand up. Not like that pathetic bar mitzvah boy in the house where Vincent is staying, the kid who just wants to get high and jerk off, or give drugs to innocent white girls so they'll let him feel their tits.

Media Boy is a Take-Charge Jew who knows that Raymond's input might make for some first-rate TV. Probably he's heard about that brawl on *Geraldo.* He'll be the one to get credit for having ushered Raymond inside. Even if the kid sees Raymond's swastika, which he probably will, race loyalty will mean less to him than personal ambition.

Raymond leaves his place in line. It's a gamble. But he can't bring himself to ask the woman behind him—a skinny black grandma with ashy skin and a gray shock of straightened hair—to please save his place. The woman's got a baby in her arms. A kid who could vomit on Raymond. Raymond glares at them both, then goes to the door where the future Michael Eisner lurks, sleek as a lizard in the sun.

Raymond says, "Excuse me, good afternoon. I'm Mister Mumble Mumble. I'm a friend of Vincent Nolan's? He's going to be on the mumble mumble today?" No need to speak intelligibly. The

kid's focused on Raymond's tattoo. The tattoo is Raymond's cre-
dential. Having it on his hand for so long has earned him the right
to use it. And it works. The fire lighting up in the kid's eyes is the
rocket's red glare of his career blasting off.

Certainly, Mr. Mumble Mumble. Come right this way.

He gives his coworkers meaningful looks, like *they'll* know what
he's doing, and ushers Raymond past a few yuppie slackers with
enough power to inquire, with their raised eyebrows, who the hell
is Raymond. It's just like the military: everything ranked by strict
tiny gradations of clout. Raymond's a friend of today's guest. Barri-
ers fall, one by one.

On TV, Chandler's fake living room has always looked vaguely
normal. In person, it's psychedelic, a funhouse video arcade. The
studio's dark except for the purple, red, and green lights on the set
and the control board. Rows of seats rise up from the sloppy tangle
of cable and wires passing for a stage. Onstage are Chandler's famous armchairs, the Chandler chairs, three of them today, the
leather chairs—Chandler's trademark—suggesting that Chandler's
family has belonged to the Harvard Club for ten generations.
Which it probably has. It's been centuries since the darker races
began conspiring to use the white man's institutions against him.

Raymond spots Vincent being led out to sit in one of the chairs.
The sight of him takes Raymond's breath away. It's too early. He's
not ready for the gunfight at the OK Corral. Though he knows not
to get excited. This is just the sound check.

Vincent has let his hair grow in. The fucker's got a two-hundred-
dollar haircut. He's wearing an expensive suit, a white shirt, and a
tie. He looks like some snotball you'd ask for a bank loan, and the
guy would turn you down. Raymond's first impulse is to grab that
powder puff from the makeup girl and ram it down Vincent's
throat. In the other seat is the little old Jew whom Raymond saw in
People. The Holocaust hero and fund-raiser for the New World
Order and the Zionist fifth column. Both men are being fussed over
by a crew of girls painting their faces. They look like two corpses
getting a two-for-one special from the embalmer.

First Vincent and then the old Jew squirm as the techies run cords up their backs. If it was up to Raymond, he'd run those cords up their asses.

When Nielsen Boy motions for him to climb the bleachers and take a seat, Raymond is paralyzed, half wanting to crawl up there and settle into the warm sheltering darkness and half sensibly paranoid that the house lights could come up at any minute, and leave him—the only guy in the peanut gallery—face-to-face with Vincent. That would spoil the surprise that, in Raymond's scenario, will not happen until after the audience is seated and the cameras are rolling.

"Is there a restroom?" Raymond says.

"A restroom?" Is this iguana mocking him? Why not pop the kid and step over his limp body and keep going till he's popped the tech crew and Vincent and Maslow? The makeup girl, if she gets in his way. Because that's not what Raymond wants. His plan involves hanging out in the bathroom until the audience arrives. Then he'll slip in with the others. He'll listen, he'll wait, he'll control himself until that part of the show when they take questions from the crowd.

For one awful second, Raymond's afraid that the kid is going to follow him into the can so they—the cut and the uncut—can bond over the urinal. But no, the kid's got a job to do. Bye-bye, see ya later. Unlike Raymond, who can take his own sweet time in the *Chandler* toilet.

"You know how to get back?" Lizard Boy says.

"I think I can find my way," says Raymond. "How long till showtime?"

"Twenty minutes." The kid's an idiot. No intelligent person would bring in a guy like Raymond and let him loose in the studio. If anyone finds out about this, the kid will lose his job.

Raymond locks himself in a stall. Someone comes in and pisses. Someone takes a shit, two stalls over. Raymond cannot believe that Vincent has betrayed him and robbed him, that Raymond is sitting on the public john inhaling a stranger's farts while Vincent is backstage drinking mimosas and spearing boiled jumbo shrimp. If Raymond could only be sure of that, he could go back and sit in the bleachers.

The Klonopin he took seems to be doing the opposite of what it's supposed to. So he's wasting two pills—pills it took him considerable effort to get after Vincent's raid on his stash—in a TV-studio toilet. The meds are supposed to cool him out. But his temperature's rising.

If only this were the men's room scene from *The Godfather*. He wishes he had a gun taped to the tank so he could come out shooting. But Raymond isn't armed. For one thing, all he has at home is his deer-hunting rifle, which he's hardly about to smuggle past Chandler's army of bodyguards. And as for a little handgun, getting one—legal or illegal—would have been so expensive and such a pain in the ass that he would have felt compelled to use it. Raymond's not going to kill Vincent. He's known that all along. Raymond's promise to his dying mother did not include shooting her nephew on afternoon TV. No matter what the guy did.

After a while Raymond takes a chance and leaves the toilet stall and goes back to the studio.

Vincent and Maslow are gone. In their place are two tech-crew grunts making small adjustments. The first two rows are marked "Reserved," which is where—if there were any justice in this world—Raymond would be sitting. He takes a seat in the next row up, close enough to the stage so that when Vincent sits in the Chandler chair, Vincent can see Raymond—but only if and when Raymond chooses to be seen. Also he can easily make his way to the stage if Chandler decides, as he sometimes does, to invite an audience member to sit with the guests. You don't want a lot of steps to fall down with the whole world watching.

Eventually, the crowd rushes in, like animals driven to slaughter, grabbing for the best seats, musical chairs for adults. You'd think they were going to some stadium-seating headbanger rock concert instead of a dull prime-time blabfest.

Raymond looks up to see one of Chandler's yuppie slaves ushering the same black woman who was standing behind him in line to one of the reserved seats, directly in front of his. They must have a special place set aside for the Welfare Queen for a Day. As she sits down, the old woman smiles at Raymond, who puts all his creativity into giving her an even dirtier look than before. Does she think they're old friends? Even the baby seems to recognize him, and twists around in the old lady's arms, trying to crawl back and fling herself into Raymond's lap. Naturally it's the white man who's got to make himself small, to assume the fetal position to keep from having his jeans drooled on by the infant, whose name—Dineesha—Grandma says over and over. You be still, Dineesha, you mind, Dineesha, you watch and see what happens, baby.

No wonder Dineesha's squirming. Raymond's writhing, too, when a girl comedian comes out and does a round of lame stand-up and then starts working the crowd to change a motley group of individuals into a *Chandler* audience. You've come here to see Chandler, right? Yo! We come to see Chandler. Raymond's drawing the line here. He will not be part of any such group. It's Communist media mind control, sending its octopus tentacles out to strangle the white race, beginning with these fools who have shown up in person so Chandler can personally brainwash them into mud-race thinking.

"And now let's hear it for Chandler." Everyone applauds. The rainbow family gives it up for this Hershey bar with a law degree who wants to get down, get real. So he becomes a TV star and gets paid millions to put on thousand-dollar suits and tell white men how to change their lives.

Raymond knows better than to applaud. He needs his hands free in case all this makes him start puking. At the same time he can't *not* applaud. Some cameraman will pick up on Raymond's resistance and broadcast his sour puss on the monitor backstage, where Vincent will be watching. Which will spoil Raymond's surprise.

There's nothing to do but fake it. Raymond claps like a trained seal.

Shiny and scrubbed, Chandler bounds onstage. The studio lights wink merrily off his brown egg of a head.

"Brothers and sisters," Chandler begins, with that famous

Chandler look, that phony eye contact deep enough to make a strong individual connection with each member of the studio and home audience.

"Brothers and sisters," he repeats. That's the first lie right there. Raymond isn't his brother. That's an insult to Raymond's mother.

"First of all, I'd like to say we have someone special with us today—"

You sure do, thinks Raymond. But you don't know it yet.

"—My great-aunt Brenda from Cincinnati and my baby niece Dineesha." The crowd loves it that Chandler's got family, a baby niece Dineesha. The camera finds them. They're on the monitor. Of all the people for Raymond to be sitting directly behind!

Raymond lowers his head and puts his hand behind his neck as if it needs scratching. Once again the white man must duck and cover in the land that his ancestors defended with their blood.

As he turns to survey the crowd of welfare queens, pimps, and slackers, Raymond's gaze snags on a kid who looks familiar. After a moment he recognizes the boy from the driveway in Clairmont. Vincent's roommate. How nice. The whole family's here to support Cousin Vincent. Obviously, that's the kid's mom, the uptight chick from *People*, that broad so ready to explode that probably not even Vincent could bring himself to fuck her. And there's a younger boy with them. Have these people no decency, bringing tender young minds to get a faceful of the hot air that Chandler's about to start spewing?

"Brothers and sisters," Chandler says. "It makes me extremely happy that a child—my baby niece Dineesha—should be with us today to witness. Brothers and sisters, how many times have you thought about how much better the world would be if we could all live in peace and love, harmony and freedom? How many people have died for that? Brother Martin Luther King, Brother Mahatma Gandhi. And how many times have *you* wished that *you* knew what to do to bring it on, to change the world, to usher in the kingdom of heaven right here on our great green earth."

The kingdom of nigger heaven, thinks Raymond. The earth

hasn't been green for fifty years. Where's this city boy been? And what's heaven doing on network TV? Wasn't the American democratic system built on the separation of church and state?

"Today's show," says Chandler, "will introduce us to two men on the forefront of the battle to do good. Two men involved in the daily struggle for the rights of men and women and children who are not as lucky as we are. Human beings who don't have our American freedoms to say what we like and go where we please."

American freedoms? If Americans think they're free, let them try breaking any of the undemocratic laws that the Jewdicial system has passed. If they think they're allowed to own property, let them try not paying property taxes. If they think they're free to defend themselves in their own homes, let them face down the FBI and the ATF like Randy Weaver, David Koresh, and those poor dead babies at Waco. And now this guy whose ancestors came over here in slave ships owned by Jews is telling *them* about American freedoms? What America does *he* have in mind? The America where white citizens like Raymond hide in the bathroom where some stranger is taking a shit while a fruitcake like Chandler has private facilities and a white butler wiping his ass?

"Today," says Chandler, "a brave young man named Vincent Nolan is going to show us how the way to start changing the world is to change your own heart. First."

For some reason the crowd applauds. Fortunately, not for long.

"Meyer Maslow needs no introduction. All of you know that he is one of our most beloved and respected Holocaust survivors and writers, one of my personal heroes—"

The Holo-hoax. But what can you expect? It's in the Negro's interest to buy into the Holocaust myth. Then the blacks and Jews can compare sob stories, the Holocaust versus the slave trade, I had it worse, no, *I* had it worse, and then the Irish can get in there with their fucking potato famine, and the so-called Native Americans. . . . They'll all get reparations at the taxpayer's expense, with a kickback in it somewhere for the Infernal Revenue Service.

"He is also the founder and director of World Brotherhood

Watch, a foundation dedicated to human rights, to making sure that people all over the globe have food and medical care and the liberty to enjoy it. Dr. Maslow is the author of a new book, *One Heart at a Time*, in which he tells us how we can change the world by turning just one heart at a time toward the path of goodness and love."

The chatter inside Raymond's head has ratcheted up to a shriek. He needs to see a pharmacist—now!

"And the really strange part"—Chandler zeroes in on this for drama—"is that Dr. Maslow wrote the book *before* Vincent Nolan came along and put his life on the line to prove Dr. Maslow's theory. What we'll see today is . . . a chay-yanged man."

The applause is nearly unbearable, but things are about to get worse. Because it's time for Chandler's trademark moment. Just before bringing out the guests, he makes major eye contact with the crowd. His eyes are practically jittering in their sockets as he gives you the guest's whole life story in his super-intense fag shorthand.

"At thirteen, he had a loving family. A comfortable house in Budapest. By the time he was fourteen, his entire family was dead. He slept in haylofts, in cellars and pigpens, constantly on the run. He was almost killed five times until he was caught and sent to Auschwitz and survived."

Chandler's run out of oxygen. "Brothers and sisters, how many of you could live through that and not want to make someone *pay?* How many of us would want revenge? But Meyer Maslow has dedicated his life to making sure that no one else ever suffers as he did, and that we forgive and forget."

Forgive, my ass, thinks Raymond.

The crowd applauds insanely as Meyer Maslow comes out nodding and strutting like a prizefighter during the walk-on, looking like some upmarket Hollywood rabbi to the stars.

"It's a pleasure to be here." Meyer shakes Chandler's hand. "And excuse me, but I feel I have to point out that I have never believed in forgiving and forgetting. I've written about the importance of forgiving but *not* forgetting."

The Jew knows more than you do. The Jew wants you to know that.

"Of course we can't forget." Chandler's so fast on his feet, he could have had a career in basketball. "None of us can forget. Nor should we."

Boo-hoo. Boo-hoo. The Holocaust. The Middle Passage. Chandler points toward one of the Chandler chairs. Whether the rabbi likes it or not, it's time for him to heel and sit so Chandler can bring out the other puppy.

Chandler begins again. "His childhood could not have been more unlike that of Meyer Maslow. Born to a mom on welfare and a dad whose life was straight out of *Les Miz*, hounded to his death because of an income tax mistake. A troubled youth, a run of bad luck, an unfortunate meeting with men like himself who'd found a way to blame their bad luck on disadvantaged minorities who are struggling to feed their children just like everyone else."

Hold on! That's Raymond he's talking about. That's Raymond and his buddies gasping for air under that shit heap of lies. The Jew and the black man are struggling, all right, struggling to take over America. And winning, by the looks of it. They're the ones onstage. The only white citizens in the room are up in the peanut gallery.

"White men," Chandler says, like it's something to be ashamed of. "White men and women who channel their frustrations and disappointments into anger and hate. And Vincent Nolan falls in with these men, and almost slips under their spell. Until one day on a visit to, of all things, a greenhouse—a visit meant to destroy and hurt, to cause its Korean owner pain—he sees the light. He sees how all God's children and all the beauties of God's earth are one."

What the hell are they talking about? That time he and Vincent went to check out the Korean greenhouse and maybe do some damage? It didn't happen like that at all. Vincent would have been down with it if they'd torched that popsicle shack just to see the special effects when all that plastic went up in flames. But they'd decided against it. He *and* Raymond decided against it. They didn't want to think about it being traced to them. Detectives, cops, lawyers, the whole nine yards. What do you get for arson? Fifteen, twenty years? For what? Flash-frying some plants? They'd gone home and got drunk in front of the tube instead.

Lately Raymond has given the subject of Vincent plenty of thought. And he's concluded that Vincent made up his mind, if you could call it a mind, to become a race traitor somewhere around the time he took all that Ex at the rave. After that he started acting weird. Raymond thought his cousin had just punctured another hole in his Swiss-cheese brain, that eventually it would heal over and he would get back to his old self. So what they're trying to pass off as a heavy-duty spiritual conversion inspired by the beauty of nature was in fact a drug OD and the sort of pathetic revelation a kid might have the first time he got high. Don't they know that? Why don't they admit it? How can they spout this crap on TV as if it were the truth? Raymond knows better than to be surprised, but he still can't help it. It's his job to correct these lies. It's his duty as a white American patriot to tell the truth, the whole truth, and nothing but the truth.

Chandler can't seem to wrap this one up. There's so much to say about Vincent. "After just a few weeks of working with Meyer Maslow, the sort of person he'd never met before—and who has met someone like Meyer Maslow and *not* been changed?—sure enough, Vincent began to. *Change.* Day by day, thought by thought. Like Dr. Maslow writes in his book. To turn himself around so completely that at the charity fund-raising dinner for Dr. Maslow's foundation Vincent proved his courage and his resolve. He nearly died. My man nearly died from an allergic reaction, but he kept on pushing, pushing, putting his life on the line, testing himself to the limit, until he said what he had to say, until the brother testified about how he turned his life around and how we can, too."

You'd think it was a Rolling Stones concert, that's how berserk the crowd goes. They're nearly high-fiving each other as they put their hands together and welcome the traitor, the liar, the thief, the truck thief, the prescription medication thief, the drug addict, a guy who is definitely not the hero they think.

If Raymond's blood has been simmering since he saw Vincent getting made up, it comes to a rolling boil the instant Vincent walks onstage. Because this time he's not sitting down under a sheet, being fluffed and powdered like some pervert poofter. He's walking on like he owns the joint, taking Chandler's hand and . . . shaking a black man's hand. The shock nearly knocks Raymond off his seat. He never thought he would live to see this. Well, jeez, why *shouldn't* he shake his hand? Vincent and Chandler are on the same page. Vincent's suit is almost as good as Chandler's. They could be two CEOs meeting in a five-star hotel for a power breakfast.

If this were a different kind of show—the old *Geraldo*, or *Jerry Springer*—they'd dress Vincent in the storm trooper clothes he never actually wore. They'd make him wear sleeves short enough to flash his tats at Mom and Pop Middle America. But this is *Chandler*, and if Vincent wants to market himself as a middle-class middle-management white sellout, Chandler's happy to go that route. Bring out Mr. Changed Man.

"It's great to meet you," Vincent says. "I'm a big fan. I've seen your show a million times."

Lies, lies! Does anybody really think they're meeting for the first time? Who doesn't know that Vincent and Chandler have been hanging out backstage, enjoying the Big Rock Candy Mountain with all the babes and free champagne? And sure, Vincent's seen the show a million times. Raymond can testify to that. Vincent used to watch it with him and the guys, calling Chandler every name in the book and talking about how the black man and his Jewish backers are sabotaging the country.

"Well, thanks," Chandler says. "It's good to meet you, too." Chandler pulls himself away from the crowd and Velcros onto Vincent so everyone can watch Vincent practically get hard from the warmth of Chandler's attention. A flush comes to Vincent's cheeks. Can the home audience *see* this, see the white man blushing? Do they know it's the only race that gets blood rising into its face, which proves that the white race is the only race with a conscience? But what is Vincent blushing *about?* Heavy eye contact with a

Negro? In another minute, they're going to fall down on the studio floor and start sucking each other off.

"Have a seat," says Chandler.

Have *my* seat, thinks Raymond.

Vincent sits, after giving his pant cuffs a tiny tug, as if he's been doing that all his life. Chandler sits, same pant-tug. Where do these guys learn this? And who could have imagined Vincent would be an A student? Raymond remembers him being a troublemaker at school. Vincent's poor mother put in her time in the principal's office.

Chandler sits in his Chandler chair and turns toward Maslow and Vincent, who are sitting close enough to hold hands if they want to.

"How amazing," Chandler says, "to see you two guys together. Not only together, but . . . anyone could tell just by looking at you how much you like and respect each other. You know . . ." Chandler's acting as if he's not reading from the prompt screen, as if he's making it up on the spot. "I'm sure our viewers would love to know what it was like for you two gentlemen to meet. Can either of you reconstruct for me what was going through your minds?"

"Well, it's strange," says Meyer Maslow. "On the day that Vincent showed up at our office, my staff and I had been exploring new ways to dramatize our cause. Because the sad thing is, Chandler, that while we are known all over the world, by the refugees and dissidents we have worked to free—"

"Excuse me, Dr. Maslow," says Chandler. "Let's see some of their faces."

The monitor lights up, and the audience watches glam shots— young and old, men, women, children, families, everyone happy and smiling, flashing more expensive dental work than Raymond can begin to afford for his kids.

"Tell us. Whose faces are we seeing?" Chandler asks.

Maslow doesn't miss a beat. "Dissidents we have freed from Communist bloc prisons. Bosnians, Serbs, and Kosovars, torture victims, prisoners of conscience who dared to criticize their governments. Hunger strikers we rescued on the brink of starvation."

Their faces flash at Raymond, who is probably the only one in the crowd who knows that this is another elaborate scam to line the Hollywood rabbi's pockets. They could take photos of anyone and make them look like refugees. Those makeup queens can work wonders. And what about the people the government killed in *this* country? Or the *white* refugees driven by poverty to live in inner-city ghettos?

"All these people," Meyer is saying, "owe their lives to Brotherhood Watch. But here at home we tend to become more involved with our own families, our own borders. I suppose it's human nature to see only what's under our noses."

"I guess so." Chandler doesn't want to admit that he does nothing all day but sit around and think about other people's problems—that is, how he can pimp them to make big bucks.

"So my staff and I were considering new ways to publicize our cause. . . . And Vincent appears out of nowhere."

"That's amazing. That's beautiful. Would you say . . . God sent him?"

"I would," Meyer says. "Others might have another explanation." He curls his lip to show what he thinks of those other explanations. "I have learned over and over that God sends you what you need."

Here's where the logic breaks down. Did God send Maslow's family, the ones supposedly killed in the Holocaust—did God send *them* what they needed? No. Which proves you can't have it both ways: God and the Holocaust. Proof that the Holo-hoax never happened. Because there definitely *is* a God. A god who believes in justice, in Vincent getting what he's got coming.

"Only later," Maslow goes on, "did I realize that Vincent would not only become an important part of our Brotherhood family, but also that he was the living proof of the ideas that I had just written about in my new book, *One Heart at a Time*."

Raymond checks the monitor, on which Maslow's book appears. If this were less important, if he were relaxing in his living room, Raymond would count the number of times they plug the book during today's show. He misses his ARM buddies. He wishes he were home with them, watching *Chandler* and cursing.

"And you, Vincent? Did you suspect that you were the living fulfillment of an idea that Meyer Maslow had written about in his new book?"

"Actually," says Vincent, "I'd read the book."

"You did?" says Chandler.

You did? thinks Raymond. When the hell was that? On the truck—the stolen truck—ride from Raymond's house to the city? It was physically impossible for Vincent to have read those books while he was living at Raymond's. The idea that someone could do such a thing totally rocks Raymond's world. Though, come to think of it, there were days when Vincent would disappear at lunch or take a long time getting home from the tire shop. Raymond had hoped that Vincent was secretly getting laid, or even copping a drink. It's sickening to imagine that he might have been reading Zionist propaganda. There was that one day Vincent's car broke down in a vacant lot, and Raymond went to get him. Vincent claimed he'd been taking a piss. Could he have been parked, reading Maslow's lies? Raymond won't let himself go there.

"I'd read all of Meyer Maslow's books," says Vincent. "And I was impressed. I'd never read anything like them. In fact the people I got mixed up with—" He lowers his eyes. Overwhelmed.

"We understand," says Chandler. "Take a minute if you have to. Have your feelings, Vincent."

Vincent works the silence, then says, "But I never imagined I could be saved the way Meyer Maslow describes saving people. I never imagined that *my* life could change."

"But you wanted to try—" Chandler suggests.

"I wanted to try," agrees Vincent. The crowd applauds spontaneously, loving how the black man puts words in the white man's mouth.

"And what made you able to do it?" Chandler says. "Able to change."

If Raymond thought he could do it without attracting unwanted attention, he'd put his hands over his ears so as not to have to hear that doo-doo about the Korean greenhouse. Raymond tries to sing a song in his head to drown out Vincent's voice. But the only songs that come to mind are the ones they played at Homeland Encampment. The trouble with German military marches is they're not singable, exactly.

Apparently Vincent has reached the end of his routine. Chandler waits a few seconds. Then, as if he's listening to the voice of his inner self instead of the million dollars' worth of audio equipment plugged into his ear, he tilts his head and says, "You know, Vincent, Dr. Maslow, I heard a story. Correct me if I'm wrong."

"What's that?" asks Maslow.

Dr. Maslow, I heard what you really get off on is sucking black men's cocks. But Chandler's not going to say that. There's no point even hoping.

Chandler says, "I heard that the first time Meyer and Vincent met, the two of you compared tattoos. You, Dr. Maslow, asked to see Vincent's swastika, and you showed him the numbers on your arm from the Nazi camp."

Vincent is trying to disappear. What healthy white man wouldn't? The alternative is to sit there while the audience imagines him involved in some macho standoff with one of those Jews who tattoo themselves. To say nothing of the fact that Vincent doesn't *have* a swastika. That would have been way too ballsy for him. Waffen-SS bolts are kid stuff. It's Raymond who's got the swastika. Would Chandler like to see it?

Chandler seems to have stepped on somebody's toes. Maslow is glaring at him.

"Do you think you could show our audience?" Chandler prods.

"Absolutely not," Maslow says. "We are not primitives. We are not Amazonian tribesmen, displaying our tribal markings. We are two men who have suffered and have come here with a message that we refuse to contaminate by indulging in tawdry theatrics. I refuse to cheapen the Holocaust for anyone's entertainment."

"All rightee." Chandler doesn't blink. If Maslow won't flash his tats, fuck him, let's move on. "Let's turn this over to the audience. Any questions for our guests?"

The lights come up. No one wants to go first. Certainly not Raymond. Let the ball get rolling. Then he'll raise his hand and start off as if he means to ask a normal question. Of course, Vincent will know it's him. That will be half the fun. Meanwhile Raymond's got his hands jammed in his pockets so his tats don't set off any alarm bells. He turns his face whenever Vincent looks his way.

A black girl stands, bouncing on the souls of her feet and jabbing the air in Vincent's direction. "So what made you join in the first place? I mean, why would a person want to wallow in all that hate?"

Vincent fixes her with his baby blues. It's like he's practicing to be Chandler.

"I guess I was an angry guy," he says. "And I blamed the wrong people for my problems."

Raymond hears a roaring in his ears so massive and oceanic that for a minute he forgets where he is, forgets to duck when Vincent looks straight at him. Damn right someone would be angry. The white race is getting shafted. And white working men like Raymond and Vincent are being forced to bend over. Though not Vincent, not anymore. Vincent has gone over to their side, and left Raymond out in the cold.

Vincent sees Raymond. Raymond sees Vincent. Vincent can't take his eyes off him. Raymond loves how the sight of him is scrambling Vincent's brain. This is why it's better to be the surpriser than the surprisee.

Finally, Vincent loses it. He goes rigid and stares into space. His concentration's shot. He can't handle the rest of the questions, can't deliver the neat, prepackaged turd he's learned to drop on command.

"Angry," he says. "Yeah. I was angry and blamed the wrong people. . . ." He's turning his head in increments, trying to locate Raymond, but Raymond slumps and hides behind Aunt Brenda and baby Dineesha.

Chandler senses something wrong, but he doesn't know what's happened. Even the rabbi picks up on the negative buzz. He's looking at Vincent, probably worried that the loser got a hold of some cocktail nuts backstage, that now he's doing his near-death thing every time he appears in public. Why not? It worked for him before.

Vincent's sudden psychic absence leaves a hole in the show, which Raymond decides to step through. He might as well go for the gold now. He's already blown his cover.

Raymond catches the eye of the girl with the microphone, and she brings it over. Only when he grabs the mike does she see his tattoos. He watches her deciding if, by letting him talk, she's doing something very right or very wrong. Raymond takes a deep breath, then asks the question he's repeated to himself until he's got it perfect:

"What I'd like to know is how honest Vincent Nolan has been with you guys about what he did before. I mean, how much has he told you?"

All right! Raymond got it out. It's not the kind of question you hear much on *Chandler*. Mostly it's some homey asking why the guests ain't got the common sense God gave them. But you never hear anything that makes you think that the person knows the real story about the guests.

Vincent is dumbstruck. Light is beginning to dawn on the rabbi. Chandler is already there. But he's still guarded and cagey as he says, "Hey, brother, why do you ask?"

That they haven't called security and hustled Raymond out of the studio is encouraging. Chandler could make that happen by moving one little pinkie, the one with the Iceberg Slim diamond ring. But he's taking a wait-and-see attitude until he figures out where Raymond is going with this.

"I'm Vincent's cousin. Raymond Gillette. His first cousin. We grew up together."

Raymond can't read Chandler's face. Maybe shock, maybe annoyance. Why didn't his staff have this in their sights? That's what he's paying them for. Someone's head is going to roll. Without a doubt, some white man's.

"Man!" says Chandler, treading water. "Can you believe that? How about that? Vincent's family." He wants the long applause to give everybody a few seconds to regroup.

Looking into Chandler's eyes is like watching a slot machine spin. Lemons apples cherries. Raymond can peer right into his skull and see that Chandler has no idea if Raymond is the good cousin or the bad cousin. Judging from surface impressions, Chandler's betting on the bad. Now what? Does he find some way to shut Raymond down long enough to go to break and remove him from the studio? Or does he go for the chance that this might really be major TV and see what comes out when he mixes the new Vincent Nolan, the reconstructed cooled-out brotherhood model, with a few drops of his volatile past? The Changed with the Unreformed. A chemistry experiment.

Chandler knows what happened on the old *Geraldo*. They must teach you that in Talk Show for Beginners. Raymond himself has watched it many times on a tape he ordered by mail from an ad on TV. *Television's Wildest Moments*. Chandler doesn't want that happening on his watch. Still, the bottom line is that he knows about Geraldo's wild moment. Everybody knows about it. Which means it must have been greater TV than all the forgettable, sharing-and-caring snoozes Chandler has hosted.

Chandler weighs his dilemma. He decides to bring it on. He hasn't become the superstar talk-show Brother of the Moment for nothing!

"Family!" says Chandler. "What a terrific surprise. How long since you guys have seen each other? Sir, please . . . why don't you come down here?"

Vincent's doing all he can short of waving his arms in an SOS signal to Chandler. Disaster! Meyer catches Vincent's vibe, and soon he too is shooting daggers at Chandler. They've worked hard to get this slot. It's supposed to be about *them* and the rabbi's book.

They don't want their big opportunity jacked by some trailer-trash cousin of Vincent's.

Screw them. Raymond's got something to say. Facts instead of bullshit. He stands and heads down toward the stage. He's taking it slow. Let them watch, let them wait, let Vincent enjoy the cameras following Raymond for a change. Maybe they *haven't* seen the old *Geraldo*. Or maybe the producers always secretly wanted to go the *Jerry Springer* route. Because they let Raymond get right up next to him, right up in Vincent's face. Raymond's so close to Vincent, he can count the drops of sweat breaking out on his forehead. Five, six, seven. Good.

He hugs his long-lost cousin. Not some Hollywood-Jew air kiss but a white man's bear hug. All right, maybe a little hard. Give the man something he can feel. Meanwhile Raymond grabs Vincent's right hand and gives him the ARM handclasp down between their chests where no one can see it. Vincent's palm gets wet in the time it takes him to wrestle it back from Raymond.

Chandler twitches his sparkling pinkie, and another Chandler Chair appears. Raymond falls back into the chair, strongly vibing Chandler not to come over with his hand out.

Chandler gets it. Chandler's good to go. Everything's clear to Chandler.

But he's a little stumped. He can't ask, How did you guys meet, or Tell us about the first time you met, like he did with Maslow and Vincent. And Chandler's not going to ask Raymond to show off his tattoo. He already sees it. Probably the cameras are being told not to look. The last thing they want the American people to see is a man who believes in something so strongly he'll have its ancient but currently unfashionable symbol engraved on his tender white skin.

"Vincent, were you aware that your cousin would be here today?" Chandler knows the answer. Silence. More silence. "I take it that you didn't—"

"It's a surprise," Vincent says.

Raymond's just figured out how to tell, from the monitors, where the camera is pointed. And right now it's pointed at him, so he gives it a big toothy grin. Let Mr. and Mrs. America *watch* the surprise he's arranged.

Chandler's teleprompter has gone blank. Has his staff fled for their lives? Chandler is flying solo.

"So you belong, or you did belong, to the organization Vincent left to join Brotherhood Watch."

"*Do* belong," clarifies Raymond. "I'm still a proud member of the American Rights Movement—"

"The Aryan Resistance Movement. A well-known hate group," the Jewish expert interrupts. "Brotherhood Watch has been monitoring their activities for years. Vincent has been extremely helpful—"

"A patriotic organization," Raymond corrects. But that's enough. He hasn't come here to debate the Jew on the subject of what ARM stands for. As much as Raymond would like to tell the truth about ARM, that approach is a guaranteed loser. He's got something better planned.

"Holocaust deniers and Nazi sympathizers." The old man is not going to get off Raymond's case. But Raymond will not engage. At least not until he's had a chance to bounce a couple of facts off Chandler.

"Cousin Vincent wasn't expecting me. I don't think he would have invited me, either. Because I know something about him that he'd rather no one knew."

"What's that?" Chandler can't help asking. Is this how you treat your guests? Invite them on the show and then invite the family to air their dirty laundry?

The audience has gone silent.

"First of all, the guy lived with me and my wife and kids for years. My wife fed him. I got him a job. He stayed on my living room couch. He was there when my kids ate breakfast. We gave him a leg up, took care of him. And then he splits. He steals my truck. He steals fifteen hundred dollars I'd saved up working two jobs. He even stole the pain medication prescribed for a serious on-the-job injury."

Just talking about a work-related injury—even if it's made up—

makes Raymond feel like some trailer troll bitching about his aches
and pains. But fine, let them see what it looks like. The hardworking, underpaid white man. Plenty *could* have happened to Raymond
in fifteen years at the tire shop. Plenty did. And what kind of work
injury will *Chandler* ever get? Back strain from kissing guests' asses?
Some bad Botox reaction?

Raymond checks the audience to see how this is going over.
What's the desired reaction? Sympathy. Raymond's a working man.
He's been hurt. Vincent hurt him. He would like the crowd to turn on
Vincent, for lying, and on Maslow, for helping Vincent lie. The crowd
should be shocked, disgusted, enraged at the self-righteous bastards
who have been playing the audience for fools, and the cherry on top
will be their anger at themselves for having been taken, for having ap-
plauded a lying thief who steals from his own flesh and blood. They
are going to be pissed at themselves for having seen this guy as a hero.
And then, if things go Raymond's way, he can use this golden opportunity to make them start seeing how this is typical of the mind-control
media twisting their brains into pretzels.

But somehow it's not working. The studio audience looks puzzled.
Maybe Raymond set it up wrong. Maybe he led them to believe he
had something worse on Vincent. Something worse than stealing.
That he killed someone, even. That's what they were expecting. Just
boosting a truck and some pills is a letdown. But wait, he did fuck over
Raymond. And Lucy. And Raymond's kids.

They took him in, they trusted him. The guy was flesh and blood.
It was tough on Raymond and Lucy and the kids when he stayed forever and then split with his truck! These poor brainwashed white people are so used to being lied to, they can't recognize the truth when
they hear it. They still want to believe that Vincent is the new prince
of peace.

"Is this true?" Chandler asks Vincent.

The cameras zoom in on Vincent.

"Is it true?" Chandler repeats.

Vincent stonewalls him. He won't let Chandler make eye contact. Raymond's got to hand it to Vincent for being a stand-up guy, for displaying qualities you'd want on your side. Well, toughness isn't everything. Integrity counts, too.

Finally, Chandler gives up on Vincent and—let's keep everything rolling here—focuses on the rabbi.

"Did Vincent mention this to you?" he asks. "Did he say he stole from his cousin?"

"How do we know it's true?" Maslow says. "Because this gentleman says so?"

This gentleman. The Jew is mocking him. The Jew in the handtailored suit and the four-hundred-dollar shoes, the Jew whose haircut cost fifty times as much as the lousy copy of *People* that a hardworking white man can't afford to buy his own wife, the Jew—specifically, *this* Jew—is accusing him of lying.

"It's true," says Raymond.

"Let our other guest speak, please," says Chandler.

"Anyway," says Meyer Maslow, "what Vincent did before doesn't matter."

"Meaning what?" says Chandler.

"What matters is what he's doing now and how much he's changed. We assumed he must have done some unfortunate things while he was with ARM, but I never asked—"

Look how the Jew has turned this around in a couple of seconds!

"You never *asked* what he did in this hate group?" says Chandler.

Wait a second. This is not about ARM and what they do. This is not about the Jew being such a saint that he accepts Vincent, warts and all, wiping out the past. This is about what *Vincent* did. Vincent stole from Raymond.

"We went on faith," says Maslow. "We took him in. We believed him—"

"Help me out, here, Dr. Maslow," Chandler says. The black man and the Jew are in this together. They have plenty to discuss. And the two white men, Vincent and Raymond, are just bystanders, looking on.

"How does this square with your forgiving but not forgetting?" Chandler—the former lawyer—is interrogating Maslow. Chandler doesn't forget. Chandler's making the old man eat it for having corrected him earlier. "Because it seems to me as if you're trying to forget the past. And to encourage Vincent to forget *his* past—"

Raymond could be furniture here! One of the Chandler chairs. He's the one who made this happen, and now it's moved beyond him. He'll be damned if they edge him out of their gay lovers' quarrel.

"Plus," Raymond says so loudly that the cameras find him on instinct, bypassing the director. "Plus this guy, my cousin, didn't *have* any spiritual conversion. He was taking drugs. Ecstasy. And if he's stolen all those pills from me, you can bet the dude is still getting high. He's probably on something now. So don't tell *me* he's changed—"

Chandler can't believe it! Why can't every show be like this?

"Is that true?" Chandler says. "Vincent, is that true?" He's tried this line of questioning. Has he forgotten it didn't work?

"And there's more," says Raymond. "There's lots the dude didn't tell you. I'll bet he never mentioned the fact that he had to take twenty hours of anger management class for throwing some little old Jewish lady in her swimming pool. In the deep end. With all her clothes on."

Chandler waits, Maslow waits, the studio audience waits, the crew waits, the home audience waits. Raymond's willing to wait. See how Vincent explains that away.

"That isn't true," says Vincent. At last. The dead man speaks. "It was the shallow end. And I fished her right out. She didn't even swallow water. She wasn't hurt. She's fine."

Raymond's going to have to shut Vincent up. He simply cannot stand the fact that Vincent's getting away with it. Raymond has got to do whatever it takes.

Just then the Jew says, "I think it's wonderful that this gentleman has volunteered to come up here and let us see exactly what Vincent left behind. What he decided *against*. The kind of person he turned his back on. And now I'm wondering if we can't get back to the heart of our show, the real reason why we're here."

Meaning the rabbi's foundation, his book. The Jew is telling

Chandler how to run his show. Will Chandler go for it? Chandler lifts his hand. A crew member checks out Raymond. As soon as they go to break, he'll be escorted out.

"We've got a few seconds before break," Chandler says.

Raymond knows that's his cue.

Raymond gets up and crosses the stage. It feels good to be moving. It's the Jew he wants to deal with. The Jew who has insulted him most, out front and in public. Vincent is just a liar and a thief, but the Jew is a danger to the entire white race. The Jew who called him "this gentleman." The Jew who said *he* was lying.

He takes another step toward the Jew. Raymond hasn't yet decided what, if anything, he's going to do to him. So how could he seem threatening? Still, just as he expected, he feels two heavy hands on his shoulders. He turns.

In fact, it's not what he thought: the beefy security bouncers.

It's Vincent, pulling him back, dragging him away from the rabbi. Raymond sees the kid from the driveway running down to get a piece of the action, then stopping behind Maslow. Will everybody just calm down here, and step back a minute, and think?

But there's no thinking, no stepping back. Vincent's face is twisted with rage. His cheeks are scarlet, his forehead furrowed, spit's flying out of his mouth.

Vincent hauls off and socks Raymond. Why doesn't Raymond deck him? It's as if his arms don't work, as if some gear has ground to a halt and needs a squirt of lubricant. Vincent keeps hitting Raymond, calling him names. Slamming his fist into Raymond.

Vincent has changed, all right. This is a million times worse than dunking some old lady in the pool. And that's what helps Raymond get through it, what lets him keep his cool until the pain takes over and eases him out of the situation.

The only thing that comforts Raymond is the proof that he was right all along. Vincent is the violent one. It's Vincent who's trashing Raymond.

D ANNY FEELS AS IF HE'S LOOKING through the wrong end of a telescope, watching water bugs skitter around, blowing whistles and trying to control the chaos that's erupted in the studio. *Slowly, slowly, brothers and sisters, let's please not rush or panic.* Then poof! The audience is gone, and two burly attendants in green scrub suits are calmly rolling Raymond out on a gurney, as if hauling bloody unconscious skinheads off the *Chandler* set is an everyday occurrence. It occurs to Danny that it might be cool to be an EMT worker someday.

Somewhere a voice asks how Vincent is. Someone else asks *where* Vincent is. Someone's sent to check on him and then comes back and says, "Mr. Nolan's not anywhere. We seem to have misplaced our guest."

Dreamily, Danny looks around. He doesn't see Vincent, either. Is all this taking a very long time, or no time at all? And where is Mom? You'd think the minute things got ugly, she'd be all over Danny and Max, shielding their bodies with hers. No sooner does Danny wonder why Mom *isn't* all over them than she is. Mom grabs Danny and Max, and drags them through a door marked "Green Room."

"You'll be safe here," Mom says, shooing them inside.

Danny could just kill her. Does she think they're babies? And what do they need to be safe *from?* Does Mom think the Aryan Resistance militia is about to descend on *Chandler* and take instant revenge for what happened to Raymond? They'll take their time. They'll come after Vincent first. They'll put him in the hot seat and cut off his toes.

"Sit down, guys," says Mom.

Danny and Max sink into the nasty couches. Does Julia Roberts chill on these before she goes on *Chandler?* Why do they call it the Green Room, when it's a gray windowless hole with a bunch of smelly old furniture and a table littered with soda bottles, cracker crumbs, pitted mounds of disgusting dips? And they're supposed to stay in this holding tank while everything happens outside?

But everything *has* happened. The main event is over. Raymond threatened Meyer, and Vincent interceded. The result wasn't pretty, but Danny didn't run away. He ran toward the . . . he doesn't know what to call it. He ran toward the . . . and then he stopped. Vincent said there were two kinds of people, those who run toward the danger and those who run away. Danny's discovered a third group. People who stop in the middle. And by tomorrow morning, everyone at school will have seen *Chandler.* Danny might as well wear a big letter on his chest, like that girl in *The Scarlet Letter.* In Danny's case, a giant red *W* for *Wimp.*

He can thank his mother for that. Mom's turned him into a coward. Dad was right about some things. She overprotects and underestimates them. Plus, she likes Max better.

Danny wonders if Vincent noticed him after the fight broke out. Did Vincent see that his instinct, when push came to shove, was to run toward the trouble? Not that Vincent needed Danny's help to turn into a punching machine. It was way more disturbing than Danny will ever admit to Mom. Danny has seen fights at school, where the trickliest bloody nose makes everyone quit and back off. But Raymond's face was covered with blood, which only seemed to make Vincent want to hit him more. Raymond's freakishly scarlet blood sprayed in fat drops as his face melted into rubbery expressions that no face should be able to make. Danny saw what he's pretty sure were teeth flying out of Raymond's mouth.

Mom stands in the Green Room doorway, hunched over, wringing her hands. It's probably how he looked when he ran toward the fight and stalled. And yet, despite how angry she makes him, Danny feels sorry for her. He knows how hard she and Meyer worked to turn Vincent into an advertisement for their foundation. And now their personal Frankenstein has blown its circuits on *Chandler*. What makes being angry at Mom more confusing is that lately Danny's been aware of how much she does for them. He knows that Armstrong blackmailed her, that her speaking at graduation is all about saving *him*. Danny's not wild about the idea, but it beats the other options, like repeating junior year.

"There's stuff to eat and drink in here. In case you're thirsty or hungry." Does Mom think they haven't spotted the sweets and salty snacks a lot faster than she has? Danny regards the table littered with broken cookies, orange cheese puffs, and dirty plastic cups. Is that what Vincent ate before the show? No wonder he went ape.

"We're fine," says Max. "Don't worry." Max certainly doesn't look fine. In fact, he looks spooked. But he does seem calm compared to how he was that night at Dad's. Once again, Max is right. Finding out about the marriage and the Bulgarian baby was worse, for them, than watching Vincent lose it on *Chandler*.

Danny looks at the monitor in the corner of the Green Room. The camera is running, but the only thing on the screen is a young guy in headphones and a *Chandler* T-shirt speed-walking across the wrecked studio.

"Vincent wouldn't just *leave*," Mom says. "I'm sure he just stepped out for a minute—"

If Vincent's gone, at least that means he won't be speaking at his school. Even when Danny got his head around the prospect of Mom giving a speech, the idea that Vincent was also involved was totally over the top. The few people who hadn't read about Danny's bizarro living arrangements in *People* would get to hear about it at graduation. Which would ruin Danny's senior year. . . . Danny's instantly sorry for thinking that. He hopes they find Vincent soon.

Mom says, "Guys, I know this isn't the right time. But we've got to talk, really talk, about what just happened. You guys lead sheltered lives, thank God. It's not often—never, I hope—that you see horrible violence like that. Violence from someone you know, someone you *thought* you knew. Someone you lived with. *Live* with."

Sheltered lives. Mom can stick that. Vincent went too far. But Raymond was after Meyer. And Vincent. Raymond parked in their driveway. He meant to hurt someone. The last thing Danny wants now is a big discussion with Mom about whether seeing Vincent beat up Raymond will leave a permanent psychic scar.

"We'll talk about it," Danny says. "Whenever. Go do what you have to do."

"I'll be back in five minutes," says Mom.

"Take your time," says Max. "We're fine here."

Finally, Mom leaves. The air feels lighter after she's gone. Max looks like he could use a drink. Danny paws through the rows of soda bottles.

Max says, very strained and subdued, "So, like, what happened just now?"

"What do you mean, what happened?" Danny says.

"I mean, with Vincent—"

"The shithead threatened Meyer. And Vincent stepped in." Danny ran toward the trouble, and stopped. But Max isn't asking about that.

"That's what it was?" says Max.

"That's the deal," says Danny. "Trust me."

The soda bottles are sticky, half full. No way Danny's going to touch them.

"Wait a second," he says. "Here's a bottle of rum. Yo ho ho. Thank you, Chandler. You know what a Cuba Libre is, Max?"

"No," says Max.

"Delicious," says Danny. "Slammin'." He mixes two rum and Cokes.

Danny and Max get hammered. Danny feels they've earned it. The Green Room looks like those cinder-block cells where TV cops interview suspects, but after a second Cuba Libre, the whole scene begins to strike him as sort of *interesting*. It's strangely relaxing to sit and watch, on the TV monitor, nothing happening in the trashed empty studio.

Danny says, "Have another rum and Coke."

"These are kind of strong," says Max.

"Drink it. You need to keep hydrated in a stressful situation. Keep that little brain moistened."

By now Danny feels kind of swampy. And through the humid, jungly haze he watches something start to happen on the monitor.

Chandler's back in the studio, giving some kind of speech. In close-up, Chandler's face is enormous. The audio's off, and Danny can't find the dial. Nor does he want to, especially when Chandler wraps it up, and here comes Meyer Maslow—kill the house lights, spotlight the guy—sitting in one of the leather chairs. Reading aloud from his book. Of course it goes on forever. Danny and Max keep watching. Hell, it's TV. It's on.

Time slips by. Finally, Mom comes in and says, "Not one person saw Vincent leave. He vanished into thin air."

"Are you okay?" Danny said. "Because you look like roadkill, Mom."

"Thanks," Mom says. "That helps."

"Sorry," Danny says.

There's a silence. Then Mom says, "What's that noise?"

"I think it's Max. Puking in the bathroom."

"Is he sick?"

"Cooba Leebrays," says Danny.

Even for Mom, she's surprisingly slow.

"Have you guys been *drinking?*"

"I don't know. Not really. Yes."

"You let your little brother *drink?* In the middle of *this?* After what we've been through today? Is this how I can trust you? Oh, Danny, you guys are *not* coming through for me. I can't tell you how disappointed I am."

"You should appreciate us more," said Danny. "You should see how bad other kids are . . ." He lets his voice trail off, ominously. "Me and Max mostly do what you want. We're pretty nice to each other. And we're pretty nice to you. Even though you might not think so. Okay, we drank a little rum. Big deal. This has been rough for us, too, Mom."

Danny is leaving out a lot. It's not the most brilliant speech. He's pretty smashed, but somehow it works. Tears pop into Mom's eyes, and she comes over and hugs him. Danny's sorry he said anything, and then again he isn't.

"I really love you," Mom says.

"I love you, too," says Danny.

Danny inhales and counts to five. Then he eases Mom off him.

After another hour or so of waiting for Vincent to show up, Chandler and his staff are all so exhausted and depressed that when Mom wonders aloud if maybe Vincent went home and fell asleep and isn't answering the phone, everyone goes for it.

Max and Danny roll their eyes. Mom and her wishful thinking.

Amazingly, and to her credit, Mom realizes that the drive home is also not a great time for them to *talk, really talk,* as she threatened in the Green Room. For a while no one says a word. Danny and Max and Mom are so separate, so wrapped up in their own thoughts, it's as if they hardly know each other, as if it's an accident or a coincidence that they're all in the same car.

Mom might as well be talking to herself when she says, "Supposedly, they're editing out the gory stuff. They'll have Chandler talking and Meyer reading from his book. Then they'll fill out the hour with clips from earlier shows. They'll make it into this whole hate-and-tolerance package. At least that's what they were saying by the time we left—"

"You better hope so," says Danny. "They could still have another meeting. And if they decide that Raymond's bloody nose is going to boost their ratings, they'll go with that. If it bleeds, it leads."

"Strange," says Mom.

"What is?" asks Max.

She says, "Your brother sounds just like Vincent."

Which pleases Danny, though he knows that—given what's just happened—it probably shouldn't.

Suddenly, everyone's talking at once, and somewhere in the middle of this jumbled group conversation, Danny finally tells his mother about Raymond parking in their driveway. It's almost as if he's explaining why Vincent *had* to hit Raymond. Of course, he should have known better, because it makes Mom so nervous that Danny's afraid she'll never let him walk home from school alone again.

"Fucking Raymond," Danny says. Raymond ruined everything.

Maybe Mom *has* convinced herself that Vincent went home without them. Because when they get to the house, she hurries inside and yells Vincent's name in the same ridiculous, panicky voice they hear when she's looking for them.

The strangest thing of all is that Mom is right. Vincent *has* been here. In fact, he's been here and gone.

Danny and Max and their mother crowd into the doorway of Vincent's room. Vincent hasn't rearranged much, but you can tell he's vacated. Checked out. It's as if a cyclone has been through, selectively taken Vincent's stuff, and left the family junk untouched.

Danny says, "Is his duffel bag here?" Even though he's sure it isn't.

"Where would it be?" Mom asks.

"Under the bed," says Danny.

"How do you know?" Mom asks. Danny doesn't answer. He's been in here a few times to check the place out when Mom and Vincent were at work. He's proud of himself for never looking in Vincent's bag even after he found out that Vincent was raiding his stash.

Still dizzy from the rum and Coke, Max nonetheless gets down on his hands and knees and crawls under the bed. "Just dust balls. I feel sick," he says, and then lies there on his stomach.

Mom says, "I'm sure Vincent will come home soon. So let's try and take it easy—"

Danny thinks, Why would he have taken all his stuff if he was planning to come home soon? He helps Max up off the floor. Then he rushes back to his room to check on his pot supply. Because if Vincent has taken his weed, that will mean that they were never really friends.

Of all the stuff that Raymond was raving about on TV, the fact (if it *was* a fact) that bothered Danny most was that Vincent had stolen Raymond's meds. It was the one detail Vincent hadn't bothered telling Danny. He'd mentioned the car and the money, but not the pills. If Vincent could steal drugs from his cousin, why wouldn't he feel free to take them from some . . . kid whose mother works in his office? What an idiot Danny was for putting his stash back in the same spot where Vincent found it. Maybe it was a test, or maybe he was just lazy. If his grass is still there, it will be a sign: Danny was right to trust him.

Danny's chest feels painfully tight as he pulls the dictionary out from the wall. He opens the coffee can.

"Yes!" he says, and with that word feels his heart start beating again.

He plays a few rounds of Minesweeper before he checks his e-mail. There's a message from Chloe, which he decides not to open. She's probably asking what the *Chandler* taping was like. She can see it for herself if she waits until . . . Danny checks his watch.

He races down to Dad's room, where he finds Mom and Max on the couch listening to the first notes of the *Chandler* theme song.

"Thanks for calling me," says Danny. "I could have missed the whole thing."

"You hate *Chandler*," Max says. "As you've told me a million times, bro." Max is trying to sound tough so he can hang on to the remote.

"Fucking loser," Danny mumbles.

"Language," says Mom, staring at the screen. For someone so opposed to TV, she's gotten into it big-time. "I was going to call you during the first commercial. Sit." She pats the couch.

"That's okay, the floor's good," Danny says.

"Please," says Mom, in such a way that Danny sinks down beside her.

Under the *Chandler* theme are the words "Faces of Love and Hate." The show starts with a close-up of Chandler. It's what Danny watched them filming as he waited in the Green Room. Staring into the camera, Chandler tells the folks at home how, this evening, they are going to see the faces of love and hate.

Most of the rum has worn off, but something about Chandler's voice starts Danny feeling woozy again, and he grabs Mom's arm. Right away, Mom's got her hand over his. Trying not to be obvious, Danny slips his hand out from under hers.

"Tonight," Chandler's saying, "we will meet two men who will show us what it means to reprogram our hearts from hate to love. To change from one kind of person to another. And another man will show us how risky and dangerous a change like that can be."

"I can't breathe," Mom says.

"Hang in there," says Max.

Mom puts her arms around their shoulders. Max snuggles up against her, and even Danny lets her arm stay there.

"This is so weird," says Mom. "I mean, we were just there at the studio—"

Obviously, it's weird. But the fact that Mom has said so means that Danny can't agree. Anyway, what's weird about it? Every day, people appear on TV and then come home and watch themselves.

And now it's as if they've all stopped breathing, or as if the three of them are breathing in unison, through the commercials. Finally Chandler comes back on, introducing Meyer and Vincent.

From there it goes pretty much as Danny remembers, except for one moment when the camera picks Raymond out of the audience, and stays on his face a beat too long, the way you do when you think you recognize somebody on the street. Then it's back to Meyer, then Chandler, yakkety-yak about change, then Meyer plugging his book, which appears on the screen, then Chandler trying to con them into flashing their tattoos, which, thank God, they resist.

At a certain point, Vincent, who is talking about how he used to blame the wrong people for his problems, suddenly looks more nervous than he did before.

"I think he just saw Raymond," Danny says.

"That's what I was thinking," says Mom.

The camera cuts away from Vincent and follows the girl with the microphone, who's handing it to Raymond.

Raymond stands up and tears right into the stuff about how bad Vincent is, all the evil things he's done to him and his family, and his dunking the old lady in the pool. Danny believes Vincent when he says the old lady wasn't hurt. Vincent probably had his reasons, it probably taught her a lesson. Taking all that into account, you could almost think it was funny.

Raymond doesn't think anything's funny. Raymond's smile is disgusting. Danny's glad Vincent trashed him.

And then that retard Chandler invites Raymond to come down on the stage. So what's about to happen will be Chandler's fault.

"Max," says Danny, "you can open your eyes, man."

"He doesn't have to watch," says Mom. "He's seen it once already."

But Max might as well watch, and in fact he probably should watch, because what happens on the screen is not what he saw.

Chandler and Raymond talk for a while until Meyer cuts in; Vincent's pretty much out of it. This time, they can see what sets Raymond off. It's when Meyer tries to get the show back on the subject of him and Vincent, and Chandler announces they're going to break.

Except they don't go to break. There's a shot of Raymond moving in on Meyer. Raymond's spitting, red in the face.

Cut to Vincent grabbing him from behind, pulling him back by the shoulders.

Then there's a shot of Danny, running toward the stage.

"Hey, that's you!" Max must have been looking through his fingers.

"Shit," says Danny. Now everybody will know.

"Shit is right," says Mom. "What were you *thinking*, running down there?"

But wait. What's happening now? According to the *Chandler*

show, what Danny is thinking is about protecting Meyer Maslow.

In the middle of the scuffle, Meyer backs up against Danny. And Danny stands tall behind him. Danny has his back.

And now it really *is* weird. Because at that point, as Danny recalls it, he had no idea where Meyer was. He wasn't thinking about Meyer, but about himself and the fight.

On TV, it doesn't look like he ran toward the fight and stopped. It looks like he ran to save Meyer.

The cameras get jittery, like they do whenever there's violence, and with the whole scene bobbing around like that, it's hard to figure out what's happening. But Danny can tell that Vincent is doing the major part of the punching. He gets in a couple of good ones. Yet when the camera moves in on him, he doesn't look angry or crazed. He looks like he's going to cry.

And that's it. No spurting blood. No flying teeth. No Raymond's face turning to jam.

The fight ends there. Fade to black. Cut to Chandler, talking. This must be the part they filmed when Danny and Max were getting wasted in the Green Room.

"This afternoon, brothers and sisters, you have seen the face of hate. And the faces of those brave men who would try to save us from hate."

"He means you, man," says Max.

"Shut up, creep," says Danny.

"Love and hate are the basic subjects we are always talking about here on the show. Underneath every word we say, behind every guest we meet. Changing from hate to love is the greatest change there is. So let's look back through some recent shows—"

And suddenly they're watching a clip from that program about the skinhead who went to work with the foundation in L.A. Danny feels Mom tense.

"This is a repeat," Max says. "We saw this."

"I never got to see it." There's a spaciness in his mother's voice that Danny finds scary.

After that they show five minutes from another program, which Danny and Max also saw, about a woman who forgave her sister's murderer on death row.

"This is boring," Max says.

"You're the one who likes *Chandler*," Danny says.

"Don't you *dare* change it," Mom says. "There's supposed to be a part where Meyer reads from his book. Oh, dear God, I hope they left that in."

Danny hopes they didn't. But no one's changing it, anyhow. They're all too limp with relief. Max, probably, because he didn't have to see the blood again. Mom, probably, because the edited version looks a lot better than it really was, which is fortunate for Vincent, for Meyer, and for the foundation. And Danny, definitely, because no one could tell that he ran toward the trouble and stopped. But even though it's a huge relief, it puts them in an odd position, bound by the knowledge that what they saw on TV isn't exactly what happened. Only a few people know that. The three of them, Meyer, Chandler, his staff, the studio audience. And Vincent, if he sees it. Danny hopes he does. The way they distorted the truth proves what Vincent always used to say about how the media lies.

And now Meyer's reading, sitting in the Chandler chair, a circle of light pooled around him. He's got his new book open on his lap, and he's singing the same old song. One this at a time, one that at a time. One heart, one brain, one—

"I'm glad about this, at least," says Mom.

Eventually, Chandler comes back on and thanks Meyer, thanks Vincent—who is noticeably not around—thanks his producers, his audience, the folks at home. "And God bless every one of you who truly believes that we can change."

Commercial break. Game over.

Fifteen seconds into the *Chandler* theme and the closing credits, the phone rings.

"Maybe it's Vincent," says Max.

Maybe it's Raymond's friends, thinks Danny. Or some lone-wolf ARM psycho.

Mom isn't gone very long before she returns, looking older than she did when she left.

"That was Roberta," she says. "She thought the show was fabulous. No one's heard from Vincent."

"Wouldn't he call here first?" Danny says.

"I hope he's okay," says Max.

"I'm sure he would. And I'm sure he is," says Mom. She takes the remote from Max and turns off the television.

"I'll call out for pizza," she says, then heads back upstairs.

"Excellent," says Max. Danny's silence is an assent, though neither of them are hungry. Danny takes advantage of the momentary distraction to reclaim the remote and switch to MTV.

Later that night, as Danny lies awake, knowing he'll never sleep, he remembers how, when he was in eighth grade, they had a dog. For two weeks. They'd bought it from a mall pet shop on a Saturday afternoon when his dad was in one of those rare good moods that meant, as Danny and Max figured out, they could mostly get what they wanted.

Much later Danny realized that those good moods were about Dad and Lorraine. But so what? They milked it for what they could get. They got a copper Siberian husky they called Tramp until they could think of a better name. And they brought it home to carry out Dad's real purpose, which was to piss off Mom. Poor Mom got to clean up dog shit everywhere, on the rugs, the floors. There was puppy shit on the ceiling until Tramp (they never had time to rename him) slipped out the front door one day while Mom signed for a package.

Everybody blamed Mom, but it wasn't her fault. A few weeks later, Danny and Max and Dad saw a TV program about puppies raised under brutal conditions by greedy, sadistic breeders. The puppies were so mentally ill they could never bond with their owners. The segment included a warning not to buy dogs from mall pet shops. Dad looked daggers at Danny and Max, as if they had known all along.

Now Danny remembers how hard it was to sleep as he listened for some rustle or yelp that might mean Tramp had come home. He remembers how long those nights lasted as he watched the numbers snap on his Chewy Chewbacca clock. It was like a preview, a trailer for the long nights he would have to get through when his parents were getting divorced.

And that's how long the night seems again, as Danny waits for the noises that might mean Vincent is home, the same noises that, he can hardly believe, used to scare him, not long ago. He misses Vincent, who, somewhere along the line, seems to have become part of their little household. Meanwhile, the friends of the guy Vincent creamed on *Chandler* are probably coming after him, and—when they find out that he's not here—they'll take it out on Danny. Which gives Danny a whole new set of noises to listen for in the dark.

Well, it's fortunate that the night is so long. Danny needs every minute to replay Vincent and Raymond's fight in slow motion, to try and see more than he saw at the time, certainly more than they showed on TV, more than the flailing arms and legs, the two men tangled in a nest of wires and cables, everyone yelling but not stopping them until Vincent had messed up Raymond.

Danny knows he should hate and fear physical violence, that his mother had raised him to hate and fear it, that everything Meyer stands for is about hating and fearing the fight. But Raymond parked in Danny's driveway. Raymond hates black people and Jews. Raymond came after Meyer. Somebody had to do something. What would Mom and Meyer have done? Try and talk to Raymond? Change him one heart at a time? Talk was not going to work. By the time they called the security guards, Meyer could have been toast.

Danny can understand why Vincent might have split. The guy gets accused on network TV of stealing from his own family, and he loses it and busts up his cousin's face. And this is after Mom and Meyer have been marketing him as Mr. Changed Man. Mr. Brotherly Love might need some time to go off by himself and think. Meanwhile Danny refuses to believe that Vincent is gone for good. Though if it turns out that way, Danny will deal with that, too. During the divorce, he'd been afraid that Dad would disappear. When actually, Dad stayed close enough so that, every so often, he invites his kids to spend the night with him and Lorraine and now the Bulgarian baby. Maybe Dad should have disappeared, moved to another city. Maybe it would be better if that's what Vincent does now.

Mom probably misses Vincent, too. She's probably worried about him. She worries about every little thing. Why should this be an exception? Danny can't handle Mom's problems right now. Because he has his own.

In the morning he's got another meeting with Graber and Armstrong. Mom has sworn that her agreeing to talk at graduation will take the heat off him. And Danny wants to believe her. But part of him suspects that they'll squirm out of the deal, or find some clever way to make him suffer more.

Danny sees the sun come up, by which point there's nothing to do but play dead and wait for Mom to call him. He gets dressed and grabs a handful of Cheerios and—without the usual drama—tells Mom good-bye. Vincent has had a good effect on their morning routine.

By the time Danny leaves home, he's feeling sick to his stomach. Perfect! Start the day by heaving in the boys' bathroom, and you might as well do it on the auditorium stage.

But the queasiness stops instantly when he finds Chloe waiting for him outside school. She leaves the kids she's talking to and comes over to Danny and, with everyone watching, hooks her arm over his shoulder. Her arm feels smooth and warm and smells like lemonade.

"What's going on?" Danny asks.

"You're famous," Chloe tells him. "Everyone's saying you were on *Chandler* and you, like, helped save this Holocaust victim from a Nazi."

"Really?" Danny needs to sound neutral.

"Everyone's saying you ran up and helped warn everybody—"

Where did that part come from? Danny shuts his eyes and counts to ten as he fights the urge to tell her the truth. The kids will find out sooner or later, and his fifteen minutes of fame will be over. No more fans lined up to watch him arrive, no more Chloe's arm around his shoulder.

"A man's got to do what a man's got to do," Danny says. He and Chloe crack up.

Danny and Chloe sweep into school, and the student body makes way. In homeroom, he gets a note asking him to show up third period in Mr. Armstrong's office. Don't they know he's a hero? They can't torture him now. They'll have a schoolwide prison riot.

Naturally, Graber and Armstrong know.

"We're so proud of you," says Armstrong. "It's such an honor for the school."

Like Chloe, they seem to think that Danny helped protect Meyer Maslow with his courage and quick thinking. Maybe that's what people want to believe. Danny's not going to correct them. He'll let them go on thinking it for as long as it takes for them to forget that anyone ever said the word *suspension*. They're not going to change their minds and resuspend him when the truth comes out.

"Isn't it amazing," says Armstrong, "when someone changes so completely." Does he mean Vincent or Danny? "And when so many good things happen as a result."

"Like what?" says Danny. "What good things?"

"Like your mom speaking at graduation."

Danny will pay for his rescue. Somehow his mother will shame him. She'll get goopy and sentimental. She'll say something about *him*. Or she'll rattle on and make no sense, like she does when she's nervous. Everyone will be wanting to laugh and desperately trying not to.

Danny won't let that happen. He'll make Mom go over every word. Line by line, sentence by sentence, he'll do damage control in advance.

Mrs. Graber's mouth is moving. "And what's also exciting is that your mom has promised that Mr. Nolan will attend and say a few words to the graduates."

No one has informed them that Vincent has disappeared. Mr. Nolan has stepped away from his desk. Can I take a message? Maybe he will show up, after all. Maybe Mom has some ace up her sleeve that she's not revealing yet.

"I thought juniors don't come to graduation," Danny mumbles. "Usually there isn't room. They're glad if we don't take up extra seats—" He can tell this isn't flying.

"Danny," says David Armstrong. "We know you'll want to be there, to support and celebrate your mother's achievements. Plus we can't help thinking that, after that paper you wrote, you'd be one of the students who would benefit most from hearing what your mother and Vincent Nolan have to say." Armstrong can't resist one last dig at the Hitler essay.

Okay. Let's see how much they want a graduation speaker. "So what about my paper? What's the deal with that?"

Graber and Armstrong look at each other. Neither hypocrite wants to touch this. Armstrong's the boss, so Graber gets to deliver the news. "Both of us read it over. And you know . . . we began to think that maybe we'd misread it. In fact, you made some intriguing points. . . ."

"So, like, what grade do I get?"

Mrs. Graber glances at Armstrong again. "We were thinking a B-minus."

"I need a B to pass," Danny says.

Graber and Armstrong exchange one last look.

"It'll count as a B," Armstrong says.

I N THE JEAN MOULIN CONFERENCE ROOM, Meyer thinks of its
namesake, a hero of the French Resistance, a brave man at a
time when courage meant something besides keeping a poker
face while Elliot Green lectures you on the liability issues likely to
arise from the mayhem that erupted on *Chandler*. *Mayhem* is a
lawyer word. *Aggravated mayhem*. Elliot warns them about how dire
the situation could be if Raymond sues and some nutcase right-
wing group fronts him the cash for a hotshot attorney. *Dire* is another legal term, which translates roughly as *money*. All their hard
work will be for nothing. Which is dire, all right.

Everyone's looking at Meyer. Depending on him to be brave.
Hasn't he been brave enough? He's survived Hitler, lost his family,
nearly died five times. He's worked like a dog, written three books,
lived seventy years on the planet so he can sit here and be read the
riot act by some ambulance chaser. Meyer reminds himself that Elliot cares about the foundation. What happened isn't Elliot's fault.
Elliot's trying to help.

Elliot says, "Get me up to speed here. Has anyone heard from
our friend Mr. Nolan?"

"No one's seen him since the show," says Roberta. It's been

Roberta's job to put everyone off when the press calls for Vincent. And it turns out that Roberta is better at her job than anyone suspected. God knows what she's telling people. But for the moment it's working.

"Thank you, Roberta," says Elliot. "That much I know. I hate to say those four little words: *I told you so.* I warned you people the night of the benefit dinner. Though I guess by then it was too late. I should have brought it up after that first night I met Nolan at Meyer's. Frankly, I took one look at your pal, and I knew the guy was trouble. Hell, I've done public defender work. And you, Meyer, you with your famous understanding of human nature, why didn't you see this coming? The guy's a wild card. A psycho. It was just a matter of time before he lost it and beat the crap out of someone."

"Just for the record," Meyer says wearily, "Vincent didn't lose it. He was defending me. Or anyway, so he thought."

Elliot sighs. "We all know what happened. Vincent continued whaling on his cousin for a good while after it was clear that you were not in danger. It won't take Clarence Darrow to make a jury see that, especially if they subpoena the complete footage and not the sanitized crap they aired after the producers decided they weren't *Geraldo* and were taking the high road."

"Excuse me," says Roberta. "But down here in the trenches, we're thrilled with the 'sanitized crap.' Elliot, do you know what this would have done to the foundation if they'd shown it unedited? If our donors saw what really happened? And just in case you're curious, Meyer's book hit eighty-four on Amazon right after the program aired."

She's right. Had Chandler shown the whole fight, it would have been quite a challenge for Bonnie to raise money for the One Heart program. Even now, there's a strong chance that Laura Ticknor might hear gossip. To say nothing of what will happen if Vincent is gone for good.

Meyer just wishes Roberta hadn't mentioned his book. He'd wanted the sales, the attention. But the price they've paid has given him yet more reason to be ashamed of his petty ambition. He should have known that Vincent's appearance on *Chandler* might lead to a dangerous brush with his past. He should have known? He *did* know. Meyer let it happen.

"Well, I stand corrected," Elliot says. "What's a broken jaw compared to a best-seller?" Roberta's the object of Elliot's spite, but Meyer is caught in the crossfire. So this is what Meyer's come to— taking instruction disguised as legal advice from a moral midget.

Meyer says, "Elliot, please. I don't have the time or patience, at my age, to be reprimanded by a . . . malpractice attorney."

Elliot sucks in his breath. Meyer wishes he hadn't said that. Elliot's working for them for free. And now if Raymond sues, they might not even have an attorney. In one sentence, Meyer has undermined Elliot's purpose, which is to prove he's not a lawyer joke, but a man of principle and conscience.

"Look, Meyer. I understand that having the guy come at you must have been pretty unnerving, especially considering your age, your experience. What you went through. I'm sure it brought back memories you'd rather not recall. But that was then, this is now. *Now* is the fact that your Nazi pal broke the guy's nose and jawbone. Now is a suit potentially big enough to take down the foundation."

If Meyer lets this go any further, things might get uglier until Elliot *does* walk out and leave them to their own devices. Meyer, Bonnie, and Roberta stare down at their pencils and pads, pretending to take notes, anything to avoid eye contact with Elliot or one another.

There's no point consulting Bonnie. She's been a basket case since *Chandler*. She's frantic about Vincent. Everybody is. But it's Bonnie who jumps highest whenever the phone rings. It's beginning to seem likely that Irene was right about the two of them being somehow . . . involved. Why would Bonnie get into something like that? Maybe it's true that, after all, women think with their hormones.

Bonnie has instructed the front desk that if Vincent calls and asks for her, Anita should ring through, no matter what. Otherwise she wouldn't be here. She'd be in her office, hovering over her phone.

"Nobody's heard from him?" Bonnie asks. No one bothers to answer.

It seems that Chandler interrogated his entire staff without finding out how Vincent slipped through security and out of the studio. And nobody has any idea how, by the time Bonnie and her sons got home, Vincent could have beaten them back to Bonnie's house, picked up his belongings, and left, removing every trace of himself, as if he were never there. Could he have hired a taxi? Where did he go from Bonnie's? The police—they aren't idiots—are refusing to treat this as a missing persons case. Unless Raymond presses charges, which is the last thing they want, the cops won't even try to look for Vincent.

Vincent's vanishing act is easier for Meyer to comprehend than it must be for the others. Meyer understands disappearance. He owes his survival to how good he got at slipping through the cracks. So he has to respect Vincent for that, no matter how much trouble it causes, no matter how immature and self-involved and irresponsible Vincent's being, no matter how inconvenient and damaging it is for the foundation.

Meyer misses Vincent. He wishes he were here now. If he were, Meyer would give him hell for resorting to violence. But someone had to step in. Raymond was coming toward him. He wishes Vincent had stopped short of breaking his cousin's jaw.

Meyer's surprised to see that he's drawn a doodle on his pad, a childish sketch of an ear. A hieroglyphic message from his unconscious: He needs to get his hearing checked! Because he can only process fragments of what Elliot's saying, thin peaks of anxiety and aggression surfacing through the steady stream of caution, catastrophe, and complaint.

"Contusion . . . lacerations . . ." Elliot sees, in his crystal ball, a magical army of personal injury lawyers about to rise up, each one promising a fortune to Raymond and his wife. Already there have been threats to sue *Chandler*, the network, Brotherhood Watch. The sharks beginning to circle them are hungry and energetic.

Maybe the reason Meyer can't hear is that he doesn't want to hear Elliot repeating, "As your attorney, I feel that I should warn you that this could get expensive."

Meaning what? Legal fees? Is some lawyer planning to buy another BMW suing a nonprofit foundation, or defending it from a punk Nazi claiming that a lumpy nose and broken jaw will spoil his handsome face and compromise his ability to make a living? No one *made* this guy come on *Chandler* and threaten Meyer.

Finally Meyer rouses himself. "They haven't got a case. Millions of people saw the guy go after me. Vincent was protecting me. A reformed skinhead saving a Holocaust survivor from his Nazi attacker. Come on. My God, Elliot, you'd think something like that would be an open-and-shut case. A case *anyone* could win."

After a silence Elliot says, "Right. Well . . . we plan to start reviewing the tapes soon. Because I know that's what you *saw*, Meyer. And we plan to argue that's what Vincent saw. But it's not at all clear. The question is how close Raymond was to you, whether he meant to harm you. And then the minor related matter of whether shredding the guy's face was excessive. And Vincent disappearing doesn't exactly help our case."

Meyer knows beyond a doubt that Raymond intended to hit him. Only Meyer saw the look that Raymond meant especially for him. If only Vincent had waited till everyone saw what Meyer saw. If only he'd put his cousin in a headlock instead of beating him senseless in the time it took security to run over and pull them apart. Where the hell *was* security? Drinking rum in the Green Room. The same poison they'd plied Meyer and Vincent with. Maybe Vincent drank too much. Meyer hadn't noticed. He'd been planning what he would say if Chandler asked about his book.

"All right. Let's take it one step at a time." Elliot's all business again, moving right along through his competent, professional, anal-retentive agenda. "I think we need to establish how much you guys knew about Vincent's background. His history. Exactly when you learned what and where and when."

"Like what?" Roberta says warily. No wonder Roberta's worried. She's got the biggest mouth. If Roberta knew anything, she's already shared it with the press.

"Let's start with tossing the old lady in the pool. The history of violence. The anger management class."

"All news to me," says Roberta.

Meyer winces and shakes his head. Why does no one understand? The old lady must have provoked him. Anyway, according to what Vincent said on *Chandler*—and even after all that's happened, Meyer believes him—the woman is alive and well and perhaps a better person for the lesson Vincent taught her about how not to treat the pool guy. Vincent rescued her right away. And if that's the worst thing he's ever done, how does that stack up against the money he's raised, the publicity he's gotten, the good work he's done for Brotherhood Watch? The good work he would have kept doing if this . . . incident hadn't happened. Meyer should have listened to the instinct warning him that going on *Chandler* was a bad idea.

"Bonnie would have known about it. She knows Vincent best." Meyer means it as a compliment. Bonnie got closest to Vincent. She's given most of herself. So why does she look as if he's slapped her? Bonnie must think he's accusing her of not having been awake, of falling down on the job. Or of getting too close to Vincent. That's a possibility, too.

"I never heard about the pool incident until *Chandler*." Bonnie sounds a little dreamy. Tranquilized, perhaps. "Are we sure it happened?"

"It happened," Elliot says. "I tracked down Nolan's former employer, who put me onto a Mrs. Regina Browner. No charges were ever filed. He wrote her some cockamamie letter about an allergy to chlorine, and she went for it. But look, it's good you didn't know, Bonnie. The less you all knew, the better. I mean, if you ask me, you should have had a record of every time the guy raised his arm and said Heil Hitler. But now that this has happened, it looks better if you didn't know. Which, I gather, you didn't. Right?"

"Right," says Bonnie.

"He's an unstable guy," Elliot says. "That much should have been clear."

"Is there more we didn't know?" asks Bonnie.

"Not that I'm aware of. For now," says Elliot. "Just what Raymond mentioned on *Chandler.* The money, the drugs, the truck, the old lady." He holds up his palm. "Don't tell me. I don't want to know if you knew more. No one needs to hear about it."

"What kind of lawyerly ethics are those, Elliot?" says Meyer. "Are you telling us to lie?"

"Of course not," Elliot says. "I've got my career to consider. You think I want to get disbarred because you let some skinhead sell you a bill of goods? I'm not counseling you to lie. You just don't have to say everything."

"Which is lying." Why is Meyer debating Elliot?

"Which is being smart." Let Elliot have the last word. It's part of Meyer's penance. But what is he repenting for? For devoting his life to peace, for saving innocent people? For never relaxing, for working himself to the bone, when he could have done nothing? He could have done other things. Years ago he turned down an endowed chair at Brandeis. They offered him a fortune for teaching three months a year.

"Look," says Elliot. "Let's talk about ends instead of means. Let's say it comes down to our feeding someone to the wolves. And let's say that someone is Nolan."

"Feeding someone to the wolves to save ourselves is not what our work is about." Meyer hates how preachy he sounds, but he needs to be clear.

Elliot pauses to acknowledge that Meyer has spoken, but he doesn't seem to have listened. "So the important question is: Do we cut our Nazi friend loose? Do we let him take the heat? Or do we jeopardize the work and the financial health—the survival, maybe—of the entire foundation? We don't have to decide right now. But let's agree it could happen."

Meyer's problem isn't Elliot. Meyer's problem is slippage. His problem is what he is doing with the rest of his one and only life. People are being imprisoned and tortured for their beliefs, and Meyer is sitting on his behind and discussing theoreticals with shysters like Elliot.

Thinking of prison reminds him of something he read this morning, a news release in the stack of papers he'd found on his desk. The story concerned a Turkish jail where there are now nineteen Kurdish leaders in custody, men and women, young and old. . . .

So fine, let Elliot drone on. At the end of the day Meyer's real work will be finding a way to free those nineteen prisoners. Which means what? Raising money, making phone calls, hosting dinners. A cycle of wasted hours and days and, if he's lucky, years. Which brings him full circle back to Elliot and this room.

That's where Meyer has gone wrong. He's strayed too far from the heart of his work.

The idea that lodges itself in his mind is so seductive that he hears himself groan aloud.

"Meyer, are you all right?" asks Roberta.

"I'm fine," Meyer says.

Whether he really is fine will depend on what he does about this seductive idea. Whether he has the nerve and resolve to act on what he is thinking. What good is the moral bungee jump if someone else jumps for you?

He's not too old to get on a plane. He can find his way to the prison. Hang around, make a pest of himself. Maybe take some reporters with him. Or go alone, pester the warden, convince him the whole world is watching.

Irene will have to deal with it. Give her dinners without him. Maybe things will change for the better. Maybe she'll gain some new respect for the man she married. But Meyer's not doing this for Irene. He's not doing it for himself. He's doing it for the prisoners. All right. He's doing it for himself.

But what a thing to do for yourself! It's not what Elliot would do to make *him*self feel better. Elliot would go for the new Lexus. The beach house in Amagansett. Only Meyer—and maybe a few like-minded individuals—would choose this particular path, would elect of their own free will to spend what funds and resources and time they have left on a trip to a Turkish jail.

Meyer wants it. He wants it all. He wants the airport waits, the rude desk clerks, he wants to fly coach, to fight for space, he wants the hours of riding with his knees up to his chin, the bad food, the bumpy landing, he wants the sudden stab of anxiety on the third-world tarmac, he wants to be the Jewish stranger in the Muslim airport, searching for the exit, the lost luggage, he wants the suspicious immigration officials. Whose suspicions will be justified, considering where Meyer will be headed.

That is *exactly* what Meyer wants. He wants to get lost on the way to the jail, he wants the heat, the dank smell of the prison, the screams, the creeping doubts about how much he can trust his translator, the loneliness, the homesickness, he wants the sick terror that wakes him in the middle of the night, alone in some frightful hotel room.

He wants to leave this conference table, this office, this life, he wants to be brought face-to-face with the reality of what he is doing, of what he *can* do. He wants to buy the ticket himself. Will it free the Kurds any sooner than the phone calls and dinners? Maybe, maybe not. Meyer wants to find out. Is this some old man's fantasy? Many old men have had worse.

Meyer's determination grows as the meeting draws to a close, and it strikes him again that this conversation was about nothing. No lawsuits have been brought. No damages have been filed. Elliot just thought they all should get together and talk about what *might* go wrong.

A waste of time. But nothing's a waste. Look for the hidden blessing. Miracles always happen when you least expect them. This pointless meeting with Elliot Green has shown Meyer the light.

A MERCIFUL SWIPE OF AMNESIA GIVES Bonnie a moment of respite until she wakes up and remembers: Graduation day! The advice to take things one step at a time was invented for mornings like this. All Bonnie has to do is get out of bed and shower and get dressed and try not to panic about what she is going to say, about the fact that she has nothing to say, and about how much easier this would be if only Vincent were here.

Bonnie likes to think in the shower. Today, beneath the hot water, she should be writing the speech in her head. But instead, she keeps dropping the soap and bumping into the shower stall. Bonnie's talked to groups before. But never at Danny's high school, with her son in the audience, and never with the painful knowledge that this is something she was supposed to do with Vincent.

Standing in front of the disorderly closet that she will never in her life have the time or energy to straighten, Bonnie tries to decide which of her basically identical suits to wear. Everything has to match and be presentable and sufficiently stylish without calling the slightest attention to itself, or to her. She settles on the tan suit that always felt lucky. Except that, Bonnie remembers now, it was what she was wearing that first day Vincent showed up at the office. Not long after that, she'd decided that it was unflattering and retired it completely. Unflattering? What does that mean? And what does that matter now?

Bonnie stares in the mirror, struggling to see the woman in the tan suit as the same person who came out to reception that day to see why Anita Shu kept ringing her line. What would she have done differently if she had known that whatever she did that afternoon would lead to what she is suffering now? She would have done exactly the same. It was entirely worth it. She needs to stop thinking about herself and concentrate on what Vincent did for the foundation. He nearly gave up his life for them. What more could Bonnie ask?

She shouldn't have taken her glasses off. That was excessive, and foolish. Still, Bonnie knows that whatever she did, or didn't do, paled beside what happened on *Chandler* between Vincent and his cousin. How sad that this should seem like a relief, and a consolation. But none of that matters now. The only thing that counts is saying something halfway intelligible and getting off the stage without ruining Danny's life.

In return for the promise of a few extra minutes of sleep, Danny and Max have agreed to let Bonnie drive them to school. She should be satisfied with that and not hope for the impossible—the chance that, on the way there, they will have a conversation. How enjoyable it would be to chat like three old friends, to talk the way they used to in those lost, idyllic days when the motion of the car seemed to shake something loose, and the boys would open up and tell her what was in their hearts. It was always in the car that the Big Subjects—life and death, the afterlife, God—came up. How cruel that she cannot remember even one thing they said. They never did have that Big Conversation about Vincent's fight with Raymond. It was almost as if what they saw on TV was what actually happened. But this is probably not the ideal morning for that. Bonnie needs to conserve her energy for the speech.

When Danny appears in the kitchen, Bonnie decides not to mention the fact that he hasn't combed his hair. It's not his graduation. That's not for another year. A year is nothing. *Nothing.* Other families have started thinking about college, but Bonnie's still not ready to face the prospect of Danny leaving. She cannot imagine daily life, rocky as it is, without him. Once someone told her that there is a word in Chinese that means the kind of pain you can produce by probing a sore tooth with your tongue. Bonnie uses a stab of that tongue-in-sore-tooth pain—her grief over Danny's departure—to distract her from the more imminent ordeal before her.

Last night, Danny asked her about her speech in a tone that implied that nothing she could say could be anything but appalling. She'd told him she was planning a brief, straightforward description of what the foundation does. The facts, an outline, her job description. That seemed acceptable.

"Don't bring up those kids that got busted last summer at the conference in Maine, okay? And no preaching. No inspirational bullshit. No advice for the future."

"Fine, no advice." That was easy enough. Given Bonnie's present state, what advice could she give? If they wanted a sermon, she'd thought disloyally, they should have asked Meyer. But Meyer doesn't have a son in the school. He's immune to blackmail. Or at least to the kind that makes you agree to do anything for anyone who promises to make your child's life a little less gruesome.

At the same time Bonnie can't help thinking that, regardless of what Danny wants, she should take advantage of this opportunity to tell these young people something useful. Useful? What would that be? Love one another. Be good. Be kind. Danny would never talk to her as long as they live.

Probably this was how Vincent felt before he spoke at the benefit dinner. And he did a spectacular job. *And* he was practically dying. Vincent isn't just a guy who beat up his cousin and split. Vincent is a beacon of light to guide her through these rocky straits.

"Good morning, honey," Bonnie says.

Danny grunts but doesn't speak.

By now Max has come downstairs, grasped the whole situation, and gotten himself a bowl of cereal. His older brother glares at him for committing the kiss-ass crime of putting the milk back in the refrigerator.

"I'll wait in the car," Max says.

"I've got shotgun," Danny says.

"Sure," Max says. "It's all yours."

Danny goes to get his backpack. Or that's what Bonnie hopes he's doing.

"I can't be late, you know that!" she calls weakly in his direction. And then because there's nothing else to be done, she goes out to the car, where Max is waiting in the backseat.

Bonnie watches the minutes flip by. Should she call the school and say she might be late? It's graduation. You can never reach anyone on a *regular* school day.

Just when she's sure that her head is about to explode, Danny opens the passenger door and flings himself in, as far from her as he can sit and still be in the same car.

"Let's go," he says. "We're going to be late."

Bonnie says, "You're kidding."

Pulling out of the driveway, she can tell that Danny has something to say.

"What is it?" The usual signal for Danny to say, "Nothing."

But now he says, "Can I ask you a question?"

"Ask me anything." Odds are it's a question Bonnie doesn't want to be asked. How come you chased Vincent away? How come you chased Dad away? What are you saying in your speech?

Danny says, "Do you think that Vincent is coming back?"

"Good question." But before Bonnie can answer, she has to start breathing again. "I don't know. I can't believe he's gone for good."

Bonnie feels Danny's disappointment. She wishes she could be more reassuring. But since when is *she* the expert on Vincent's future plans? Obviously, and in more ways than she wants Danny to know, she's already proved how good she is at misreading Vincent completely.

"Want to hear something strange?" asks Bonnie.

"What?" Plainly, Danny couldn't be less interested in hearing something strange.

"I keep thinking about that dog that you kids and your dad got at the mall. About those nights after it ran away, when I'd listen for it to come home."

Lately, Danny's acted as if any mention of his childhood is a weapon Bonnie's using against him. Trying to infantilize him, or, alternately, kill him with boredom. But now he turns to her and says, with genuine astonishment, "That is so fucking *awesome!*"

"Language!" says Bonnie. "What's awesome?"

"I've been thinking about that, too. *Dee dee dee dee . . .*" Danny hums the theme from *The Twilight Zone.*

How young and innocent Danny still is, to see every coincidence as a supernatural occurrence. First kids believe in Santa Claus, then in the paranormal. When did Bonnie quit believing? Bonnie is still a believer. She believes in Meyer. She believes in the foundation and its goals. She believes that just *wanting* to do good means, in and of itself, that you are diminishing the quantity of evil in the world. She believes that Vincent became a better person when he lived with her and her children and worked for Brotherhood Watch.

"You know," she says, "when you were little, you read my mind all the time. I'd be driving you somewhere in the car, and I'd think something—and, out of nowhere, you'd say it."

It happened. Bonnie knows it did. The fact that she remembers means that time is not lost. Those years existed and still exist. Their lives coincided and overlapped. This person began life inside her. No one else could be closer. Bonnie concentrates on the road, partly so they won't get killed, and partly so as not to burden Danny with the gummy intensity of her emotions.

"How old was I?" asks Danny.

"Seven, eight. Maybe older."

"*What* did I mind-read?" asks Danny. "What kind of stuff did I pick up on?"

Bonnie thinks for a long time. "Gosh, you know, I can't remember."

"Great," says Danny.

"You know what I *do* remember? How guilty I felt about the dog, because I'd been annoyed at your dad for buying this obviously deranged puppy from the mall. As if the whole point was to annoy me. And then when it ran away, and I saw how sad you were . . ."

"Dad *liked* to annoy you," Danny says.

"Did he?" says Bonnie. "Really?" Why did she think she was paranoid for suspecting what even a child could see?

Max says, "I remember that dog."

"How could you? You were hardly born," says Danny.

"I was too born," says Max. "Moron."

"Shut up," Danny says.

"Was I or was I not born yet?" Max says.

"Of course you were born," says Bonnie.

"*I've* been thinking about that dog," Max says.

Danny says, "That is *strange.*"

"Why?" says Bonnie. "We're a family. We went through stuff together. We *should* be thinking the same things."

Not even Max wants to be thinking the same things as his mother.

"All right," Bonnie says. "Look. The dog is the last thing that ran away. Till now. First the dog and now Vincent."

Their father doesn't count. They knew in advance he was leaving, though it was like any slow death, shocking when at last it occurred.

"But you know," says Bonnie, "I'm not sure it's fair to connect Vincent with a dog raised in such a way that it couldn't interact with humans." Bonnie doesn't want them knowing that she lies awake listening for Vincent's return. The question she wants to ask her sons is: Do *they* think he'll come back?

"You can drop us off here," Danny says.

"We're two blocks from the school," Bonnie says.

"That's okay," says Danny. "You can drop us here. We can walk."

Both boys jump out of the car.

"See you later. Love you," she says.

"See you," says Danny.

"Good luck," says Max.

"Retards say good luck," Danny says.

"What *do* you say?" Max asks him.

"Break a leg," says Danny.

"So break a leg," Max tells Bonnie.

"I hope not," Bonnie says.

"Don't tell her that," Danny instructs Max. "Now she'll worry that she's going to break a leg." And then, miracle of miracles, Danny smiles at Bonnie.

Bonnie smiles back. "Love you," she says.

"Love you, too," says Max.

"Go ahead, Mom," says Danny. "It's okay. You can get there before us."

Bonnie has a sudden desire to make the kids get back in the car and drive on without stopping. No graduation speeches, no office, no work, no going back to the house. No missing Vincent. Hit the highway, start over. The new American dream. The spirited wacky single mom, taking the kids on the road, the quirky impossible heroine of so many novels and films. But ultimately they would have to stop, and what would they do then? Bonnie's having Vincent's fantasy. He's never coming back.

As Bonnie pulls away from the curb, her eyes fill. She's been on the edge of tears ever since she woke up. She knows what lies ahead of her. Everyone cries at graduations. The tears per person ratio is probably higher than at weddings, about which there are usually more mixed feelings. Maybe it's the spectacle of all those young people leaving school without a clue to the future or to the dog-eat-dog world they're so eager to enter.

Maybe no one will think it's odd if Bonnie bursts into racking sobs in the middle of her speech. She can blame it on "Pomp and Circumstance." She can say it's a Pavlovian thing. The song has made her cry ever since her own sixth-grade graduation. What sensible person wouldn't cry? Whose crazy idea was it to spin graduation as marking a new beginning? Even in sixth grade she knew that she would never see sixth grade again. She'd been so overcome by grief they'd practically had to carry her out of her grade-school auditorium. The fact that "Pomp and Circumstance" goes straight to her tear ducts in a way that "The Wedding March" never has should have told her something before she got married.

Bonnie's already miserable, and she hasn't even parked. Each sorrow piles on another, a layer for Vincent's absence, another for how she has failed her kids. Another layer for how her life has gone, her broken marriage, how old she's grown, how much she misses her parents. Layer upon layer, weighing on her heart . . . No need to "share" *that* with the graduates! It will be traumatic enough for Danny if Bonnie sticks to what they worked out. But how will she get through the part where she apologizes for Vincent's absence? Something came up. He's home with the flu. The guy left town for a while.

The truth? Roberta would kill her. They don't want *that* news getting out. Vincent might still come back, and it's hardly going to do the foundation a favor if their donors think they're supporting a program designed around a here-today, gone-tomorrow Changed Man instead of the steady, dependable Changed Man they all admire so much.

For one blessed moment, Bonnie accepts it all. She appreciates what Vincent's done. She's satisfied with that. They never asked for a lifetime commitment. A moment later, she feels crazy. She needs to see him. At once. So much is still unresolved. *Was* there anything between them? Could she have fallen in love with him and somehow not have noticed?

She can't get used to his absence. It's like a death. Except that no one's dead. She hopes. The fact that he packed his duffel bag and straightened up his room put an end to Bonnie's fear that a hit squad from ARM might have kidnapped him when he stepped outside the *Chandler* studio for a breath of air. Nazi thugs don't drive you to Clairmont and wait while you make your bed. Unless, of course, they waited while Vincent got the money and drugs that Raymond claimed he stole. Was Raymond telling the truth? She'd never thought that Vincent was on drugs. And he stole nothing from her and the kids. Which either meant he was never a thief, or that he *had* changed, after all.

So another man left her. Leaving after a few months and one clumsy mistake of a kiss is nothing compared to bailing after thirteen years of marriage and two kids. So why should she feel worse about this than she did about Joel? Because Joel was about the past, and Vincent seemed like the future. A future with Vincent Nolan? Bonnie needs therapy. Now.

She can say that Vincent has gone on a retreat. She can start her speech that way. Sometimes you need a break from your life to see where your life is going. That wouldn't be a total lie. It's true. The guy has retreated.

Bonnie takes the last parking space in the faculty lot. Go ahead, let them tow her. As she introduces herself to the guard at the door, she sees, standing beyond him, an angelic blond girl in a white satin dress. The girl spots Bonnie and steps forward and gives her a single red rose.

"I'm . . ." Bonnie misses the girl's name. She's been sent to meet her and take her to Mr. Armstrong's office. Bonnie's getting the VIP treatment. Already she's choked up. Why didn't she have a daughter? Why didn't she have more children? She wishes she had a toddler who still loved to cuddle. Why should Joel be the one to get the Bulgarian baby?

Bonnie and her beatific escort weave through the crowd of kids converting their discomfort at seeing each other in caps and gowns into manic activity and squawks of raucous laughter. Bonnie has never felt so alone. How different this would be if Vincent—or Max and Danny—were with her.

Bonnie's precisely on time, so why are Linda Graber and David Armstrong waiting for her in the hall, peering down the corridor like sailors looking for land? From a distance Bonnie can see on their faces an expression she knows all too well, the taut desperation of longing to see a particular person.

"Great to see you!" David Armstrong kisses her cheek as if they're old friends. In fact, the first time they spoke was when he called to strong-arm her into this. Bonnie only knows who he is from seeing him at PTA meetings at which his main function seemed to be leading the parents in a round of applause for the terrific job the teachers are doing. Armstrong reminds Bonnie of a clean-cut, bespectacled, 1950s game-show host.

"Great to see you, Bonnie. Really great."

"Welcome." Linda Graber shakes Bonnie's hand. "We're so happy you could be here. I so admire what you do, and what I respect even more is that you're still doing it. Most people would have burned out by now." Is Linda implying that Bonnie's stuck in a job that anyone but a masochist would have quit ages ago?

"I guess the same could be said for what *you* do." So instantly, instinctively, Bonnie and Linda have fallen into that special relationship you have with a teacher who doesn't much like your kid, a relationship that Bonnie has had with too many of Danny's teachers. Now she tries not to stare at the moles on Linda's neck and chest, above the Frida Kahlo shawl that goes with the center-parted, rolled-up dark hair.

"May I ask . . . where's Mr. Nolan?" Smiling rigidly, David Armstrong peers over Bonnie's shoulder, as if Vincent's absence is a childish prank that Bonnie will soon tire of.

"I don't know," she says. "I honestly don't know if he's going to be here or not."

That's all the raw material Armstrong needs from which to manufacture shock and disappointment. How could Bonnie *not know?* Obviously, she's lying. Or making excuses.

And she *is* lying. Mostly. She's ninety-nine percent certain that Vincent is not going to show up. But there is that one percent of her that almost dares to imagine that this could turn out to be like some cheap Hollywood romance. At the very last minute, Vincent will come through. He knows when and where graduation is. She'll look up and see him at the back of the auditorium. And she'll know that he has decided. Chosen Brotherhood Watch. Chosen her.

How depressing that her fantasies have regressed back to that scene in which Dustin Hoffman appears at the back of the church in *The Graduate*. But Vincent's appearing would mean more than that. This is not about some confused rich kid having sequential affairs with a woman and her daughter. If the miracle happens, if Vincent comes, hundreds of young people will witness someone choosing good over evil. They will remember it all their lives. It will be more like a religious event than a high-school graduation. Except that only Bonnie and Danny will know what it really means. Everyone else will just assume the ex-Nazi showed up late.

Why is Bonnie fooling herself? Vincent isn't coming.

"Where is he?" echoes Linda. Didn't they see *Chandler*? Are they so eager to have a speaker who just trashed his cousin on TV? But that's not what they saw at all. They saw Vincent protecting Meyer.

Vincent didn't care what anyone thought. He was punching out his past. Bonnie doesn't believe in violence. But is one guy hitting another guy really the end of the world? Raymond parked in her driveway and terrified her child. Raymond came after Meyer. It's not that Raymond deserved to be hit. But he wasn't exactly blameless.

On the drive home from *Chandler*, Danny finally told Bonnie about finding Raymond in the driveway. Bonnie was as frightened as if it were occurring right then.

"And you didn't *tell* anyone?" she said.

"I did," Danny said. "I told Vincent."

Both boys were jacked up and babbling, saying more than they meant to. "Fucking Raymond," Danny said.

Bonnie let the language go. Danny was right. Fucking Raymond. It was Raymond's fault that she and her boys were going through this. No one told him to come to the show. If he hadn't spoiled it, it would have been a great program, a whole hour about Meyer and Vincent and the foundation. Vincent would have gone home with them. They would have been celebrating. . . .

Graber and Armstrong are waiting for her to say something. "I *know* that Vincent knows when graduation is. He was looking forward to doing this." It's all she can say. And all they can handle. Meanwhile they'll settle for Bonnie, who is at least physically here. Against formidable odds, they have found an acceptable last-minute replacement, a speaker who is not being indicted on child pornography charges. One speaker will have to do. They'll let her explain to the crowd that the celebrity former skinhead canceled at the last minute. Not that the crowd much cares. The students want their diplomas. And the parents would just as soon not hear from a guy who could spoil this happy occasion by bringing up subjects like hate.

Once again, tears threaten. Bonnie swallows hard. She'd rather not break down in front of Linda Graber and David Armstrong.

"We really appreciate this," Linda says.

"It's a pleasure," says Bonnie.

"You never know," says Dave, confidentially. "This could work both ways. Some of these kids have very wealthy parents looking for a tax-deductible charity."

What a vulgar, awful man, making this about money! Rather than what it's really about, which is flat-out blackmail. Instead of struggling over Danny's paper, which is what she should be doing, Bonnie's taking the easy way out, pulling strings for her kid, which hardly puts her in the best position to tell Dave Armstrong to go to hell for suggesting that she shake down the wealthier parents. Besides which, Bonnie will accept any donations the parents want to make. It's not for her. It's for Meyer's work. Whatever that is now.

Lately, Meyer has been talking about going on a series of solo fact-finding missions to Turkey and the Middle East. By now it's reflexive for Bonnie to encourage Meyer, partly because his ideas are often so marvelous and surprising. Secretly, she's terrified by the thought of him jetting into some hostile outpost and relying on charm to protect him.

It's admirable that a man of Meyer's age would have the courage and the integrity to leave his comfortable life and see, up close and personal, what his fellow humans suffer. How inspiring that someone who has achieved what he has achieved should push himself, should ask more of himself. He *is* a saint. An angel. Of course, he has his flaws. But all told, he is a good man, a man who is trying to do good.

Unlike selfish Bonnie, who can't help wondering: What do Meyer's plans mean for *her?* Meyer sounds as if he means to spend the rest of his life on the road, bouncing from one scary airport, one filthy jail cell, one torture chamber to another. Yesterday, he told Bonnie that Irene had accused him of wanting to wander off and stage a theatrical public death, like Tolstoy's last hours in the deserted railway station. And Meyer had told Irene: What's good enough for Tolstoy is good enough for me.

But what about the foundation? Without Meyer, it will be nothing. Everyone is leaving. First Vincent and now Meyer. Meyer isn't a young man. This can't be good for his health.

Just then, an air raid signal goes off.

Linda squeezes her eyes shut. Dave chuckles.

"Don't panic," Dave says. "It's the first warning before assembly."

"Euphonious, isn't it?" Linda says.

"What do they need to be warned about?" asks Bonnie.

"Us," says Linda.

"Heh-heh," says Dave.

"Tardiness," says Linda.

The brain-frying buzzer sounds again. Danny listens to this all day. No wonder *annoying* is the most common word in his vocabulary. This buzzer is constantly interrupting his thoughts, his daydreams, anything he might be learning. Naturally, the kids come home wanting only to gobble chips in front of the TV and be numbed out by its soothing drone. How could Bonnie have not heard the sound track of her children's days? It's only a buzzer. She's got to relax if she plans to get up onstage and talk. Suddenly unable to recall one sentence she planned to say, Bonnie struggles against a sudden urge to sit on the floor and put her head between her knees.

"Are you all right?" asks Dave.

"I'm fine," says Bonnie.

"Nervous?" says Linda Graber.

"Not at all," says Bonnie.

"Do you do much of this sort of thing?" Linda's on to Bonnie. She knows that Bonnie is lying about not being nervous.

So Bonnie might as well lie more. "Constantly," she says.

After the second buzzer, Linda and Dave turn, zombielike, and head for the auditorium. All around them, the seniors hold their mortarboards onto their heads and stampede.

As they navigate the rush, Armstrong chooses this moment to tell Bonnie the plans for the ceremony. The hall is noisy, the kids are loud, she and Dave keep getting separated. She hears maybe a third of what he's saying. Prayer, chorus, diplomas. Bonnie nods and fakes comprehension. She'll figure it out. Somebody will signal her when she needs to begin her speech.

Dave opens a door and ushers Bonnie and Linda down a corridor that leads over cables, past amplifiers and costume closets, the usual backstage mess. It reminds Bonnie of *Chandler*. She and Vincent and Meyer went there together and waited in the Green Room.

"The auditorium has some structural problems," says Dave. "Every time a lightbulb burns out, we have to send a midget through the infrastructure to change it. It would cost over a million to fix."

"That's too bad," says Bonnie.

The three of them stand awkwardly in the wings, from which they can see a sliver of stage and a few rows on one side of the auditorium.

"I need to check a couple of things. Can I leave Bonnie with you?" Dave asks Linda. Bonnie feels like a child in a fairy tale, dropped off at the witch's for day care.

Linda turns to Bonnie. "So Dave told you about the order of the graduation program? I know it's a little complicated, but I'm sure you'll catch on."

Bonnie smiles.

"It's a miracle you could hear Dave, walking down that noisy hallway." Linda wins! How good she is at ferreting out a lie. The kids must be helpless before her.

"Well, actually," says Bonnie, "I *couldn't* hear—"

"So you have no idea what the order is," Linda says.

"Basically, no," admits Bonnie.

Linda sighs. "All right. First the pledge of allegiance, then the nondenominational prayer. Then the choir. Then the awards. Then the choir again. Then they'll hand out the diplomas. Then you. Then the valedictorian. Then Dave will say a few words. And we'll hear one more time from the choir."

This is going to last fifty years! How many songs is the choir singing? And they've got Bonnie talking *after* they give out the diplomas, when all the kids will be busy looking to see if they've got the right one? No one ever schedules the speeches after the diplomas. No one is that thoughtless.

Look for the hidden blessing. Bonnie might as well talk when no one is listening. What does Bonnie have to say that these graduates need to hear? Meyer would tell her to do her best, to try and make the most of this chance to change one young heart at a time. As always, thinking of Meyer helps her forget her personal problems and concentrate on what she can accomplish. If only she didn't keep thinking how different this would be if Vincent were here. She could speak for a minute or so, and then let Vincent take over. He was brilliant at the dinner. His first time speaking. Dying.

Bonnie cannot accept the possibility that she might never see Vincent again.

Dave reappears and stage-whispers, "The parents and faculty are getting settled."

Bonnie needs to locate Danny. She doesn't want to start talking and make accidental eye contact with him and get stuck. She moves to the edge of the curtain, from where she can see the audience.

Linda grabs her elbow and bumps her onstage, where a group of dignitaries—the district superintendent, the principal, the head of the PTA—have come from the opposite wing and are taking their seats in a row. Four empty chairs remain as Bonnie is perp-walked out between Linda and Dave. Is that chair meant for Vincent? Dave and Linda exchange looks. It would be awkward to have it removed. Might as well leave it empty.

Bonnie's fixated on the empty seat. Linda and Dave make her sit next to the chair that would have been Vincent's. Bonnie scans the crowd for Danny, but they've already lowered the lights so that all she can see is that the first dozen rows are empty.

The heartbreakingly wobbly orchestra strikes up "Pomp and Circumstance," and the music starts working its magic. Dear God, it was composed to be played by a crappy high school band. Those sour notes make it soar, the rhythm mistakes make it all the more wrenching.

Bonnie nearly dissolves again. It's too much trouble to fight it. Why not surrender and let the sobs shake her until something snaps? But what would be the point? She already feels that spongy exhaustion that follows hours of weeping.

The graduates file into the first rows, repainting the front of the auditorium in a garish purple that must be the school color. The principal rises and stands at the podium and waits till everyone figures out that they've started the nondenominational prayer, a moment of silence. A lengthy moment till everyone bows their heads, which is fine with Bonnie.

The silence ends. Then Kathy Sojak, the music teacher, approaches the choir and raises her arms and makes the grotesquely clownish faces that every kid in the school can imitate to perfection. What a bad person Bonnie is for having laughed at Danny's Mrs. Sojak imitation. She was thrilled that Danny was trying to amuse her. A better mother would have told him it wasn't nice. A decent human being would have asked Danny to imagine *being* Mrs. Sojak and making those faces she can't help making because she so loves the music.

Parents always get everything backward. After the PTA meeting at which the Linda Graber skin-condition Web site was mentioned, Bonnie told Danny she thought it was mean. But that was before she'd met Linda. Now the site seems like a restrained response to how Linda makes you feel.

In any case, Bonnie's stopped noticing Kathy Sojak's funny faces, because now she's being torn apart by the chorus's wrenching version of "Bridge over Troubled Water." What a touching song it

is. Why did Bonnie never like it? She'd just thought that it was
Simon and Garfunkel sentimental twaddle. But now she sees it's the
hymn for our times, and the kids believe it. The singers' faces are
shining, flushed by their nearness to the light, by being the closest
they're going to come to the flame of pure belief.

Like a bridge over troubled water, I will see you through. Who is
that *I*, exactly? Who will see *Bonnie* through? No one, no one, no one.
Bonnie's on her own. Everything depends on her. She takes care of
everyone, and no one takes care of her. Which is another reason to
cry, if she could just let herself go. Danny is somewhere in that room.
Bonnie's not allowed to lose it.

At least the choir has stopped singing. And now they're giving
out the awards. History, English, school service. Each with a name
attached. The Brenda Barlow Medal for Women's Sports. Bonnie
hates to think the names might be those of students who died
young. She prefers to imagine that they have grown up and given
money to the school, funded prizes like the ones Bonnie and Meyer
invented for Brotherhood Watch.

Like the Laura Ticknor Prize that Meyer announced at the benefit dinner. What if Laura Ticknor finds out what really happened
on *Chandler*? Or that Vincent has disappeared?

There's no time to think about any of that. They're giving out
the diplomas. Alphabetically. In order to get their diplomas, the
kids have to file past Bonnie. Ninety percent of the kids are white,
the rest are Asian, a few blacks. Every last one seems lit from within
by the pure flame of personal sweetness. Every kid is beautiful, and
yet there is a huge difference in the signals they are transmitting, in
a language that mostly speaks about confidence, or its lack. They
think high-school success is predictive of the future! Adults joke
about how misguided that is. But maybe kids are right. To watch
Bonnie talk to Roberta is to know more about who they were in
high school than about who they have become since.

By the time they reach the B's, Bonnie can take one look at the
graduate bouncing or slinking up to the stage and predict exactly
how much applause the kid will get. It's brutal, like a game show:

Popularity Contest. It's so clear how liked each boy or girl is. The winners and losers find out along with their diplomas. But of course they already know. Everybody does. Can't anybody stop this?

Poor Vincent! How many kids cheered for him when he graduated high school? Maybe that's what makes someone join ARM. Now she's thinking like Vincent, blaming everyone but himself, blaming his high school student body for not applauding enough. You don't become a Nazi because no one liked you in high school. At the benefit dinner Vincent got enough applause to make up for what he missed senior year. And then he almost died, so some of the good effects of the attention may have been lost.

Next year, Danny will have to go through this when he gets his diploma. *If* he gets his diploma. So much can still go wrong. Danny's going to college. Bonnie has to start dealing with that. College tours and so forth. Why can't Joel help? Give Danny a fraction of the time that, whether he likes it or not, he's about to lavish on the new Bulgarian baby.

What letter of the alphabet are they on? Bonnie's heart speeds up. She hasn't got time to go over what she talked about with Danny. Something about the foundation, what they've accomplished, what they do. Even though she'd promised not to preach, she did plan to quote Meyer about changing one heart at a time. But how did she intend to begin and get from one point to another?

Soon she'll go to the podium, open her mouth—and nothing will come out.

She looks out into the audience, back to the last row where the most infantile part of her still believes that Vincent may yet appear. Her white knight come to save her. Her personal Dustin Hoffman. But no one's going to rescue her. She can only hope that Danny will eventually find in it his heart to forgive her. Forgive but not forget. All right. She'll settle for forgiveness.

Apparently, no one has told Dave Armstrong that Bonnie is incapable of giving a speech. That all this was a huge mistake. Dave rises to the podium, and Bonnie hears her name, and something about Brotherhood Watch. Something about Vincent. *What* about Vincent? Bonnie seems to have missed it.

Then she distinctly hears Dave say, "Bonnie Kalen is a model to us all. As a woman, as a human being, doing something few humans do, and even fewer women, working to make the world a better, safer, more caring place. And if I may inject a personal note, raising two sons as a single mother in a nontraditional family and sacrificing of herself to shelter people in need, to take in and reform a man who spent years lost in the wilderness of prejudice and hate—"

Did Dave say what Bonnie thinks he said? Did he just give the crowd *way* more information than they need about her personal life? About her being a single mother? Taking in a Nazi? And what was that part about *even fewer women?* It will be years before Danny will forgive *or* forget or consent to be in the same room with her. And why is Dave making it sound as if this is about Bonnie? Bonnie promised Danny that she wouldn't talk about their family, or herself.

The students are used to ignoring Dave. But the parents love where he's going with this. Bonnie is not just some snobby do-gooder working to help foreigners with unpronounceable names. Bonnie is one of *them*, a parent, with a parent's problems and challenges, except that she's being useful. Making the world a more caring place. The graduates will applaud anything because the ceremony is almost over.

The applause lasts long enough for Bonnie to walk over to the podium and peer into the crowd. On the way, she realizes that she's still clutching the rose she got from her meeter-and-greeter.

A sudden shift of the light beams in, as if someone's playing with a mirror. Bonnie squints in the searchlight of the graduates' up-turned baby-bird faces. What do they want from her? To make it short. Which is what Bonnie wants, so at least they agree on that.

Dear God, how pretty their skin is, how bright and clear their eyes. How much Bonnie loves them, with a pure undifferentiated love for their youth, their innocent hearts and souls. Even the angriest, most damaged kids are succumbing to the spell of the day and its promise of a future. What future are they imagining? What does their future hold? Bonnie refuses to guess. Love, grief, the loss of parents, the leaving of children, the death of love, more grief. And now the tears rise up so insistently that Bonnie's sure she's about to lose it. Standing here and trying to think of something to say must be a milder version of how Vincent felt at the benefit dinner, trying not to die.

What a brave guy Vincent is. And finally he snapped.

The graduation audience waits. Bonnie has nothing to tell them. A minute passes, then another. She has to say something. For Danny. For Vincent.

The silence is horrifying.

Bonnie shuts her eyes, then opens them. The entire school is listening.

She says, "If I had to pick one word that Brotherhood Watch represents, guess what it would be." Bonnie's channeling Meyer. It was always a good line. Everyone likes to guess the one-word sound-bite. Meyer would have said it on *Chandler* if Raymond hadn't wrecked things.

Bonnie says, "I'd say that word was: *change*. The man I work for, a great hero, Meyer Maslow, believes that the world can be changed. One heart, one person, one man or woman or child at a time."

Bonnie needs Chandler up here now, milking the crowd for a response. Bonnie's losing her audience. Time to kick things up to a higher level. "I only wish you could meet my friend Vincent Nolan. I wish that he could be here. Because if you saw him, you would know how much a person can change." This works better. Mentioning Vincent gets the audience's attention. Many of them must know about him. They'd thought he was going to speak.

There's no reason why Bonnie has to explain why he isn't here. And no one's going to ask her, yelling out from the crowd. That in itself is liberating. She feels lighter, in a way.

"But the fact is," Bonnie hears herself saying, "change is the one thing—the only thing—you can count on. Nothing stays the same." Can Bonnie get back to Brotherhood Watch? She's having an out-of-body moment. "And the thing is, you can't be prepared. And that part is hardwired. It's not only human nature, it's the nature of the universe. Right now, you kids think you'll always be young. If your parents are together, you think they'll stay together. You think everything's going to continue pretty much on track. But I promise every one of you. I can guarantee it. Nothing's going to be anything like it is today."

She is trying to reassure them. Whatever they're worried about, or afraid of, will improve or stop mattering. So why does it sound like a threat? She needs to put the brakes on. She is certainly not going to surrender to the temptation to list all the things in *her* life that unexpectedly changed. She never expected her parents to die so soon, never expected Joel to leave, never expected Meyer to decide to take off for Asia, never expected to turn around after a brawl on *Chandler* and discover that Vincent had disappeared.

The kids and parents and teachers wait.

Bonnie looks back past the last row.

And there he is. Standing there.

Vincent.

THE SCHOOL GUARD NEARLY BODY-BLOCKS VINCENT. The guy probably would do the same no matter what Vincent looked like, but what makes it a no-brainer is that Vincent's tattoos are showing.

Vincent had considered whether to hide them or not. It felt like time travel back to that first day he walked into Brotherhood Watch. Except that it's all turned around. Back then, when he *was* a Nazi, he hid his tattoos. And now that he isn't, he flashes them. He wants these kids to see what permanent harm you can do yourself if you're screwed up and immature and pretending to believe something you don't really believe just because it's convenient and, for the moment, it feels good.

The guard is black, about Vincent's size. Vincent could take him if he had to. Vincent's not going to have to. This is not three months ago, when just talking to a receptionist—poor Anita Shu, who, Vincent later learned, is in love with an American boy her parents will never accept—was a major challenge. Since then, Vincent's gotten up and spoken to five hundred rich New Yorkers. He nearly died. He was on *Chandler.* He's definitely a changed man.

The guard's island accent rolls toward him.

"Good morning, sir," he says.

"Good morning. I'm Vincent Nolan. I'm supposed to speak at the graduation."

"Right." The guard gazes at Vincent and nods. Frankly, it doesn't surprise him that the white dude with the Nazi tattoos is speaking at graduation while he's working as a security guard for six-fifty an hour.

The *ex*-Nazi with the Waffen-SS bolts, Vincent wants to explain. This is from another life. I'm not like that anymore. The thought makes Vincent feel like a jerk. Let the guy think what he wants. Vincent's got work to do.

The guard says, "I saw you on *Chandler*, man. I saw you on *Chandler* trashing that bad boy." And with that, he waves Vincent through.

Vincent likes how this has gone down. Like a key in a lock. Which is everyone's secret desire. Show Mr. Spielberg to his table.

The last few days, which Vincent has spent camped out in the HiWayVu Motel by the side of the thruway, have hardly been what you might call showing Mr. Spielberg to his table. If the motel clerk saw Vincent on *Chandler*, he was not about to say so. The kid was Indian, Danny's age. Vincent paid ahead, in cash.

The room was the black hole he expected. Nothing. Nothing. Nowhere. No more Bonnie, no more Bonnie's kids, no more Bonnie's house, no more pizza dinners, no more good wine, no more big TV, no more instant family that *liked* him, no more decent people who gave him everything and asked for nothing in return.

No more Bonnie was the main thing—the fact he kept coming back to. He wished he could talk to her about this, about what was happening, what he was feeling. But part of the point of his being there was taking a break from Bonnie.

He'd lain down on the lumpy bed and tried reading the books he'd brought along, but nothing held his interest. Certainly not *Crime and Punishment*. He couldn't even stand the title. He'd turned on the remote and flipped through the channels, and within a few minutes was watching himself on *Chandler*. He remembered it being messier. Chandler's people cleaned it up. So maybe Vincent's luck *has* changed, because if they'd shown the whole thing, it would have been a disaster for Brotherhood Watch. No matter what he did after this, Bonnie would never speak to him again. On the other hand, there's always the chance that Raymond's friends will track him down and make him pay, which will mean that Vincent's luck has changed back again. For the worse.

It had felt great to hit Raymond. Like nailing a mosquito that's been torturing you all night, like stretching when you've been stuck in the car, like scratching a nasty itch. Phoning Bonnie, scaring the kid—Raymond had it coming. And then taking a swing at Maslow. Raymond was asking for it. Peace Through Change is fine, but it's a gradual process. Sometimes you need to move faster. So, actually, if you look at all this from an Old Testament point of view, Vincent's become more Jewish, more eye-for-an-eye than Maslow. Now that's a thought that would never have crossed his mind all the time he was in ARM.

But why wasn't Maslow grateful to Vincent for jumping in to protect him? Why didn't he say thank you? When they finally pulled Vincent off Raymond, Vincent caught Maslow's eye. And Maslow looked away.

Right then, Vincent knew beyond a doubt that his days at Brotherhood Watch were numbered. All they had to do was figure out how to cut Vincent loose. They already had the Iranian waiting in the pipeline.

Vincent got the message. And now he needs some quiet time in order to think things through. R and R. Rest and recreation. Retreat and reconnoiter. Maslow, more than anyone, will understand why there are times when you have to keep a low profile. Too bad Bonnie will never figure it out. Vincent always wondered about those guys the foundation helped. Didn't they have the instincts to get the hell out of Dodge before the showdown began? Why couldn't the Iranian dude have split *before* things got heavy? If it had been up to Maslow, he would have left Europe when the going was good. Too bad his family made the mistake of sticking around.

And now, in Vincent's humble opinion, Maslow should leave Brotherhoood Watch if he plans to stay alive. Get away from those women breathing down his neck and pickling him in their goodness. Their *care*. The guy can't even take a dump without running it by his whole staff. Vincent and Maslow both need to get out. The difference is that Maslow has a golden parachute the size of Manhattan. And what does Vincent have? What allowed him to make his break when he slipped out of *Chandler*?

The Warrior keeps his vehicle running. So maybe Vincent does have a shred of instinct left. He came to *Chandler* prepared with Raymond's truck keys and the money to pay the parking fee. It had only been a few days since he took the Chevy out for its weekly spin.

As he sneaked out of the studio and headed for the garage, Vincent felt very cool and controlled, considering that he'd just pulverized his own cousin on national TV. For just a few seconds, the memory had made him dizzy. What cured him was getting into the truck and sailing up the highway to Bonnie's.

The bridge wasn't even a problem. That's how much momentum he had. He flew across the Tappan Zee, hardly noticing the part where it nearly dips into the water.

He'd driven to Bonnie's house and taken what was his. Only what he had brought with him or bought, not one thing more or less. Which means he is a better person than the guy who left Raymond's. He even thought he should leave them something. But what? Money would be an insult, and anyway, Vincent would need it. A note? Saying what? Thanks for everything. Best of luck. Don't do anything I wouldn't do. See you in some other life.

That he hadn't stolen any of Danny's weed also proved how much he had changed. He knew it would break the kid's heart, and a joint or two wasn't worth it.

When Vincent checked into the HiWayVu, he'd signed in as Jesse James. He could have written anything. The desk clerk was reading *Dianetics*.

For two days, Vincent lay low. Stayed in bed, watched TV. He bought a fifth of Jack Daniel's, mostly to wash down the Vicodin. He ignored the maids when they knocked. Eventually he made himself get dressed and cleaned up enough to order out for pizza.

There was still a surprising amount of coverage about Tim McVeigh. Vincent had been so busy, he'd missed most of it when it happened. Now it struck him as strange that he hadn't noticed the bizarre coincidence of his own nearly dying on the same night the poor bastard was killed by lethal injection. Vincent got the good needle, and McVeigh got the bad one.

Lying on top of the dirty spread in the HiWayVu Motel, Vincent had plenty of chances to make up for his inattention to Tim McVeigh's sad fate. The networks kept airing the shot of him leaving the jail in leg irons, that lizard thing he did with his head, that trapped baby-ferret twist. Vincent found it fascinating, but almost too depressing to watch. The reporters outside the prison where McVeigh died were like sharks snapping their jaws in the bloody foam.

Vincent would never have done what McVeigh did. Brotherhood Watch didn't save him from that. That wasn't the path he was heading down when he detoured through their office. They'd started with a guy who, in return for a couch to sleep on, would smile and nod his head and go along with Raymond's bullshit. And something or someone—Bonnie? Maslow? Bonnie's kids?—had turned him into a believer. Or as close to being a believer as he is likely to come. The only hitch was that his ideas about justice and retribution and forgiveness will never be the same as Meyer and Bonnie's. Let *them* turn the other cheek. Let *them* be the Christians.

One problem—in fact, a major drawback, given his current situation—was that they'd changed him from a guy who made plans into a guy who let shit happen. After two days at the HiWayVu, Vincent found himself wishing he was watching the giant TV in the basement with Bonnie's kids. Only a fool wouldn't see that living at Bonnie's house was better than hiding out in a cheap motel. Pretty soon Vincent began to notice that he was missing Bonnie all the time. Wishing she were there. Fat chance he could have persuaded her to leave the kids and share his swinging bachelor pad at the HiWayVu. What did he imagine them doing here? Having sex? Maybe. Sure.

Watching *Good Morning America*, he jerked off thinking of Bonnie.

He pictured Saturday mornings in bed, watching cartoons on TV. Except that Bonnie hated TV. He must have been thinking of someone else. Or maybe she would make an exception. Maybe true love would turn her into someone who liked watching cartoons with him on Saturday morning. True love for *him?* Unlikely. Still . . . Bonnie took off her glasses.

By the end of the fourth day, Vincent was starting to think he'd been hasty. Possessed by that old devil fight-or-flight. God's epinephrine shot.

Okay, he felt guilty for kicking Raymond's ass. But Maslow has stuff to feel sorry for, too. Maslow isn't perfect. He didn't say thank you. He'd made Vincent think that he and Bonnie would find some Iranian to take his place.

Vincent *had* been hasty. Very immature. But people make mistakes. And Vincent's brief break from the workplace and home doesn't have to be forever. Taking a few days of personal time is not the same as cashing it in. Vincent hasn't sent in his letter of resignation. He can still go back. Hang with Bonnie and the kids. Enjoy the perks of his brotherhood life until they fire his ass. Every month he spends there is psychic money in the bank that leaves him better prepared for the future.

The question is how to jump back into the stream without making too many waves. Should he appear in Bonnie's kitchen? Stroll into the office? It all seemed primed for disaster. The logistics were paralyzing.

He paid for another night at the motel. He ran through the options again. Going back to a home and office where they know you stole your cousin's truck and money and drugs, and then apologized by knocking his teeth out on national TV has got to be trickier than coming in from the cold as a recovering Nazi and saying you want to save guys like you from becoming guys like you. So far there's been no evidence that Vincent saved one single human being from becoming him. Which doesn't mean it can't still happen. . . .

And that was when Vincent thought of graduation at Danny's school. He and Bonnie were supposed to give a speech. Is any of that still on? What if Vincent showed up at the school in time to talk, and they could take it from there? Risky, but ideal. A public event had obvious advantages as a point of reentry. Bonnie would sooner burn in hell than embarrass the foundation. It was the ultimate version of what you heard about breaking up with a girl in some crowded place so she wouldn't make a scene. Margaret announced she was leaving him at the dinner table. She was picking chicken off a bone. Very cool, very surgical. She'd informed Vincent that he had to move out as if it were a mildly interesting fact she'd heard on the evening news. Strangely, the thought of Margaret no longer had the power to wound him. Now it was missing Bonnie that hurt.

By the time he finished giving the graduates whatever brilliant advice he came up with, Bonnie would have fallen in love with him all over again. And he'd have her on his side when it came time to deal with Maslow.

He called the school to check when graduation was. All he had to do was show up. And he'd be *in.* Talking at graduation was not like crawling back to Bonnie's house. They wanted him to appear at the school. He'd be doing a public service. Also it seemed sort of sexy, him and Bonnie speaking. They could take their show on the road. They'd see how it worked out.

Of course, there was the question of what Bonnie thought of him now. She'd seen *Chandler* live, in living color, not the PG-rated TV version. She knows he wasn't the guy she thought. Maybe she doesn't want him. Vincent wouldn't blame her.

Bonnie took off her glasses. Vincent is betting on that.

Meanwhile it felt terrific to check out of the motel.

Too bad he couldn't stash his duffel bag there. Leaving it in Raymond's truck was going to be a problem. In post-Columbine America, tattooed white men are not encouraged to carry duffel bags into schools. So much for your free country. The bag had to stay outside. He just took the money and pills, which is also dicey in an educational setting.

Vincent could have brought in a private arsenal and a pharmacy, that's how pleased the school guard is to meet Chandler's famous friend. He turns door patrol over to his buddy and escorts Vincent to the auditorium and opens the door and stands with him behind the last row.

Bonnie is key. It's Bonnie Vincent is looking for, from the back of the room.

Bonnie's at the podium, talking to the crowd. Or *supposed* to be talking. Her mouth is open, but no sounds are coming out. Poor Bonnie looks crazed as she pauses and wonders where to begin. Bonnie! Get it together! She's talked to groups before. Vincent addressed a major crowd, and he happened to be dying. Vincent roots for Bonnie as if she were a horse he has money on. Come on, Bonnie. Come on. He wants her to look good up there, if just for herself and the kid.

With each second Bonnie stalls, her pals on stage—wardens and prison matrons in black robes—seem more upset. No one's looking at anyone. No one knows what to do. Bonnie has to pull this thing out of the fire.

Bonnie says, "If I had to pick one word that Brotherhood Watch is about, guess what it would be?"

Excellent decision: Bonnie's quoting Maslow. How sweet. It's sexy, that in this crowded room only Vincent and Bonnie—well, and maybe Danny—know that.

Bonnie says, "I'd say that one word was: *change*. The man I work for, a great hero, Meyer Maslow, believes that the world can be changed. One heart, one person, one man or woman or child at a time."

It's good that she's saying something. But it's not great to hear her repeating the tired crap the boss says all the time. Just don't let Bonnie start preaching about forgiving without forgetting.

Bonnie says, "I only wish you could meet my friend Vincent Nolan."

All right! We're getting somewhere! Bonnie's calling him her friend. So she must still like him. She must still like him a lot. *This* gets Vincent's attention. And for some reason, everyone else's.

"But the fact is," Bonnie says, "change is the one thing—the only thing—you can count on."

Where is Bonnie going with this? Get back to Maslow—and
Vincent!

Then Bonnie begins to ramble about how everything they expect
to happen is not going to happen, because something else will happen,
and about change being hardwired—a phrase he can't believe she's
using—and even about their parents splitting up and . . . Vincent has
to help her! He's got to get her attention and shock her back into talking about something concrete. *Talk about the foundation.* That's what
Bonnie told *him* before the dinner at which he'd nearly died. *Nearly*
died. Didn't die. The difference is all that counts.

The crowd of kids and parents wait.

Bonnie looks back toward the last row. It's as if she's looking for
him.

She finds him in two seconds. She can't believe it's true. She's
overjoyed to see him. She doesn't try to hide it.

Which still won't make this easy. But the brightness he sees in
Bonnie's eyes, sparkling behind her glasses, is the green light that
makes it possible for him to start walking toward the stage.

The crowd watches Vincent walk down the aisle. Mr. Changed
Man has learned a lot since that first day he tiptoed into the foundation. Onstage, the blond guy with the nerd glasses shoots a worried look at Bonnie. Bonnie smiles and mouths Vincent's name.
Another key in the lock.

Doesn't Bonnie want to finish her speech? Apparently not. She
says, "Here he is. Vincent Nolan."

Vincent feels like Elvis again. The crowd is going nuts. As Bonnie gives him the podium, he kisses her on the cheek. It's total theater. And totally real. The crowd loves it. Everyone's clapping. He
catches her eye as they separate. He almost starts to say something,
but what? How happy he is to see her.

Vincent waits for the applause to die down. He says, "I'm really
glad to be here. But I have to say, I'm getting a little nervous about
public speaking. The next to last time I talked to a group, I nearly
died. And the last time, someone nearly got killed."

There's a tiny stir of unease from the folks behind him onstage.

Maybe they were hoping to pretend that no one knows what happened on *Chandler.* They know a little part of it, which is bad enough, and it's created a tiny charge, but Vincent has defused it. He's not saying *who* nearly got killed; no one is going to ask. The crowd exhales another sigh. Another wild burst of applause.

Now he can move past that and tell them what they need to hear. Which is . . . what, exactly?

He'll give them the basic love message. A duck could be somebody's mother. He'll tell them they have to *do* something. Get off their butts and get moving. Do good. *Be* good. Love your fellow humans. Be conscious. Change one heart at a time.

Everything he says will be true. He'll believe it with all his soul. He'll make it up as he goes along.

It will come to him when he needs it.

V INCENT'S CHASTE LITTLE PECK on the cheek is the public kiss that an exuberant kid might give the favorite guidance counselor who helped him make it through high school. But as he pulls away, their eyes lock. And even Bonnie can see that he has come here because of her. It's as if they have a second or two to find out everything in the world they need to know. The glance is like a conversation, or like the promise of one. Bonnie can't imagine what they will say, but she's looking forward to it. She's looking forward to everything now. How much can change in a heartbeat.

The crowd rips into a round of applause. What are they applauding? Would they be cheering like that if they'd seen what really happened on *Chandler*? Probably they wouldn't care. They're cheering for a guy who was on TV and who is taking time from his busy famous life to come here and to talk to *them*.

And probably they're right to applaud. So what if the guy screwed up? The fact is that Vincent has come out of hiding and shown up here because he's trying again. Trying to be a human being. As is Meyer, and Bonnie, and, she hopes, her kids. Shouldn't Vincent get credit for trying?

Everyone's a mixed bag. That's why they call it *human*. What was it that Vincent said about Raymond and his friends? They couldn't deal with the gray areas. But that's where they all live, all the time. Add up all the virtues and failings, they've all got something in each column. Even Raymond. Hate is a serious minus. But at least he's clear on the fact that it's wrong to steal from your cousin. Which is a plus in Raymond's column, and a minus in Vincent's. The problem, thinks Bonnie, is how efficiently love erases the calculations.

Vincent waits for the applause to die down. He says, "I'm really glad to be here. But I have to say, I'm getting a little nervous about public speaking. The next to last time I talked to a group, I nearly died. And the last time, someone nearly got killed."

No one knows how to take this. A tiny shiver goes through the crowd. If they hang on, the moment will pass. A few people laugh nervously, but not the people onstage. They have a different view of Vincent. They're observing him from behind. They can, if they want, watch his right foot rubbing, like a cat, against his other shin. It's pure little-kid nervousness, and the sight of it moves Bonnie more, she knows, than it should.

Vincent stands behind the podium, gripping it with both hands, leaning forward as if he's trying to reach every kid in the crowd. The parents can listen in if they want, but this is between him and the graduates.

He says, "I can bet that when I say just one word—*future*—everyone in this room will imagine something different. And have a different feeling about it."

Obviously, two safe bets. But what future does Bonnie imagine? Domestic bliss with a former skinhead who beat up his cousin on *Chandler*? Stranger things have happened. He gets along with Danny and Max. He's nicer to them than their father, who, unlike Vincent, has all the surface makings of a perfect dad. Dear God, what would Bonnie's parents think now? Maybe they would see beyond the surface to what she admires—what she loves—about Vincent. Who cares what anyone would think? It no longer feels like a choice. What happens now will happen.

Vincent seems to be speaking again. Bonnie needs to pay attention.

"Though maybe," he's saying, "there are some of you out there who can't imagine any future much beyond tonight's senior prom."

Every kid's tiny chuckle adds up to a laugh. Please, Bonnie prays, don't let him tell that story about the Latvian girl who ditched him for the Puerto Rican.

"I don't know what I can tell you about the future," he says. "Except that it's both way longer and way shorter than you might think."

He's getting metaphysical now. It's like listening to Meyer. Bonnie wishes Meyer were here to see how Vincent's got them hanging on every word.

"So you need to act fast," Vincent tells the kids. "Watch yourself. Do your best. Don't smoke, don't drink . . . well, don't drink too much. Don't let your heads get turned around. If something goes wrong, don't blame it on some . . . group that makes less money than you do."

The parents get a big kick out of this, and everyone claps, even those parents who routinely blame everything on their secretaries and maids. The teachers and administrators and staff applaud, a group justifiably attuned to inequities of pay.

"The main thing," Vincent says, "is that I don't want you guys becoming guys like me."

This is a little tough for the kids. They *sort of* know what he means. That is, most of them know that he used to be a white supremacist. On the other hand, he's the one onstage, and they're out in the audience, and they're listening to *him*, so what exactly *is* the part they're not supposed to be? He can only be talking about what he *used* to be. And so, no matter what he says, everything about him and his situation—at least at the moment—telegraphs the fact that you can start off as one kind of person and end up as another. Actually, it's inevitable. Isn't that what Bonnie just tried to tell them?

They weren't about to listen to her. But they see it before them now in every cell of Vincent's body.

"Be fair," he's telling them. "Try to do some good." He's so simple, so fully present. They're on the edge of their seats.

Bonnie can't get over the fact that Vincent has just told them more or less what he said that first day he walked into Meyer's office. I want to help you guys save guys like me from becoming guys like me. That's what he claimed he wanted to do. And that's what he's doing. Or trying. Are there guys in the room like him? Yes and no. Maybe. Who knows?

Bonnie feels as if she's zipping back and forth across the chasm between that afternoon and now, between who Vincent was and is, between who she was and is, between everything she believed that day and everything that's happened since. It's like trying to recall a dream that slips away, second by second.

Soon the ceremony will be over. Bonnie will look for Danny and see if he wants a ride, which of course he won't. Then Bonnie and Vincent will be left alone. And what will happen then?

Bonnie is about to find out. But now, for just a few seconds, she wants to leave the present and think back to that afternoon she met Vincent. It's as if she believes there is something there that might help her step more bravely into the difficult future ahead.

She closes her eyes and thinks of the story that Vincent told her and Meyer that first day, the story about the rave. She imagines the flashing lights, the deafening music, the feeling of an overwhelming love like pounding wings in her head. For a moment, she almost imagines that she can hear the thrumming wings. Then it passes, and Bonnie opens her eyes to find that the roar in her ears is the applause of a crowd of people cheering the messenger who has come to offer them a vision of the meaningful life before them.